To Barbara
Happy birthday
June 2016
With my love,
Prue

THE HORDENS OF HORDEN HALL

Book Four

Other Books by Prue Phillipson

Heir Apparent

The Hordens of Horden Hall Series

Vengeance Thwarted (1)

Hearts Restored (2)

Rebels Repentant (3)

Height of Folly (4)

HEIGHT OF FOLLY

Prue Phillipson

KNOX ROBINSON
PUBLISHING
London & New York

KNOX ROBINSON
PUBLISHING

34 New House
67-68 Hatton Garden
London, EC1N 8JY
&
244 5th Avenue, Suite 1861
New York, New York 10001

Copyright © Prue Phillipson 2014

The right of Prue Phillipson to be identified as author of this work has been asserted by her in accordance with the Copyright, Designs and Patents Act 1988.

All rights reserved.

ISBN 978-1-910282-32-8

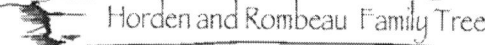

Horden and Rombeau Family Tree

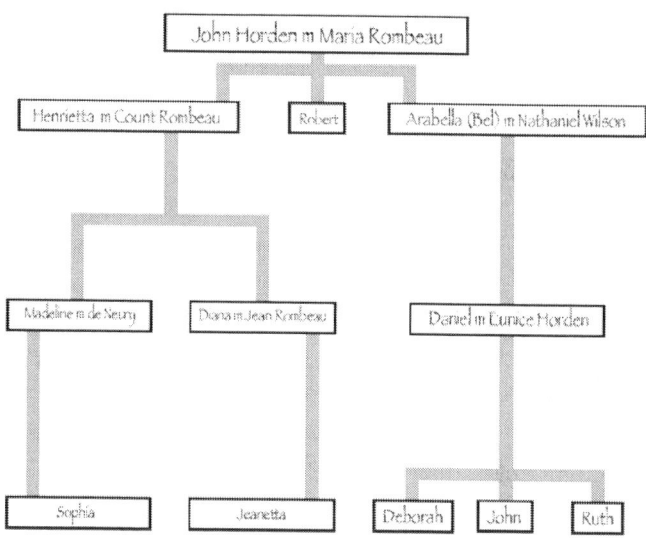

CHAPTER ONE

Horden Hall, Northumberland
New Year's Day 1700

"So, my girl," she asked herself, "what will you make of this new century? Eh?"

Deborah Wilson Horden stood before her cheval mirror – a Christmas present from her parents, Sir Daniel and Lady Eunice.

"They are sensible gentlefolk so why," she demanded of her reflection, "did they think I want to look at a six-foot-tall scarecrow?" She thrust her hands upwards through her flaxen hair and grinned at the effect. "Yes, scarecrow – an apt image. There is the straw on top. And the face? Roughed out of lumps of cloth, the nose too long and the chin too square. The forehead much too high – for what brains does a scarecrow need standing in a field all day watching the world go by?" She peered closer. "They've done better with the eyes." She widened them appreciatively. "There are depths in there. Green-blue ocean depths! Oceans this scarecrow has never crossed nor is likely to." She pulled down the corners of her mouth – too large of course – and hopped, feet together, her bed-gown flapping round her, to the window.

"Well, look at that, Scarecrow. It's snowing!"

The narrow, pointed window still reminded her that the room had been a Catholic Chapel in the days of her French great-grandmother. She leant her elbows on the stone sill. Out there the statue of old Sir Ralph Horden, the first baronet and her great-great-great-grandfather, was wearing a jaunty cap of snow. Around him the expanse of lawn was unbroken white. She wagged a finger at him.

"It'll melt and all will be green again, you old rogue. Those distant trees will grow fresh leaves, become heavy with summer, golden with autumn and certainly white again. You will still wave your sword at me and my life will be just the same. No one will put me out but I will never marry. It would be the height of folly to suppose a *scarecrow* could attract a man. I will be the eccentric unattached sister, aunt, great aunt – as I will surely become – part of the furnishings of Horden Hall."

She turned from the mirror and flung herself onto her bed. Am I still weary, she wondered, after last night's New Year's Eve revelry? The house is very quiet. Even the servants must be asleep. She sat up. No, I am not tired. It is the new century that has upset my contented soul. The Deborah Wilson Horden of my youth would have greeted it with joy. She rocked herself on the bed. New things to learn, new people to meet, history to unwrap before my very eyes.

She sprang to her feet again and walked up and down her long narrow room till she stopped at the mirror again and told the scarecrow, "In two years' time, you Thing, you will be thirty. Thirty with no future." She cocked her head on one side. "But a past. Oh yes, you certainly have a past. And that's what you can become – 'The Legend of Horden Hall.' Word will go down from generation to generation that the mad old woman at the Hall has a history. Murdered her lover, didn't she? 'Tis said she went on a wild ride to Edinburgh to save him from the gallows and he ended up dead – but not by the hangman. She'll never speak of it, that's for certain."

"Deb, have you someone in there?" She started. Her father's voice sounded just outside the door.

"Oh Father dear," she muttered under her breath. "Do you suppose I've had that bearded mining engineer from Newcastle in my room all night? You thought he'd gone home after the First-footing but he crept back in."

She opened the door. "I'm talking to the scarecrow in the glass.

Height of Folly

Come over here beside me. It's only when you are by me that I don't look like a freak-show."

He slipped his arm round her waist and gave her a squeeze.

"Not that old grumble again?"

He drew himself up to his full height of six foot-three and grinned at their reflections. She thought, the grey mixed with his fair hair scarcely shows. He is still a handsome man at over fifty and has kept his slender figure. I like him best without the wig he puts on for formal company. But he is excited about something. Is it just the new century or has he something to tell me?

He squeezed her waist again. "Happy new year, daughter."

"Happy new century," she reminded him.

"Indeed, and it's going to be a great one. We will have peace now the religious wars are over. Science and industry will advance apace."

"Is there to be no more fighting? King James is exiled but is still alive and has a son whom many would wish to see on the throne."

He dismissed this with a wave of his hand. "A mere remnant of fanatics."

"Of whom your son is one."

"What? John? Nonsense, girl. Look, I came with a great surprise for you and I find you talking to yourself in a pessimistic mood. Put that behind you and listen to what I have to say."

"Very well, Father." She sat down on the window-seat and folded her hands on her knees. He took the chair by her little desk and turned it round to face her with his eyes bright and a smile on his face.

"Have you not always wanted to travel abroad, my Deb?"

She lifted her brows and nodded, not daring to hope.

"You shall. When John and Jeanetta go on their visit to her family you shall accompany them."

"I see." It was better than nothing though she disliked what she had seen of her French cousins when they visited London and she and John first met Jeanetta. At least she would cross the Channel and be in another country. She would live for a few weeks or perhaps months in a French château. She could show off her fluency in their language.

"Are you not delighted?" he asked.

"Why yes, Father, but the extra expense to you?"

He chuckled. "I'll tell you what happened last night after you went to bed. You know Bill Warner, the mining engineer?"

She nodded. "With the beard."

"He was the last to go. I could see he wanted me on my own. Well, the long and the short of it is that his coal company – he is a member of the Guild of Hostmen – wishes to lease many acres where our land meets Upper Horden Manor's. They are certain of rich seams there and will pay handsomely. Don't pull a face. Plenty of woodland will be left at the back which will screen the workings from the Hall. Deb, I do believe we are on the way to being wealthy and you shall reap the fruits of it."

"Oh Father, why me? You will need a dowry for Ruth in a few years' time. And will not Mother expect all excess to be given to the poor?"

He laughed uneasily. "I daresay, I daresay, but *I* have the last word and you are to see the best sights of the great continent of Europe."

Now her heart did lift. "Do you mean it is to be more than a visit to the Château Rombeau?"

"Indeed it is. John can leave Jeanetta with her family after a suitable stay when we all trust she will find herself with child at last. She says she must be in France to produce a baby. Nonsense of course, but John encourages the notion. I thought you and he could visit the Loire and Rhone valleys and even take ship to Italy before the birth was due. Young gentlemen are expected to make

Height of Folly

the grand tour these days. At twenty-five he has crossed the Channel only once – for his wedding. And Ruth went to be Jeanetta's bridesmaid when *you* should have gone but –"

"And left Grandmother Bel alone when Grandfather Nat was ill?" Deborah still gulped with sorrow when she thought of Grandfather Nat. "Was he not my lifeline all my childhood? He always had time for my questions, taught me Latin and Greek, never thought I should exchange a book for a sewing sampler."

Her father held up his hand. "I know, Deb, I know. I was too busy with the restoration of this place after the fire and your mother – well, that is all past history. But what say you to my great idea?"

She jumped up and spreading out her arms as he rose too she gave him a prolonged hug.

"Dearest Father, it is a wonderful idea. But who is to be in charge? Am I to keep little brother from all the temptations we will encounter or is he escorting me because he is a man?"

Her father laughed. "Both, I would suggest. You will have to settle that between you. Of course a woman cannot travel alone. At the same time I rely on your good sense when decisions have to be made."

She took both his hands and led him to the window-seat to sit beside her.

"Political decisions, Father?"

"What do you mean? You will be sight-seers only."

She shook her head. "I was serious just now when I hinted that John has Jacobite leanings. Will he not meet French gentlemen who believe that James is the rightful king of England?"

"Maybe, maybe, but King Louis has recognised William whatever he thinks privately, and John would never revert to his mad episode at Killiecrankie. He was a child then. Now he's conscious that he is heir to Horden. If he views Catholicism with sympathy it is only for Jeanetta's sake. He has small interest in politics. He never speaks of such things to me."

She gave an exasperated sigh. Surely, she thought, Father can see John's restlessness. His Scottish adventure when he was thirteen has not frightened him into placidity, rather given him an appetite for risk and excitement. Jeanetta encourages him. She wants to see him as a romantic hero. *She* is fretting not only because she has failed to produce a child but because Horden is too dull, too rustic, too English. When she gets John to France who knows what ideas he will lap up.

Her father stood up, patting her on the arm. "Have no fears on that score, Deb." He noticed she was still in her bed-gown. "Get dressed, my sweet, and come down for breakfast all together. The first of the new century! The servants have been creeping about because your mother was still asleep but she is up now. I told her I was going to break the good news to you. Of course she says I am not to spend money till I have it. Well, I know that. Your great adventure may not come about for a year or two but I promise it will happen – in the providence of God."

She got up and nodded at the scarecrow, telling it silently, you have no idea, Thing, what this may lead to! You might even meet a very tall man.

When her father had gone she twirled round the room till she lost her balance and fell on the bed laughing with excitement.

CHAPTER TWO

Dover, April 1705

The wait for the grand tour had taken five tedious years and now here they were still waiting just to get out of England – three days on the white cliffs praying for a fair wind.

There had been setback after setback. The mine had to be deeper than Bill Warner thought. He could only pay the promised lease when he could afford the latest ventilation equipment. That was not until 1702. But that was also the year war broke out in Europe and a land tax was imposed to pay for it.

John and Jeanetta were fretting and there was no sign of an heir to Horden. Sir Daniel wrote to Jeanetta's father, the Comte Rombeau, for his opinion on the state of the war. He assured Sir Daniel that people were still travelling and the fighting was confined to the Netherlands and Austria and would not be allowed to stray onto true French soil.

John told his father, "Jeanetta will pine away if we don't go soon. We will be perfectly snug at Rombeau."

"Is not Rombeau near the border?" his mother Eunice cried. "You shan't go into danger."

Jeanetta pouted. "Sixty miles away."

"Is not that scarce two days' march?"

Jeanetta gave up trying to convince her mother-in-law but Sir Daniel was another matter. She would hang on his arm and let her great black eyes search his until her pleading wore him down. Then news came in the summer of 1704 that the Duke of Marlborough had won a great battle at Blenheim by the Danube.

"I am sure," Daniel told Eunice, "the French will capitulate soon. We must let the young people go."

Prue Phillipson

Jeanetta sang and laughed. She was again the captivating girl John had fallen in love with at the age of thirteen. None of them realised quite how homesick she had been when he had brought his bride home to Northumberland.

Deborah at thirty-two skipped about in her room from wardrobe to trunk, delighting Grandmother Bel who sat on the window-seat to watch the preparations.

"If your father could afford it I would join your party. I feel thirty-seven not seventy-seven just seeing you packing."

"Oh Grandmamma, I'd love you to come."

"Just come back safe and sound, my precious, before the Lord calls me."

And now here they were, Jeanetta moaning at the wild wind and waves. On the fourth morning she and Deborah and John had stepped outside the inn door to be buffeted again by a south-westerly and to see over the higgledy-piggledy roofs of Dover that the Channel was still a chaos of grey and white heaving water.

Clinging to John, Jeanetta propelled him back inside the shelter of the porch. Deborah was laughing at the sheer exuberance of it all, taking gulps of salty air.

She said, "Your candle to Saint Antony last night has done no good."

Jeanetta pouted and John frowned. He could laugh at her himself but no one else was permitted to do so.

The innkeeper stepped up behind them, rubbing his hands. "Come, ladies, there'll be no sailing today. Sit you down to a good breakfast. You won't get food like this from the Frenchies." He waved them to the laden table set in the bow window, the least dingy part of the room. Even there the tiny leaded panes admitted little light when the clouds outside hung so low over the sea.

They sat down and John, tucking the linen napkin under his chin, grinned at Deborah. "You have longed for this for five years

Height of Folly

and now the fates decree that we must stay in England."

Deborah smiled back. Being stuck in Dover was no hardship at all. She was alive in new places, observing new people, their clothes, their work, their accents. If they stared at her for being so uncommonly tall, she stared back or laughed till they looked away. It amazed her to recall how few new people she ever saw at home from one day to the next. Now she was jostled by them here in the inn and out in the streets and she made notes and lightning sketches in her diary of the more eccentric characters she saw.

All the way from Northumberland she had been content to let John lord it over her. He was the seasoned traveller after his one trip to Château Rombeau for his wedding. She let him manage the coach stops, the bargaining with inn servants, the choice of accommodation here in Dover, a dirty town, crammed with disgruntled travellers, while she drank in every new experience like heady wine.

Horden Hall and the last sight of Grandmother Bel, their father and mother waving and sister Ruth, struggling to hide tears because she was not coming too, all seemed far away in both time and space.

"You must eat," John was telling his wife. "If we do sail tomorrow you will certainly be sick and if you are already weak –"

She pushed away her plate. She had toyed with the eggs but the curled slices of baked ham underneath were untouched. He pushed the plate back to her.

She stood up. "Don't fuss me. I shall return to bed. I couldn't sleep for Deb there snoring all night."

Deborah laughed. "That was the old gentleman above us. I do not snore."

Jeanetta lifted her narrow shoulders, her eyes staring out at the violent sea. She was almost whimpering. "Those waves out there. I verily fear we will never get to France or if we venture we will be

Prue Phillipson

drowned on the way."

"Rubbish!" John snapped. "They won't sail if it's not safe."

"I only want to stand on French soil. Send Maria to me and Matt must sit outside the door. I trust no one here." She pushed her way between the tables and made for the stairs. John got up reluctantly to find their servants. They had brought only Maria, Jeanetta's over-anxious French maid and Matt, the senior groom, a lover of excitement, desperate to come travelling.

Deborah sighed for Jeanetta. She is still pretty, she thought, in a helpless sort of way even when pouting. But where is John's lost passion? They were Romeo and Juliet once. Love will never come to *me* again but I want it for them — and for my sake. Bickering and snapping are poor travelling companions.

John came back to the table and sat down. "Of course breakfast is cold now."

All the same he cleared his plate and Jeanetta's. Deborah studied him as he ate. He had been competent on the journey but he would always be her little brother since she overtopped him by several inches and his face was still round and boyish. He wore his own dark hair curling onto his shoulders. She loved him. She desperately wanted him to be happy in his marriage.

She reached across the table and pressed his hand. "John, I was thinking about that evening in London when you confided in me that Jeanetta loved you."

"Eh?" He looked up, astonished.

"Yes, you told her about your great Scottish adventure and she said she had never met anyone so brave and she asked if she could kiss you and you said yes and told me she was the most beautiful girl in the world and you intended to marry her."

His face flushed up. "And you laughed and said I was a little boy and I'd probably never see her again."

"Ah but you clung to that memory. Even the distractions of

Height of Folly

Cambridge University didn't wipe her out of your heart."

"So why are you saying all this now?"

"Because I don't want you to lose her. Changing coaches in London reminded me of that visit when Great Aunt Henrietta brought her granddaughters over from France to show them London."

"And hoped to wed one of them to me. Jeanetta knew that and was determined *she* would be the one."

"Are you saying it was a trap? She didn't love you truly? I saw you together before the end of that visit. Oh I knew *you* were smitten. But she loved you too. And she still needs you. She looks to you to be gentle and patient with her moods. We will get to France at last and she will brighten up and be your lovely girl again."

John ran his hand through his hair. She had embarrassed him, she could tell.

She added, "And think of the obstacles you overcame to get her. Puritan Mother accepting a Papist daughter-in-law!"

He grinned and scratched his head. "I never did see how *she* came round."

"It was Grandfather Nat, of course. Surely you remember his dying speech to Mother." She intoned it in Grandfather's low voice. "'They love each other, Eunice. They can have a marriage like Bel's and mine. Say not it will be two beliefs in one family for is there not one Lord? The nearer I get to meeting Him the more I am sure that He yearns less for outward ways of worship than the love of a true heart.' He was very ill at the time and that impressed Mother deeply."

John nodded. His deep, luminous brown eyes had become round and solemn as they had been when he had seen the colour and ornament of a Catholic Chapel for the first time as a little boy. He pushed back his chair and stood up. "I'd better go and see how she is."

She heard his footsteps go up the wooden stair. Bless him, she thought, he is persuadable as a child. But under *wrong* influences too? I pray not.

In the waiting years since that first day of the new century she had become convinced that her warning to their father was right. John's heart – if not his head – *was* with the Jacobites. She sat gazing at the fury outside and recalled comments he had thrown out to her on the spur of the moment. When the Protestant Princess Anne, Willliam's appointed successor, lost the last of her twelve children, John had muttered, "Is not God removing them so that James can come back?"

In 1701 the Act of Succession became law. The crown must pass to James's nearest Protestant heir. "Who would that be?" he asked Deborah because he knew she would know.

"The Electress Sophia of Hanover, and then her son, George."

"They are foreigners! James may be in exile but he has a son."

"Brought up a French Catholic. Do you not recall how James was besotted with power and put all his Catholic friends in high places when he was king? We need moderation as Father always says." John just pursed up his lips and frowned.

Then in September of that same year of 1701 James died.

"The young prince is the true King of England and Scotland," John declared. "They say Louis swore to James on his deathbed to recognise his son as King. Perhaps he will send him over with a French army to back him."

"And what would you do if we were in France at the time? Join in?"

John laughed it off. "I'd have to wait and see the outcome."

Deborah snapped back, "England will go to war with France first to prevent Louis putting his grandson on the throne of Spain and making a great league against us and the Dutch and the

Height of Folly

Emperor. Louis' generals won't let him take risks for a thirteen-year-old boy whose upkeep at Saint Germain already costs a fortune."

"Well, I don't understand Europe at all," John grumbled. "Father fought the Dutch when he was young and we didn't exactly win but now we are their allies and have a Dutch King."

That however was not for much longer as William died in February 1702 and Anne succeeded. John borrowed the newspapers and read that in Scotland many were openly declaring that the young Prince James Frances Edward Stuart was now James the Eighth of Scotland and Third of England. "I have to agree with that," he told Deborah, "but don't tell the parents I said so."

"And what do you intend to do about it?" she asked. "I suppose Jeanetta wants you to raise a troop of Northumberland Catholics to march on London?"

He made a great show of being offended. "You think she and I are fools because she's not as clever as you?"

Deborah sat listening to the howling of the gale. Maybe it is all noise with him, she tried to reassure herself, like that wind out there. But I do believe he was secretly received into the Catholic Church before they married and goes in when he takes her to their private Mass in Newcastle. Mother believes he has a walk by the quayside. How blind she and Father are! God send him wisdom and for us a calm day tomorrow.

CHAPTER THREE

Next day, rising early in the cramped room the three of them had shared with Maria, Deborah looked out of the tiny window and saw blue sky. She listened. The groaning wind was still. She told herself gleefully, my prayer has done more than all Jeanetta's candles. We will sail today. For the first time ever I will leave the shores of England.

She stirred Maria on her straw mattress on the floor. "Fasten my corset before your mistress wakes, then I can attend to myself. See the day is calm. We can sail but we must be at the quay early for there will be a great crush for the packet boats."

Maria had slept in her clothes and was up in a moment. On tiptoe she peered out of the window.

"Oh Mistress Deborah, there are still waves. Madam will be fearful."

But she came over and tied Deborah's laces. Deborah patted her arm.

"They are *blue* waves, Maria. That makes all the difference."

"Does it, Ma'am?"

Sadly, it didn't. They soon found themselves wedged on board with four times as many passengers as there were berths below decks. John insisted that Jeanetta must lie down. The fare for the crossing was only a guinea a head but Deborah saw him slip extra silver into the steward's hand to procure a side berth for her.

"I shall stay on deck in the fresh air," Deborah said. "I must see the coast of England disappearing from sight."

Matt had seen their baggage bestowed and was joking on deck with a group of other menservants, but Jeanetta kept Maria at her side and implored John too not to leave her. While they were still in harbour she cried that the motion of the boat was making her

Height of Folly

ill.

Deborah clutched the wooden side as the sails were spread and the boat surged into the waves. Oh glorious, glorious, she was telling herself, when suddenly the sensation of rising up and leaving her stomach behind as the boat plunged again made her gasp with astonishment. So that's what sea-sickness is, she muttered, but I shall not succumb to it. She took deep breaths of the sharp air, much colder as they found themselves in the open sea. She looked back at the land to keep her eyes and mind occupied but the white cliffs were rising and falling. She looked at the horizon but it too was heaving up and down.

She realised that the face of a moustachioed gentleman holding onto the side next to her had turned a greenish white. Meeting her eye he tried a grin. "One can never become accustomed to it."

She laughed. "It's my first voyage. You are much travelled perhaps."

"Back and forth all the time. Even so –" He turned his head and was copiously sick over the side.

Deborah jumped back as some of it blew towards her. Her foot slithered from under her and she sat abruptly down on the deck. The stench told her that she had slipped in a pool of vomit.

The moustachioed gentleman extended his arms at once and, clutching him, she hauled herself upright. They swayed together till they both grabbed the side again.

Deborah had never been gripped and held like that by a man since the time of Ranald Gordon. She looked at this man with a new intensity. That he had flecks of vomit adhering to his moustache was, she felt, irrelevant. Who was he? He spoke English well but looked French. His dress was more flamboyant than that of a travelling English gentleman but it was his face she studied, especially his eyes. They were so dark they were almost black but shining with intelligence and humour. His lips were curvy and full.

Prue Phillipson

The colour was returning to his cheeks and she could tell that their natural tone was a ruddy red.

Ignoring the state of her skirt she smiled at him. "Thank you for your assistance, sir. May I know your name?"

He smiled back, studying her too from top to toe.

"Le Vent. Edouard le Vent. I must say you are an unusual young lady to be treating with indifference the damage to her apparel. May I also know the name of my interlocutor?"

"Deborah Wilson Horden. Le Vent? The wind? And you travel back and forth all the time like the wind?"

He lifted his brows and nodded several times, compressing his lips, assessing her. She enjoyed his scrutiny. He produced a handkerchief to wipe his moustache with a flourish. She thought, he is not ashamed of his sickness and I shall not be ashamed of my unpleasant condition. It seems to impress him that I can rise above such things. He is not as tall as my Ranald but at least he is not shorter than I. We are the same height and that does not appear to have frightened him unduly.

"You understand some French, Mistress Horden?"

"I read it easily but have had little practice in speaking it. Your English is excellent."

"I love your England." There was a pause before he added in a low, almost reverend tone, "and your wild, beautiful Scotland."

He can't possibly know my connection with Scotland, she thought. There was no reaction when I gave him my name. Why the special emphasis then on our northern brethren?

She realised they were still bouncing along in the waves and her stomach had adapted itself to the motion. Their dialogue appeared to have taken his mind too off his sickness. He was patently interested in her and she was a little disconcerted to find how excited that made her.

"You have visited Scotland?" she asked.

Height of Folly

"Several times and you?"

"Once." She threw the word out lightly but it was there with her, the moonlight night, the horse beneath her, the exhilaration, the desperation, the fear.

"And you come from – ?" he asked

"Northumberland."

"Ah – so near to Scotland – and yet –?"

"We are not a travelling family." She laughed at herself. "Till now, I should say. How long do you think before we reach France?"

He shrugged. "I have known nine hours for a crossing and I have known three, less if the wind is most favourable but that is rare. Let us guess at four today."

"I believe I can stand here, holding on like this for four hours. I have no wish to join my brother and his wife below."

"No no, it is hell below decks. Even here in the air –" He waved one hand around and Deborah reluctantly turned her head and surveyed the deck. Figures were huddled, white-faced on the benches, and more were prone on the boards despite the vomit that sloshed around on the deck. Seamen leapt among them none too gently when they had to adjust sails. Deborah looked quickly back at the water creaming by the gunwales. She gulped and swallowed and breathed in deeply.

"I am all right here." She looked boldly into his eyes. "Are you?"

"With your company, Madam, I am indeed."

He *was* interested in her. He asked where in Northumberland they lived and she found herself telling him he must have passed not far from Horden Hall if he had been to Scotland from London.

"We are but four miles north of the town of Newcastle and our land reaches nearly to the Great North Road which is the stage-coach route into Scotland."

Prue Phillipson

"Your land? You are big people? Aristocracy? I am perhaps addressing *Lady* Horden, the *Countess* of Horden?"

His black eyes were bright with humour but he was not teasing her. She laughed freely. "Mistress will do very well. My father is quite a small baronet."

He held out a hand about five feet above the deck. "Small so? And his daughter so tall?"

It was the first allusion to her height but it was impossible to mind it, his smile was so charming.

"I think you know I meant 'lowly' in the hierarchy of our English people of title. A baronet, especially one created by James the First to raise revenue, is not a nobleman. Although with a different emphasis he is certainly a *noble* man." She thought fondly of her father. One day she would tell him of this encounter.

"You alluded to James the Sixth of Scotland. I understand that natives of Scotland refer to the young James in exile as the eighth James. They were not so happy with Dutch William I believe and your Queen Anne has no living heir?"

Ah, so we are onto politics, she thought. She answered cautiously, "There are many who agree with the English government that the union of our two countries is desirable. Scottish trade would prosper. But yes, there are those who wish to see a Stuart on the Scottish throne. The difficulty lies in the Presbyterian form of religion which Scotland has embraced as its national church. There is a general suspicion of Catholicism." She gave him a very straight look. "Of which no doubt you as a Frenchman are an adherent."

He tossed his head and waved one hand in a dismissive gesture. "Catholic, Protestant – I keep away from such things." A sudden squall of wind blew a shower over them. He clasped his hands together and pointed them upwards for a moment before grabbing again at the side. "Of course I pray for a safe landing."

Height of Folly

Was he mocking religion? She couldn't be sure. Or was he implying like Grandfather Nat that God could not be confined to one sect? If that were so she could agree with him heartily.

He was hanging onto his hat now as the squall passed. Her own was held on by a silk scarf fastened over it. She didn't mind the rain on her face but it was over quickly and sunshine suddenly lit up the waves.

"May I know where in *la belle* France Mistress Horden is heading?" he asked now and, seeing her eyes widen with excitement, he looked round. "And yes, there she is, the line on the horizon. My beloved country." He placed one hand over hers for barely a second. "And your very first visit to it."

The touch expressed an intimacy they couldn't have reached in so short a time. She knew it in her rational mind but the feel of his fingers through the fine calf leather of her glove spurred her to talk freely. She told him of the Château Rombeau and her sister-in-law's family and their mutual great-grandfather. She even explained that she had felt unable to leave her sick grandfather and travel to her brother's wedding.

"I should have attended on the bride with her own cousin's daughters but how could I overtop them all? The bridal procession would have excited ridicule rather than solemnity." Was she drunk with the heady sea air that she would make fun of her own height to a virtual stranger?

He gave her such a merry understanding smile that she did not regret it.

"That was, perchance, a stronger reason than your grandfather's illness for your withholding your presence?"

She was about to deny it vigorously when she acknowledged for the first time ever that he was probably right. Grandmother Bel had urged her to go. 'My Nat is not so near death. He will be here when you return.' And he *had* lived three more years. She smiled. "There is a nugget of truth in what you say. I am a firm believer in honesty and the hardest thing is to be honest with oneself. I admit I did not want to be conspicuous. My sister-in-law is slight of build and her bridesmaids were mere children. My young sister took my place. She is both petite and pretty."

"I admire and share your love of honesty. To be open and frank with all men is admirable." He paused very deliberately and added, "Though it may not be given to all in all circumstances."

She nodded. "You are thinking of the demands of tact and courtesy." I am liking this gentleman more and more, she thought, and then Maria appeared at her elbow.

"Oh Mistress Deborah, are you well? Master and Mistress sent me to find out." The poor girl's clothes were more stained than Deborah's. Her pallor was a shock. She seemed hardly able to stand.

"I am as you see, Maria, in good health if a little discommoded as to my dress. How are my brother and your mistress? He at least could come up here for some air."

"Oh they are both quite laid out and say they only want to die. I too. The motion is as bad everywhere." She retched over the side but nothing came up.

"I am quite empty but still sick," she moaned.

"Go and lie down if you can. Tell them I am not ill at all."

Maria brushed sodden, sticky hair from her eyes. "You are the only one in the boat then." She scurried below.

"*La pauvre fille!*" exclaimed Monsieur le Vent.

Deborah turned to him with renewed pleasure. It *was* possible to keep sickness at bay if the mind was pleasantly engaged. She said, laughing, "Life is seldom kind to Maria, which is sad since her mistress needs a *cheery* companion. S*he* sees the black side of everything, yet she will have none but Maria as her lady's maid."

He inclined his head towards her. "While *you*, I am sure, are

Height of Folly

happiness itself."

"I try to be." She was looking beyond him to the coast of France becoming clearer. This was to be the most thrilling moment, the landing on a foreign shore. She met his eyes again. "Oh, Monsieur le Vent, pray let us converse in French from now on." She broke into French herself as she went on. "Tell me how it will be in Calais and what we should see in Paris when we get there. I have read books but to be told by a real Frenchman − ! And please correct my accent and many mistakes."

He took this seriously and though he could not fault her grammar he showed her how to achieve a French r and avoid an English inflection in her sentences.

She practised everything he pointed out with the same assiduity she had always shown in the business of learning. She well remembered how it had astonished her family when she was a child. I had just started to study Hebrew, she recalled, when Ranald came into my life. This man is as pleased with my dedication to learning as Ranald was, though he, God bless him, was in men's eyes a rough, uncouth giant.

Monsieur le Vent now asked where they intended to stay in Calais and also in Paris. He wants to meet me again, she told herself, exulting. I have attracted a man. They were so engrossed that she didn't notice the approach of Matthew their serving-man till he called "Mistress Deborah" over the bodies of passengers blocking his way.

"What is it, Matt?" His sun-bronzed face showed no signs of seasickness.

"Captain says he's seen you standing all this way and begs you will come into his cabin and drink a glass of wine with him."

"Oh, that is most kind of him but I prefer the air out here" − she looked at le Vent − "and the company."

Le Vent shook his head. "No, pray go. The wine will sustain

you."

Deborah realised her legs were aching and her throat dry. "Very well but I'll see you again, Monsieur le Vent," she said, and left him smiling. It is good to take every opportunity for something new, she thought, and I have never been in the cabin of a captain of a packet boat before.

Picking her way among the bodies she found that the motion of the ship had quietened somewhat. All the same she grabbed Matthew's hand which he held out to her so that she would not slip on the deck. Outside the cabin door Maria was waiting with a clothes brush.

"It's dried on you, Mistress Deborah, and will brush off. Matt came for me. It's not so bad now, the swaying up and down. There, you're fit to be seen. But poor Mistress below! I don't know how I can make her presentable till we can get where she can change all her clothes."

The captain appeared at his door now, a weather-beaten man of middle years, with very tight white breeches and blue coat. He had been smoking a pipe and though he tapped it out on her entrance the smell lingered. He was not a cultivated man like Edouard le Vent but he sat her down on a hard chair screwed to the floor and she was glad of the rest. He perched on the edge of his bunk while his servant poured out two glasses of wine. Deborah feared they were not very clean glasses and took out her kerchief to wipe her lips and then, she hoped surreptitiously, the rim of the glass.

"Your good health, Ma'am."

"And yours, sir."

"I can't abide to see a lady standing."

"The benches were crowded and had become as soiled as the deck."

"Ay, but how am I to set a sailor to the hosing down with the passengers all about?"

Height of Folly

"I understand your dilemma, sir. Your ship was perfectly clean when we came aboard."

He nodded. "'Tis always the way. They cannot abide even a calm sea some of 'em. And it takes twenty-four hours or more to quieten after a storm. The English Channel is never a mill-pond. There's always waves."

Deborah sipped her wine slowly and he seemed content to drink his and say no more till he finished it and set down the glass, fitting it into a hole in the table. He rose to his feet.

"Tide'll be low at Calais. We'll heave to outside the harbour."

"Oh, does that mean we'll have a long wait?"

"Nay, they send boats. We'll have you all off. The more of you as gets in a boat the less the fee for each passenger but my advice is not to be parted from your baggage. If you see it lowered into a boat get in after it or you may never see it again."

"Certainly we will keep it by us. But what is the fee we must pay? I thought our fare took us from Dover to Calais without more expense."

"Ah dear Madam, we get you as near Calais as we can. After that it is the French watermen who have to earn a living. If they're greedy they may charge two guineas a boatload but it should be less."

"Two guineas!"

Deborah had risen when he did, thinking she must leave him to his duties.

"Nay, sit you down. I'll about my business and you'll be called when we are ready. I can't abide to see a lady standing."

Deborah did as she was told but she was determined not to be shut in the cabin and after the Captain left she opened the door a little and stood by it peeping out. There was plenty of bustle now, but between the comings and goings of sailors and reviving passengers she could see the French shore and mean little houses scattered beyond it. Their ship was still moving but shouted commands were followed by the hauling in of sails and the clang of the anchor going down.

She noticed rowing boats putting out from the shore. These must be the watermen coming to meet the ship. We need to assemble our party together, she decided, and see that Matt has our baggage ready. I trust we can be in the same boat as Monsieur le Vent.

She was about to step out when she heard the captain's voice, speaking low to someone round the other side of the cabin. "Well, Edouard, was all that talk with the lady to some purpose?"

Then she heard le Vent's reply. "It might lead somewhere, *Mon Capitaine*, one can always hope."

He *is* attracted to me, she thought. Holding herself very still with the door a mere crack open she was inwardly skipping like a child.

Then the captain said, with a hoarse laugh, "For the future Madame le Vent?"

And the answer came, also with a laugh. "God forbid. If I ever wed it would not be to a post. Something more curvaceous and not nearly so clever. A man must dominate, *n'est ce pas?*" They moved away still chuckling.

Deborah clenched her fists against her lips and a quiver of pure fury shook her whole body. Men! Never again will I go to meet one halfway! The fury exploded at herself. Fool, imbecile ever to imagine – but what did he mean, "One can always hope"? What could he *possibly* mean? Does he think I am wealthy, that he can travel with us and we will *pay?* I will certainly *not* get in the same boat with him.

Now she slipped out and mingled with the crowds gathering on deck and with much relief spotted John and Jeanetta emerging from below. She made her way to their side, all solicitous for her

Height of Folly

sister-in-law who was moving with great caution like an old lady unsure of her footing.

John said, "Well, Deb, you had the best of it. I stayed down there for Netta's sake but I have never felt so ill in my life."

Maria was following and Matt was waving from a corner of the deck where their luggage had been assembled. The air was full of shouts as the boats drew alongside. The watermen yelled their prices while the seamen encouraged reluctant passengers down the sides and ladies squealed at what they were expected to do.

Deborah strode forward and seeing a boat with a hulking boatman the size of Ranald Gordon she called to him in French that they would travel with him. He was ready with his arms to lift her down as she began to descend but she said, "I thank you, I can manage."

Jeanetta was held by John's arms till the boatman grabbed her and set her down, a soiled miserable bundle on the seat next to Deborah.

"I shall be ashamed to set foot on my native soil like this," she moaned.

"We will have a night in the hotel and you will be as fresh and pretty as a picture in the morning."

John, Maria, Matthew and their luggage were now safely stowed.

As they were rowed away Monsieur le Vent put his head over the side and called, "God speed you on your travels, Mistress Horden." She gave the merest flip of the hand in acknowledgment.

John looked at her in surprise. "Who was that that knew your name?"

"Oh some forward Frenchman that engaged me in talk on the crossing."

John grinned and shrugged. *He doesn't believe I could attract a man,* she thought, *and he is right.*

So what was le Vent's purpose, she asked herself, and a cold

27

fear suddenly gripped her stomach. I learnt nothing about *him*. I prattled about our home, our family and our destination in France. The captain knew him. He makes the crossing frequently. What if he is a government agent looking for conspirators? He can now investigate John Wilson Horden and find that he fought against government forces at Killiecrankie when he was a mere lad. He may even learn that one Ranald Gordon, a notorious rebel, brought John home to Horden Hall and there captured the heart of John's tall sister Deborah, the mad girl who heard he was in prison and rode to Edinburgh to plead for his life. Will the Hordens now be tainted with the name of Jacobites – even Father who fought in the Dutch wars for Charles the Second but dutifully accepted the end of the Stuarts when the Prince of Orange superseded them? What have I done?

The boat came alongside a low wooden jetty raised a foot or two above the shore. As Deborah stepped onto its planks she knew she should be exulting in her first moment on a foreign land. Instead she was bewailing her innocence of the big world and wanting the comfort and security of Horden Hall. She was cold, wet, and her clothes stank, but much worse was the fear that she had unwittingly stirred a pot of danger for herself and her family. Grasping Jeanetta's hand and helping her over the slimy timbers she was overwhelmed with shame that she had babbled for so long and so foolishly to that man with the sinister black eyes and flamboyant moustache.

CHAPTER FOUR

A change of clothes and a night's sleep transformed them all. Monsieur le Vent did not call at the Hotel Angleterre which boasted 'the best reputation for cleanliness in all Calais.' I will not let the villain trouble me, Deborah told herself, as they sat down at an early hour to what the *patron* called an English breakfast. He can be my warning light not to seek men's company. That's all. This is my first day in France. Oh to see Paris soon!

She voiced this thought aloud and Jeanetta immediately squealed, "No, we must set out at once for Château Rombeau. Mother and my brothers will be so eager to see us. Maman would have sent their carriage for us if she could have been sure when we would land. John has sent word ahead that we will be there this afternoon."

John, Deborah noticed, had been looking on his wife with fond, admiring eyes. She was a picture indeed this morning with her high colour, jet-black hair and all too-perfect features. Deborah took pleasure herself in watching her rapid changes of expression, the brilliance of her eyes and the lively gestures of her delicate hands.

"Yes, Deb," John said grandly, "I've hired a carriage from the inn."

"Should we not take the *diligence?*" Deborah said. "I read that it is much the cheapest way of travel."

Jeanetta flapped her hands in horror. "You saw one yesterday, a great clumsy vehicle. They crush in thirty people with their luggage and bounce you horribly. If you and John wish to travel like that when I am safe at Rombeau I am sure I shan't mind. But today I shall go home in comfort."

She put her hand on Deborah's wrist so that the contrast in sizes was all too obvious. "Dear Deb, we can take the Rombeau carriage to Paris any time when you are with us." She removed her hand to make one of her flourishes. "Of course I know Paris so well. And Versailles! Papa is much at court and Maman is forever dragging us there to see the fashions but did you know the King lays down rules for his visitors, unless he goes hunting and then everything bows to that. But you will love Rombeau in the spring. The gardens are so pretty. You are to have your own room overlooking them in our wing of the château. My uncle the Vicomte de Neury and Aunt Madeline with their daughter Sophia and her family are in the other wing. Her husband was killed in the Dutch wars and she has only her two girls. My parents and brothers occupy the central rooms. The place is much bigger than Horden of course."

Deborah smiled sweetly. The Rombeau family can patronise me all they want, she was thinking. They can't stop me enjoying the beauty of their gardens and my own room where I can read and write up a copious diary. I shall save money under their roof so I can tolerate today's extravagance.

So they travelled as conveniently as was possible on bad roads little recovered from the ravages of winter. Deborah was fascinated to compare the countryside with Northumberland. There seemed to be nothing as charming as the stone-built cottages about a green and a church as in Nether Horden. What intrigued her were a number of wayside shrines where the statue of the Virgin Mary was crudely painted, and black-shawled women were huddled on their knees before her. The fields were showing a greening from rising crops but the few scattered hovels of the peasants suggested a poverty-stricken land. She remembered that France had suffered famine in the last decade and she began to wonder if the Rombeau and Neury families had to share the Château for financial reasons.

Deborah considered the family members she would meet and

Height of Folly

was pleased to realise there were no unattached men she would have to avoid. Jeanetta's brothers were no more than boys. She was a little sad that she would not be seeing again Great-aunt Henrietta, Grandmother Bel's formidable elder sister. She had died since John's and Jeanetta's wedding which she had been so eager to promote. But her daughter, Diana, Jeanetta's mother, Deborah was curious to meet again. She had married a Rombeau second cousin who had inherited the title and land but Grandmother Bel had told her all about the brief attraction between this Diana and Deb's own father. 'She threw herself at your poor father with such vehemence that he was hard put to it not to catch and hold her, being the gentleman he was even at fifteen years old.'

Perhaps Father and I have the same inability to judge character, she thought. Yet I am over thirty and should know better by now. Well, I will dismiss le Vent from my thoughts and reserve my opinion of these Rombeaus. When I saw them thirteen years ago I was still recovering from Ranald and could scarce trouble myself to make their acquaintance.

She knew that the Château Rombeau was on the edge of hilly ground facing east over farmland and John had described to her its fantastic ornamentation with little pointed turrets and heraldic animals so she was not surprised when the carriage turned into gates decorated with wrought ironwork displaying flowers, birds and the crest of the Rombeau family, a snake entwined around an olive tree.

Jeanetta was bouncing up and down with excitement. "Look, look, Deb. See the gardens and they have made the fountains play for us. And there, look, the Château. Is it not beautiful?"

Deborah peered from the window. In her eyes it was grotesque. She thought of the simple front of Horden Hall, its twisted Tudor chimneys its only ornamentation apart from crude Sir Ralph of whom she had grown quite fond over the years.

"Why, Jeanetta," she said, "it is indeed very splendid."

As they drew closer she put her hand over her mouth to repress a laugh for the family members were assembled on the steps to greet them, all small and stiff like a puppet show waiting to have their strings pulled. The cocked hats of the men perched on their full-bottomed wigs and the *fontange* of the women, including even the young girls, exaggerated the heads and they were all the colours of the rainbow, the males in velvet suits with a million buttons and the females in silks and satins. The moment of string-pulling came as the carriage drew up and the tableau on the steps came to life.

John handed out Jeanetta. The first to embrace her was a plump, middle-aged Jeanetta who must be her mother, Diana. She had the same beautifully arched brows that always showed an air of surprise. Deborah was very glad her father had escaped the clutches of this harpy. Her cheeks were fiercely red and her neck and bosom impossibly white. Her voice was shrill like Jeanetta's and her manner extravagant.

As the brothers and father stepped up to greet Jeanetta, Diana was free to notice Deborah.

"Oh my, how you've grown!" she exclaimed.

Deborah smiled down at her. "On the contrary I was this tall at age eighteen."

Diana was not put out. "Ah well, I remember you and your grandmother would walk everywhere in London and we were raised up in the carriage. So, fancy this being your first visit to France." She turned to John. "And how is my sweet son-in-law? I congratulate you on how well my dear Jeanetta is looking. You made a safe and easy crossing then?"

Deborah chuckled at John's embarrassment at being kissed on both cheeks.

He mumbled, "It was not so good but we are all recovered today."

Height of Folly

Deborah found herself being presented then to all the family in turn and was surprised to see that Madeline, the Vicomtesse de Neury, Diana's sister looked like an old lady and her husband the Vicomte a bent old man leaning on a stick. They are only in their late fifties at most, she thought.

Their daughter Sophia gave her the kindliest and most natural greeting of all. This is the lady who lost her husband in the wars, Deborah remembered. She doesn't know that I am also widowed in a sense and regret that I will never ever have a family. These are her two girls, Louisa and Francesca. They are sixteen and fifteen I believe and were the bridesmaids I would have been numbered with at John's wedding eight years ago. How absurd I would have looked!

The most imposing character was Jeanetta's father, Comte Rombeau. Though he too was short he made up for it in breadth and girth. He wore a crimson coat over an embroidered waistcoat which hung to his knees, hiding his breeches. His white-stockings clung tightly about his very round calves. Deborah gave him a low curtsey so she could meet his eyes which protruded eagerly above his plump cheeks.

"Mistress Horden, you are welcome to Rombeau." He said this in English but hurried on in French, "Sadly our countries are at war but relationship overrides such things. I admire your general Marlborough but we too have a great general, the Duc de Villeroi, and now that the armies are all emerging from winter quarters we may take our revenge for Blenheim but you are not to fear. You are under our protection and safe within the walls of Rombeau."

He released her hand which he had kissed and flung his arms wide to embrace his great estate. "When you are rested you must allow me to escort you about the place."

"I shall be charmed, sir." Deborah made a point of answering him in French. Some of the family had tried out their English on her with varying degrees of accuracy so she was happy to show off her French.

They went inside and Deborah studied the elaborate furnishings of the salon as they called the first room for entertaining. Wine was served and formal speeches passed for conversation till they were shown to their rooms to be made presentable for dinner which had been held back for their arrival.

"Their normal hour is two," John whispered to Deborah as they climbed the marble staircase. "They copy the King at Versailles. You'd better wear something fine but keep your best for a ball. They are sure to give several balls while we are here."

"I have my sixteen-year-old sea-green gown but it will be mighty crushed. If my trunk is in my room now I can shake it out but I thought this fine grey silk I have worn under my travelling cloak would do well enough."

John pursed his lips. "*They* are all so splendidly colourful. Still I suppose it doesn't much matter what you wear."

"No, you are quite right, John." That, she thought, will be the story of this visit for me. But I am here in France, the fulfilment of a dream. She followed the footman into the bedchamber she had been given. He bowed several times at the door and finally backed out with an ill grace. He expected a tip, she realised. Well, I will receive scant service from the *domestiques* while I am here but that suits me admirably. She went to the window. And there is, as Jeanetta said, a fine view over the gardens with an abundance of blossom when our northern countryside is still half asleep. She turned back to study the room. The bed is very high but there is a flight of three steps by which I can climb in and the curtains are handsome. I trust there are no bugs here as there are in all the inns.

She lifted the damask coverlet and fingered sheets of the best linen. A fragrance of flowers rose from them. She shook her head

Height of Folly

in disbelief. No bug could live here. Why, I am to be a princess this summer!

A tap came at her door. She flung the cover over and called *"Entrez!"*

Sophia put her head round the door. Her plain, wholesome face was scarcely painted at all, Deborah noticed, and her smile was genuine if a little nervous. "I believe you have no maid of your own, Deborah? May I call you Deborah?"

"Of course. Are we not second cousins? No, I have shared Jeanetta's Maria till now."

"Then you shall have Suzette. She is the orphan of a tenant so I adopted her. She has few words of English but you speak French perfectly. Here, Suzette. Lady Horden is your new mistress." Then she hissed in English behind her hand. "If you cannot stomach her, Deborah, pray say so at once."

A thin girl, her face marked with smallpox, edged round the door. Deborah had seen plenty of worse cases. Newcastle had had its share of outbreaks over the years. She went to her at once and took her hand and spoke to her in French. "Well, Suzette, we shall be friends, shall we not?" She looked at Sophia and said in English, "I am not *Lady* Horden you know. That title belongs only to my mother. John will not be Sir John until he inherits Horden from our father."

"Oh pray let Suzette call you my lady. It would make her so happy. She had no aspirations to be a lady's maid but my own maid has been showing her how things are done for I knew I must find her a place one day. Thank you for accepting her."

Sophia slipped out as unobtrusively as she had come in.

The girl was looking up at Deborah with round brown eyes like a devoted dog. She seemed in awe of her new mistress's height. It came home to Deborah what she was taking on.

I'll be obliged to keep her with me, she reflected, when we

return home. If I make a friend of her I could never cast her off, but Mother does not approve of ladies' maids. The poor girl will see a sad contrast to this place with its swarms of servants.

Beaming at Suzette she began to tell her what her English home was like. "We Horden ladies roll up our sleeves, bake bread, polish silver, tend the gardens. And my favourite outdoor task is clearing undergrowth in the woods and chopping logs for the fires. When my Grandmother Bel lived in the parsonage she had only one servant. She picked her own apples and blackberries to make into pies, grew vegetables and kept hens. Since my Grandfather's death her hens have come to join ours at the Hall and Grandmother runs out in her apron to feed them." She had nearly added "while Jeanetta is still a-bed," when she remembered Jeanetta was a great lady here, daughter of the master himself.

The girl's eyes grew wider than ever. No wonder Jeanetta finds us a puzzle, Deborah reflected, and cannot feel truly comfortable in John's home. What does *she* ever *do* at Horden? Plays tolerably on the virginals and puts a few stitches in the altar cloth she has been two years embroidering. I can never forget the look on her face when mother told her of her poverty-stricken Puritan background. I'm afraid Father cringed to hear her speak of it to a child of French aristocracy, and a Catholic to boot.

So what will Suzette's role be at home? She must learn English as none of our people speak French. Maria has picked up English but has always found the cheerful informality of Horden under my parents' influence quite distressing. I will have to shape this girl into another mould if she is to fit in and be happy.

Suzette was now hovering beside the trunk which had been carried up. Deborah sighed. She knows that her first task is to unpack for me but do I want anyone handling my things? She may look like a devoted dog but she has a human tongue in her head and can amuse them all below with tales of the eccentric lady's

Height of Folly

belongings. Reluctantly she fumbled for the key in her hanging pocket and handed it to the girl. I don't know her, she was thinking, but I am sorry for her situation in life and as darling Grandmother Bel would say, "Just love everyone around you and you will always be happy."

That must be my secret for this sojourn in strange places but I must also be wary because there are characters about like Edouard le Vent. If one's trust is thrown back in one's face one must walk away, not fuming, but a little wiser.

She sank into an upholstered chair, put her feet on a footstool and watched Suzette take out her clothes and hang them in the closet or fold them on shelves as appropriate, handling them as if they were the most expensive silks. Every few minutes the girl cast anxious glances at her.

Deborah smiled. "*Très bien, très bien*, Suzette!" All the time she wondered, how can I get rid of her so I can be alone?

CHAPTER FIVE

Horden Hall, May 1705

Sir Daniel Wilson Horden knocked at his mother's bedroom door at eight in the morning. "A letter with an earl's crest for you."

There was no reply.

His daughter Ruth came running up the stairs. "Grandmother Bel is feeding the hens. Let me see the letter. What does an earl's crest look like? How does Grandmother know an earl? Is he her secret lover?"

Daniel ruffled her fair curls. "No, silly girl. It is the crest of Lord Branford whose son Henry was my friend at Cambridge and afterwards in the King's navy."

"Ooh, was he the one whose head was shot off right next to you?"

"Who told you that?"

"Grandmother Bel. She says I have to thank God always that the canon ball missed you or I wouldn't be here at all. So when I have naughty thoughts I try to remember that."

"Well, we will go and find her. The old earl wrote and commiserated with her over the loss of your grandfather for *they* were at Cambridge together. They keep up an intermittent correspondence."

As they went down the stairs and through the rear door to the stable-yard Daniel was seeing the bulge under the fallen sail, ripping it apart and finding the head of his friend, the eyes wide open and astonished at his sudden end, the ears protruding as they always did but no longer a comic feature. He drew a deep breath and took Ruth's hand as she skipped beside him.

"Good morning, Mother," he called to the fenced area of the

Height of Folly

hen run, "Lord Branford has written again to you."

"Oh the dear old man!" Bel cast the last scraps from her basket and came trotting out latching the gate carefully behind her. Daniel watched her with loving eyes. She had a man's hat pulled over her thick grey curls and a maid's apron over her old worn dress. Seventy-seven now she had shrunk in height with no spare flesh on her from her endless activity.

She took the letter, chuckling. "I know not why I call him old. He and I must be much of an age for he was younger than your father when they were at Cambridge. He always says it was your father who helped him through to his bachelor's degree. Come into the parlour and hear what he has to say. Yes, you too, Ruth, if you like."

Eunice was in the parlour turning a torn linen sheet into aprons for the kitchen maid. Daniel was a little wary of his wife's attitude to their acquaintance with an earl. Mother Bel made nothing of it herself but Jane, their longest-serving maid, always presented such a letter on the best silver salver. Eunice had given up telling her that 'an earl is just a man like the rest of us.' But his mother sat down on the settle next to her, broke the seal and abstracted her spectacles from her apron pocket.

"We'll all share it. My, it's a mighty long letter. What can he find to write about?" Her eyes were glancing rapidly down it. "I see he's interested in the news in my last letter to him that Deborah was to go to France with John and Jeanetta. So he writes that by coincidence his grandson Frederick, Henry's son, has also set off for –"

Daniel started up. "*Henry's* son. You must be mistaken. Henry had no son."

Bel put the letter closer to her eyes. She was shaking her head. "No, it is so. He writes that Henry fell in love while he was still at Cambridge and when you and he enlisted in the navy he married secretly before joining the ship."

"Nonsense." Daniel held out his hand for the letter. "He would have told me. This is some hussy trying to win a fortune for her child. The earl's old wits are addled if he accepts her tale."

"He is as sane as I." Bel kept hold of the letter, her lips compressed as she scanned the closely written pages. "He tells me that his grandson Frederick who is a widower has recently departed for the Continent and he would like to know where Deborah is going in the hope they can meet. Why, he is as good as proposing his grandson for your daughter!" She faced Eunice. "Well of course *you'll* not care that he is heir to a great estate in Hertfordshire as well as a fine mansion in the Strand, and nor do I of course, if he's a good man. But if Deborah could find a husband that made her happy –"

Eunice, as small as Bel but plump in her middle age as she had never been in her Spartan childhood, laid a restraining hand on Bel's arm. "Slow down, dear Mother Bel, and let us hear how Henry Branford, with whom Daniel was so intimate both at Cambridge and in the navy, could possibly have produced a son without him knowing of it."

"Of course he couldn't and pray never let me hear you again linking Deb's name with some bastard."

Bel looked up at Daniel rearing over her from his great height. "Sit down, son. Draw a chair up close if you like but have the patience to listen." She laid a finger on a sentence of the letter. "Before you sailed for the wars did Henry ever speak of a dream wherein he was cleft in two by a cutlass? He had no pain but immediately found himself in heaven."

Daniel struck the side of his head with his palm. "By the Lord, he did, he did. He said he couldn't tell his family for they would take it as an awful presentiment. He told *me*, laughing it away as he did most things. How can his father speak of that?"

Height of Folly

Again he held out his hand for the letter.

Bel wouldn't yield it to him. "It was because of the dream he determined to marry the girl he loved. In the dream he was seeking her in heaven and couldn't find her so he told her they must be made one before God so they could meet in heaven."

Daniel shook his head. "He never added that part of the dream. If there is any truth in this at all it must be that some girl trapped him into marriage because she was with child. He was guileless, that I do know and easily led. I had only to say I wanted to serve in the navy and he said, 'I too!' He was not very clever either. But it seems this girl – why, Eunice, she must be a woman of our age now – *she* is clever. She has beguiled the father as she did the son."

"At all events," Bel said, "she has convinced the earl that this Frederick is legitimate. But more than that he writes affectionately of his daughter-in-law. She is a 'noble' character." Bel was now reading directly from the letter. "They were married and Henry was killed before she could write to him that she was with child."

Daniel interrupted with a snort. "It was the other way about. She told him that she was with child and he felt obliged to do the honourable thing and marry her."

Bel frowned. "Just hear what the earl writes and do your snorting afterwards. He says, 'Her family wanted to engage her to a second cousin in the next village but Henry loved her. He insisted on their marrying before he went to war. To do it quickly he had to write to me for more funds, for clothes he told me, but he spent the money on obtaining a licence. They were wed in a church where they were not known and he was recorded as Lieutenant Harry Branford. She had no notion who he really was. So they married without the knowledge of our family or hers and Henry died unaware that his wife had conceived a son.'"

Daniel saw from Eunice's small frown that she was considering this seriously. The piquant face tapering to a tiny chin that had fascinated him when he first saw her was fuller now with a suspicion of another chin below as she cocked her head on one side. Her smoothed back mousy hair was streaked with grey. We can't escape it, he thought, we are past our middle years as Henry would be if he had lived. I wonder whether she'll recommend Mother to give the earl details of Deborah's whereabouts. Certainly she'll care little about rank. All she'll want to know is that a prospective son-in-law has been brought up to fear God and keep the commandments.

She turned her head to Bel. "I am trying to put myself in the shoes of this woman when she heard Henry had been killed. How did she learn of his true identity? Why did she not go at once to the Branford seat in Hertfordshire and present the child to his grandparents?"

Bel had read on a little way.

"The earl is blaming Henry for that. He says Henry rushed into the marriage in a passion of love. Well, that *I* can understand. I was so desperate to marry my Nat that I proposed to him in the public street. But because it was all done in haste Henry left no word with his wife about his family nor had he any papers on him about *her*. When he failed to return she had to search the news sheets that listed casualties. *Then* she found his true identity. What could she suppose but that he was ashamed of marrying so far – in the world's eyes – below him? She believed she must raise her boy herself. She would not approach a grand family to be rejected, but of course she carefully locked up the certificate of her marriage."

Eunice nodded. "It is the curse of our divided land, the gulf between the great and the humble. She feared the Branfords would take the boy and reject *her*."

Daniel was now caught up in the story. "Lord and Lady Branford were *kind* people. I knew them."

Height of Folly

"But *she* didn't," his mother pointed out, looking down the page. "She loved Frederick as dearly as she had loved Harry as she always called him. She was happy to keep her boy with her on her father's farm, for her parents forgave her secret marriage to her naval officer in pity for her loss. They were glad too to have a clever grandson. Her brother had boys to take over the tenancy of the farm but young Frederick proved himself a scholar. He did so well in the local Dame School that he was given a scholarship to the Grammar School and from there he was indentured to a law firm and qualified as a lawyer. Ah now I see why the earl says Frederick is a widower. He married a local girl but sadly she died in childbirth two years ago."

Daniel was still impatient to read the letter for himself. He demanded, "But, Mother, when did Lord Branford learn of the young man's existence?"

"Why, only in the last year. Just after he got my letter he learnt that his sister Hermione's grandson, his sole heir, had been killed in France. The other children are all girls. Frederick's mother read the society papers to keep in touch with the Branfords' doings and saw that there was no descendant left to inherit the earldom to the great grief of old Lord Branford. At last she saw that it was her duty to break to Frederick what his lawful inheritance was. Very tentatively and with much misgiving she wrote to Lord Branford and enclosed a copy of the marriage document."

"Which he would scrutinise, I trust, as a probable forgery."

His mother looked sadly at him. "You are in a most sceptical frame of mind, my boy." She looked back at the letter. "But you are right that he got his lawyers onto it and they were sent to the church where the ceremony took place to examine the records. They even spoke to the priest, old and retired from the living but still in the neighbourhood. He remembered the circumstances and could describe Henry well."

Prue Phillipson

Daniel heaved a sigh. "I still doubt this woman's complete veracity but I suppose if she had been a fortune hunter she wouldn't have kept silent so long. Poor Henry with his protruding ears! I wish he had told me. He seemed so light-hearted. But now I think of it I recall a time when he asked me if I was secretly betrothed. Eunice's grandmother had hinted so much to him." He looked at Eunice as he said it. "I dismissed the subject. My feelings were so confused at the time." Eunice nodded, smiling. "So he said his family too had a young lady in mind for him but he couldn't fancy her. Maybe if I had bared my heart to him then he would have admitted his secret love for a farmer's girl. I can see that my reticence may have held him back. Yes, I think I can believe all this now and maybe the old earl's wits are *not* addled."

Bel had now read to the end of the letter. "Well, it is plain from this that the good old man has taken Frederick and his mother into his own home and heartily approves of them both. In fact as soon as he saw the lad he knew it was Henry's son. He has the ears."

Daniel got up. The sight of Henry's head was there again. He paced the parlour and then turned on his mother. "Whatever the truth of all this I can't put this unknown boy forward for our precious Deborah." He laughed abruptly. "Why are we speaking of him as a youth? He must be thirty-five or six and has been married. This is no Mother's boy. This is a mature man."

Bel laughed. "Which is just what Deborah wants. She will be thirty-four in September and if she is ever to be a mother she should waste no time meeting a suitable husband."

Ruth popped her head over the back of the settle. Daniel had forgotten her presence. She has crept round out of sight, he thought, just so we *would* forget.

"Oh let Deb get married, then I can be a bridesmaid again and as it would be here at home I wouldn't have to go to France and be

Height of Folly

seasick on the journey."

Eunice put her hands up to clasp hers on the back of the settle. "You bad little eavesdropper. I didn't know you were there."

"I'm not bad. Grandmother Bel said I could hear the letter."

"True, I did, Eunice, but of course I knew not what it contained."

"Well, what did I hear? It was an interesting story. I'll write it all in my diary."

Daniel held up his hand. "Now Ruth, stop there! I know not that we want this to be public knowledge. You leave that diary of yours where anyone can pick it up. Your mother and I will have to consider carefully whether we fulfil Lord Branston's request to inform him of your sister's whereabouts. That is the end of the matter for the present. Mother, do you think I might now have the perusing of his letter myself?"

Bel clutched it tightly and screwed up her lips. Then her eyes twinkled and she handed it over. "But remember it is *my* letter and *I* will have the answering of it."

Eunice looked startled. Bel squeezed her hand. "Nay, my daughter, if this man should ever meet your girl it is she who will decide where it might lead. We all know Deb has a mind of her own. No one will push her into a marriage against her will."

Eunice shook her head. "It is not her *mind* I fear, Mother Bel. It is her untried girlish emotions. We all saw what happened when Ranald Gordon appeared on the scene. More than fifteen years on I do not feel she has mastered her inner passions. She yearns for any man's attention, poor child."

Ruth was listening wide-eyed.

"You," said Daniel sternly, "are long overdue in the library. I left you a page of mathematic problems to work out and I will come in half an hour to see if they are done."

Ruth turned her pretty mouth into an angry pout and marched

from the room.

Eunice said, "Why, Dan, you will be making that biddable girl into a rebel with so many sums. She is fifteen. Too old for lessons like that."

"No knowledge is ever wasted."

"I wonder about that. Look at poor Deb with all her great learning. She never stopped acquiring more and more but it has got her nowhere."

"Well, she will be conversing this minute with her French cousins in their own language. Is not that something?"

"Yes, but Hebrew!"

They all laughed and Mother Bel rose, slapped her man's hat on her head and announced that she would be out in the garden "for the weeds are all up apace" and she would pray for dear Deb's future while she worked.

CHAPTER SIX

Deborah was reading Racine's 'Andromaque' on a marble seat in the château gardens. She had lately made this seat her own and Suzette had learnt that if no excursions were planned that day she was to take a cushion out and set it on the rose arbour seat for her mistress and then disappear for an hour or two. Deborah could send for her since there were always gardeners about and footmen frequenting the paths to bring wine or iced cordials and sweetmeats to anyone out taking the air.

Looking about her Deborah found a wry pleasure in reading of dark tragic passions when the roses were in flower, their petals pure whites and pinks and their scents engulfing her in sweetness. It was mid-morning and growing hotter but half of the seat was shaded by the hedge that formed the arbour.

I can sit in the sunlight or in the shadowy corner, she reflected. I can enjoy the beauty around me or dwell on my own passion for Ranald and its tragic end. I can revel in Racine's elegant language or weep with Andromarque. Will the pain of lost love ever leave me? Should I not thank God for these days of ease and peace? Yet there is talk that Marlborough has forces poised to invade France itself but no one here seems perturbed. I long to be travelling to Paris but an apathy of summer lies over the château. Have I to wait till Jeanetta conceives?

She returned to her reading but from time to time lifted her eyes as figures passed along the main walk some thirty yards away. The gardens were copied from Versailles she had been told by the count who had insisted on being her escort on the day after their arrival. They were laid out very symmetrically with long straight vistas, and in between circular spaces with gravelled paths twining round centrally placed statues or fountains. Here and there however near the high walls were secret bowers like this one, in its semi-circular hedge of yew.

Occasionally she heard voices from behind the hedge where there was an Italianate garden surrounding a fountain. The splashing of the water usually made the words indistinct but today she began to hear the unmistakeable cough of the Vicomte de Neury, Sophia's father. She had made little headway in his acquaintance for he rarely appeared in the public rooms and then seldom spoke. Sophia would make an excuse that he preferred writing in his study. The vicomtesse also kept to their own part of the château and showed no interest in Deborah.

Deborah could tell that the vicomte had someone with him whose voice was very low for at one point the vicomte said quite plainly, "Speak up, man. You know I am hard of hearing."

The other replied, with a low chuckle, "That may be, sir, but I am wary. Even fountains have ears."

Deborah dropped her book into her lap. That voice! She knew it. Where had she heard it before? It was no one at the château. The speakers were moving away now, she could tell. Where could she go to see who it was that had spoken? She laid aside her book and stood up. She must walk in the opposite direction till she came to the diagonal that led back to the Italian garden. She didn't want to be seen herself so when she reached the turning she peeped round a tall fir on the corner to see if the men were still in sight. There they were, heading by the opposite diagonal for a gate in the wall that led towards the stables. Beside the small hunched figure of the Vicomte stalked a tall man clad in a dark cloak despite the warm day. His hat was pulled well down on his head and made her think of Shakespeare's conspirators in *Julius Caesar*. She couldn't possibly tell from his back a hundred yards away who it was. She bit her lip in frustration. That voice!

She now stepped out into the centre of the path for they were

Height of Folly

going to disappear through the gate at any moment. But as they reached it the man turned sideways to speak to the vicomte. She realised he was saying goodbye. Oh he was too far away to see his features! And then her figure must have caught his eye because he turned fully round, raised his hat, waved it and passed out through the gate in the wall.

That flamboyant gesture! Last seen as he looked over the side of the packet boat as she was rowed away. Edouard le Vent! She shivered.

"What is *he* doing here? But the impudence of that wave! He knew I was coming here so if he wanted to see *me* why is he going away? But of course he didn't. I am a post." Angry and flustered she began to retrace her steps to the rose bower. "Why is he dressed like one disguised? And what business can he have with the Vicomte de Neury? Is he an agent of the *French* government?"

She heard her name called and saw John pausing on the main walk. He came down the path to join her.

"Not reading on your marble throne, Deb?"

"Yes, no, I mean I've left my book there."

"You look – troubled. Were you mumbling to yourself just now?"

She was only too eager to confide in him. "Yes, John, you recall the man on the boat who wished me a safe journey."

"Why yes, he knew your name. You said you'd been talking to him on deck."

"I've just seen him."

"Here! How could that be? You must have been mistaken. Where is he now?"

"He was talking with the Vicomte de Neury by the fountain. He passed through the gate to the stables. I suppose a groom was waiting with his horse there and he will be well on his way."

"You don't suppose he came seeking *you?*"

"He saw me – at a distance – he raised his hat and went. So, no, I do *not* think he came to see me. But he had *some* curious business here."

John took her arm and drew her back by the side path and looked toward the garden wall. The vicomte was ambling along by it as if returning to the château by that route.

"See how tiny he looks from here. You couldn't recognise anyone you hardly knew from this distance."

"He waved his hat to me."

"Any gentleman might raise his hat to a lady he saw watching him. I would myself."

"John, I heard his voice when they were behind the hedge. He sounded – I know not how it was – like a spy! Maybe one playacting a spy."

"A spy?"

"And he was dressed up as one – well, a long dark cloak and his hat pulled over his ears."

John laughed now. "I think you are touched by the sun, sister. Come get your book. The family are planning a picnic." She fetched it and as they walked on John asked, "I suppose you know not the name of this mysterious man though you gave him yours."

"Yes, he was called Edouard le Vent."

John stopped still and grabbed her arm to face him. "Le Vent!" His mouth stayed open.

"What! You've heard of him?"

At once he was on his guard. "Oh well, yes." He gave an embarrassed laugh.

"How? Where?"

"Here perhaps. Or no, maybe in Dover or on the boat. Someone who travels a great deal. Maybe he gambles mightily or deals in fine wines. I've heard the name bandied about."

Deborah was both intrigued and alarmed. "You can't fool me,

Height of Folly

John. The name startled you. But you didn't recognise him on the boat?"

"I've never seen the man. I told you. I've just heard the name. It's nothing. Let us go and see the picnic preparations. They do such things on a magnificent scale here. There'll be every servant in the place carrying tables and trays down to the glade in the woods by the stream. It will last all day. They hang lanterns in the trees when it gets dark and there'll be musicians and dancing. Oh, I was going to tell you — Netta is feeling sick and doubts if she'll come down. That's a good sign isn't it?"

Deborah had to smile at his round eager eyes. "Mother was sick when she was carrying Ruth but there are many other causes. Don't hope too soon. But John, be honest with me. What do you know of le Vent? There is something sinister about him."

"No no, just an odd character. Playacting. You said it. The name is tossed about. You say he was talking to Neury? No one else."

"Not that I saw."

"Well, I wouldn't mention it to anyone. Better not."

"What? A name bandied about and yet not to be mentioned?"

"Perhaps old Neury lays bets with him and wouldn't want it known. We'll keep his secret eh?" He seemed desperate to drop the subject but then suddenly asked, "Tell me, what did le Vent speak of on the boat?"

"Very little. I told him about us and Horden and coming here."

"And me? You mentioned me?"

"Yes, why would that matter if he is some eccentric as you say?"

John laughed. "No indeed, not at all. I wager he's a gossip who likes to know folks' business. Harmless of course. Forget him. Ah here is Netta up after all." He looked crestfallen. He is desperate for a son, Deborah thought. I mustn't harass him about this.

Jeanetta approached, holding hands with her two young cousins, Louisa and Francesca, Sophia's daughters.

Prue Phillipson

"We made her get up and come out," they shrieked.

"I am better out in the air and will enjoy the festivities even if I can't eat much." She pulled the book from under Deborah's arm. "Urgh, Racine! How can you read such gloomy stuff?"

She seemed about to hurl it into the bushes but Deborah grabbed it. "I took it from the château library."

"Oh! I suppose they would have to buy his works because the King made much of the man, but he was quite a heretic you know. The Pope didn't approve of him. You girls shouldn't read him," she told them, chuckling, and skipped ahead with them like a young girl herself.

Deborah followed, heavy-legged. Is John afraid of le Vent because of his boyhood adventure with the Jacobites, she wondered. Pray God he is not already entangled with them again! Was the vicomte reporting something to le Vent or was it the other way round? I dislike mysteries. And is it not a further puzzle that if le Vent wanted secrecy he should reveal himself to me by that saucy wave. I could spread news of his coming to all and sundry. Should I tell Comte Rombeau that his gardens are used for secret meetings between de Neury and some mountebank? Why does de Neury live here at all? Is there no Château Neury? Should I make a confidant of Sophia and find out her family history?

She realised John was silent too. He had not hurried ahead with his wife. He was plodding beside Deborah in a cloud of thought.

Seeing they were approaching the château where there was an immense bustle going on, she asked abruptly in a muted voice, "John, what do you know of de Neury?"

His head jerked up. "Why? Nothing much. He keeps to himself."

"Has he not got a mansion of his own somewhere? Why do he and the vicomtesse live here and Sophia and her girls?"

"Oh that! It was after Sophia's husband was killed. He was at

Height of Folly

some siege when King Louis's forces were fighting the Dutch. The French rebuilt a Citadel and held the place but the Dutch took it and the French had to surrender. Sophia's husband ordered his men to lay down their arms but the Dutch shot him anyway."

"Oh." Deborah considered this. "It must have been the Siege of Namur. That was about eight years ago. It all ended with the Treaty of Ryswick."

John laughed. "Of course I should have expected you to know all about it."

"I followed the course of that war in the papers as you could have done. But what has Sophia's husband's death to do with the de Neury family coming to live here?"

"Their home was close to the border so they feel safer here. Jeanetta says her uncle went a bit mad. He hates the Dutch and would like them wiped off the map. Her Aunt Madeline thought he might go out and shoot a few. That's why he won't talk to us. We English fetched William of Orange over to be king instead of James."

Deborah watched John's face closely when he threw this out. "Oh," she said, "does that suggest a connection with this man le Vent? A Jacobite plot perhaps?"

John waved his hand in a dismissive gesture. "Forget that man. As I said he's an adventurer, an eccentric. Now I beg you, sister, to put your curiosity to rest and enjoy today's festivities. Next week you and I have been promised the carriage to visit Paris and Versailles."

"Do you mean we are to begin our great travels then?"

"Nay, we will come back here afterwards. I must know if Netta – " He lifted his brows. "You know what I mean. It seems her father has to show his face at court so we'll go with him but he'll stay there when we return. Of course you know the French nobility are obliged to spend time at court. If the king observes anyone's absence without due reason, well, they might as well be dead meat."

"Should you not keep your voice down?"

But the racket of shouted orders, the running of feet and clattering of dishes was loud enough to drown all conversation. Deborah decided she must enter into the spirit of a French picnic on so grand a scale and inwardly indulge her delight at the prospect of Paris and Versailles so soon. The count's company was not so welcome. He took over every activity and talked incessantly but that she must endure patiently.

A footman approached her as all the servants did with a mixture of diffidence and derision. She knew they all regarded her as grotesque. He was bearing a letter on a silver dish. Deborah saw Grandmother Bel's handwriting and grinned with delight.

John was already moving from her side to join Jeanetta so she called after him, "From our grandmother."

"Good. I'll see it later."

She wandered back along the main walk away from the crowds till she found a carved bench with stone snakes entwined along the arms. She was soon engrossed in the letter. Amidst the minor details of Horden life Grandmother Bel had inserted the news that a member of the Branford family – Deborah might remember that the old earl had been at Cambridge with her dear Nat – was travelling in France and had been sent an introduction to herself and John in remembrance of the link between their two families. So she was not to be surprised if the card of a Lord Frederick Branford should be presented at the château door. 'He is about thirty-five we reckon and a widower,' Grandmother added.

Deborah smiled to herself. What is she saying between all these lines? Am I to consider him as a suitor, officially proposed by my family? They do not know that I am suspicious of men, on my guard, armoured against flattery. Well, we will be away for some

Height of Folly

weeks visiting Paris and Versailles so if this Frederick calls here he will be disappointed, unless of course they entertain him in one of their many spare guest rooms till we come. I wonder what connection he is with the old earl. Grandmother Bel avoids mentioning the son Henry, Father's Cambridge friend, the poor lad who lost his head to a canon ball. Perhaps she shows her letters to Father and believes the memory still upsets him.

She got up and inserted the letter into her hanging pocket and walked briskly back to join the family party. She was not surprised to find they had already set off for the picnic place, some in the carriage, the younger ones walking. No one had noticed her absence or they didn't care. She set off with her great strides and soon saw the colourful figures disporting themselves in the glade.

I am not much enamoured, she was thinking, of the name Frederick.

CHAPTER SEVEN

Lord Frederick Branford was in a constant battle with his servant-companion, Will Smythe, over his reluctance to spend his grandfather's money.

Will was a solemn, heavy-jawed, stalwart man in his fifties, a long-standing retainer of the Branford family, so much respected by the old earl that he had agreed to send only Will and two footmen, Peter and Joseph, in Frederick's retinue.

"Will has travelled extensively," the earl told Frederick, "and you are too old yourself, my boy, to be accompanied by a tutor as young men are these days on their grand tours. But trust Will in everything. You are clever and well-read but have scarce been away from Cambridge and its countryside all your days."

There had been a long embrace then from his grandfather and Frederick couldn't help a moment of puzzlement that having been so lately found he should be sent away where he had no wish to go, but, sadly, it seemed to be obligatory on a member of the nobility to broaden and cultivate his mind to take his place in society.

The embrace from his mother was even longer and more poignant.

"It is what I always dreaded," she told him. "That revelation would lead to separation." She, who had been a radiant, laughing mother all his childhood, was struggling to raise a smile to lighten their parting.

"I'll be back in a year." He gulped when he said it. A year felt like a life sentence.

But they had set off and Frederick almost immediately found that the hardest thing was learning to travel in luxury.

"My Lord would not wish you to take the *diligence*" was Will's

Height of Folly

first piece of advice when they arrived in Calais. And when they reached Paris, "My Lord would like you to stay in one of the hotels in the *faubourg* Saint Germain. They have the best reputation." And all the time, to porters, waiters, beggars, street singers, "A few coins or we will be in grave trouble, my lord."

"To anyone whose services I use I will be generous but I dislike those who pester me when they have done nothing for me."

"It is the safest way, my lord."

Frederick was happiest when he could walk about Paris and view Notre Dame, the Louvre, the Tuilleries Palace and the Invalides hospital, but Will never left his side, warning him of all sorts of dangers if they quitted the main thoroughfares. When they were to go more than a mile or two he insisted that they use the hired carriage and the services of its driver as well as Peter and Joseph. Peter was a shy, quiet youth with a stammer but excellent with horses. Joseph was much older but clever with his hands. If a carriage wheel came off he could fix it. Frederick had no trouble with their company. He had always been friends with the farmhands on his grandfather's farm. Unfortunately Will Smyth expected them to treat Frederick with distant respect.

The weather turned wet and Will allowed him a day indoors in the Paris hotel to write letters home. Then he laid out a programme for the next few days which included an opera and a visit to view, but not take part in, the gaming tables which were a great feature, he said, of Parisian life.

"I'd like to move on," Frederick said, wondering if he had any authority to say such a thing. "Paris is a very dirty city and all this rain is turning everything to a noisome slime."

Will looked out of the window at the clearing sky and made no comment.

The evening became quite radiant. It seemed that Will controlled the weather too. Frederick had no wish to go and see the gaming tables or an opera and he wondered why he should not saunter down to the banks of the Seine on his own. As a small town lawyer he had taken strolls on June evenings to walk by the Cam. With great daring he managed to slip out of the hotel without Will seeing him.

He had strolled about for an hour or so and admired the prospect of the city from the Pont Neuf but, worried that Will would send out search parties for him, he decided to take a shortcut back to the hotel. He soon realised this was a mistake. He thought he had an idea of the general direction but quickly found himself among streets that grew narrower and turned this way and that until he was hopelessly lost. There were still swarms of people about so he hoped to pass unobtrusively among them, but he was disconcerted to find that nearly all stared at him, many laughed and many shouted words of jeering abuse. His own French was stilted and somewhat limited and he could make nothing of these coarse sounds. Perhaps he had been wrong to decline Will's advice to buy a whole new wardrobe of Frenchified fashion on their arrival. He had been shocked enough at the expense of dressing him up to befit an English lord on his travels. To play yet another role to deny his Englishness was more than he could stomach.

"The English are not loved here, my lord," Will warned him. "We are allied with their hated enemies the Dutch, my lord, and have won a great battle against them."

Frederick had begged Will to refrain from adorning every sentence with 'my lord' but that he couldn't be persuaded to do. Now, hemmed in by blackened houses and ragged crowds, Frederick longed for a return to his former existence, his quiet Cambridge house, his daily walk to his office and return to his mother's plain English cooking in the evening. The death of his wife and baby in childbirth had been a shattering blow but the brief happiness he had had with her had slipped into a golden

Height of Folly

sliver of time that would always shine in his memory. He had taken his mother into his home and gladly embraced again the dependence of his youth on her strength and steadfastness. That was until she had heard of the Branfords' lack of an heir and had broken it to him that it was now incumbent on him to fill that place.

Among the many uncomfortable changes that ensued probably the worst was this travelling abroad. A rough shoving by a boy with a barrow of onions made him clutch at the sword that dangled at his hip, another awkward sign of his new life. The boy passed but now a bent old woman accosted him in a high croaky voice.

"Are you lost, sir? You are not safe in these streets."

He grasped her meaning and nodded vigorously. She put her hand on his sword arm and guided him round two corners to a small filthy courtyard from which there appeared no exit. Straightening up suddenly she gave a manly shout and two men appeared from a doorway and seized his arms. It was three against one for the woman was certainly a man. The shawl had slipped from her head and revealed a chin with a scruffy beard.

Frederick had one second's thought of his own idiocy in placing himself in this danger. What would Will, what would his grandfather say if he never returned?

He made no resistance. "Take my purse," he gasped at them in French. "Take anything but let me live."

They were grinning. "Ay that we will, take everything."

First they removed his sword, then his hat, new curled wig, coat and waistcoat, feeling in the pockets and sharing out the coins from his purse among themselves. How thankful he was that he always entrusted his passport and other papers to Will who had soon noticed his habit of leaving such things by his bedside in inns. But now he realised the robbers intended to strip him naked.

"Nay, for God's sake!" he cried in English. Laughing they took his shirt, shoes and fine silk stockings.

"*Petits pieds!*" roared one of them as his small white feet were exposed to the filthy ground. They felt the fine cloth of his breeches and looked at their own hulking frames.

"Too small but they'll sell." They ripped them off him, fingering the fancy buckles and belt.

Frederick stood trembling with shame and shock in his linen drawers.

"Wrap yourself in those ears," yelled the one disguised as a woman.

Frederick couldn't help putting up his hand to those obtruding features which had been the bane of his life at school. The men laughed, slapped his face and disappeared by the doorway from whence they had come. Now Frederick realised to his horror that the courtyard was filling with others who had come to gloat at the spectacle of a half-naked Englishman.

Well, he thought, I am alive and I am determined to stay so. Thank you, good Lord. I might have been a mangled corpse. I must face this out.

He straightened his spine, drawing himself to his full height of five and a half feet, and grinned round at the crowd. "Good people, as you see I have been sorely robbed, but there must be a kind heart among you that will find me a covering and guide me back to the *faubourg* Saint Germain where you will be amply rewarded.

There was a fight then to be his escort. The largest man, who looked like a carrier of coals, took the soot-encrusted sack from his shoulders and enveloped Frederick in it and marched him off, keeping others at bay with an extended fist.

When they emerged onto a main thoroughfare where elegant ladies and gentlemen were strolling Frederick kept his head bowed and prayed that no one who saw his dirty face and half-naked state would ever recognise him again. Then he heard Will Smythe's

Height of Folly

voice.

"Oh my lord! Whatever has happened to you?"

He lifted his head and saw they were actually near the steps of their hotel.

Will must have come out in a panic to look for him.

"Can you not see I have been robbed? Reward this good man and get me inside quickly."

The man wanted his sack back and haggled with Will over the coins he was handed. Frederick couldn't help thinking that if he'd fallen into *his* hands first he would have fared no better than he had. Paris was a fearful place and he was a fool to have ventured out alone.

Will told him so as deferentially as he could when they were back in their hotel room, where Will habitually slept on a mattress on the floor across the doorway.

"I know, I know."

Frederick was making plentiful use of the water in the ewer and basin provided on a marble-topped stand. First he cleansed his whole head and neck. Then Will emptied the dirty water out of the window and refilled the basin from the jug. Frederick, drying those obtruding ears, told him, "I will never again trust a suspicious-looking woman and I shall be glad to leave Paris as soon as possible."

"My lord, this is a hazard of travel anywhere. I advise you to carry one of the good pistols his lordship gave you. The sight of a firearm frightens most robbers."

"Perhaps we can go on to Versailles tomorrow. Surely one is safe in the palace of the King?"

Will pursed up his lips. "They say there are pick-pockets everywhere but serious violence - ? I think not, my lord. And see, letters have come from England in your absence. We should strive to keep to our expected route so that correspondence can reach us safely."

When he was clean all over and clad in fresh linen and his bed robe Frederick took the letters and seeing one in his mother's hand opened it first. How shocked she would be if he wrote to her of his latest experience. He would spare her that anxiety though he might tell her when he was safe home, if that should ever happen. Shaken though he was, he felt a little proud of how he had escaped without injury.

He sat on the bed to read her letter while Will summoned a serving-maid to replenish the ewer with fresh water and brush patches of soot from the floor. Glancing at her as she worked Frederick met her scarcely concealed grin. Yes, he thought, the adventure of the English lord must already be a mighty source of merriment among the hotel's domestics. The sooner I am gone from here the better.

He finished his mother's letter and when the maid had gone he said, "Will, let me see my grandfather's letter. My mother is telling me to follow the suggestion he has made in it."

With no one else to confide in he needed to treat Will as a friend, difficult as that was, so, when he had read Earl Branford's letter, he summoned him to sit by the bed, which he did with great reluctance, perching on the edge of the chair.

"Well, Will, I am to seek out a young lady while we are in France. What do you think of that?" The intimate question embarrassed Will. He placed his fingertips together and looked up at the ceiling. "Well indeed, my lord should be always on the look out for an English lady of appropriate rank. The Branfords must have an heir." He met Frederick's eyes for a second. "It is some time since your sad loss, my lord."

Frederick waved a hand to dismiss that still painful subject and a rare moment of intimacy vanished. He laid his hand on the letter. "This is a *particular* lady we are to encounter if possible. She

Height of Folly

is the granddaughter of a friend of his lordship from his Cambridge days."

Will's eyes lit up. "Ah that could be a Horden from Northumberland, my lord. I was a boot-boy and had the honour to clean the boots of Sir Daniel Wilson Horden when he stayed with the young lord, with your father I should say, before they joined the navy. Is this young lady travelling in France then, my lord?"

"She is staying at the Château Rombeau for the present and Grandfather has sent a letter of introduction to the count there who is evidently her brother's father-in-law. We could be welcome there for a short stay while I make the young lady's acquaintance." He grinned at Will. "Surely we should be safe there even from pick-pockets?"

Will was nodding solemnly. "Indeed, my lord. But I feel I should say, knowing a little of the history of the Hordens that the lady would hardly be your equal in rank. Her grandfather, Nathaniel Wilson, of whom I have always heard his lordship speak warmly, became no more than a village parson, although I have seen papers by him on theological subjects in his lordships' library. He made a name for himself in a small way. It was because he married the daughter of Baronet Horden that he took the name Wilson Horden and they provided the heir, Sir Daniel, who was in turn the friend of your father at Cambridge and a fine, handsome young man as I remember him, unusually tall and with very flaxen hair. He survived the war and married a second cousin whose name I forget but who came from a merchant family in London. Her father, however, was a little mad I believe and became a dissenting street preacher who died in the London plague. I know of these things for his lordship kept up a correspondence with the late Reverend Nathaniel until his death. It is only his great affection for that gentleman that would lead him to propose his granddaughter for his own heir. However, my lord, we will certainly accede to his wishes."

Frederick suppressed the chuckle that was rising in him at this the longest speech Will had ever made to him. "Well, Will, I thank you for all that information but we mustn't run ahead of ourselves. My grandfather does not say I am to *court* the lady with his blessing, merely that as there is a friendly connection of long-standing between our families it would be a courtesy to greet the lady and her brother while we are still in northern France. As to rank you know I never aspired to be of the nobility and such distinctions come very hard upon me."

Will got up. It was plain that he felt uncomfortable and Frederick knew well that what he had just said would make him more uncomfortable still. Will was only too conscious of his master's inadequacy as an English earl's son travelling abroad. The scrape I have been in tonight, Frederick was realising, has shamed him even more than me. Poor Will!

"Is it your wish then, my lord," Will said, "that we make for the Château Rombeau tomorrow?"

"No, we will take in Versailles first for that is westward of Paris I believe whereas the château" – he looked back at the letter – "appears to be in the other direction, towards France's eastward border. There is no fighting there I trust."

"None at all that I have heard of, my lord, though there is no news of the great Duke of Marlborough's movements as yet. Very well, I will alert Joseph and Peter to have the hired carriage and the luggage carts ready for the morrow." He bowed and departed.

Frederick put his head in his hands, not sure whether to laugh or cry. He took up his mother's letter and kissed it. "Dear, sweet mother, have you any idea of the pickle you landed me in when you disclosed the true identity of my poor father."

CHAPTER EIGHT

Paris began for Deborah with the waddling figure of Comte Rombeau filling her vision and assailing her ears with his booming commentary on every building of note. On the third morning he was seized with gout and waved a pained hand at her from a couch in the hotel.

"Today was to be Notre Dame. So sad. You and your brother must go alone. No no, not altogether alone. Suzette must walk behind you. No French lady would walk without her maid. But myself – ah it is my tragedy."

And our delight, Deborah said to herself as she backed out with a sympathetic smile.

At Notre Dame it was a shock to see John cross himself with the holy water and genuflect before a statue of the virgin. He did it so easily, even casually, that she was more convinced than ever that he was now a communicating member of the Catholic Church. None of the family had forgotten how impressed he had been by a priest and his chapel as a little boy but it was only to Deborah that he had vowed to become a Catholic when he grew up. It was something a little boy might say in a moment of wonder and no one had made any connections when he fell in love with his French cousin. All the years since then he had continued to take communion in the village church with the rest of the Horden household.

She tapped his arm. "Is everyone expected to do that? I reverence Mary but do not worship her."

He flushed up. "It's what they do. Look at Suzette."

She was kissing the ground before the statue.

"Well I shan't do it. It's against my conscience."

John just shrugged his shoulders and no officials rebuked

Deborah. In fact the crowds parading around seemed in no way struck with the awe which began to overwhelm her. She had read about the cathedral before, of the thousands of men who had added towers and windows and carvings decade after decade, but she could only gaze now and marvel that somehow a magnificent wholeness had been achieved. When they went outside again she stood so long just looking at the West Front that John had to take her arm and drag her away.

In a few days the comte's gout had eased enough to allow them to travel on to Versailles. There Deborah was oppressed rather than uplifted by its grandeur. "It is such a mass of buildings, wall upon wall of little windows. The scale of it and of all this regimented nature leading up to it quite staggers me."

Worse was the interior of the block allocated to courtiers and their relations. The few rooms for the Rombeau family's use were small, evidently partitioned out of a larger one. The long passages were dirty and crowded with people passing up and down, even pedlars selling ribbons, buckles and a variety of food stuffs. The sanitary arrangements were extremely primitive.

Comte Rombeau's wide frame was again swaggering ahead of them as they explored the buildings and gardens. When he was not bowing to acquaintances he was turning round to see how delighted Deborah was with all this magnificence. John grinned at her wickedly. He had exhausted his own adulation at his last visit and found amusement in her efforts to maintain her enthusiasm. "The Hall of Mirrors and the Orangery," she declared with truth, "are very fine."

On their last morning the count managed to insert them into the crowds pressing into the King's bedchamber for the daily ceremony of his dressing. Deborah thought this extraordinary and though they only saw some of the final layers of Louis's elaborate costume being put upon him she would have liked to hide away.

Height of Folly

Instead she had the mortification of meeting the King's eye and hearing him ask an attendant why the lady had climbed upon a box to look at him.

Comte Rombeau pushed forwards and fell heavily on his knees. "Forgive me, your majesty. She is sister-in-law to my daughter and is a very tall English lady."

The King waved a jewelled hand to dismiss the matter, but Deborah heard a courtier mutter, "She could be added to the menagerie as a new attraction." There were giggles as the Rombeau party retreated quickly and the comte's affability with her was sorely strained from then on.

She was very glad next day when she and John climbed into the carriage without him to begin the journey back to the Château Rombeau. In her eye she pictured with pleasure her quiet reading bower until she remembered the mysterious visit of Monsieur le Vent. All this sight-seeing had put him out of her mind. Would he return? Why had John started at hearing his name? For the sake of harmony she refrained from questioning him again. He was edgy, anxious to be back for news of Jeanetta.

They were travelling amicably enough now, the road passing through misty morning fields, when they saw in a dip of the road ahead of them a thicker patch of fog. Shouts came from it and all sorts of strange shapes loomed out of it.

"What's to do here?" John called to the Rombeau coachman. "Slow down and approach cautiously."

A horseman emerged, seeming to trail wraiths of the mist behind him. He shouted to them, "Nothing to fear. Just some peasant woman evicted for not paying her rent. She and her boy were pushing their cart in the middle of the road. Idiots!"

He galloped off.

As they drew nearer Deborah could make out on either side of the road the scattered hovels of a small settlement next to a stream meandering through the valley. In the middle of the road was an upturned cart that must have been piled with the items of furniture and baggage that were now strewn across the road. A carriage approaching from the opposite direction was held up too and a woman in a shawl was wailing and wringing her hands at the edge of the road while a skinny lad struggled to pull the cart right way up. People running from the houses were doing nothing to help but were making off with anything they could carry.

Deborah saw that a gentleman had descended from the other carriage and was remonstrating with the plunderers. His servant seemed to be remonstrating with *him* and urging him back into the carriage as the poor sticks of furniture were dragged off the road and the way opened. But Deborah's heart went out to the poor woman and her son. She jumped down and ran to her.

"Where were you going?" she asked her. "Have you some place to take these things?"

"My brother's if he'll have me."

John had followed but at that moment a burly man trotted up on a pony and began laying about with a whip. "Leave the goods alone. She owes me them for the rent."

Deborah was caught in a rush of people trying to dodge the whip and found herself pushed against the gentleman from the other carriage. He looked round and seeing this shape looming over him grabbed her arms and held them tight against her sides. His head butted her chin.

"I've been fooled once," he muttered in English. "Not again." Then to her in French, "You were trying to pick my pocket. I warn you I have a pistol in my belt."

Deborah was too astonished to speak but the man's servant hauled him off her.

"Get in the carriage, my lord. And let's get out of here before more harm's done."

Height of Folly

The gentleman found himself lifted bodily in. His mouth hung open as he looked up at Deborah's face. "God in heaven! Is it really −? No surely − ?"

He was trying to touch his hat and bow to her as the coachman whipped up the horses and the carriage escaped from the general melée.

John came up and grabbed Deborah's arm. "They do well to clear off. This is not our business."

She saw his hat had been knocked awry and there was a red mark on his cheek. Matt and the Rombeau servants were fighting off several ragged boys trying to raid the carriage where Suzette was cowering on the floor squealing.

Deborah pushed some coins into the woman's hand and shouted at the man with the whip, "Let her alone. Take only what is yours in law and let her and her boy go to her brother's." Something about her imperious tone, her height and her fluent French made the man lower his whip and the villagers melted away to their houses leaving a few broken bits of furniture and the woman's bundle. Her boy loaded it onto the cart which he had finally managed to set upright.

"You can't have my few clothes," the woman screamed at the man.

"Nay, they'll be full of fleas," the man yelled, "but I'll have the cart. You took it from my shed."

John drew Deborah back to the carriage.

"For pity's sake, let's go. We can't judge between them."

With great reluctance she climbed in and comforted Suzette. The Rombeau coachman clicked to the horses. As they passed the woman she was shouldering her bundle and taking her boy by the hand to go on their way. Her hunched weary shape stabbed at Deborah's heart.

She shook her head at John and gave a long sigh. "At home I

would have taken her up and deposited her at her brother's door but we can hardly impose that on the comte's servants. And you, John? Did the whip catch you?"

He put his hand to his cheek. "The merest touch. What was all that to-do at the other carriage?"

Deborah thought of the face of the gentleman who had threatened her with his pistol. She couldn't help breaking into laughter.

"I suppose he took me for a man in woman's clothes. He must have been attacked by one before. 'Not again,' he said. He was English and his servant called him 'my lord' but he was not a very heroic figure when he was hauled back into his carriage. Although," she added, thinking of when she had first noticed him, "he had got down himself to protest at what those thieving villagers were doing. That took courage for he was quite small of stature. But oh the redness of the poor man's face when he looked me in the eye. I'm not sure even then that he was certain I *was* a woman."

John joined in her laughter.

The Branford hired carriage went on its way towards Versailles as the sun broke through the mist and touched the summer fields with flashes of brilliant green.

Frederick sat hunched and silent as Will persisted in haranguing him.

"But my lord, I implore you not to concern yourself with the affairs of other people. Will you give me an assurance that you will not leave the carriage again if we encounter troubles like that?"

Frederick shook his head, sat up straight and looked Will in the eye. "They were robbing that poor woman. The horseman galloped straight into the village when he could scarce see ten yards before him in the fog. The poor boy swung away from him and the cart went over. But the man didn't stop for a moment. He might have

Height of Folly

killed her and the boy."

"He is not permitted to stop. He was a King's messenger."

"I care not who he was. There is such a thing as humanity."

"But you see, my lord, you again laid yourself at risk from robbery. Where there are crowds of desperate people there is always thieving."

"And why are they desperate? Are not the fields producing food?"

"Ah yes sir, and prices will come down at harvest time. This is the hardest month for many. Larders are empty. Rents are high."

"Well well, it may be so but I do not believe we would have witnessed a scene like that in England. But now, tell me, Will, was that not a man who accosted me in the crowd? There was very little bosom that I could see under the bodice and when I looked at the face there was no beard but certainly a strong jaw. The hair piled up under that straw hat was so fair I thought it might be a wig."

Will was grinning in a way Frederick didn't like. "Assuredly it was a tall lady, my lord. I saw her get out of a fine carriage with a count's crest. She went to the poor woman with an air of feminine compassion, though it is true that she moved like a man with large strides. She fell up against you because she was pushed by the surge of the mob fleeing the man with the whip, my lord."

Frederick burned even more fiercely with shame. "You think it was a *grand* lady? And I pinioned her arms to her side and threatened her with my pistol! You gave me not a moment to make my apologies before you whisked me away."

"Do not be anxious, my lord, you are hardly likely to meet her again in the whole of France. She doesn't know your name. Let us forget the incident and endeavour to have no more such encounters. Keeping one's distance from trouble is what I have learnt wherever I travel, my lord."

Frederick fell silent again. The sprinkling of 'my lords' did nothing to mitigate his sense of being told off like a naughty child.

Deborah and John reached the Château Rombeau on a baking hot afternoon. Jeanetta was lying down. All the family appeared to be lying down and Suzette assumed that Deborah would wish to do the same.

"I get bag of ice for my lady, put on head."

"Thank you, no, Suzette. I see the fountains are playing and I'll stroll round where the air is moist and cooler."

"Is my lady's head not aching?"

"Not at all."

"You wish me attend you?"

"No. *You* lie down yourself with a bag of ice and let me be alone for a while."

Suzette giggled nervously. It was a habit with her lately. Deborah found it irritating but couldn't stop herself from provoking it. This being waited on and followed about was absurd and she longed to break through to the real Suzette and make a friend of her. She knew the giggles only covered Suzette's inability to make sense of her new mistress of whom she plainly remained in abject awe.

Deborah went out through the empty passages into the garden which throbbed with heat and stillness. She reached the first fountain and stretched her hands into the veil of spray, tilting her head to let it spatter her face and even run down her neck.

"You long for the cool of Northumberland, *n'est-ce-pas?*"

She swung round. Edouard le Vent stood ten paces behind her.

"You – again!"

He grinned and she felt those black eyes boring into hers like gimlets. He stepped up smartly and seized her hand and kissed it.

"No." She snatched her hand away, took a step back, tripped on the rim of the pool and sat down in the water.

Height of Folly

He leapt to her aid with both hands outstretched but the absurdity of the situation convulsed her. Am I to fall over every time I meet this man? She nearly asked it aloud. She rejected his hands and leant back exulting in the cool cascade, her fury turned to laughter. He laughed too. After a few moments she did stretch a hand to his and he hauled her out.

"My dear Mistress Horden, may I escort you to the château to change your apparel?"

"I am not your dear Mistress Horden, I am a post, a post with sharp ears."

She looked to see him disconcerted but though it was plain from his eyes that he was instantly alert to her meaning he remained all smiles.

"Ah, you do not know that all the packet boat captains wish to marry me off but I tell them the wind can settle nowhere. Nor may I say would I ever aspire to an English baronet's daughter and certainly not to one so *formidable* as Mistress Deborah Horden. I admire your humour and your spirit and repeat may I escort you to the château?"

"I will walk about and dry in the sun, thank you." She unpinned her straw hat which the fountain had not improved and shook out her abundant flaxen hair. She knew it was her best feature and took delight in displaying it to him.

"Ah that is indeed a sight for the eyes."

"Then you may earn the pleasure of it by answering this question. Why do you keep appearing at Château Rombeau? Is it because I told you we were to stay here?"

She began to stride along one of the diagonal gravelled paths and he had to hasten to keep up with her at least till he answered her question.

"The Château Rombeau is but one of many havens to which this wind blows."

"And to what purpose does it blow here?"

"Ah that is man's business." He made great flourishes in the air with both hands.

"Politics? Have you forgotten that England's most renowned ruler of recent centuries was a woman?"

"But I am French and we see women in a different light. Their *raison d'être* is to be beautiful, which you are." He checked his steps to face her. "But you have strength and dignity too which frightens men – unless perchance they are of unusually large stature?"

He was shooting her meaningful looks, his eyebrows and moustache working gleefully.

He cannot possibly know about Ranald Gordon, she thought. To cover her discomfiture she scoffed, "Dignity? In wet, steaming clothes? Come, Monsieur le Vent, you trifle with me. Always you turn away from my legitimate curiosity. You know much of me and my family and my French relations too and I know nothing of you."

"The wind is unattached. As your lovely English Bible tells us, 'it bloweth where it listeth.' It has blown me to Scotland and back again and there I saw people of great families like the Campbells, the Frasers, the Gordons" – again a darted glance loaded with mischief – "and small people whose names no one remembers. But I pass by and they know not when they will see me again." He bowed. "And, my dear lady, nor do you know, for if I can be of no service to you now I will take my leave."

Another bow and flourish of his hat. His face she could see was glistening with perspiration but his dress made little concession to the heat of the day. He was equipped for riding and she noticed their walk had brought them near the door in the wall that led to the stables. He strode towards it, turned, bowed again and was gone.

Height of Folly

"Infuriating man!" she said out loud. But she was not angry, she was frightened. Her brain was absorbing what he had said and her thoughts were galloping. *He has delved into my history. He has probed my connection with a Gordon, a lowly and illegitimate one but still by birth a Gordon and one who fought for James! Am I being investigated for something that happened so long ago? And has he learnt about John's boyhood adventures too? If he is a spy who are his masters? The English government? Do they suspect a Jacobite rebellion while we are at war with France? But those Scottish clans he named I thought they had all accepted the status quo, some for reasons of expediency perhaps. Maybe things are stirring and I am ignorant. But why did he hint of his discoveries? To warn me? And what of the Vicomte de Neury? Is he being investigated? Le Vent must have been with him today and perhaps met John too. Does de Neury know my past and John's? Dear God, please do not let that time rise up again to trouble us!*

She had begun walking again in her agitation and found herself by one of the marble seats. She sank down, breathing the name 'Ranald' in a choking voice. She thought he had been laid to rest but that cauldron of emotion bubbled up all too readily. She shivered. A tiny breeze had curled round her and awakened her awareness of her saturated gown. She stood up abruptly and marched with long strides back to the château. Nothing had changed there. A footman was asleep by the door. Heavy heat lay over all the rooms. Leaving a damp trail behind her she made her way to her bedchamber and gave herself to the excited ministrations of Suzette.

CHAPTER NINE

There was rejoicing in the château and letters flew to Horden Hall. Jeanetta was with child. She was in the highest spirits Deborah had ever seen her. Sickness had passed and she pranced about like a wild colt to John's evident alarm.

There had been no more reappearances of Monsieur le Vent and when Deborah again questioned John he maintained he hadn't seen him on that second visit but was prepared to agree that he might be working for the English government and investigating the activities of English travellers in France.

Deborah frowned. "So why would he proclaim his presence to me and hint that he knew of Jacobite connections from our past? Do not spies sneak about and keep their discoveries secret?"

John laughed. "He has taken a fancy to you, sister, and this openness is his way of telling you that you need fear no harm from him. He has found out things but decided they are no longer matters of suspicion."

Deborah was sceptical about the first part but thought there might be truth in the second. "I am still puzzled though that you had heard the man's name bandied about before as you put it."

"That would be his cover. Let everyone think he is a travelling gambler, buyer and seller, a seizer of opportunities. Who would then imagine him as a dealer in secrets?"

"And his visits to Vicomte de Neury?"

"Gambling I feel sure. Sophia is worried about her father, Jeanetta tells me. She is afraid he has a hidden vice. Look, he is a nobody, a family hanger-on. Now tell me, Deb, do you wish to go travelling again when we are not sure where the war may strike next? I am inclined to wait here until our child is born. Jeanetta is fearful of my leaving her."

Height of Folly

Deborah was trying to keep up with reports of the progress of the intermittent fighting. Marlborough had had to withdraw his army from the Moselle because his Dutch allies had sent no reinforcements and France had hailed this as a victory but since then Marlborough, by a clever double bluff, had broken through the famous Lines of Brabant, believed to be impregnable. Again the Dutch held him back from pursuing his advantage and heading direct to France. It seemed certain then that for the moment the fighting would be confined to the country south-east of Brussels.

"Surely, John," she said, "you would not want to wait till January. We could explore the Loire valley as we intended, see Orleans and perhaps go by water to Nantes on the coast. I have heard of no fighting in that area and we could be there and back before winter sets in."

John crinkled up his face in just the way he used to do as a boy when she tested him on his Latin irregular verbs. "I'll talk it over with Netta."

A few days later on a wet day when Deborah had wearied of reading in her room she sought John for his answer and found him in the billiard room directing his young brothers-in-law, in a game. His function seemed to be to prevent them from quarrelling as they constantly accused each other of cheating.

"Oh leave them to it," she said to John, "and tell me what Jeanetta said to our travelling again before winter."

"I haven't asked her. I know she doesn't want me to go."

"Then *I* shall ask her. We have been here an age and time hangs heavily."

She went to the billiard room door and opened it just as a footman was lifting his hand to knock.

"Ah my lady, Madame la Comtesse is sending all over to seek you. An English m'lord has come with letters of introduction desiring to make your acquaintance and that of your brother."

Deborah exchanged glances with John. To her dismay she found her neck and cheeks burning.

"Why John, it must be that Lord Frederick Branford." She was laughing to cover her confusion. She had shown John Grandmother Bel's letter and he had teased her at the time but had evidently forgotten all about it.

He slapped the side of his head. "Oh yes. You think the old folk are after a husband for you."

Deborah flapped her hands at him. "Nonsense, don't say such things."

But she couldn't help a sideways glance at the large mirror in a gilt frame along one wall of the billiard room. Suzette had piled her abundant flaxen hair on top of her head which was how she had been taught to create ladies' coiffeurs but it gave Deborah even more height. She wished now she had arranged it herself. Her gown was a simple light green silk over a flecked petticoat. The big cream collar and cuffs contrasted with the natural colour of her sun-bronzed face, while the close-fitting bodice only emphasised the flatness of her chest.

I would make a handsome man, she thought, with my hair cropped and a coat and breeches. Well, Lord Branford will hardly see in this towering Amazon the dainty, amenable second wife he may be seeking but I suppose I must go and meet him. She beckoned John to come too and they followed the footman to the salon.

Four Rombeau ladies were sitting in a semicircle, Madeline de Neury, her daughter Sophia, Comtesse Diana and Jeanetta. The gentleman they were facing was seated in a high-backed chair and Deborah could see nothing of him when she entered the room except for one foot in a highly polished shoe.

Diana waved a gracious hand. "Ah, here is my dear Jeanetta's

Height of Folly

husband and her English sister-in-law. Deborah, my dear, may we present Lord Branford?"

The gentleman leapt to his feet and faced them. Deborah needed only one glance before she was struggling not to burst out laughing. She saw his eyes lift from her chest to her face and the blood rush up his cheeks. Oh the poor man! Her heart went out to him in his horror and confusion.

Graciously she held out her hand and he bowed over it. She could see he would have liked to sink through the floor. She noticed how red even his forehead glowed against the white of his neatly curled wig.

"I am delighted to make your acquaintance, Lord Branford. And here is my brother, John Horden."

John, shaking his hand, evidently did not recognise him as the man in the carriage, which was a relief to Deborah. Her task now was simply to put the poor man at his ease and pretend to everyone else that they had never met before.

They all sat down and refreshments were brought in. Deborah deliberately placed herself next to Lord Branford while John shared the couch with Jeanetta.

Amidst the bustle of questions about coffee, chocolate, fruit cordials or wine she made Lord Branford meet her eye and put into her steady look a wealth of humour, reassurance and kindly feeling. She was rewarded by seeing his face return to a healthy English colour and his eyes lose their shock and embarrassment. He even managed to lift his head and give her back an apologetic smile. She could read much in those expressive eyes. They were a pleasing light blue, honest and guileless as a summer sky. They told her he was overwhelmed by shame but mightily thankful for her tact and thoughtfulness. She creased up her own eyes in a mischievous wink.

When he was engaged with the footman over his choice of

beverage and sweetmeats she was able to study his profile. Why, he is the very opposite of me, she decided. My forehead is too high, my nose too long and my chin too square. His features are neat. Perhaps his nose is a little short compared with his upper lip. His chin is smoothly rounded and very precisely shaved. He has small hands and clean nails. And yes, he is small. He is an inch at least shorter than John. He can never compare with Ranald in manliness but I believe I could enjoy his company.

There was some general talk then about where he had been so far, what he had seen and what had most impressed him. Although it seemed that his French was passable the ladies did him the courtesy of speaking in English. As always it was Diana who dominated the conversation. Her sister Madeline, the Vicomtesse de Neury, Sophia's mother, hardly spoke and Sophia too was usually quiet in company.

Diana fluttered her fan at their guest and excused the absence of her husband, the comte. "He is at Versailles. His Majesty must have his favourites about him, you understand, my lord. It can be trying but duty is duty you know. You will stay a while of course and I shall send word that we have another guest and he will beg leave to come home and make your acquaintance. It matters nothing that our countries are at war. My grandfather was English. John and Jeanetta are second cousins as well as husband and wife. Is that not charming? Later you will meet the Vicomte de Neury, the husband of my silent sister here. He is the only one of us who dislikes the English – for borrowing a Dutch king, but then he dislikes all foreigners, the Dutch above all. But you will be wise and ignore him as we all do." She sprinkled this speech with so many laughs that Lord Branford could only smile and bow in reply.

He is shy, Deborah decided, but whether that is because he is still recovering from the encounter with me, I can't be sure. He certainly doesn't swagger like an English nobleman in the presence

Height of Folly

of French aristocrats of equal rank.

The Vicomte de Neury appeared when a lavish dinner was served at two o'clock. As they were introduced Deborah was pleased to see that Lord Branford overtopped the little vicomte.

John had already teased her about their new friend's small stature. "If you hoped for another six-foot-five giant you must be sorely disappointed."

"Now look," she whispered to him, "Lord Branford is not so insignificant."

He had changed from his travelling clothes and presented a smart trim figure in a purple coat and embroidered waistcoat which Deborah was sure he must have purchased in Paris. John just raised his eyebrows at her which was infuriating.

There was no chance at the dinner table for any private talk with Lord Branford but afterwards everyone noticed that the rain had stopped, the sun had been shining while they ate and the garden paths were dry.

"We must let our English family learn all the latest news from England," Diana announced. "John and Deb, pray show Lord Branford the gardens."

"I shall come too," Jeanetta declared, grabbing John's arm.

"Should you not rest, my pretty?" her mother cooed.

"No indeed, I have never felt so alive."

Deborah found this was a happy arrangement. Only the very broad walks permitted them to walk four abreast and she and Lord Branford soon strode ahead of the young couple. Deborah was pleased to find that though he was not tall he had a good stride and walked as one accustomed to the exercise.

The moment they were out of hearing of the others he turned to her.

"I cannot tell you, Madam, how grateful I am for your discretion over our first unlucky meeting. I was wretched when I realised I had manhandled a lady. Did I cause you any hurt?" He was blushing again. "My serving-man gave me no chance to apologise –"

Deborah checked him, "It was nothing, my lord. Pray, let it not be mentioned again between us, except –" she hesitated and looked laughing into his eyes – "do tell me the reason for your exclamation of 'not again!' Can it be that you had recently been attacked and robbed by a man in woman's clothing?"

"I had indeed – it was in Paris – but that in no way excuses my disgraceful conduct."

"But it *does*. We were all in confusion. I was thrust against you by the mob."

"Were you not angry with me?"

"Not in the least. I was angry for that poor woman and her boy, but your mistake was only comical. I told the tale to my brother, convulsed with laughter."

"And he doesn't know the blackguard was I?"

"Not at all. He was not close enough in the crush."

"And you are telling no one of my shame?"

"Certainly not. Perhaps your serving-man will know me if he sets eyes on me but I am sure he is discretion itself."

Lord Branford nodded. "I am afraid Will Smyth is all too ashamed of me as his master. I do not meet his standards in any respect and he is only too anxious to keep my escapades from the public eye."

This revealed a very intriguing aspect of Lord Branford. The sentiment chimed neatly with her own inability to play the great lady and keep Suzette happy. She looked down at him with deepened interest.

Perhaps her failure to reply at once struck him because he asked suddenly, "I know not how much you may have learnt of my history from your family in Northumberland. I am aware that my grandfather wrote a long letter to your grandmother. Did she tell you I am a mere novice among the aristocracy?"

"She described you only as a member of the Branford family." If Earl Branford is his grandfather, she reasoned, how can he be new to the aristocracy? Is he perhaps illegitimate, like my poor Ranald who was a bastard Gordon?

Lord Branford hesitated. "Your grandmother was being very discreet."

Ah, perhaps I am right. Deborah encouraged him with a little chuckle.

"Discretion is unusual in Grandmother Bel. She is the most open and frank character I know."

"Then I should say she was being thoughtful, leaving it to me to speak of my true status if I wished. Perhaps I should not allude to the circumstances on so short an acquaintance but I thought you might already know – but if you did not –" He tapped his cane against his calf in his confusion – "The truth is I fear I must betray myself constantly among high society."

Deborah was more and more intrigued. They had come by chance to her familiar reading bower. John and Jeanetta were not in sight. *They are deliberately throwing us together*, she realised, *and later John will tease me without mercy about my 'petit gentilhomme.'*

"Let us sit down for a moment, my lord. You have roused my curiosity."

He seemed happy to talk, but first he begged her not to call him 'my lord'.

"It is a relief to speak with a friendly English person. Will Smyth is my sole companion and I cannot cure him of the habit of punctuating every sentence with 'my lord'. The truth is I have not grown-up with it. I did not know I was the heir to an earldom till recently. My mother was a farmer's daughter called May Haywood."

He glanced at her to see if this shocked her.

"How delightful." She said it heartily but her imagination was busy. Earl Branford had only had one son, Henry, killed in a naval battle. Had he had some escapade with a farmer's daughter? Ranald was a Gordon only because a despicable member of that clan had taken advantage of a serving-girl and then abandoned her. Surely, she thought, Father's friend would not have behaved like that. And this gentleman is not hesitating over a shameful secret. He *wants* to tell me. He has just admitted how short he is of friendly English company. As there cannot possibly be any attraction of a romantic sort between us I see no harm in lending an ear to his revelation. His candour is refreshing and I am enjoying it after the horrid mysteries of Monsieur le Vent.

Lord Branford was regarding her with his eyes alight with eagerness.

"May I really tell you the story as my mother told it to me?"

"Of course."

So there unfolded a pastoral idyll of a girl on a day in early summer seeking eggs in the hen-run, the men of the farm in the fields and her mother at market. She saw a young rider showing off to her by jumping a hedge into the lane. Thrown into the ditch he got out unharmed but wet and muddy. Her laughter triggered his and from that moment mutual laughter bound them together and grew swiftly into love.

Deborah listened wistfully to the tale of their secret meetings at an anglers' hut by a stream. She was thinking, did not Ranald and I fall in love as swiftly? Did we not laugh together too? She had not expected to be stirred so deeply by Lord Branford's story. So she asked casually, "Was this when your father was a student at Cambridge? For that is when my father knew him."

"Yes, he had a fine mount from home and loved to exercise it when he should have been at lectures. Your father perhaps had no

Height of Folly

horse there and couldn't accompany his friend?"

"Indeed he hadn't. His family then kept only the horses needed on the land. My parents didn't set up a carriage till the day I was born."

"And my mother and I had no access to any but the plough horses on her father's farm."

She laughed. "We seem to have got into a competition for the humblest origins which is not the usual way of the world. Despite all, you are the heir to an earldom. Pray fill in the rest of the tale. I know our fathers graduated and then joined the navy."

So he told her how his father had feared that he might not survive the navy and was desperate to secure his lovely girl as his wife. He described a secret marriage and then his mother's heartbreak when her Harry went to war and did not return.

Deborah stared at a faded rose hanging over the back of the marble seat. I am like that flower, she thought. Ranald and I also had our secret wedding and he was dead the next day. But this man's mother was *truly* married and blessed with a child. What would my life have been if I had borne Ranald's bastard son? She began pulling apart the browning petals of the rose and scattering them at her feet.

Lord Branford went on to explain how his mother had been long finding out what had happened to his father since the navy had no record of his marriage. He himself was born by then and her family had accepted her situation as a widowed mother. He was animated in his devotion to her for the happy childhood she had given him. Laughter had quickly come back into her life and his memories were all of joyous days on his grandfather's farm.

She watched him as he talked. He had sat back on the seat and was gazing up through the bower of roses. Why, he is far away, she realised. He hasn't noticed me destroying this sad flower. Studying his face she saw a tear at the corner of his eye ready to drop. He must have become aware of it too because he suddenly brushed it away and looked at her as if he had just remembered where he was.

"Oh forgive me, Mistress Horden. I had become lost in my memories. The truth is I miss my mother very much. I was sad to leave her and she was sad to see me go. I was never apart from her in my life before. During my short but lovely marriage she was nearby and ever since my wife died we have lived together again."

There we differ, Deborah thought. My closest bond is with my father. But she was now very curious about his story. "Do I understand that your mother knew the true identity of your father but had no wish to restore you to his family?"

"Yes, she was sure they would reject us as lying peasants or, if they believed the evidence of the marriage certificate, would take me out of her life altogether, send me away to Eton and perhaps into the army and she would never see me again."

"So what changed her mind?"

"Well, I was a grown man, had married and sadly lost both wife and child. And then she read in the papers of the death of the one remaining heir to the earldom. She believed it was her duty to approach the earl, my grandfather, and reveal that he had a legitimate heir after all."

Deborah clasped her hands under her chin and cast him a look of true sorrow.

"I should have said before how sad I am that you had such a grievous loss not so very long ago. But I believe you are going to tell me that your dear mother's fears about the Branford family were unfounded."

He acknowledged her sympathy with a bow and a sweet smile before readily plunging into the concluding part of his story.

"You are right. My grandfather is a most kindly soul. He was very alone at his country seat in Hertfordshire, his wife having died

Height of Folly

some years after they lost their son, and his daughters married and living at a distance from him. He took both me and my mother to his heart and his home. But of course I needed" – he hesitated – "grooming, shall I say – for my future role and this travelling is part of it. Mother has had to accustom herself to a changed life, not in our own little home in Cambridge, but in a private wing of her father-in-law's grand mansion. And I" – he lifted his shoulders and gave her a rueful grin – "have given up my work as a lawyer and must learn to be an earl. Now you see why I am a novice at the business." He laughed and blushed. "I fear I have talked far too long. A true aristocrat would be courteous but aloof on so brief an acquaintance."

"And I wouldn't have enjoyed his company half so much. Pray do not let anything *groom* away your natural self, Lord Branford. Ceremony is not something we Hordens have ever stood upon."

She looked up as John and Jeanetta appeared at the end of the path, arm in arm. "Here are my brother and his wife. *Her* family are a little more conscious of their status. Perhaps you will not be telling *them* your story?"

He stood up and gave her his hand to rise too. He was chuckling and shaking his head. "No indeed. But you were such a sympathetic ear, Mistress Horden."

John and Jeanetta stopped before them. Deborah was touched to see John's childish shyness asserting itself before a nobleman he scarcely knew. "A bit warm eh?" was all he could manage but Jeanetta had her mother's loquacity. She seized Lord Branford's arm and demanded to walk with him. "For," said she, "Deborah has had you to herself quite long enough."

They returned to the house in time for the afternoon refreshments that were always brought into the salon or carried about the house to wherever the family could be found. Deborah suffered John's teasing and curiosity over what they had talked about for so long. She had no intention of divulging Lord Branford's story. John would tell it to Jeanetta and then it would be all round the family in no time at all.

She herself was warmed by the encounter. The few men she had met in her life at Horden regarded her with nervous apprehension which developed into jocular familiarity from her brother's friends or remained a wary 'keep her at arm's length' from slight acquaintances. Everyone in the neighbourhood knew the rumours of her Scottish adventure but didn't know the full truth. One thing they were sure of was her great learning and were either in awe of it or discounted it as unbecoming a woman.

I find it liberating, she thought, to meet a man who knows nothing about me and rouses in me no physical attraction. Frederick Branford lacks the great height and exuberance of Ranald Gordon, nor has he the flashing black eyes and alluring smile of horrible Edouard le Vent. But he has opened up to me with sweetness and innocence. I see into his heart and there is no guile, no mystery. Can I have a friendship with a *man*? I have never achieved intimacy with a woman my own age. Grandmother Bel is my only true female confidant at home. I thought I might make a friend here in Sophia de Neury but she is very reticent. Well, Lord Branford will move on and I suppose our paths will not cross again. If Grandmother Bel or his grandfather had plans for us they would drop them sharply after one look at us together.

CHAPTER TEN

Will Smyth had a bed in the dressing-room that adjoined Frederick Branford's heavily ornate bedchamber. When he came to prepare his lordship for bed they had their first moments of intimacy since Fredrick's walk in the gardens.

It was at once obvious to Frederick that the usually stolid Will was agog with questions but he still managed to introduce them with circumspection.

"And did you have a pleasant stroll in the grounds, my lord? I believe they are copied from Versailles."

"Very pleasant." Mischievously Frederick refused to help Will.

Will busied himself laying out his master's nightshirt very precisely on the bed. "So would you be thinking of moving on in a few days, my lord, now that you have fulfilled your grandfather's wish that you call upon the Hordens at their French retreat?"

"I don't mind how long I stay here," Frederick chuckled.

Will couldn't hold back his curiosity any longer. "I was told by the French household, my lord, that Mistress Horden is uncommonly tall. I have not yet set eyes on the lady but surely she is not by any chance –"

"Yes, she is, Will, and a more gracious and forgiving character you could not imagine. She is delightful."

Will straightened up and looked him in the eye. "My lord, I hope you won't be taken in. You appreciate that for a lady not in the first flush of youth and of no great social standing you are a very desirable prospect. I am sure she would be only too ready to forgive your unlucky rough handling."

For the first time in their enforced companionship Frederick snapped back at Will with real anger. "It is no such thing. I would be honoured beyond words if she were to look upon me in that way, but of course I could not so aspire. She is as far above me in her nature as she is in her physical height. She is a goddess among women."

Will bent hastily to his duties again, murmuring, "I'm sure I beg your pardon, my lord."

Frederick drew a long, slow breath and calmed himself but said not a word more to Will that night about Deborah Horden. His mind was full of her but Will was not the one to receive his confidences. If only his mother had been here! He would have described to her Deborah's open, easy manner that surely hid profound emotions, those speaking eyes, suggesting ocean depths, that glorious flaxen crown of hair, her tall, regal figure! He could watch her forever. And he had had the nerve to tell her his story. How had he dared to ramble on so long? But she had listened, commented, asked questions, sympathised. And above all, she had humour, a quality he loved and longed to share. Will Smythe hadn't a humorous bone in his body. That was why he missed his mother so much. She would smile at the world even if her heart was sad. Deborah Horden was another, he felt sure, whose natural demeanour was cheerfulness. Laughter played about her. He went to his bed and she inhabited his dreams all night.

Deborah meanwhile had taken her chance to speak to Jeanetta alone when she saw her in the glasshouse picking an orange.

"They are so juicy, Deb. Come and try one. I have a craving for them now."

Deborah took one to eat later with the help of a napkin, a knife and a plate. She couldn't afford to let the juice dribble down her bodice as Jeanetta was doing.

She asked her straight out, "I believe you wish to keep John with you till the birth of your child. Is that right?"

Jeanetta raised her eyebrows as she squeezed the last of the

Height of Folly

orange into her mouth. She licked all round her shapely lips and considered the question.

"Oh I want him here for the birth of course though he will die of fright if he is in earshot of my screams." She cackled uneasily when she said it. "Sophia tells me it may not be as bad as I fear but Maman shrieked horribly when the boys were born for I remember covering my ears with pillows."

Deborah ignored this. "So you are saying you won't mind if John and I go away for some weeks before the bad weather makes travelling difficult?"

Jeanetta spread out her hands. "I would have come too but Maman says I shouldn't be bounced about in a carriage." She added with a roguish smile, "You'd like to have Lord Branford for company, wouldn't you? What a pity he's so short! John and I were laughing at the comical pair you made when you walked ahead of us in the gardens. I'm afraid you're never going to find a man like that Ranald Gordon John told me about."

Deborah started and Jeanetta rushed on, "Oh I know he always warned me that you didn't want to talk about it but surely it doesn't matter now. It's so long ago. But how romantic it was! That great big highlander and you rode all night to save him from the gallows and then he got stabbed to death in prison. Such a shame!"

Deborah did *not* want to talk about Ranald, certainly not to Jeanetta of all people, but she said in a neutral voice, "He was not strictly a highlander since he was born in Edinburgh. But no, I'll never meet another man like that. How did you like Lord Branford when you walked back with him?"

Jeanetta took another orange, bit into the peel and spat the piece onto the ground before digging off the rest with her dainty fingernails. "Dreadfully bad for the skin, I'm sure," she tittered. "Lord Branford? Rather dull, lacks the poise and polish one would expect from a man of his rank. Really hadn't much to say for himself."

Deborah turned to go. "Will you tell John then that you don't mind him leaving you for a while? He seems to think otherwise."

Jeanetta grinned, dropped the rest of the peel onto the ground and bit squelchily into the pulp. "If you like," she spluttered.

Returning to the château Deborah met John coming to look for his wife and told him herself what she had just said.

He looked a little furtive. "Well, she may *say* that, you know. Doesn't want you to think her anxious. I'll talk to her. Let you know in a day or two."

Three days passed in picnics and evening parties laid on especially for Lord Branford and Deborah had no chance of private conversations. On the fourth day she went out alone in the gardens after breakfast and took her book to her rose bower but intended to look out for either John or Lord Branford. It had struck home when Jeanetta had said, "You'd like to travel with Lord Branford too." She would, very much. If they could make up a party and go together that would be more interesting than with John alone. The Comtesse Diana had pressed Lord Branford to stay longer and meet the comte to whom she had sent a message about his new guest, but his coming, she giggled, would depend on the severity of his gout at the time.

Deborah hadn't been reading long when she heard footsteps and looked up to see Lord Branford turn briskly off the main walk at sight of her. He came up eagerly. She rose to greet him and he begged leave to join her for a few minutes if he was not interrupting her reading.

They settled down on the seat and he began at once, "Mistress Horden, I have just had a rather odd encounter. I wonder if you can tell me who the gentleman is with a curling black moustache

Height of Folly

and very black sparkling eyes. Is he one of the family whom I haven't yet met?"

Deborah shivered. "What! *He* is here again! No, he is a mysterious visitor who makes me feel decidedly uneasy. Pray tell me how and where you met him."

"He slipped out of a side door with your brother and the Vicomte de Neury."

"With John! Are you sure?"

"Well, I was at a distance, actually admiring the orangery, but I *thought* it was your brother. They seemed to be saying goodbye to this strange man and went back into the house. He was turning to pass along by the garden wall when he must have spotted me and he came on to meet me with hat raised and flourishing gestures. I wasn't sure if I was supposed to know him but I stepped out of the glass-house and to my surprise he greeted me by name and asked if all my kinsfolk in Hertfordshire were well when I left. 'All high Tories I believe, the Branfords,' he said then. 'An ancient family. Hertfordshire is a pleasant part of the world and close to the capital. I love your England and of course your wild, beautiful Scotland.'" Deborah started at the words but Lord Branford didn't notice and went on, "I am afraid I stared at him speechless. He bowed, told me he wished me well on my travels and left me standing there. After a moment to recover my composure I thought I should follow him but he moved very swiftly and I just caught sight of him disappearing through that doorway which I believe leads to the stables."

"And he will have a servant there holding his horse and he will have vanished as mysteriously as he appeared. Lord Branford, what was the tone of voice in which he said 'your wild, beautiful Scotland.'"

"That was a little odd too. He lowered his voice and spoke the words liltingly, poetically perhaps."

"Even reverently?"

"Well yes, as if they were a sort of incantation."

"Then I am sure they are a code or password and you didn't give the right answer so he left you alone."

"A code! A password? What can you mean, Mistress Horden?"

"I am more convinced than ever that he is in the pay of the English government. He calls himself Edouard le Vent, moving hither and thither like the wind. I'd wager it is not his right name."

"But why would he come here?"

"He seems to know the movements of every English traveller coming to France and they are all suspected of plotting to overthrow the Protestant crown and replace Queen Anne with the young Prince James. He must have learnt some code words used by Jacobites and is trying them out to test people's innocence. You passed the test and he lost interest in you."

"But the Vicomte de Neury? How would he be involved?"

"That I don't understand though I am sure he speaks with him every time he comes. What concerns me is that you say my brother was with him."

"I certainly *thought* it was your brother but that need not alarm you. If you are right about this man your brother will have passed the test as an innocent traveller like me."

Deborah felt a chill at her stomach. Was John an innocent traveller? Could he be mixed up in some conspiracy after all? Why was he with the Vicomte de Neury? She knew the Vicomte disliked the English for putting a Dutchman on their throne. Could there be secret movements in France to restore a Catholic Stuart? John had not hidden from her his sense of the rightness of young James' claim, had even said the French would have to send him with an army to seize the throne.

"I fear my tidings have upset you," Lord Branford said, getting up. "I would not for the world –"

Height of Folly

"No, no, not at all. Pray sit down again and I will tell you how I first met this Monsieur le Vent." She began to laugh. "It's my turn to tell *you* a story."

He sat down very readily and she felt how pleasant it was to have him there to share her anxiety.

So she described their turbulent crossing to Calais and how she had talked with this seemingly charming man and given him so much free information about her home and family. In the telling she had to reveal that she and John had both been to Scotland when they were younger without explaining any of the circumstances.

"So there *was* a connection," Lord Branford said, "which might have roused his suspicions – added to your relationship to a French Catholic family. So his interest in you and your brother is understandable, but how did he know who *I* was and why should he suppose I was a likely rebel against the crown? He said my family were 'high Tories.' How could he know such a thing and what did he deduce from that?"

"He could have found out from the Vicomte that a new English visitor had come here. He would ask your name and I presume he has made it his business to know the allegiance of English nobles. It was the Whigs that were in the ascendancy in Parliament when William was brought in and when the succession was proclaimed for Queen Anne I believe some 'high Tories' were doubtful about disposing of the true line so arbitrarily."

Lord Branford nodded slowly. "I think you may be right."

He is weighing it up as a good lawyer should, Deborah thought.

"Yes," he went on, "I recall now my grandfather telling me he spoke in the House of Lords to that effect – that there was irony in the proposal to diverge now from the principle of an hereditary monarchy when we fought Cromwell over that very issue. Of course my grandfather has since accepted that a Stuart would not do unless he renounced his Catholicism."

"But there you are then. *You* are suffering now from the price of fame."

"It makes me very uncomfortable. I liked being a nobody."

"I too." And they sat and laughed together.

Deborah didn't have to wait for a chance to question John. As soon as she and Lord Branford had returned to the château John sought her out and getting her apart into a corner of the salon hissed in her ear, "Would you believe it, Deb, I've met your mysterious *Mr Wind*. He must be as you thought in the pay of the government. I suppose de Neury pointed me out to him. He wanted to know – all smiles and flowery gestures of course – why I was at the Battle of Killiecrankie. I more or less said I was kidnapped and made to fight. Well, it's true. I was so young I didn't really know what I was doing. I'm sure I satisfied him. Now look, about that other business – when we are to go off travelling again. You were right there too. Netta's quite happy for us to go so we can set off as soon as you like."

Deborah was puzzled. Why is he so excited and breathless, she wondered. There is more going on than he is telling me. But if I can get him away from here for a while it can only be a good thing. Maybe le Vent's questions have alarmed him. Could he have been on the verge of participating in some Jacobite conspiracy that de Neury is hatching?

All she said was, "Shall we go then when Lord Branford also plans to leave? He feels obliged to wait and see if the comte comes but that we should know very soon."

John grinned at her slyly. "Are you proposing to travel *with* Lord Branford?"

Height of Folly

"Not in his carriage of course but we could make up a party. There could be safety in numbers and we might receive more respect as acquaintances of an English lord."

"We couldn't afford the places where he will be staying."

"I don't think he has very grand ideas but we will see."

"Are you smitten with him, Deb? He really is too small for you, you know."

"I am *not* smitten as you put it but people can be good company however small they are."

"Very well. I shall sound him on the subject and make arrangements." And he walked off leaving her frustrated that he had got the upper hand in that conversation when she had intended to put him through a severe interrogation herself.

Next day the comte sent word to Diana that he was obliged to stay in Versailles and would she give Lord Branford his apologies. Perhaps the noble lord would return and visit them on his way back to England after his travels.

Plans were laid then for them to set out in two days' time and Deborah looked forward to shaking off the somewhat stultifying atmosphere of the Château Rombeau.

CHAPTER ELEVEN

Frederick Branford took a bold step and informed Will Smyth that they were going to visit the Loire valley.

"But, my lord, we were to be heading south in late August. Your grandfather's letters will be arriving in Lyons."

"And they can wait till we arrive. Now that we have made the acquaintance of the Horden brother and sister I would like to pursue our travels together at least for a short while. After a day or two I will propose that they come in my carriage and you, I hope, will not mind accompanying their man Matthew in theirs. As we will drive along together Mistress Horden may be happy for her maid Suzette to travel in the second one with you. We will keep Peter with us along with the hired carriage's driver in case of trouble and you can have Joseph."

Will stood for a moment with his mouth open but recovered himself quickly.

"Very well, my lord."

Frederick chuckled to himself. He had triumphed. Will was offering no arguments against the plan. This is my new decisive self, he reflected. I am growing used to having a manservant. Mistress Deborah likewise had a lady's maid imposed upon her. We had a pleasant laugh together on the subject.

On the morning they were to set out John Horden accosted him after they had risen from breakfast. He appeared to have waited deliberately till Deborah had gone up to her room to check Suzette's packing.

Frederick thought he looked rather red and flustered. "I hope you don't mind, Lord Branford, but de Neury has asked me to take a letter to a friend of his at Saint Germain. It's not out of our way,

Height of Folly

you know, and Saint Germain has some very fine architectural features which I'm sure you'd like to see."

"By all means if your sister is agreeable."

John reddened even more. "That's it, you see. She may kick up a bit of a rumpus because that's where the young Prince James has his court and this fellow le Vent has been going about hunting for Jacobite conspirators everywhere. Deb said he spoke to you the same day he spoke to me. It's all nonsense of course. France has troubles enough with the war. She's not wanting to harbour English rebels, is she?"

Frederick was in a dilemma. He mustn't upset Deborah and he was too new in their acquaintance to arbitrate between brother and sister.

John rushed on. "If *you* said you were sure there was no harm in it she'd be easy in her mind. De Neury says the man is just a friend he corresponds with. Nothing political at all."

"So why does he not send the letter by a servant?"

"He could of course but he's told me about how interesting the place is and I really want to see it."

"In that case I am sure we would all like to see it. Here *is* your sister."

Deborah was descending the great staircase. What a splendid figure she looked in her long travelling cloak! Frederick felt like a dwarf as he stepped forward to give her his hand on the last step.

"Mistress Horden, your brother is telling me there are interesting things to see at Saint Germain and we can easily take them in on our way."

He saw her brows rise as she looked at her brother. "What things, John?"

"Buildings and such. What you like looking at."

"Yes, there is the palace which King Louis gave to our exiled James and where his son now lives."

Prue Phillipson

"Oh, come on, Deb. I'm not going to see *him*. I'm not going near his court. We can look at the palace from afar. De Neury has asked me to hand over a letter to a friend if we happen to be calling there to see the sights."

That's not how you put it to me, John Horden, Frederick thought. Well, le Vent passed us all clear of suspicion so there can be no harm in it. But that may be just why the vicomte is using John. We know nothing of *his* plots or whether le Vent still has his eye on *him*. He looked at Deborah to see how she was reacting.

She pursed her lips in a charmingly thoughtful way. "I have read," she said slowly, "that there is a mighty long stone terrace there built by André Le Nôtre, from which you can see the Seine valley all spread out and on a fine day pick out the Cathedral of Notre Dame. I *would* like to view *that*, but I would also like" – she lowered her voice – "to drop the little vicomte and his letter in the river."

Frederick couldn't help chuckling as he saw the mischievous gleam in her eye.

"But you'll go along with it, Deb," John cried. "After all, le Vent told me he was going back to England so his sniffing round here is over for the present."

Deborah raised her eyebrows again. "He told you that, John?"

"Well, put us all at our ease, you know."

Frederick could see John Horden was certainly more at ease now.

"If Lord Branford is happy –" Deborah began.

And so a few minutes later instructions were given to Peter and Joseph and to the Rombeau coachman and the party set off.

The August day was ablaze with sunshine and even the solid mass of the Palace of Saint Germain and the great terrace spreading in both directions seemed to Frederick to be melting and shimmering in the heat.

They had all descended from the carriages to mount to the terrace and see Paris but a heat haze hung heavily over the Seine valley.

Frederick noticed that John was fidgeting from one leg to the other and Deborah was watching him with a frown on her face.

"*You* do not have to play post-boy, John," she said. "Give the vicomte's letter to one of the servants."

"I'd better just take it myself. It's not addressed on the outside. De Neury told me where to find his friend." And he hurried off in the direction of some of the lesser buildings that clustered at the side of the palace.

Deborah sighed and turned to gaze into the fuzzy distance. Frederick wanted her freely laughing self to reappear.

"Pray do not be anxious, Mistress Horden," he began. "Your brother will return in a few minutes and we can resume our journey. At least the motion of the carriages creates a little breeze."

She looked round and smiled at him but he could tell her thoughts were far away. They walked up and down on the terrace and watched the other sightseers but an hour passed before John came running. When he saw the heads of the many strollers turning to look in astonishment and some alarm he slowed his pace and sauntered up to them with a laugh.

"They must have feared I brought bad news, a battle lost or some such thing."

Deborah snapped at him, "And where is your apology to Lord Branford for keeping him waiting in this heat? He will be regretting ever proposing to travel with us if this happens again."

Frederick made deprecating noises as John flushed and stammered his regrets.

"Didn't realise how long – they – *he* urged me to take a glass of wine."

Frederick instantly imagined a group of conspirators, heads lowered, drinking round a table.

Deborah too picked up on 'they.' "Who have you been seeing? What people are these you have been meeting?"

John tossed his head. "Just a few friends of de Neury's friend. Why are you so suspicious, Deb? I'm sorry about you waiting in the heat. We could go down into the small town and find some refreshment."

This they did and Frederick made sure that ale and cheese and French loaves were sent out to all the servants at his own expense.

When they were ready to resume their journey he ventured to suggest the rearrangement of the carriages that he had already proposed to Will Smyth.

"You said 'after a few days' my lord." Will reminded him, his face as pugnacious as a bulldog.

"And now I have proposed it to my friends and they have agreed," Frederick told him. He didn't say John had agreed readily while Deborah had been reluctant. He guessed she had prepared fierce words with her brother if they had been on their own. I *hope* that was the reason for her reluctance, he reflected, as he handed her into his own carriage. I want harmony between the two of them. What he really wanted was for John not to be with them at all but he would scarcely admit that even to himself.

With an ill grace Will gathered Matt, Suzette and Joseph into the second carriage and the coachmen took their places. This was how they travelled for the next few days till they reached Orleans. John gave his sister no more alarms and though he was quiet and thoughtful, Deborah herself shed her anxiety and threw herself into enjoying the trip and, Frederick hoped, his own company.

Height of Folly

At Orleans they sent the Rombeau carriage ahead to Nantes and Frederick paid off his hired carriage so that they could take to river transport for a change. From Nantes they went on to Saint Nazaire to see the Atlantic Ocean.

"Nothing between us and the Americas," cried Deborah stretching her arms to the waves. "Is not that an astonishing thought?"

She had plucked off her hat which the wind was threatening to blow away and her hair ballooned out into a flaxen cloud behind her. Frederick could only gaze at her in delight and wonder that he should have met such a woman. She was so different from Mary, the wife he had lost, a slight figure, smaller than himself, with dainty features, fawn-like eyes and a clinging nature. She had been in awe of his strong mother and devoted to him but her constitution was always delicate and childbirth had been too much for her. He had however been made to feel a man. She looked up to him in all senses and he delighted in being her protector.

This Deborah Horden was a tower of health and strength. He could never aspire to be anything more than an admirer from afar. He had told her his story but would not presume to delve into hers. She was a free spirit, with sudden enthusiasms, as she showed now when she exclaimed that she must find a way down to the shore and walk to the very edge of the sea.

"I want to see those waves breaking at my feet."

John refused to attempt the descent because he was wearing new shoes but she found a rough path down and Frederick accompanied her, with Suzette picking her way carefully a few steps behind as usual and then looking up with eyes and mouth agape as the great breakers tumbled in towards them.

"She has never seen the sea," Deborah told him. "I saw it first when I was ten and my father took me on a boat down the Tyne."

Frederick felt a sharp pang of memory.

"I saw it at Holkham Sands. Mary and I went to the Norfolk coast after our wedding. There were seals basking and she was quite frightened of them – like giant slugs, she said." He gulped on the last words. He could hear Mary's voice and suddenly he wanted her beside him, looking up and seeking reassurance that the monsters wouldn't come up off the sandbanks and attack them.

Deborah looked down at him with instant sympathy. Yes, she was warm-hearted this sturdy north-countrywoman.

"It's still a raw grief?" she said and he nodded.

They went back to find John at the hotel where they were to stay the night.

After two days in Nantes Frederick hired a carriage again and they began their journey south. Will Smyth expressed satisfaction that they were on their correct itinerary though Frederick knew he didn't approve of their mode of travel. He was deprived of the pleasure of chivvying his master at every opportunity, nor did he care for the company of Matt who in his view was too high-spirited for a manservant.

Although it was now early autumn the weather was still benign. As they journeyed they met some anti-English sentiment from mobs in the cities but most landlords were happy to take their money. Frederick was impressed by Deborah's interest in the news. There was much talk that King Louis had offered peace terms to The Hague. Deborah commented that he was trying to split the allies and the Duke of Marlborough was more likely to be spending his time on diplomacy than planning more campaigns before winter.

One day they were quenching their thirst in a tavern in Lyons when a man claiming to be a retired French officer leant across to Frederick and remarked, "You English will never beat a French army fighting for the land of France."

Height of Folly

Deborah replied in her impeccable French, "But sir, France has forces in the Low Countries, Northern Italy and Spain. Her own borders are not breached. Perhaps their heart is not in it now." The officer, floored by this imposing lady speaking his language so well, withdrew quickly. Deborah gave Frederick a mischievous smile. How much my enjoyment is enhanced by her presence, he reflected, but we must part company soon when they return to Rombeau. The prospect left him desolated.

The next day in Lyons was stormy and they stayed indoors and wrote letters, Frederick to his mother and grandfather, while Deborah said she would write a general letter for her grandmother, father, mother and sister. John said he would write to Jeanetta to tell her they would be starting their return journey after they had seen Marseilles. No letters from her had reached them though John had had one from his mother-in-law, Diana, to say that the pregnancy was proceeding perfectly.

"Jeanetta is no correspondent," he told Frederick. "Writing letters is such a bore, she always says, but she makes me write in French which is mighty hard on me. I can talk the lingo now well enough but spelling it – !" He put his hand to his head.

"I'll correct it for you," Deborah offered but John refused and Frederick wondered uneasily what messages he might be sending to the Vicomte de Neury.

Before autumn turned into winter they reached Marseilles where Frederick felt overwhelmed by Mediterrranean colour, noise and smells, the brilliance and bustle of boats on the blue water, the piles of fruit and vegetables shouted for sale by the roadside, the stench of fish. As they strolled along, smiling at their assaulted senses, they were suddenly startled to hear roaring shouts and a great clanging, rattling noise. They looked up to see two galleys rowed into the harbour manned by slaves.

"They are chained to the benches!" Deborah cried in French which was now coming more readily to her lips. "How can a civilized people allow such horrible practices!"

A captain, smoking a pipe on the quay, turned and glared at her. "The slaves are allowed time to earn money ashore when they are in harbour so they can buy their freedom."

"Takes 'em most o' their lifetime," muttered a wizened old man passing by. "I knows. I was one of 'em."

Frederick had his hand in his purse at once and was picking out a coin to give him when the whole purse was snatched from him and the man disappeared into the crowds. Will Smyth, always at hand, reproached him sadly.

"My lord, I have advised you many a time. Keep a few coins loose in your pocket for such eventualities. Never produce a whole purse to public view, my lord, if you'll pardon my saying so."

Frederick saw Deborah watching him with a smile of sympathy. He shrugged his shoulders at Will.

"You had better see if any of these stalls will sell you a gentleman's purse. And you needn't remind me that it's for the second time nor can I promise it won't happen again." Will compressed his lips and stumped off.

"I had no such troubles in Cambridge," Frederick ruefully told Deborah.

"Nor I at Horden though one has to be on guard on the streets of Newcastle where there are many beggars. Are you wearying of this travelling, Lord Branford?"

"A little."

"But will you go on into Italy now we are so far south? You know you are welcome back at Château Rombeau to meet the comte."

Frederick saw with dismay that the moment of parting was imminent. His grandfather had been very emphatic that the

Height of Folly

galleries and antiquaries of Italy were to be the focus of his travels. If the weather held it was essential to take ship to Genoa and spend the winter in Florence or Rome.

A daring idea leapt into his mind. "What of yourself, Mistress Horden? Your brother of course must return for the birth of his child. But you also hoped to see Italy, did you not?"

"Indeed I did." She was gazing at him very intently. Could it be that she had the same thought as he had?

He put it into words. "Would it be presumptuous of me, on the basis of the longstanding friendship of our families, to offer to be your escort?" He knew he was blushing. He couldn't believe she would consent.

She made no reply at once but looked about for John who had wandered off to purchase some gift for Jeanetta.

"Ah, there he is," she said. "I think he's returning." Her eyes, Frederick saw, were very bright. Her whole body as she stood up to wave to John seemed tense with excitement.

John sauntered up. There was no sign of Will yet.

"John, John," she began, "Lord Branford has just made the most *sensible* suggestion."

Frederick's heart swelled with delight at her choice of the word 'sensible.' It was so unromantic that it would surely convince John of its propriety.

"You want to get home to Jeanetta as quickly as possible, do you not? You and Matt could travel some of the stages on horseback with a pack animal for your baggage. I on the other hand wish to go into Italy while we are so near. It was planned that we would go by sea but Father forbade me to travel alone. I must have a man with me. Lord Branford is travelling in that direction too and has three men to look after him. What do you say?"

Prue Phillipson

Frederick was staggered at the speed with which she had clad his tentative proposal with practical details. She was a wonder and it was wondrous that she had agreed. He looked at John.

"Well, that's a sudden idea, Deb. What would the old folks at home say, d'you think? I mean is it proper and all that? Wouldn't I be sort of abandoning you, you know." He laughed uneasily at Frederick. At the same time Frederick could see the idea growing on him as he spoke. No doubt he would like to be free of his sister's supervising eye.

Deborah frowned at John. "Of course it's proper. Our father and Lord Branford's father were close friends as were our grandfathers. We know Lord Branford very well now ourselves and as for Will Smyth no one could have a more protective escort than he."

"Well, dash it all, it certainly makes sense," John began and then Will Smyth came up and handed his master a small leather purse.

"Pray put it away at once, my lord, before eager eyes catch sight of it."

Frederick knew he must face Will alone with this plan so he proposed returning to the hotel where they were staying and ordering a dinner to be served.

When he and Will were in his room he said straight out, "Will, Mr John Horden is to return shortly to Rombeau for the birth of his child."

"That I understood, my lord. We can then proceed with the itinerary which the earl laid down – without any more divergences or distractions, my lord."

"With the company of Mistress Horden and her French maid." He said it quickly, not looking at Will's face.

There was an ominous silence.

Frederick added, "So you can book passage to Genoa for two more in our party."

Height of Folly

Will heaved a deep sigh. "Have you considered this carefully, my lord? Will it not be interpreted that you and the lady are affianced? Although even if that were the case would it not be damaging to the lady's reputation? I trust it is *not* the case, my lord. Your grandfather must be apprised of any suitable lady to be a future Countess of Branford so that he can approve your choice."

Frederick frowned as fiercely as he knew how. "There is no question of an engagement and don't let me hear you mention such a thing again. But have you forgotten that it was my grandfather who proposed us meeting with the members of the Horden family for old times' sake." He was thinking to himself, I am a grown man, a widower, and if I were ever to remarry it would be my own choice for my countess. But he had learnt to confide much less in Will now that he had more congenial company.

Will had put on his most obstinate expression, standing feet slightly apart and hands on his hips. "I must speak, my lord, and risk your anger again. I am sorry that your grandfather failed to warn you that many young ladies would be after you. If Mistress Horden has asked you to escort her to Italy it is only as I predicted. She has set her sights on you, my lord."

"You *are* making me angry and I'll have you know, Will Smyth, that *I* asked Mistress Horden, not the other way about."

"But she acceded readily, my lord."

"You can sprinkle 'my lords' all you like but they do not lessen your rudeness in raising this matter to me."

Will's eyes blazed with fury. He turned on his heel muttering, "No one ever called me rude before." At the room door he bowed stiffly. "I will go and make the arrangements you requested, my lord. Which day shall I book passage and do you wish oars or sails, my lord?"

Prue Phillipson

"Let us say three days from now. And sails of course. I hope you are not suggesting a horrible slave galley. Those feluccas in the harbour go to Genoa, do they not?"

"Yes, my lord, but they also keep close inshore like the oared vessels because of Barbary pirates. But you know best my lord." He bowed again and went out.

Pirates! Frederick echoed. Will is maliciously trying to frighten me. But into what dangers am I leading Deborah Horden? If we miscarry her family will never forgive me. Yet they say the route by road is mighty hazardous too especially as we draw in towards winter.

Even as he was half-regretting his impetuosity he was thinking how stalwart and unperturbed Deborah had shown herself in every situation they had met. Her confidence in the language and in dealing with the native French had already frequently smoothed their way. I believe I am looking on *her* as *my* protector, he was ashamed to admit to himself as he changed into fresh linen and prepared to go downstairs. Nevertheless, he was thinking, this is my first great adventure. Maybe it should have come when I was much younger for now I cannot foresee where it may lead and that is unsettling at my time of life.

CHAPTER TWELVE

"Letters! At last!" Daniel could hear his mother calling from the kitchen. His heart sang with relief.

Letters were brought to the back door of Horden Hall and he knew his mother was more likely to be in the kitchen than any other room on a wet November day that had scarcely become light. She came bounding into the hallway under the ornamental plaster archway with the letters bundled in her apron. She was young again.

Daniel had emerged from the estate office and Eunice from the parlour. Eunice's face was crumpled with tears of joy. "Thank God, thank God, thank God."

His mother extracted one from her apron and peered at it. "This must be the latest. Deb dates them outside and inside. Oh what can have held them up? Is there fighting going on? They have come in a bunch all together."

"Let us spread them on the library table," Daniel said. "Read them in order."

"But I must just look at the last first that we may see the dear souls are well." Bel's rheumatic fingers were already trying to ease the seal apart.

Daniel took out his pocket knife and slit it for her. "Go on then, Mother. You will have your way." He handed it to her and she took it to the library window to get what light she could.

"It is headed Lyons and then further down, Marseilles. Where are those places? Are they somewhere near Rombeau? But what is this? Deborah and John have parted, she for Italy and he back to Rombeau."

Eunice cried out, "Have they quarrelled? Please God it is not that. I trust neither on their own."

Prue Phillipson

Daniel felt sick at heart. It had been such joy to hear anything after so long a wait but now this could only be bad news.

His mother was having trouble with the dim light.

"Let me." He took the letter from her and glanced quickly through it. "She is with Lord Branford. We must look back at these other letters. Mother, what have you done, agreeing with the old earl that they should meet? Now he has got hold of our Deb and has dismissed her brother and is prancing about the continent with her. She will be infatuated as she was with that Ranald and the next thing we'll hear is that she's expecting his child."

Eunice sank down onto one of the library chairs and put her head in her hands.

"Why did I ever let both my children go? You did it without my consent, Daniel. I thought it was the war we had to fear but that has been nothing. And now they are apart and she is in a strange man's clutches!"

Bel was unsealing an earlier letter with Daniel's knife. "This is clearer writ, with a better quill. You shan't blame *me*, either of you. Hear what Deb writes of Lord Branford when he came to Rombeau. 'He is a little man. I am a giant to him. He is shy and not at all earl-like.' Well, her head will not be turned by *him*."

Eunice lifted her eyes to Daniel's. "But she should not be travelling alone with an unattached young man. When I think how my father kept me confined!"

"We are all getting over excited." Daniel saw he must take charge. "We will do what I said first. Lay the letters out in order of date. I see how it is. John and Deb have set off travelling again shortly after her last one to us when she described Paris and Versailles. That was despatched by the Rombeau servants when they were back at the château. The delays have happened since then. Once John and Deb were on the move again in a hired carriage letters sent to England from French inns may have been

Height of Folly

intercepted and scrutinised. At all events they have come."

So he read aloud the account of the Loire valley, Orleans, Nantes and the Atlantic waves. 'Suzette was frighted by the great rollers pounding in.'"

"You see," his mother interrupted, "she has her French maid with her and John has Matt. Lord Branford seems to have a host of servants too."

Daniel dismissed this with a wave of his hand. "Servants don't count."

Eunice slapped her hand on the table. "Servants are people too. I won't have you say that, Daniel."

Bel squeezed her shoulders. "You are right, Eunice, and we needn't feel so anxious about them. From what we know of Lord Branford he was not used to so much attention but it is well that he has it now."

"But let us see the next one where they speak of parting company." Daniel could see Eunice was still tense with anxiety. "John is so young and innocent and Matt is not a solid character. He will go along with any mad scheme of John's. And they are travelling in a hostile country too. What happens if they are surrounded by a French army?"

Daniel was already studying the latest letter. He looked up. "I wager the armies will all be in winter quarters now. John will be safe back at Rombeau and Deborah and Lord Branford will be in Italy where there is no fighting at all."

"So you are a little calmer now, son?" Bel was pushing her spectacles back up her nose and giving him her twinkling smile.

"I may seem calmer but it irks me sorely that she is travelling with this man we have never met."

"And she and John have not fallen out?"

"No, Deb writes of it as the most natural thing that John should be eager to get home for Christmas with Jeanetta and her family and be in time for the birth in January. She points out that she and Lord Branford both wish to go into Italy which indeed was the plan for her and John this winter."

Eunice said, "And you truly think John may be safe in Rombeau now."

"If he and Matt took horse and stopped as little as possible."

She lifted her face and tears were still running down. "I cannot bear to be away for the birth of our first grandchild. I want to see my baby John as a father."

"They will come to us as soon as is wise in the springtime."

Bel clasped her hands before her face. "And that I should live – God willing – to be a great-grandmother!"

"If only he had married a local girl," Eunice said.

Daniel laid down the last letter and got up to pace about the room. "It is Deborah I am thinking of. What can be her real state of mind? She has had weeks of intimacy with this man. She speaks of him as pleasant company but what is she hiding from us? What are *his* feelings about *her*?"

He could say no more. Tears were welling up. Experiences were happening to his precious girl and he was cut off from them. He gathered up all the letters and took them to the estate office to study more closely. His mother and wife were following, clamouring for them. "You'll get them all back," he managed to say and went in and closed the door.

Deborah and Frederick Branford had indeed reached Italy but were still far from their destination of Genoa. The *felucca* in which they had been travelling had been forced to put into port by bad weather. Deborah was thankful that neither she nor Frederick Branford had been seasick but she was happy to find herself in harbour at San Remo though the boat still rocked a little and Suzette for whom the voyage had been a terrible ordeal was still

Height of Folly

feeling ill. Deborah was the only member of the party with fluent Italian so the captain addressed her.

"It is almost nightfall, good lady. I know of an excellent hotel in San Remo and can conduct you there at once."

Before she could answer she found Will Smyth at her shoulder. He appeared never to be ill by sheer strength of character.

Now he whispered urgently, "Don't trust him. We will fare better on the mattresses under the awnings. The masters of the *feluccas* always want the passengers to go on shore for they and the crew can be more comfortable without them."

She could see that Lord Branford was ready to follow the captain who was gesturing for them all to go ashore.

Deborah smiled at Will. "We'll try the inn." He stepped aside, shaking his head.

Lord Branford held out his hand to help her onto the steps. "They can surely give us a supper and now that we are off the sea I am quite hungry."

She took his hand even though her stride was longer than his and she could manage perfectly well herself. His grip was firm and she liked the feel of it. She could hear Will muttering behind as he helped Suzette. Peter and Joseph followed. Peter was permanently hungry for the 'b-b-beef of old England.'

It was dark now but the captain carried a lantern and led them up an alleyway at right angles to the coast until they came to a stone stairway between two buildings. Turning to Deborah he told her that the *patron* up there would give them fine entertainment and she and her maid would have the prettiest room in San Remo.

Will bustled forwards. "What said he, Mistress Horden?" She knew he hated to admit that his Italian was very meagre. His eyes had opened wide when he had first heard her speaking it as eloquently as French.

"We are to go up," she said.

Prue Phillipson

The captain was holding up his lantern to point the way and indeed there was an open door at the top of the stairs from which candlelight shone and voices could be heard. Will shook his head again but obviously thought it his duty to venture first. He only murmured to Lord Branford, "Let them see you have a pistol in your belt, my lord," as he began to mount the stair.

Lord Branford looked round at Deborah. "I really dislike wearing this thing." She caught the gleam of his teeth as he smiled at her. "Can you see your way? Pray take my hand."

"I need to lift my skirt and hold onto this rail. These steps are none too clean. Suzette, take hold of me if your feet slip." And so they made their way up towards the light and noise, Deborah delighted with this first mysterious taste of Italy.

The room they entered was a general common room where rough-looking men sat about drinking. It opened at the left hand end to a kitchen from which floated a strong aroma of onion and garlic. Next to the kitchen, at the far end of the wall opposite, were two doors. The right hand one stood open showing a narrow stair leading up. What was below, Deborah wondered. She couldn't imagine what this place would look like in daylight.

They had emerged into the centre of the room and the men at the tables glanced round and then grinned at each other. No one else appeared to greet them.

Will Smyth walked over to the kitchen door and called out in English, "Is there no service here?"

A stout woman ambled out wiping greasy hands on her apron. Deborah stepped towards her and asked in Italian what chambers there were available for their party and could a supper be served there. The woman looked up at her with her mouth hanging open. Deborah realised that both her height and her Italian had astonished her. She gave her a winning smile. Then the woman peered round at Lord Branford, cocked her head on one side,

Height of Folly

suppressed a grin, and counted them all on her fingers before screwing up her face and babbling something very fast at Deborah.

Deborah couldn't help chuckling at Lord Branford. "I think she takes us for husband and wife and can give us the best room. I will explain."

After more talk she turned to him again. "She has two rooms. Suzette and I can share one and you and Will the other. She can give Peter and Joseph mattresses in here. Well, we would have been more crowded on the *felucca* and not as warm."

"Not so likely to be robbed though," Will muttered.

Peter piped up. "Are we to be f-f-fed, Mistress Horden?"

Deborah laughed. "Nothing comes before your stomach, does it, Peter? She says, if I understand her dialect of Italian, that she will see what she can do."

The woman picked up a candle from one of the tables and beckoned to the four of them that were to be privileged with separate rooms. They followed her up the narrow stair in the corner into what seemed by the lowness of the ceilings to be attics. To the left at the top was a very small room containing nothing but a wooden bedstead. To the right a larger one boasted a set of shelves too and a rickety table. Between on the outer wall of the square of landing was a roughly boarded up door.

Deborah indicated the left-hand room. "Suzette and I can be very snug here." She said it brightly though she had to bend her head and shoulders to get in, the tumbled bedding looked none too clean and there was a strong smell of mould.

Lord Branford peered in. "No, I protest. Will and I could bed down there."

But Will had already carried his lordship's valise into the other room. He popped his head out again to say, "I noticed a bolt on that other door, my lord. Mistress Horden and her maid can lock themselves in. I will bring a blanket out here and sleep on the landing."

The woman had by now lit a candle in each of the rooms and was preparing to descend. Deborah asked her if they could after all eat in the common room.

"I don't want you to have the trouble of carrying food up that narrow stair," she told her sweetly. The woman grunted and descended.

Deborah could guess at Frederick Branford's rueful expression as Suzette laid her mistress's small travelling bag on their bed. The candle was in a bracket attached to the wooden bed head and lit up the cobwebs that linked wall and ceiling in a festooning net.

"This is the worst we have ever seen," he said. "You can't spend the night there."

"Nonsense. We'll survive. And if our door is bolted Will has no need to be on the landing. Let us go down and see if they can do better in the provision of supper."

Unfortunately this proved not to be the case. A man-servant with dirty hands threw onto the table a wooden platter containing slabs of rock-hard cheese, a few hunks of stale bread, a small knob of butter and several raw onions. These had to be washed down with a very inferior wine. There was a jug of water but none of them dared to touch it.

Frederick Branford said, "If we can sleep after this it will be a miracle."

But Deborah found that by the time she had persuaded Suzette to use the chamber-pot they found under their bed and then to get into the bed beside her mistress, both keeping on their outdoor clothes, she was so tired that she fell asleep as soon as she had curled her long legs to suit the shortness of the bed.

She didn't know how long she had slept before Suzette woke her, squealing that she was bitten all over and Deborah realised

Height of Folly

she too was being attacked. The grimy skylight above them showed no vestige of daylight. Their candle was out and she had no means of relighting it. This was truly misery. She thought of the scented linen at Castle Rombeau and wondered if John was enjoying it now. To Suzette she could only say, "When we are safely out of here we will laugh about it. Let us just cuddle up together and pray for morning."

Deborah thought she had scarcely gone to sleep again when cries and shouts invaded her dreams. She tried to pull the covers over her head, desperate for sleep. But then there came a thunderous knock on the door and Will Smyth's voice yelling, "Come out. There is a fire below. Wake up."

Deborah's stomach lurched. She was out of the bed and dragging Suzette after her while he was still speaking. Her feet found her shoes. She felt about and located Suzette's and thrust them at her. Straightening up she banged her head. Which way was she facing? She flung out an arm and struck the door with her knuckles. Now she felt frantically for the bolt and dragged it back. Smoke met her, acrid and stinking. The foot of the stairway was lit by a sinister glow showing all round the doorframe. From underneath it the smoke was curling in evil swirls.

She was sickeningly reminded of the time when she and John were trapped as children in the Catholic Chapel in Newcastle. An inflamed mob had deliberately tried to burn down the door. Fire will pursue me all my life, she was inwardly screaming. I was born when Horden Hall was on fire. Mother was always afraid of her fire baby. Oh God, Father will learn that his girl was burnt to death in a stinking Italian inn.

No, we must get out. My life can't end here.

She stood on something – her small travelling bag. She picked it up and slotting her left arm through the leather handle dragged it up to hang from her shoulder, leaving her hands free. Then she clutched Suzette's hand and they stepped onto the square of landing.

She was aware of two figures, one scrabbling about near the floor over to her left, the other reaching out to seize her hand.

Lord Branford's voice choked at her, "I opened our skylight. Too narrow to get through. But there are people down in the street. I can hear Peter yelling from below that we mustn't go down the stairs. That end of the floor has collapsed. But this disused door leads to the roof. Put this round your mouth." He was fumbling at her face with his neckerchief. She grasped the ends and tied it behind her.

Suzette was coughing and crying at once. Deborah pulled her small kerchief from her sleeve. "Hold that to your face."

Will Smyth's voice was spluttering, "This *has* been a door. I've pulled back a bolt, my lord, but it's still not opening."

"Can we smash it with something?"

Deborah peered down the stairs. She recalled something she had seen last night. She must go down and look. She grabbed the wooden rail and almost fell down the narrow flight feeling the heat increase.

Lord Branford was shouting, "Deborah! No!"

"I've found something," she yelled back. She was sure the door was on fire on the other side but beside it stood a great iron shape with a neck like a bird, used she supposed to hold the door open. It was already warm to the touch and very heavy when she lifted it. She thanked God for all the outdoor work she loved to do at home. Would she ever see those beloved woods again? Rapidly remounting the stair she made out Lord Branford peering down to her. The smoke was clearing through the skylight he'd opened in the larger room. He looked different. What was it? Of course! He was not wearing his wig. His head looked small, with a close crop of darkish hair. And his ears stuck out. Her father had spoken only

Height of Folly

once to her of his dear friend Henry's head rolling on the deck with its protruding ears.

"Use that." She thrust the ornament at him.

He passed it at once to the substantial hands of Will Smyth, who stood up as far as he could and attacked the panels of the door. There was little space for him to swing it on the small square of landing so Deborah pushed Suzette back into their room and clambering onto the bed felt at the pale square in the ceiling. Was day dawning? Her hands touched a wooden rim and she found the little window would yield to pressure. She forced it as wide as it would go. There was a creaking, cracking noise and it tore away and slithered down the roof. She pulled down Lord Branford's neckerchief and took a deep breath of fresh air.

She jumped down and ordered Suzette up. "Go on, breathe."

Crashing and splintering sounds came from the landing. She could see the same pale light filtering through gaps in the woodwork. Will was panting. He was too tall to get his full force behind the blows.

"Let me." Lord Branford seized the thing from him and with both hands smashed it into the half broken wood. A large chunk flew off and he fell against the gap. Deborah could hear him gasp as he tore his cheek and hand on the splinters. But he drew in the weapon again and with two more blows had opened up a hole big enough for a body to pass through.

Shouts were still coming up from the narrow street below. Deborah could hear both Peter's and Joseph's voices, so they were safely out, thank God.

Lord Branford had now knocked out the worst of the jagged bits of wood protruding from above and below the hole.

"I'll go first and see what the footing is like the other side. When I've helped the ladies through you bring up the rear, Will."

Prue Phillipson

Deborah marvelled at the steadiness of his voice after his exertions. She saw him bend down and insert his right leg through and feel for the surface out there.

"It's level. We can manage."

She glanced back down the stair. The door at the bottom seemed to be glowing now. Desperate, she turned back to their only way of escape. Frederick Branford was manoeuvring his lithe body sideways through the hole. Keeping a grip on a slither of wood above him he straightened up. She could see him against the sky.

"Is there a way? Is it daybreak?" she called out.

"No, moonlight. There is a narrow ledge till we can reach a sloping roof which seems to lead to a flat area. It is all higgledy-piggledy tops of houses built on the hillside. The men below have seen that I'm out and are trying to call directions. I think the *patron* must be with them who knows the way. We must go straight ahead."

Deborah was coaxing Suzette through the hole. She was small enough to do it easily but squealed as her skirt caught on splinters and pulled her back. Deborah kept unhooking it for her. She saw Lord Branford grip her arms and raise her to her feet. But when the girl looked down and saw how far above the street they were she screamed and swayed. He held her tight.

"Deborah," he hissed as she was about to follow. "I must get her to a safer spot before you come. There isn't room on this ledge. I'll come back for you."

Deborah could now see that sloping tiles came down on her left to this two-foot wide ledge and a steeper slope went down into the darkness below. She was no lover of heights herself but she said in her heart, I can and will walk that ledge. The wind has dropped. There is no reason why I should fall off. He called me Deborah in his urgency. I like that.

Height of Folly

She saw him slide one hand round Suzette's back so he could grip her arm and hold her other arm at his waist. Evidently he meant to edge her along sideways. She could hear him saying, "Keep your head turned to me, Suzette, look only at my ear. Now move your feet with mine. Pretend we are doing side steps in a dance. There, that is very good." Suzette was gasping with fright but had set her feet in motion and was not looking at the drop below.

Oh Frederick, Frederick, Deborah was saying to herself, if she panics you will both fall together. But they were nearly at the end. He was telling her, "Look now. A slope of tiles leads to a wide flat roof. We are going to sit down on that and slide together." Deborah couldn't think how he could move her onto it but somehow he lifted and swung her shrieking off the ledge and they went rolling down out of sight.

It was only two seconds of horror and then she saw their heads appear. They had reached somewhere where they could stand up and feel secure.

Deborah at once gathered her skirt up and gripped a clutch of the material in front. She looked Will Smyth in the eye. "I can do this. Follow me as quick as you can before that fire breaks through."

She compressed herself into as small a shape as she could and edged into the hole. Her travelling bag caught at one side but Will inserted his hand to free it. As she straightened up on the ledge she felt desperately for any protruding piece of the wall at her side.

He called out, "Wait there for me now, Mistress Horden."

"I can manage, thank you, Will." She wasn't going to hesitate or she would never be able to do it.

She gritted her teeth and placing one hand lightly on the tiles beside her she turned her body and walked forward on the ledge. Then came a horrible moment when she felt an urge to steady herself and her hand dislodged a tile. It tumbled down in front of her and bounced over the ledge to crash to the street below. She froze, unable to move. She heard Will coming through the hole and Lord Branford shout, "Deborah!" That set her in motion again and she completed the distance to the slope where she could see the area of flat roof and Suzette standing quite confidently on it. She sat down at once and bumped down the tiles into Lord Branford's arms.

At the same moment there was an explosive sound and she swung round to see a sudden rush of flame from the hole behind them. Will wobbled on the ledge. Deborah gasped and Lord Branford cried, "God help him!" The moment passed. Will almost ran forward and leapt onto the tiles and came tumbling down beside them. In one hand he was clutching his lordship's valise.

He got to his feet and looked back. "The door below gave way, my lord. The stairwell acted like a funnel. The whole place will go now. We need to get off here. These houses are built jammed together."

There was more shouting from the street and the top of a ladder banged against the flat roof. Peter's head appeared a moment later.

"It's s-s-steady, Mistress Horden. I'll help you. Jo and some Italian fellow have hold of it below."

"Help Suzette down first," she ordered him. "I can manage alone."

Will Smyth had stepped up to the edge and looked over. "There is a crowd just clamouring for entertainment. Who is putting the fire out?" He glared at Peter. "Why were we roused so late? You and Joseph made your escape. Why were we exposed to such danger?"

"Truly we c-c-couldn't help it, Mr Smyth. We were w-w-wakened by the floor c-c-collapsing at that c-c-corner. The f-f-fire had been smouldering b-b-below and suddenly c-c-combusted."

Height of Folly

"You and the other men were all dead drunk."

Deborah led a quivering Suzette to the ladder.

"Will Smyth, your inquiries can wait. Peter, get this poor girl down."

Lord Branford stepped forward to coax Suzette and actually lifted her feet one after the other and placed them on a rung. As soon as she felt Peter's arms either side of her she was able to loosen her grip and move her hands down.

Deborah watched her progress for a few moments and then turned to meet Lord Branford's eye. He had a gash down one cheek where he had fallen against the splintering wood, his poor head was wigless and his ears stuck out. His hand dripped blood. He was a pathetic sight but for the glow of admiration in his eyes. His gaze up at her was intense, awestruck. She was desperate to tell him how brave he'd been, how calm. He should be so proud of himself.

She said it aloud. "Lord Branford, you should be so proud of yourself."

He shook his head vigorously. "You," he said, "you were magnificent."

He turned quickly to Will. "And you, Will. You even saved my valise."

Will was looking over the edge again. "They have reached the foot. Would you wish me to assist you, Mistress Horden? I can go first and steady you."

Deborah just shook her head. "You may grip the ladder as I get on." First she handed Lord Branford his neckerchief. "Bind that round your hand."

She descended with care and found herself greeted by cheering Italians. Suzette broke from among them to cling to her, sobbing with relief.

"Oh my lady, I thought we were going to die."

Prue Phillipson

Deborah realised she too was shaking. Now that she was on solid ground it came home to her how near they had been to death. Flames were curling round the broken door through which they had just passed. Was nothing being done to quench the fire?

She demanded this of a stout man who pushed his way to the front of the crowd. He was so like the captain of the *felucca* that for a moment she thought it was he, only this man was distinctly wider in girth. They are brothers, she realised, and this is the *patron* we never met last night.

"I am desolated," he cried out to her and to Lord Branford who had now descended too. "My livelihood is gone! But that you English should have suffered such danger, that is a million times worse!"

Will Smyth stepped off the ladder and several hands laid hold of it and carried it away.

"How did the fire start?" he demanded in English.

"Is no one trying to put it out?" Deborah asked. She was looking about to get her bearings. The steps they had climbed yesterday must be further down the hill round the corner, beyond this building with the flat roof.

The *patron* threw up his hands. "A vagrant was sleeping in the storeroom below. He must have been smoking a pipe – oh where can I take you to clean up, to recover, to eat and drink. I am desolated. I was out with friends. Did my wife make you comfortable?"

"Is your wife and all your household safe?"

"They are, God be praised."

Now a voice shouted from the back of the crowd, "Are my passengers alive and well, Pedro?"

That *was* the captain of the *felucca*. Deborah turned to Lord Branford who was obediently winding his neckerchief round his hand. She saw him as a young brother, heroic but vulnerable.

Height of Folly

"Frederick," she said without thinking, "you need to have those wounds dressed." She felt Will Smyth stiffen at her familiarity. She found herself gabbling on. "Perhaps we can sail on in the *felucca* today. I think I will feel safer at sea. There is little wind now. What a blessing that we left the bulk of our luggage aboard!" She thought, I was calm before. We were all calm but are now all of a tremble. Frederick – Lord Branford – seems scarcely able to speak now.

He was gulping, swallowing. He drew out his pocket watch with a quivering hand and tried to read it by the moonlight.

"I think it's still night. We must go somewhere else. A drink, tea or coffee – if they have such things. We could all lie down for a while."

Will Smyth shouldered his way to the captain of the *felucca*. "Get us to a decent eating place where we can rest. You sent us to that hell hole and must make amends." Deborah followed to repeat this in Italian more tactfully phrased.

"I'll rouse Luigi," the captain shouted to his brother. "You'd better help your fire-fighters or you'll be in trouble for it spreading to all your neighbours. Come this way, my lady," he said to Deborah. She turned to make sure Peter and Joseph were following. Suzette was still holding tightly to her skirt.

They were led away along the hillside a little distance to the head of a steep cobbled alleyway where there was a glint of the waters of the harbour at the bottom. Before they entered it Deborah looked back and could now see the building they had been sleeping in as a whole column of flame between the other houses. There *was* activity, the clashing of buckets, the sound of a pump, and people frantically carrying out furniture and other possessions from the houses nearby. The crowd that had watched the English party's escape had all headed down round the corner to view the progress of the fire. She thought of the fire of London which her poor mother had lived through but could hardly bear to recall. How fiercely it had spread! Could that happen here? She wanted to run. The sight of the sea ahead was reassuring.

It was suddenly dark in the alleyway. A cloud had spread over the moon. A wind rose up from the sea and a spattering of rain began.

"Thank the Lord. It may put out the fire." Deborah spoke into the darkness. She could sense the shape of the captain ahead of her and felt Suzette panting beside her. Frederick Branford was close behind with Will, Joseph and Peter for she could hear several footsteps. In fact there was much stumbling and bumping into each other as the way down was steep and the cobbles were very uneven.

The rain grew heavier.

When they reached the quayside the captain led them to a tavern, shuttered of course, but he hammered at the door and yelled "Luigi."

A shutter above was thrown open. "Is that you, Giorgio?"

"Open up. I've brought you customers."

By the time they were all inside they were drenched but a fire was soon roaring in the hearth. Luigi, a youngish man with a great mop of black curls, brought wine and ale and they all crowded, steaming, onto two wooden benches, Will Smyth directing Peter and Joseph to the end furthest from the fire.

Presently a young woman with a shawl round her nightgown padded in on bare feet carrying a tray of bowls of some sort of broth, which looked and smelt good.

"Why did you not bring us here last night?" Deborah said, looking round for the captain but he had slipped away.

They ate and drank while Will again interrogated Peter and Joseph about the outbreak of the fire. They had to admit they had been drinking late with the Italians and it was the *patron*'s wife

Height of Folly

who had woken them, coming screaming from the kitchen premises where her household slept. It seemed the vagrant had woken and escaped from the storeroom below leaving that door ajar. This had caused the smouldering room to burst into a mass of flame. The rotten floorboards by the attic stairs had given way but they could all reach the door to the stone steps.

Joseph protested, "The serving-man who had a little English kept telling us there was a safe way from the attics. The *patron* appeared when we were all safe in the street and assured us in gestures that you had another way out."

"Yes," snapped Will, "when we had broken down the door and got onto a narrow ledge. Is that how we protect his lordship? What sort of report can I make of this night to the earl?"

Deborah saw Frederick frown in distress. He laid a hand on Will's arm.

"No, Will. There was nothing they could have done. If I tell my grandfather of this night it will only be to praise your bravery and Mistress Horden's ingenuity in finding us a weapon and displaying such courage. We owe our lives to her."

Will gave a curt nod and Deborah thought, he disapproves of me even more than before. But at least he hasn't said, "I told you not to come ashore, my lord."

Will pursed up his lips and shook his head slowly from side to side. "I did warn you, my lord, that you would be better aboard ship."

Deborah smiled ruefully at Fredrick. Oh Will, she was thinking, you are a stalwart servant but that speech diminishes you a little in my eyes.

She now questioned Luigi and learnt that they had six children asleep and no spare rooms. He ran a tavern only but she and her maid could lie down on the table and the men on the floor. He would bring bedding. It was still two hours to dawn.

She looked down at Lord Branford. "Frederick, I couldn't sleep." The name slipped out again. 'Lord Branford' was too absurd after all they had been through. Had he not called her Deborah? She was past caring for Will Smyth's opinion. "You should have some salve for those cuts. How is your hand?"

"It's nothing. No, I do not want to sleep now." He went to the door and looked at the sky. "See, the moon is out again. The squall is past. I would rather stroll here by the harbour."

"I too." The confined space in there with a fire in the hearth repelled her.

"We will walk in the air," she told Luigi. "Take care of these people."

She saw Will's scandalised face as she tucked her arm into Frederick's and stepped outside. Suzette squealed, "My lady!"

"Stay here and lie down on the table when the kind man brings you a pillow. Try to sleep. Mr Smyth is in charge."

She pulled the tavern door to behind them and stepped out briskly. Frederick peered up at her.

"You are so bold with Will. He frightens me, Mistress Horden."

"Pray let us stop this formality. We are nothing but a man and a woman whom God has chosen to save from death. Let us please just be Frederick and Deborah from now on."

"I would like that but – to be honest with you – I am mightily in awe of you."

A laugh burst from her. "Oh pray don't be. I was terrified on that ledge."

"So was I, but you walked it quite boldly."

"And you," she said with feeling, "managed a trembling Suzette who might so easily have dragged you down."

"I feared she would. I prayed. That was all and she came."

"Then you are a better person than I. I was too engrossed in myself to pray. I thought only, I must do this to make a good

Height of Folly

impression on you and on that Will Smyth who resents my company on your travels. I was driven by pride not courage."

"You are too honest with yourself."

She stood still and faced him. "That's impossible." Her shoulders began to shake. "Oh, Frederick, Frederick, I want to laugh. We are alive. Nothing else for the moment matters. Giving thanks, yes, of course. But I want to laugh because your Mr Smyth is so solemn. And here we are telling each other how we felt. It's happened, it's over. We are all safe, even the wicked old tramp who was the cause of it. We expected adventures and we've had one. I left home for this. There is the moon shining on the water between the two capes of Nero and Verde and it is *so* beautiful."

He looked too and nodded. "It is indeed."

She could see his face turned up to her again. What could she do to reduce the adulation in his eyes? He looked such a little shrimp of a man and in her company that must be how he saw himself. She longed to say, can you not forget I am so tall? Why should inches worry you any more than your earldom bothers me? She took his arm again and they walked on.

CHAPTER THIRTEEN

It was two days before Christmas when John Wilson Horden, riding with his manservant Matt Baker, reached Château Rombeau.

Striding in from the stables, travel-weary but aglow with anticipation, he surprised Jeanetta and her mother in the salon. There she was, heavy with child, but jumping up to receive him with shrieks of joy.

"It's John, Maman!" Her hands were all over him. "Oh, you have been so long. Your letter that you were on your way came weeks ago."

Diana rose from the couch. "It is not *weeks,* Netta, maybe a fortnight. You shall not start scolding him the minute he's here," and she gave John her customary pecks on both cheeks. "The comte only arrived yesterday from court but is in bed with his gout. I shall tell him you are here and you may come up and pay your respects."

The moment she left the room John circled his wife's enlarged waist and whispered, "I have been about the *king*'s business."

"What? King *James!*"

"Sh!" He covered her mouth with his hand. "No one must know but plans are afoot."

"You won't go away again?"

"Not yet. No indeed. I am here for this one's arrival." He patted her bulge. "But many pledges are being made to the young king and his time will come. When we return to England there will be much work for me to do."

"But I am hoping that when James is King he will make you a Chevalier of France and King Louis will want us to live here."

"He might raise me to Baron Horden and I will be expected to run the estate there. Of course I don't want Father put out of it but

Height of Folly

he'll have to come in on the right side. It can all be done in peace, you know, if the country accepts that James has too much support to be resisted."

She put up her hands to his face and pulled it down to kiss his lips. Then she breathed at his ear, "I think you'd like just one exciting battle before it's all settled, wouldn't you, John? I can never forget how you described that charge down the hill at Killiecrankie. That was when I fell in love with you."

John swallowed uncomfortably. He had never told her the whole truth of what happened at the bottom of that hill. Plunging so fast with his sword outstretched he had leapt a fallen body and cleft the face of an enemy soldier – unintentionally. He could still feel the squelch as the body dropped from his sword-point with the head a one-eyed wreck. And his own wound proudly born had come from being thrust to the ground by his friend when a musketeer took aim at him. He had been pierced by the spike from a fallen shield. Only Deborah had been told the true story. The strange thing was that he still longed for the thrill of that moment of joining battle. This time he would not be a boy but a man in command of his actions, a man in command of other men perhaps, a man proving himself a hero in the service of his true king.

He patted Jeanetta's rear. "Well, you know they let William in with hardly a fight. James the Second had mismanaged everything. This young prince – I should say king – is a true warrior. He is not much older than I was at Killiecrankie and he has been bloodied in action already with Louis's forces. When he is seen riding into London with a fine army at his back they will welcome him in. How can they want a German prince who knows nothing of England, not even the language, when Anne goes to her Maker? If I am riding in that procession I will be so proud – whether or not we have to fight. Now listen, sweetheart, I must report to your uncle Neury."

"But first you must see *mon père* or he will be aggrieved."

"What? In my dusty riding clothes?"

"Yes, yes, yes." She took his hand and pranced with him to the stairs. He was overwhelmed with delight at her liveliness. He had feared languor and grumbles at the weight of her burden. This was a Jeanetta so different from the one at Horden. Was it the baby or being with her own people or both? He only knew that he could love her again with his early passion. It was wonderful to have her at his side, looking up into his face with those very arched brows and a mischievous smile.

Half an hour later he was knocking at the door of the Vicomte de Neury's study. He knew now to give the correct signal, two sharp taps followed by two lighter ones, and walk straight in, closing the door quickly. The little man was perched on his stool, alert as a magpie in the black coat and breeches he always wore and very white linen. Before his massive desk John thought he looked smaller than ever. His face seemed to grow all to the point of his nose and his head jerked up and down as he began at once in a low hurried voice to probe John with questions.

John produced a paper from the inside pocket of his riding coat. "Here, sir, this will tell you everything. These are the people le Vent suggested I should try to contact and the forces they could raise."

"What! You have travelled with this on your person. Are you mad?"

"I'm sorry, Vicomte, I can't memorise all these French names."

"But what if you had been taken with them?"

"Surely your government troops are on the same side. Is there not contact between Saint Germain and Versailles all the time? Does not our King James send his own agent, Colonel Hooke, to

Height of Folly

your King Louis –"

The vicomte threw up his hands. He had turned quite pale. "Silence, please. We never name names out loud. I see how little you understand France or HCM." He whispered this and John realised he meant King Louis, always referred to as His Christian Majesty. He went on, "Only HCM may authorise activity between S G and V . But you and I know that our windy friend has his suspicions about some of the Scottish lords with whom the colonel you mentioned is negotiating. So our windy friend is doing his own recruiting and when he is sure of complete loyalty in everyone we can combine with the main force when the time is right. So it is sh-sh here just as much as it will be when you get back to England. Do you understand?"

John nodded solemnly. He felt there was something a little absurd in the vicomte's whispering of initials in the secrecy of his own office. The château walls were thick and his door solid oak.

Now he beckoned John even nearer and hissed in his ear, "There are secret Catholics like you in your county of Northumberland, are there not? The colonel you mentioned is at work mainly in Scotland. Northumberland will be your field of activity."

John nodded again. "Le Vent told me that."

The vicomte put his hand to his lips. "Will you never learn? Our windy friend we call him."

John suppressed a grin. This was serious business. "But, sir, I know not how soon I can be back in England. My wife is to give birth and my sister is travelling and may be away for months. I would be expected to wait for her return here."

The vicomte tut-tutted. "Nothing can be done in a hurry. Have you forgotten that HCM is engaged in a war? That is surely enough for the present."

John felt a little dashed. "Yes, I see, of course." The action he was looking for might still be years ahead.

He saw the vicomte was now peering at the paper he had given him. John half expected him to cast it into the mean little fire that burned in his hearth. Instead he gestured that he should move away and, turning his back, fiddled with some levers and knobs and inserted the paper into the depths of the vast desk. He swung round quickly to see if John had been watching him. John pretended to have been poking the fire.

"Would you like some more coals on, sir?"

"No, no, no." He sat down on his stool again. "It will do very well."

Everything about him, apart from his linen which John suspected his wife took care of, proclaimed parsimony. The black clothes had a rusty look and the wig was ancient and unfashionable. John wondered, not for the first time, why he was part of this conspiracy. What could he gain for himself or his family?

"And my friend at S G," he asked suddenly, rising to his feet and pacing about. "Did he read my letter in front of you? Of course it was in code. Perhaps he hadn't time to decipher it. But I have heard nothing from him."

"Oh yes, sir, he and some friends invited me to have a glass of wine with them and he read the letter and told me to say he took good note of it."

The vicomte drew his sparse grey brows together and glowered suspiciously at John from beneath them.

"That was all he said?"

"Yes, sir, but he seemed very pleased with the letter."

De Neury nodded his head a few times. "Well, we will await our windy friend's return. You have done well, John. But your sister and that English lord? They know nothing of this?"

"No, they met le – *him* here of course. It is a part of his

Height of Folly

disguise to proclaim himself openly to people but I have left them believing he is a spy for the English government. They think his task is to interrogate travellers and discover secret Jacobites. They have no idea he is on our side."

"Good, good, good." Then his mouth curled in a leer. "They are travelling together – your sister and this lord? They are betrothed – is that the way of it? An odd couple they'll make to be sure."

"They would indeed, sir, but that's not the way of it. He is a friendly escort, that's all. It seemed quite proper. His father and our father fought in King Charles the Second's navy and our grandfathers were friends before that."

The vicomte's brows, which were very active, shot up. "Ah, we need English nobles. Could he not be recruited – this lord?"

"I doubt it. He seems a peace-loving sort of fellow. Our windy friend didn't reckon he'd get anywhere with him and my sister's mighty clever so we've got to keep her in the dark."

"Well, well!" The vicomte sank back down on his hard stool. His bony figure seemed to grate against it but there was no comfortable chair in the room. He gave a ghastly grin in John's direction and a dismissive wave of his hand. "It will be hard work for us all, but you are doing well."

John backed out of the door with a perfunctory bow. As he descended from the Neury wing of the château he could still see the vicomte as a magpie in black and white plumage solemnly secreting bits and pieces into its nest and taking them out to look at from time to time. Does he imagine he is directing operations, John asked himself. He hardly ever leaves the château. At Saint Germain I thought his friends didn't take him seriously. There was much laughter about him when I presented his letter. I wonder what le Vent thinks of him.

Any more thoughts on the matter were soon obliterated by the festivities for Christmas and the opening of the new year of 1706.

Prue Phillipson

Hostilities were still in abeyance because of the time of year and Château Rombeau knew how to entertain itself with balls, masques, visiting musicians and lavish feasting.

John feared that Jeanetta was throwing herself into everything with more zest than was wise and shortly afterwards, a little before her expected time, she went into labour. He was instantly banished into the company of men as almost all the women in the château seemed to be involved in the lying-in. Most of them crowded into the very room where his poor darling was suffering.

He walked out into the gardens in the early morning after a sleepless night though the air was biting with frost. Why will they not leave her with one or two comforters, he asked himself. Her cousin Sophia is the gentlest and quietest. At my sister Ruth's birth Grandmother Bel and the midwife were the only souls Mother wanted near her. There was little fuss made and within five hours baby Ruth was there and Deb and I were taken in by Father to see her. Mother and the little thing were as serene as day. I recall my surprise that it was a girl because Mother had been so sure it would be a boy. Jeanetta and I expect a boy but what if it's a girl? We will have to try again and I hope it doesn't take as long to conceive next time.

Finding himself near the chapel on the outskirts of the grounds where the local villagers also came to worship he went in and flung himself down before the statue of the virgin. The place was deserted at this early hour, the priest not being inclined to take more than the bare minimum of services especially in winter.

"Now Our Lady," he said aloud, "you know what this is all about. You went through it yourself so please spare my Netta any more pain and I won't care if it is a girl or boy as long as she and the infant are all right. She anyway, for I find I love her again to distraction and she can always have more now she's managed this far."

Height of Folly

He stayed on his knees for longer than he had ever done in his life till he was stiff with cold.

Two hours later Matt found him curled up asleep on the velvet-cushioned seat in the Rombeau family pew with the rug from before the altar pulled over him.

Matt was the same age as John and had begun service as a stable-boy in Horden Hall but here in the hierarchy of Rombeau he had quickly discovered a new status as John's valet-de-chambre. He pulled the rug off his master and shook him by the shoulder.

"Master John, wake up and come and see your son. He's a brave one."

"What!" John was on his feet, grabbing Matt's arm to steady his stiff legs. "What! It's a boy. You've seen him before I have?"

"Ay, the count carried him down to the assembled company. I've been all over hunting for you."

"God be praised, but how is my lady wife?"

"The countess her mother says she is calling for you, so make haste."

John rubbed some life into his thighs and set off across the gardens so fast Matt gave up trying to keep up with him.

The family came milling out of the salon to congratulate him but he thrust them aside and rushed up the stairs shouting, "Netta, Netta, I am here."

More attendants were in the room but melted politely away as he burst in. She was sitting up in bed, her black curls glossy on her shoulders, her face high-coloured and radiant.

"Where were you? He was born an hour since. Is he not beautiful?"

John moved to clasp her in his arms but drew back at this.

"I don't know. Where is he?" The handsome lace-curtained crib was empty.

"Why, Father took him to show everyone. And Maman is

crowing over Aunt Madeline because Sophia could only produce girls."

John laughed and kissed and hugged her. "Are you all right, my precious?"

"No, I am sore as hell and exhausted but go and bring him back. I want to see you with him. What are we to call him?"

"He's to be Nathaniel to please Grandmother Bel and John for me of course."

"But my father thinks he must be Jean after him."

"It doesn't matter. John – Jean – it's the same name. Let me go and get him."

He almost tumbled down the stairs but the comte was coming to meet him clasping a small red-faced wailing bundle in his arms.

John gasped. "Oh God, what's wrong with him?"

The comte laughed. "He's hungry, what do you think? Take him to his mother. I'm not climbing the stairs again with my legs."

John eased the bundle from the Count's arms as if it were delicate porcelain.

Finding it continued to squirm and emit thin little cries he bounded up the rest of the stairs and laid it on the bed in front of Jeanetta. "Make it stop."

"Oh bother. I don't like that noise either. The nurse has been sent for but is not here yet so I suppose I'll have to –" she opened her nightgown and approached the baby towards her breast. The effect was instantaneous. His lips closed on her nipple and the little face relaxed.

John sat down on the bed and chuckled.

"I say, he is rather a nice little fellow, isn't he? I wish I could show him to Father and Mother and dear old Grandmother Bel. And I wager Ruth would be wanting to play with him straightaway."

"Well, you must write and tell them and Deb too I suppose. She and her little paramour might be in Florence by now."

Height of Folly

"Nay, he is not that. She couldn't fancy him that way."

"But she could fancy his wealth and title. Gracious me, at her age she would jump at any man. The problem for her is that *he* could never tolerate feeling so small beside her. Poor old Deb. She'll never get to have one of these." She looked down at the baby who had gone to sleep. "Put him in the cradle. I must sleep too. Let Maria come in now. You can go and write your letters before dinner."

John inserted the bundle between the lace curtains and watched the cheek settle on the silk pillow. "He's ours. What a funny tiny little thing!"

He made to kiss Jeanetta again but her head had drooped back and she frowned him away.

He crept out disappointed but that was soon forgotten in the hours of celebration that followed. He found himself gloriously fêted and Jean Nathaniel toasted so often that he had no recollection of Matt getting him to bed that night. It was some days before he could face the exertion of writing letters.

CHAPTER FOURTEEN

The March day was bitingly cold but Deborah minded it very little. They had been in Florence for a week and she was utterly absorbed by it. She and Frederick Branford were sitting at breakfast in the window of their hotel. They had been silent, enjoying the veal cutlets and eggs in clean dishes on a linen cloth.

As she set down her knife and fork she burst out with all that had been in her mind. "Oh Frederick, I feel I haven't lived till now. I knew so much but I hadn't *felt* it. I hadn't drowned in frescos and sculptures and buildings and music as I have here. Yesterday the Medici chapel with the Magi coming to Jesus! The colour, the wonder of it! I will never hear that story read without seeing it in my mind's eye. And then that concert last night in the hall of the Palazzo Medici! The sweet sounds cascading over me, the paintings on walls and ceiling blazing their colour and brilliance into my very brain, the thousand lights! It was almost too much. Can we perhaps just walk this morning by the Arno? I am drunk with so much man-made beauty."

"By all means. At my Cambridge home I loved winter walks."

"Will I ever see Cambridge I wonder? I mustn't forget England has her own splendours." She said it without thinking but his reply brought her up short.

"I would be honoured if you would allow me to show you Cambridge when we return to England."

She looked hard at him across the table, forced to think of *him* rather than her own ecstasy. He still bore a scar on one cheek but he was wearing a new neat wig covering his ears. He was a being in his own right, much more than a pleasant companion who acquiesced with all her suggestions and smiled at her enthusiasms. What was behind that 'we return to England'? She hadn't been

Height of Folly

thinking of anything but the teeming, exciting present. Would she ever be back in the old life at Horden Hall? Why did he speak of them returning together? What was he presuming from their shared experiences?

A serving-man hovered by their table. "Post, my lord and lady."

They each received letters which put an instant stop to Deborah's musings on how she should answer him. She looked at hers. "From home, not from John. And yours?"

"Two from Mother and one from Grandfather."

They had hardly begun reading when they looked up and both cried, "They know about San Remo."

Deborah saw Frederick's expression of alarm change to laughter at their simultaneous exclamation, mirroring her own laughter.

"But it *is* serious," she chuckled. "How did it get into the newspapers?"

They returned by unspoken agreement to their letters to read more.

'Imagine your mother's horror' Deborah read in her father's hand, *'on learning you had barely escaped from a fire. She wants you and John both home at once so she can cease from suffering this endless anxiety. She is quite angry that you wrote nothing of it yourself in your latest letters which speak only of minor inconveniences as you travelled from Genoa through Italy. I tell her I can well understand your silence on such a fearful adventure and that you would never suspect we would hear of it. Hoping you will have settled in Florence by the time this reaches you I am addressing this there. I have to presume Lord Branford is still with you and I would wish you to convey to him our thankfulness for the courage he showed. As you will see in the newspaper article I enclose, your own bravery is recorded with astonishment. I may say your father is* not *astonished. It is how I would have known my Deborah would behave.'* Tears blinded her as she read this. She

longed for her father's arms about her but, quickly brushing her hand over her eyes, she unfolded the crumpled paper and saw the heading '*English travellers' narrow escape from Italian inferno.*' She looked up at Frederick.

"Father has sent me the paper. It is all here, our names and everything."

"How could it possibly have reached a London journalist?"

She shook her head. "Someone in the crowds watching? They must have inquired who we were." She looked back at her letter and discovered a welcome piece of news. "Ah they have heard from John of the safe arrival of a baby boy. *They* have heard and we have not or maybe his letter has not traced us to here. Well, God be praised for that."

"Is the child in line to be Comte Rombeau as well as Baronet Horden?"

"No, Jeanetta's brothers come before him at Rombeau. He is all Horden and she will have to get used to that. Ah I see Mother has added sentences too. She will not be happy till I am safe at Horden and she goes on −" but looking ahead at what she said she refrained from reading it out. '*Your travelling alone with an unattached gentleman cannot be right. Of course he must see you safely back to Rombeau now when I trust you and John and his little family will join you and return with you, weather permitting. All the world knows now that you and Lord Branford have been together for weeks and weeks. There are not lacking those who will believe the worst. I fear you have put yourself in a very compromising position, yet without sin, I hasten to believe. Dear Deborah, you are innocent of the world and believe good of everyone. We do not know Lord Branford ourselves but what are your feelings towards him and his to you? It cannot be that you have spent so much time together without arriving at an answer to that question.*'

Height of Folly

She looked across at him, the difference in their height not being so conspicuous when they were seated. *Have* we resolved such a question, she wondered. He is a true friend but I cannot ever see myself in bed with him. Will that do for an answer, Mother?

He met her eyes. Oh how could she get rid of that look of admiration in his? You sweet man, she thought, I am tall enough without you setting me on a pedestal.

"All is well – with your family?" he asked.

She had to be honest. "My father thanks you for your brave conduct in our little adventure and my mother thinks we should not be travelling together."

"Oh." He was startled.

She thought, I had forgotten how easy his face is to read. But of course I knew from our first talk in the garden that he is as transparent as the day. I must continue to be direct with him. "Does that concern you, Frederick?"

He frowned and bit his lower lip. "Maybe it should." Then to her surprise his face broke into a smile. "But no, it does not." Was it a brave smile, against his heart's wishes? She was quite pleased to find that she wasn't sure after all. He went on quickly, "I know you could never look on me as anything but your loyal friend and admirer. Forgive me for smiling but my mother says the same as yours." He looked back at her letter. "She says I am to blame for jeopardising your good name. If I thought I had I *would* be grieved but anyone who meets you would not dare to impugn your character. You are so far above the run of humankind –"

Deborah held up her hand. "No, pray stop there. At home I am an object of ridicule, 'that tall thing at the Hall with too much learning for her own good.' Now can we just go back to being Frederick and Deborah and forget all this nonsensical anxiety from our mothers?"

Prue Phillipson

Again she watched his face. The eyes showed wistful sadness as he appeared to agree heartily. So what *were* his true feelings?

She pushed back her chair and stood up. Suzette immediately appeared at her elbow. "My lady dress to go out?" Suzette was very proud of using English now.

"Yes." She looked at Frederick who had risen too. "Ten minutes?"

"Certainly. Perhaps I could also read the newspaper article later?"

She nodded and smiled. So far she had barely skimmed her eyes over it.

Frederick found Will Smyth waiting for him in the anteroom to his bedroom where Will himself slept.

"Plans for today my lord?"

Frederick was astonished to see in his hand what looked like the same sheet of newspaper Deborah had been sent. Will was making no effort to hide it.

"Yes, my lord, the earl inserted it in a letter to me and has left it to my discretion whether I show it to you or not. I believe he wanted to spare your feelings but I observed in the dining-room that Mistress Horden has been sent a copy too."

Frederick thought, Grandfather with the best of motives appointed Will to be both my guardian and my servant-companion but I am tired of being constantly spied upon. He held out his hand for the paper and took it to the window while Will laid out his cloak with the fur collar.

Had the writer of the article seen their passports and travel permits? There were their names as Deborah had said. 'We have learnt of the narrow escape from death of Frederick, Lord Branford from Hertfordshire travelling with Mistress Deborah Wilson Horden from Northumberland. It seems that a fire broke

Height of Folly

out in their hotel in the Italian town of San Remo and they had to scramble over roof tops to escape. A number of their men-servants sleeping in a room below got out without difficulty but Lord Branford had to break open a hole in the attic wall and carry to safety Mistress Horden's terrified maid. Mistress Horden herself climbed out and walked alone along a narrow ledge before Lord Branford could go back to help her. Both the lady and gentleman behaved with the extraordinary courage and cool-headedness one would expect from the English travelling abroad. Whether the couple are related is not known but the crowds in the streets observed that they enjoyed a moonlight walk together afterwards as if nothing calamitous had befallen them.

'Later inquiries showed that the fire must have been started by a vagrant who had crept into a storeroom and left a smoking pipe behind. The patron, Pedro Donelli, was from home at the time and was horrified to learn of the danger to his honoured guests. His hotel was destroyed but by the providence of God no lives were lost.'

Will Smyth remarked when he saw Frederick had finished reading, "It is not very accurate of course, my lord."

"No indeed, Will, it leaves out your own splendid part in the escape But how did it get into a London paper?"

"That I think I can guess, my lord. We were returning to our *felucca* in the morning when I observed that Luigi fellow speaking with a seedy-looking individual on the deck of a vessel sailing for England that day. I thought he must be trading goods of some kind. I am certain the fellow handed over money."

"But Luigi was not at the fire."

"Ah, my lord, when you were out walking with Mistress Deborah in the night he questioned Peter and Joseph. He spoke pretty good English and must have spotted a way of making even more money out of the episode. He charged us heavily for the supper he gave us and for sleeping us – if you could call it that – on floor and table for an hour or two. I assumed he was just curious about how we came to be in such straights. I was busy myself calming down that silly girl, Suzette."

"Well, you are probably right, Will." He was thinking, Will is always finding fault with Peter and Joseph so they took their revenge in the way they told the story. He put the paper in his inner pocket and added, "I must go down now and join Mistress Horden."

"Yes, my lord, but while we are on that subject I wonder if you realise how *our* situation has changed. Formerly we ate our meals together and discussed our plans. Now I eat at a table alone or with Peter and Joseph and Suzette in a corner reserved for servants."

"Oh dear." Frederick was genuinely embarrassed. He had been enjoying Deborah's company too much to appreciate the consequences for Will.

"I don't see how that can change much at present."

"Well, my lord, all I can say is, I don't know how the fashionable world will react to this story but it is what I warned you. Gentlemen and ladies do not travel about unless they are married or brother and sister or have proper chaperones."

"Thank you for your advice, Will. We are going for a walk now. You and Suzette may follow a few paces behind us."

Will's heavy-jowled face contorted so much with suppressed words that, sorry as he was for him, Frederick wanted to laugh. He managed to reduce it to a placatory smile, took his cloak, hat and cane and descended to meet Deborah who was already waiting near the pillared entrance. It was pleasing to look down on her from the stairs but he knew he would soon be gazing up at her and cursing his missing inches.

If I were but six foot and one inch, he moaned to himself, or if

Height of Folly

she were an average height for a woman but with the same amazing qualities that she has I believe I could be in love with her as I was with my Mary. But I fear I am too much in awe of her. She is far cleverer than I though she does not flaunt it and she has a very direct way with people. Yet I know if she met my mother and grandfather she would show them only her grace and charm. She has a ready humour and I could imagine a smaller version of her seated in my mother's parlour in our Hertfordshire home enjoying a laugh with her. They have the same bright outlook on life.

But all that, he thought, presupposes a situation that can never happen. She will always look down on me. How can she help it? And even if, as Will Smyth suspected, she had ambitions to join the aristocracy, how could I, who already have so little presence among my new circle, make myself more of a laughing stock by introducing such a towering figure as my countess? So what is to be the outcome? I do love her company and she seems happy enough with mine. But how are we to fade again into polite acquaintanceship now that we have gone so far with our intimate 'Frederick and Deborah'. I would truly delight in showing her round my old haunts in Cambridge but I cannot foresee her coming to Hertfordshire as my wife. It is a dilemma and Mother is right I suppose. I should not have let it happen.

"Ah to sniff that chill air from the mountains," she said as she linked arms with him and they set out for their walk.

For Deborah the walk was not as comfortable as she had hoped. The letters and the newspaper article would not stay at the back of her mind where she had dismissed them. Questions had to be answered. How long could she stay exploring Italy with Lord Branford? The separation from John had been made without much thought to their itinerary but it was plain that the family at home expected the young heir to Horden to be brought there this summer. She then should be back at Rombeau to accompany them home to England. Lord Branford would certainly not let her travel back there alone but he had not yet seen all the places he was supposed to see. She had been so overwhelmed with the wonders of Florence that she had thought they would stay longer and then go on to Rome. But now – that article and those letters! Had she really lost her good name? Would no other man ever look at her after this horrid publicity? And they had forgotten about the war. Where would it break out again when the armies emerged from winter quarters? It was said that Marshal Vendôme was wintering a substantial French army near Mantua. That was less than a hundred miles away. Father would be keeping a close eye on the news and would be worried about them.

She stood still as they reached one of the four bridges over the river.

"There are too many imponderables, my lord."

"My lord!" he repeated. "Do you mean, Mistress Horden, which path should we take now?"

She laughed, shaking her head. "I meant, Frederick, how can we escape from this dilemma we find ourselves in?"

Will Smyth and Suzette had stopped too at a discreet distance. He never talks to the poor girl, she thought, and she is too shy of him to venture a word. Now they are simply standing staring across the river.

She made Frederick look up at her. "I should go back to Rombeau and then home to England with John. Can I travel only with Suzette?" She had no sooner said it than she realised how little she wanted to part from Frederick. I think I love him, though never as I loved Ranald. I loved Ranald for his size and because he was the only man who had ever loved me for mine. Oh that dance we did together! It was the first time in my life that I loved my long stick of a body. He wanted me so much. Frederick *likes* me and is

Height of Folly

less in awe of me than he was at first. We get on well, mostly because he accedes to everything I want to do. But I should not allow our friendship to continue without telling him of Ranald and that I am not ready to do. This dilemma is much bigger than I thought.

Frederick said, "You are worried about that unfortunate newspaper article? I assure you I will go with you wherever you wish to go. I long to see my mother again and it is no hardship to curtail my travels."

"But you should not. I can hire a carriage and a *vetturino*. We have spoken with several travellers who highly recommended them."

"I have never heard of two women alone being entrusted to their care. No, I beg you, let me accompany you back to Rombeau. If it makes you happy we will set off tomorrow." He turned and called Will to him. "Could we be ready for a journey back to France tomorrow? Mistress Horden would like to return to Rombeau."

Will looked from him to Deborah and curled his lip. "You are in a hurry, Mistress? You want the shortest route via Turin to Grenoble by Mount Cenis? In winter? I did the Alpine crossing with the earl when I was Peter's age. There was plenty of snow and ice though the month was May. You are carried by porters on a kind of litter –"

Deborah blushed at her own folly but Frederick interrupted in a voice she had never heard before. "Don't take that tone with a lady, Will Smyth. We could make our way in easy stages to a port to take ship to Marseilles when the weather was clement. No one said anything about crossing the Alps in winter."

Deborah saw Will squirm at the rebuke. But he squared his shoulders and let the whole heavy weight of his personality bear down on Frederick. When he spoke it was in his most clipped and impressive voice.

"My lord, you surely would not consider missing Venice and Rome. The earl has sent most particular letters to titled friends who have houses there and would welcome you to stay with them. We can be very comfortable in Venice and Rome. But I have a suggestion, my lord. If Mistress Horden is determined to return to Rombeau as soon as possible we could lend her Peter who is young and vigorous and they could depart as soon as I could arrange for a *vetturino* to take charge of the journey. I should explain, Madam, that a *vetturino* gives you a price beforehand which includes accommodation and provisions on the way. I would be happy to seek out a reliable man."

Deborah had read all about the various modes of travel before they left home but she let Will Smyth finish and then looked down into Frederick's eyes to see how he took this suggestion. He met her gaze and his blue eyes were not sunny but frowning and pleading.

"Of course you could have Peter," he said, "but I would much rather accompany you myself as soon as it is practical."

Deborah thought, I *must* leave him. I could never be accepted by those grand people in Venice and Rome. They would think I was Lord Branford's 'woman' and ignore me. I note that many of the young nobles provide themselves with female company in each new town. Frederick is too newly widowed and I hope too fastidious to indulge such desires but our mothers certainly believe the world will think that is the way of things with us.

She stared Will into silence. "Very well, Mr Smyth. I will be most grateful to have Peter's services and will set off as soon as the weather is a little warmer. You could perhaps return via Rombeau, my lord, to collect Peter or I can send him back to join you. John and Jeanetta will not want to travel with a very young baby so we will probably stay there a little while." She didn't give him time to

Height of Folly

answer but turned on her heel as she spoke. "Let us go back to the hotel. Poor Suzette is shivering."

Suzette immediately followed, just as if I were towing her, Deborah thought, and Will Smyth has fallen in beside his master as if to preclude us linking arms again. I admire his impudence. Peter is a pleasant lad, very shy of me but I can break that down. Well, I am committed and can see a little more of Florence before I depart.

But Florence was not the same any more. She had set her face against further intimacy and asked Suzette to sit at table with her. Lord Branford was downcast. She indicated a nearby table for him and Will Smyth. When she visited the Uffizzi Gallery for the second time she kept Suzette at her side. She even considered moving to a cheaper hotel but as a warmer wind came up from the south she decided to bring her departure forward. A letter had finally arrived from John begging her to come and make the acquaintance of her new nephew.

"I hadn't really considered," she told Lord Branford in a rare tête-a- tête at the foot of the hotel stairs, "that I am now an aunt. I must enter into my new role. I will leave tomorrow and thank you for your great kindness in sparing Peter to escort me."

"Deborah, I don't think I can bear this. We have been so happy together – "

She swallowed hard but kept her fixed smile. "I know, my lord, but the time has come. You will fulfil your appointed journey and back home your appointed destiny and I mine. Let us not say a fresh goodbye tomorrow. The *vetturino* is to be here at first light." She pressed his hand quickly and ran upstairs to her room to set Suzette to the packing of their bags.

CHAPTER FIFTEEN

Early May 1706 Château Rombeau

"Deb is here," John called to Jeanette as he stood at their window and saw his sister's tall figure emerge from the carriage. "Dear old Deb. But mind, not a squeak to her about your uncle or our windy friend."

He ran out and down the great staircase to embrace her. "So, here you are, all on your own. You travelled with just Peter and Suzette. I got your letter that you'd sent poor Frederick packing."

"I did *not* 'send him packing.' I wanted to come back to see what you and Jeanetta had produced between you."

"And you shall. His nurse is in the gardens with him just now. He's fretful a bit in the afternoon so she walks about with him but she'll be back presently." He led the way into the salon and clapped his hands for refreshments. It thrilled him that she should see how easy her little brother was in this grand place. All his childhood she had put him down because he was not at his lessons. But now he was someone, son-in-law to the Comte Rombeau, father of the heir to the baronetcy of Horden. He had feared she might overtop him again by becoming the Countess of Branford but that seemed safely out of the way.

When the wine and sweetmeats arrived he waved away the servant and poured her a glass with his own hand. "To Deb, to celebrate her safe arrival."

She looked travel-weary but the wine refreshed her.

She asked, "And how is everyone at the chateau?"

"Sleeping off the afternoon as usual on a hot day. I daresay they'll put on a party for you presently."

"For me! They hardly noticed I was here before."

Height of Folly

"Any excuse for a party will do."

"Le Vent has not been back?"

John was startled that she should think of *him* so soon, but covered his surprise with a laugh. "Oh no. He's satisfied that you and I and indeed Lord B are all dutiful subjects of Queen Anne. Ah here is Netta to greet you." He saw she had got Marie to titivate her face. How beautiful she looked with her trim figure, high-colour, sparkling eyes and raven hair beside Deborah who had risen as she entered. Suzette had already whisked away her hat and cloak and she stood slightly stooped with weariness, a thin, angular figure, her flaxen hair untidy, and her face sallow.

"How well you look, Jeanetta! Motherhood must agree with you."

"But you, poor Deb, are quite exhausted."

"Well, we came as fast as possible from Grenoble but there were many delays on the sea passage from Italy waiting for a fair wind. I'll be happy to have a short rest here till you are ready to return to England. Oh course they are longing to have you back and to welcome the young heir to Horden."

John looked anxiously at Jeanetta but fortunately they were interrupted by the arrival of the nurse who appeared at the salon door. "He's asleep, my lady. I'll take him to his bed shall I?"

"Show him to his new aunt first," Jeanetta said.

On the long journey Deborah had thought about this moment. I shall meet a nephew, she had chuckled to herself, an interesting new experience. I have not handled a baby since Ruth was born and I was too young and far too recently overthrown by Ranald's love and horrible death to be able to appreciate a tiny sister. Now I am a mature woman, learned and much travelled. I shall engage myself seriously with this little one's progress and upbringing.

She smiled and stepped towards the nurse and said, "May I

hold him?"

Nothing had prepared her for the physical sensation of taking him in her arms, the feel of his little shape, the weight of his sleeping head on her arm. Her whole body seemed to lurch, to yearn over him. It was like a convulsion. Oh God, I must have a child. I must bear one myself, my own.

Despite the upheaval that was going on inside her she stood very still, just gazing at him till she heard John say, "Well, Aunt Deb, do you like the little fellow?"

"Of course I do. He's beautiful." She handed him back to the nurse and turned to them both with a bright smile. "You must be so proud of him, so happy. Now, if I may, I will go and change these clothes. Suzette will be unpacking and I feel rather hot and tired." She turned and left them, sure they would look at each other and say, "Poor old Deb, going to stay a spinster for ever. What are babies to her?"

She made her way to her old room where Suzette had indeed begun the unpacking. "Leave me awhile. I need a sleep," she told her.

The moment she was gone Deborah clambered up and flung herself on the bed and hid her face in the pillow. She was shaking with suppressed tears but now she let them pour out.

What have I done, fool that I am, she demanded of herself. How can I ever become a mother now? I have cast off the only possible man in my life. That is indeed the height of folly. Did I not tell myself on the first day of this century that for a six-foot pole like me to think of getting a husband was the height of folly? I remember the words. But I had one in my grasp and have thrown him away. And he was so kind, so sweet. He did everything to please me. If I'd said, 'marry me' he would have done. Indeed I believe I could have compelled him to ask me. Am I to mismanage my life for ever? Have I slammed the door on my last chance of

Height of Folly

motherhood?

She lay there tormented. He *was* kind but what if she had told him the story of Ranald? Would his kindness have stretched to accepting second-hand goods?

There came a tap on the door and John put his head round and called, "Deb, I was forgetting, letters came for you a day or two ago. Deb, are you there?"

She sat up and pulled back the bed curtain a little. "Just having a rest."

"Sorry, did I wake you?"

She was sure it was dim enough behind the curtain for him not to see her red eyes. "No, let me have them. Are they from home?"

"Two are and one from Rome. Lord B I guess, pleading for reconciliation perhaps. You should have grabbed him you know."

She took them without a word. He was looking at her a little curiously. "You *are* all in, Deb. Do you want Suzette? She's waiting in the gallery."

"No, I sent her away. Tell her to go to the kitchens for something to eat for herself. I'm sure Peter's there already. He was perpetually hungry on our journey."

"As you wish." John went out again.

She broke the seal of Frederick's letter first. It was the only communication that had passed between them since the parting in Florence. She saw the words, '*Honoured Madame*' and her heart sank. But then he went on, '*Nay I cannot write that. We have been through too much together. I am hoping, dear Mistress Deborah, that you will soon reach the Château Rombeau and am therefore directing this there. We have made a stately progress from Florence to Rome via Sienna and are now delayed in Rome because Joseph has been ill. It is for this reason that I am presuming to write to you. If you are safely at Rombeau when you read this you will have the company of your brother and also the*

Prue Phillipson

services of his man-servant, Matthew. Could you then instruct Peter when he is suitably rested to set out for Venice where we hope to arrive in June if Joseph is well enough to travel? We will stay at the Leon Bianco which was recommended by my grandfather as a favourite haunt of the English. As you can imagine Will Smyth is in good spirits now we are following our original scheme. He is scrupulous in pointing out buildings, works of art and sculptures which I am to appreciate but he cannot rouse me to enthusiasm as my late companion did.'

Sienna, Rome, Venice, she mused. I have missed such magnificent places. And does he mean he has truly missed *me?* She read on.

'I have prayed for your safe journey and trust that your return with your brother and his family to Northumberland will also pass without hazards of any kind. I too am looking forward to being at home in Hertfordshire later in the summer. If you or any of your family are ever in that neighbourhood I trust you will do me the honour of calling upon us. My mother and grandfather would be delighted to make your acquaintance.

'Pray convey my humble duty to all at Rombeau and my regrets that I will not now meet the count. If hostilities permit we will be returning via the German states and the Low Countries, but the French under Marshal Vendôme have inflicted a defeat on the Emperor's forces at Calcinato and have strongly garrisoned Turin so we await developments.

'If our paths do not cross believe me I will always remain, your devoted friend,

Frederick Branford.'

She flung the letter down on the bedcover. That's it, she decided. He is satisfied never to see me again and assumes I feel the same. He was obliged to write to ask for Peter back and of course that saves him coming by Rombeau on his return journey.

Height of Folly

Yes, that's the end of it.

Or was there an underlying sorrow? She picked the letter up and reread it. 'We have been through too much together.' 'My mother and grandfather would be delighted to make your acquaintance.' Of course he had to say *that*. He misses 'the enthusiasm of his late companion.' Well, how could he be inspired by a cold fish like Will Smyth? It was the enthusiasm he missed, not me.

The tears were welling up again and with them memories. I slid down that bumpy roof of tiles into his arms, she reminded herself. His hands gripped me and stood me upright on the flat roof and the fire burst from the hole we had just scrambled through. I was shaking but he was so calm. He had been praying, he told me afterwards. A man like that has his own rock within that will never fail him. What does his size matter to me? But it is *my* size that matters. He could never love this long body. 'A post' that hateful le Vent called it. And not even virginal! Ah if only it were I think I would write back to his lordship a letter of passion – in the manner of Grandmother Bel – regretting my hasty parting from him, begging him to throw up his grand tour and come to me. Oh the poor man would be mightily embarrassed and would not know how to answer. He would have to ask his mother.

Struggling with hysterical sobs she broke open the letters from home. Her father and mother had written parts of one letter and Grandmother Bel the other. All were delighted that she was on her way back north, her mother particularly praising her for separating herself from Lord Branford's company. She urged her to persuade John and Jeanetta not to delay their coming with the baby now they were all reunited.

Her father let more emotion slip out. After warning her to listen for news of the movements of the armies now that spring had come he wrote, '*You cannot imagine how much I long for my*

Prue Phillipson

Deb's company again. Home is not the same without you. If it has been hard for you to part from Lord Branford I feel for you but perhaps you can meet again in more convenient circumstances. I certainly would be happy to entertain him here for his father's sake. Henry was my closest friend.

' Your letters on your journey north were most welcome but told us only of the progress of your travels and that the man Peter was a loyal and capable escort for you and Suzette. I should assure you we are all ready to make that young girl very welcome at Horden Hall. But when you come I trust you will confide in us what your feelings are for Lord Branford. It cannot be wrong for a father to wish to know what is in his daughter's heart. '

No, dear father, she thought, not wrong, but as I couldn't speak intimately to you about *Ranald*, how can I open my heart about the great dilemma of *Frederick*? If he *did* love me would you advise me to marry him without disclosing my past – just so he could give me a child? I do not think so. This I must face alone.

She turned to Grandmother Bel's letter. Here, she thought, love will cascade forth without restraint or much punctuation. Maybe I can talk to *her* when I get home.

'My darling Deb, my heart bled for you that you felt you had to break away from Lord Branford after that unfortunate newspaper article. The world is a silly place and I have tried to ignore it all my life. As our dear Ursula always said love love love and all will be well. God knows she had a rough time of it in life with her poor hideous, lovely face but she never ceased loving.

' Of course I know you may not feel sensual love for Lord B and if you don't well no harm's done but if you do and he for you I pray heartily that you will still come together somehow. As you know I loved your grandfather Nat just from his letters after one short meeting and I determined to find him again which I did in the worst circumstances possible and it was I who told him we

Height of Folly

were destined for each other so we were never parted again after that. So who knows how it will be with you and Frederick? You can still have many years with him as I had with my Nat or maybe there is another to come into your life you are still young.

'*And now there is a baby Nathaniel. I am so thrilled that they are choosing that name to remember his great-grandfather. John is a terrible correspondent and has not described the baby at all. Pray do so my sweet Deb and delight your ever loving grandmother Bel.*'

Deborah was smiling by the end of the letter, though it left her breathless. Dear Grandmother! She has forgotten all about Ranald, that great hairy figure that still darkens my future. But maybe I can hang on to her principle of love and stop thinking of my cursed inches. Grandmother was blessed. She was just a little shorter than Grandfather and what a marriage they had!

She climbed down off the bed and decided to get changed now without Suzette's help and prepare herself to meet everyone at the family dinner.

But the sooner I can be on my way home to Horden the happier I shall be, she said aloud, as she struggled to untie her laces without pulling them into knots.

Two days' later, wanting to write home with a date for their return, she sought John and met him coming from the Neury's rooms in the château. She beckoned him into the library. There was rarely anyone there and as she expected it was empty.

First she asked him what he had been doing up there.

He bridled a little. "Not your business but the fact is old man Neury's taken a fancy to me and likes me to play chess with him sometimes."

"*Can* you play chess? I tried to teach you when we were children."

"I know I know. You were too quick for me then but he's shown me the rules again. He always wins but that suits him well. What did you want with me anyway?"

Deborah accepted the explanation for the present and sat down at one of the tables to discuss the matter. "We have to arrange our journey back to England soon."

"Oh." John prowled about the room and then flung himself into the rocking chair beside the unlit fire at a distance from her.

"The fact is Netta doesn't really want to go back to Horden. She can't see that it's necessary at all."

Deborah sat bolt upright. "Not go back? She's *married* to you and that is your home."

As soon as she said it she realised that if she married Frederick she would have to live in Hertfordshire. Well, that wasn't going to happen but for a few seconds she understood and sympathised with Jeanetta. Then she burst out, "They want to see the baby. She can't deny them that."

"Oh I daresay she'd be happy for me to take him for a visit –"

"A visit! John, you *live* at Horden Hall. It's your ancestral home. While father is alive it's your duty to help him and when – God forbid – his time comes to depart this life, you take over."

"I know all that but he doesn't need me now and afterwards – well, I can appoint a steward."

"A steward! The baronet not live at Horden Hall!"

"Well, Father leaves it to the coal company to manage those seams they found. I wouldn't know anything about that."

"You could learn. I have read much about mining and coal production and distribution since the beginning of seventeen hundred when we first knew we had coal at Horden."

"Well there you are. You like that sort of thing." He grinned at her, rocking the chair back and forth. "You can be Father's right hand man now. You should have been a boy anyway. And you'll be living there the rest of your life."

Height of Folly

Deborah crushed down the hurt these words gave her and went back to the main point. "John, are you telling me you want to bring up little Nathaniel, the heir to Horden, as a Frenchman, a mere hanger-on in his grandfather's château? How could you think of such a thing?"

"I know. It's been deuced awkward. Netta and I have had words about it, but the thing is she doesn't really like life at Horden."

Deborah didn't want to hear of marital disputes. She remembered the inn at Dover where she had urged John to be tolerant of Jeanetta's moods and keep her love. But she couldn't stop herself blurting out, "Oh I know Horden's not grand enough for her, we don't have armies of servants and the ladies of the house delight in work which never did suit her. But she can continue as she did. Father likes her around as a pretty ornament and Mother tolerates her."

"But that's it. Here she has her own mother. I know her father's away in court a great deal but they both pet and indulge her and give parties and balls and picnics and such which she loves."

"And you would give in to all that? You would be her appendage. Are you not bored to tears here sometimes?"

He rocked more vigorously. "There are good hunting and shooting parties –"

"Oh John, you disappoint me. I never thought you would turn out so feeble, so lazy." She got up, exasperated. It was a long time since she had spoken to him like that. Nothing was resolved. Should she speak to Jeanetta herself and risk a serious family rift? She had no status with the comte and comtesse. Her longing to be at home in Horden had intensified while they were talking.

John had stopped rocking and his jaw was set. Had she angered him at last?

"I'll show you one day whether I'm feeble or not." He stood up and glared at her. Then he stalked past her to the door and turned at it. "I suppose you can write to them at home that we'll come in August when Jean is eight months old."

"Jean?"

"Nathaniel then. He's Jean here. You and the nurse can manage him if Netta won't come. We had such a hellish crossing on the way she's frightened, but the baby seems a tough little thing. He's scarcely ailed anything since he was born which Mother Diana says is pretty miraculous."

Deborah caught him and grabbed his arm as he was going out. "John, you can't tell me Jeanetta would let the baby out of her sight for months? Of course she would have to come."

Even as she said it she realised neither John nor Jeanetta spent much time with the baby. The nurse brought him to be played with when he was newly cleaned up and fed. Oh if he was mine! she wanted to cry out, but that thought was too full of pain.

John shook off her arm. "If we both went it would just be to show the old folk the baby and keep them happy for a while. I would have to come back here. I expect I'll be travelling back and forth from France to England for some time. Anyway, you'd better write. They keep plaguing me with letters asking when we're coming."

"But August is nearly three months off."

"Say July then, but you'd better say nothing about Jeanetta. Let them suppose she's coming. I might persuade her. God knows I don't want to be apart from her but I don't want her miserable, that's all."

This time he got away and bounded up the stairs no doubt to tell Jeanetta what a pest his sister was.

Deborah turned back into the library. A supply of writing paper adorned with the Rombeau crest was always on display on a desk in the window with ink filled up and pens newly trimmed. With a deep sigh and a foreboding of unpleasantness to come she sat

Height of Folly

down to write what should have been joyful letters. But I must make them *sound* joyful, she told herself, however heavy my heart is. As she picked up a pen a summer shower blew against the window panes, veiling the green of the garden.

Well, *I* will not weep. I will say I am safely arrived here, to Maytime beauty, and in only eight little weeks I will be with them. Nothing shall take away that joy.

Upstairs Jeanetta rolled on the bed, inviting him in. She was in a playful mood and he would not spoil it. He bolted the door and began to unbuckle his breeches. Deb would have to eat her words when he led a troop of soldiers from the great Catholic families of Northumberland to join the banner of King James. If only the word could be given soon. The news was that Turin was under siege by Prince Eugene and the Duke of Savoy and a battle was looming between Marlborough and the Duc de Villeroi's forces south of Brussels. It was certain that King Louis would not spare French troops for the Jacobite cause till these threats were over.

If I go to Horden, he was thinking, as he cast his breeches on the floor, I can visit these people on le Vent's list. It is like the time when the highlands were raised under Claverhouse. There were long delays and I wanted swift action because I was a mere boy. Now I see how these things must be carefully planned to seize the moment.

He leaped onto the bed. "Have at thee, girl." Jeanetta squealed with delight.

CHAPTER SIXTEEN

On a day of continental heat the stagecoach, bearing Deborah, John, Matt and Suzette with baby Nathamiel and his nurse passed through Durham County on the last stretch of their journey home. Deborah sat still, utterly absorbed with the prospect of seeing her father again and anticipating the joy of Grandmother Bel.

John kept looking from the windows and remarking on the signs of new coal workings. Crossing the Tyne Bridge he pointed out the mass of coal-barges in the river.

"Look there, Deb, the north-east is the engine of the whole country. Whoever controls this trade will have London in their power."

Deborah wondered if the prospect of being a landowner here was at last exciting him. She herself was not so sure that she wanted to see Newcastle as a coal town with tentacles of industry creeping into the countryside.

At the staging inn in Newcastle the Horden carriage was waiting for them. Suzette, who had chatted to Nurse Forêt all the way, a solid woman with not a word of English, fell silent, sensing her mistress's suppressed excitement. The baby, muffled up, was bright red and cross.

As they approached Horden Hall Deborah saw beyond the trees the tops of the mine workings on Horden land. Her heart sank a little. With all these new mouths to feed would her father have to lease even more land for coal. She was glad that when she stepped down from the carriage and looked about with moist eyes at the dear old place no changes were apparent and here came everyone running from the house to greet them.

Her father's welcome was the most emotional. He couldn't hold back his tears. Her mother's was for John first and then the baby.

Height of Folly

"Poor little precious and no mother!" Eunice took him from the nurse and, sitting down on the steps, undid his wrappings and pulled up his dress to reveal his moist pink legs. Everyone gathered to coo and gloat over him, and then Deborah found herself embraced by her sister.

"Ruth!" She held her at arm's length, astonished and a little disconcerted.

Fifteen months had changed her from an undeveloped girl into a stalwart young woman. Her fair hair was browner and swept up smoothly. Deborah thought, it will always look more kempt than my flaxen mop. Her face is not so prettily petite as it was but handsome. Her breasts and hips are fuller but her waist is neat. Despite the heat she is wearing a tight corset under her dress. She is Mother's build though taller, but still shorter than John. Oh, men will turn to look at *her* all right.

Ruth said, "Oh Deb, you look exhausted and much thinner!" She turned back to the baby and begged to hold him. He was gurgling now at his freedom to kick.

Eunice yielded him up and finally turned to Deborah and hugged her.

"My dear girl, are you well?"

Deborah exclaimed, "Just a little wearied by the heat. Ruth has grown into womanhood! I hardly knew her."

Eunice pursed up her lips with her old disparaging smile. "Seventeen in September and looking for a husband soon."

Deborah laughed. "I know. She was born on my birthday. I'll be thirty-five."

Her father squeezed her hard. "Nothing wrong with thirty-five. It's a joy to have you back."

That was very comfortable but it would be Ruth's marriage prospects that would concern the family from now on. And Deborah winced to see Ruth cradling the baby. He was to be hers while he was here without his mother as long as the nurse kept him clean and fed. Ruth was eyeing Suzette curiously too. She'll be demanding a lady's maid next, Deborah thought. Well, that I don't mind. Suzette will have to serve all the ladies, including Grandmother Bel.

And where was Grandmother Bel? Now she appeared in the doorway holding out one hand, but clutching a stick in the other. Deborah ran to her.

"I fell asleep and no one said you were here."

She had aged but she was still all love. "What no Jeanetta? I couldn't believe she wouldn't come with her baby. Ah let me see him." Deborah helped her down the steps. She sat down as Eunice had done on the bottom one and demanded to hold him.

"I never thought I'd live to see a great-grandchild. He's a beauty and so big and bouncy. Little Nat! How *my* Nat would have loved to see his namesake."

Deborah saw that Ruth was now engrossed with John who had paid her some compliment on how she had grown up. Deborah recalled that it was he who happily played childish games with her. I tried to teach her lessons as I tried with John and the children at Nether Horden's Dame School to please Grandfather Nat but I could never get down to their level. Their pace of learning was too slow. Yes, John will be her confidant now. She never really was mine.

The baby began to cry and Nurse Forêt declared him to be thirsty. Jane who had come with the other servants to greet them took her upstairs to feed him. I hope, Deborah thought, that Nurse will attempt some English now. Our people have no French. I am sure she understands most of what is said to her.

Later as they assembled for their first meal in the dining-room, Deborah was thinking, I must get used to this but, God help me, home feels different now.

Height of Folly

For John the strangeness lay in the absence of Jeanetta. Up to the very last day he had hoped she would change her mind and come. He made passionate love to her with the luggage standing in their room. She was languorous in the heat-wave that lay over northern France too and finally pushed him away.

She put her hands behind her head, lying back on the pillow. "You might have left me with another child. I wonder if I can bear to go through all that again."

"Come with me," he said.

"You'll come back soon. You only have to show them baby Jean and they'll be satisfied."

"But I have to do work for the cause. You know the commission le Vent has given me. You want me to be somebody, don't you? I am no one here."

"And I feel no one at Horden. Your mother always looks at me as if I should be at work, earning my keep. Here everyone wants to look after me. It's so comfortable. Well, do your commission as you call it and come back quickly."

With these words in his ears John wanted to start straight away making contact with Catholics in Northumberland. Le Vent had asked him to recruit more of the humbler sort to the cause. Catholic nobles like the Earl of Derwentwater were already secured. He had spent much of his childhood at Saint Germain and was certain to be prominent in the uprising. But how am I to set about *my* task? John wondered.

It would excite too much curiosity if he just rode off and stayed away a night or two. Horden Hall was a more intimate place than the Château Rombeau. Everyone expected to know everyone else's whereabouts. He was hampered too by not knowing when King Louis would be prepared to commit forces to send with James. He wanted to be armed with news.

Prue Phillipson

In the next few weeks he studied the newssheets more than he had ever done. Marlborough was taking town after town in the Low Countries following his great victory at Ramillies. Would this kill off French help? Could disaffected Jacobites raise enough forces in England and Scotland on their own? John struggled to understand politics but he heard Deborah discussing with their father the Treaty of Union agreed between the English and Scottish parliaments on the twenty-second of July. It had still to be passed as an Act of Union but for the Jacobites it might offer a chance to exploit Scottish discontent with the idea of one nation.

Besides, with government troops busy across the channel there would be fewer forces here to control an uprising. The Jacobites could proclaim James as King of Scotland first and hope that England would accept him. If the two countries were to become Great Britain, he was unsure whether the task would be harder or easier.

As a Catholic it was his duty to go to Mass but now that he had no wife to take he had no excuse for disappearing to Newcastle and he had to commit the sin of attending the Parish Church or risk upsetting the whole family. Their shock and amazement that Jeanetta had not accompanied him was bad enough. He feared that they thought him inadequate as a husband because he could not command his wife.

His sisters also monopolised his baby as soon as the nurse had dealt with his physical needs. Deborah even carried him in his basket to the woods and set him down to gaze at the waving leaves while she pruned dead wood or cleared undergrowth. Deb had no sense of the fitness of things. He too could work at that sort of task to fill his time but after his long sojourn at Château Rombeau he couldn't see that as right for the future master of the Hall. And, as he had told Deb, his father was managing the estate competently. What help could he be?

Height of Folly

His mother liked him near her. "Come and tell me more of your travels," she would say as she went into the kitchen to make tarts with the raspberries and blackcurrants from the kitchen garden. He perched on a stool and tried to describe Paris, Versailles, the Loire and Marseilles.

"I have to live them all through you," she said, "for I cannot go there myself."

"You and Father should go abroad. I would look after things here."

She patted his knee with a floury hand. "I have no desire to go where men are fighting. There is no sense in this war even in the *world*'s notions of sense."

"I know. I can't see where it's leading at all but there *are* times when you have to fight for what is clearly right."

"Our Lord didn't fight."

She always ended up preaching and he would wander off, not too obviously, to spare her feelings.

One day she said to him, "You are fretting at being away from Jeanetta."

"Of course I am," he snapped. "We're neither of us great hands at letter-writing and I don't know what she's doing this minute which makes me mad."

"John, has she eyes for someone else? Is that why she wouldn't come?"

"No! That never crossed my mind. Of course the men who come to parties and balls flirt with her. She's so pretty. She likes that. It's flattering, but she always laughs at them afterwards with me. Still, I can't stand this. I'll have to go back soon."

"And take our little Nat? We will miss him so much. It is she who should come here to you. You know what the Bible says of a dutiful wife."

A few days after this conversation she was taking some mending out to the bench under the parlour window. "Come with me, John. I have an idea to put to you."

When they had sat down, warmed by the August sun, she said, "Your father says Nether Horden Grange is empty now old Mistress Carr has died. Would Jeanetta come if that were yours? It is a pleasant Elizabethan house with plenty of room for the nurse and Maria, her lady's maid, and another servant or two."

John shifted on the bench and stroked his chin. A house of his own, free from parental eyes! But Jeanetta would need a cook, grooms and their own carriage horses.

He picked up a spool of silk that had rolled onto the grass and looked into his mother's face. "Would you call it a *mansion*? There's stabling there, isn't there?"

She took the spool and put it in her workbox. "A mansion? Hardly, though a new wing was added when there was a tenant with a big family. And yes, it has stables. Mistress Carr was left a goodly portion and kept her own carriage. Your father's allowance would not extend to a carriage but you could stable your own mounts and use our carriage when it was available. I suppose your father would excuse you rent, but of course, John, you *could* find some profession. You need to be occupied."

"Profession! I only ever fancied the army or the navy and you wouldn't hear of either." He got up and prowled about before stopping suddenly in front of her. "I tell you what, Mother, if Father would spare me a few days I'd like to go about the county a little and find out the latest methods of husbandry and such so I'm more prepared to take over Horden when the time comes."

She actually laughed. "Well, John, I've never heard you show that sort of interest before. Your father would be delighted. The only difficulty is that he himself is a pioneer in the latest ways of managing land and knows there are many backward practices in outlying places. You can learn all you want from studying *his*

Height of Folly

methods."

"I'd still like to do my own survey. It will mean more to me if I've seen for myself what goes on. Then if we did take Nether Horden Grange I could manage the land there in the best way. After I've had a little tour round – say a week or two – I could go back to France and bring Jeanetta over. I might even leave you the wee boy so you'd know I'd be back soon. Deb would be pleased. She's determined that the first words he speaks will be English ones. Nurse isn't even trying to talk our lingo. She gabbles to him in French all the time."

His mother laid down her work and took both his hands in hers. "If you will bring Jeanetta here where she belongs at your side, dear boy, I will get you leave from your father to make your little tour of the county. It is good you should be known as a man of ideas and interests. Is it safe to return to France afterwards? Will you not be arrested as an alien?"

He laughed. "As the son-in-law of Comte Rombeau I can go anywhere I please." He was thinking, there it is again, 'get you leave from your father'! I am a man and should come and go as I like, but I will put up with it for now.

Somehow his mother persuaded his father it would be a good thing for him to study the farming methods in the county. "Take a notebook and pencil and let me see what you have found out," was all he said. "Matt can go with you."

John had every intention of taking Matt. Matt knew all about the people he had called upon in France on their way from Marseilles. Matt wanted adventure as much as he did. It had not been hard to convince him that James was the true king of the whole country of Britain. He rode off, alight with purpose at last. He would test all the Catholic houses he could trace with the password of 'your wild, beautiful Scotland'.

From the first he found himself accepted as an emissary of

Prue Phillipson

Edouard le Vent and the days passed in a whirlwind of gathered heads, whispered words, glimpses at caches of weapons, oaths before icons of the Virgin and promises, promises, promises. At each manor house or farmstead he remembered to ask brief questions about the number of their sheep and cattle, what crops they grew and whether the land was loam, clay or – as it often was – very stony.

He and Matt rode home on an early September afternoon under a drooping yellowing sky. He saw the grey solid shape of Horden Hall sitting against its sombre curtain of trees and grinned at Matt.

"The old place is not finished with history yet. You and I don't want it to settle into its fields and woods and think its day is done."

Matt, curly-haired, more sun-burnt than ever and now more a friend than a servant, chuckled back. "And that old devil," he pointed to Sir Ralph, "can keep on waving his sword. He may see action again before he crumbles to dust."

As they drew nearer John saw his mother sitting sewing on the bench as if she had never moved. Now she set down her work and held out her arms in delight. Grandmother Bel was coming down the front steps and waving something in her hand. She didn't scamper as she used to do but held onto the rail that had been put up for her. The hectic two weeks he had been away seemed so long that he thought she must have aged during his absence. He dismounted and flung the reins to Matt. When it came to unsaddling and grooming Matt was again the servant.

Grandmother Bel held out a letter. "There you are, John. From France. It is not Jeanetta's hand but I'm sure she will have put in a message. Eh, I could never have borne to be away from my Nat as long as this and my baby too." She sat down beside his mother. "Have you any work for me there, Eunice? I can't abide my hands idle."

Height of Folly

"I was thinking of going indoors till I saw it was John come home. We may have a thunderstorm."

John walked a little way across the grass towards the statue of Sir Ralph and broke the seal. He had recognised Sophia's hand which chilled his stomach. What if – after all his activity of the past two weeks – he was to learn that her father, Vicomte Neury, had died, his desk had been opened and the plot discovered?

But no! He ran back to the others. "Mother! Grandmother! Netta's with child again. See how good the French air is for her. But Sophie says she's more sick than last time. I must go to her."

Deborah, hot and grubby, came round from the kitchen garden carrying Nathaniel's basket. Ruth followed Grandmother Bel from the house. Everyone could hear horses' hooves at Horden Hall and would come to see who had arrived.

He greeted his sisters "Deb! Ruth! Another baby for you. But I must take this one home." He pounced on the basket and lifted the child out, the long clothes trailing. "Hey young sir, you're to have a brother or sister next year. What do you say to that?" Nathaniel chortled with delight as he was thrown in the air and caught again. "I reckon he's pleased."

Deborah looked from Eunice to Bel and back to John. "Is this true?"

They nodded, smiling. Ruth skipped with glee. "I'll have this baby all to myself!"

Deborah's face was bleak. "But you're going to take Nat back to France? You call France his home now?"

John was unmoved by her disappointment. She had become too obsessed with his child. Nat was his and Jeanetta's and he was fun to play with now. He popped the baby back in the basket where he immediately raised a howl.

"Tell Nurse to start packing all his things," he said to Deborah. "I'll not be back till t'other's born." and he ran indoors to prepare for his departure. How thankful he was that he had achieved his work for le Vent before this news came!

Deborah bit her lip and picked the baby out again and cuddled him. "See how he treats him. Nat was so happy with me. I propped him up and he watched me while I was hoeing the cabbage plants. Now he's to be snatched away and if we ever see him again he'll be a little French boy and won't even know who we are."

Grandmother Bel was patting the bench. "Come and sit, my Deb, and let me have a little loving of him. Don't be sad. He should be with his father and mother so if she can't come here he must go to her."

"But they leave him to the nurse all the time at the château." And Deborah, to her own disgust and shame in front of her sister, broke into sobs.

Her mother tut-tutted. "Oh Deborah, that's not like you!"

But Grandmother Bel put an arm round her, enveloping her and the baby together. "You've been keeping these tears pent up since you came home. I know that. And this little one was your principal joy and he's to vanish away."

Deborah nodded.

"Are you also weeping for Lord Branford?" her mother asked. "You have told us nothing of your feelings for each other and your father is quite hurt about it."

Grandmother Bel flapped her free hand at her. "Let her alone for now, Eunice. Hark! Was that not distant thunder I heard?"

Deborah, choking back her sobs, had heard nothing and Grandmother was getting deaf.

They all got to their feet and her mother gathered up her things. "I didn't *hear* anything but the sky *is* darkening. Go to your room, Deborah, and compose yourself. Can you manage Nathaniel?"

Deborah inserted him, protesting, into his basket and picked it

Height of Folly

up. Ruth, puzzled, peered up into her face. Then they all scurried indoors as, without lightning or thunder, a few large drops of rain began to fall.

Deborah delivered the baby to the nurse who had already received John's orders to pack his things.

She said to Deborah in French, "He cannot go tomorrow surely? A baby needs so much for every day. Men! They do not understand babies at all. Ach! He is all wet and dirty again. He smells." She babbled on to the baby in half scolding, half joking terms and Deborah left her to it and went to her own room.

I suppose I am a little squeamish, she admitted to herself, as Jeanetta surely is and thankful to have someone else to deal with him, but oh! without him what is there here for me? And Father is hurt, is he? He has been very sweet and tender to me but I have not been able to confide in him, for what is there to confide? There have been no more letters from Frederick and why should there be any? His last was a goodbye.

She sat on the window seat, her head turned to see the rain blackening Sir Ralph's statue. There came a knock on her door. She knew it at once. Her father's knock. So there was to be no escape. 'Deborah is upset. You had better go to her' her mother must have said.

"Come in," she called.

He came in, shut the door and came straight over to her and sat beside her.

"So what's all this, my girl? Is it John's sudden decision to go back to France and take Nat? It was bound to happen sooner or later but with Jeanetta expecting –"

She shook her head vigorously. "Of course he must go. I'll get over it."

"And it's nothing to do with Lord Branford?"

She compressed her lips and breathed hard. How could she say it wasn't? He waited. She looked at him sideways, lifting her eyes to meet his.

"There you are, you see," she said at last. "I look *up* to you. For Frederick I have to look *down*. How can he stand that?"

"What! Is it still that old height problem? Are you saying you two could have made a match of it if he had been as tall as I?"

"I don't know." She burst out with tears again. "But he was – he is – a good man. Not exciting, not wild like Ranald, but steadfast. I didn't love him till we were parted but now I think about him all the time and there are no other men in my life so how can I ever become a mother? And *Ruth* will be wed in a few years' time. All I will ever be is an unwanted aunt."

"Ah that's it, isn't it? Well, we must look among friends and acquaintances. John has been meeting many local people lately and we can ask him if he came across any of suitable age and status. We will have a Harvest Ball in the grounds."

Deborah looked out at the teeming rain and her shoulders began to shake.

"Well Father, don't do it for me."

"Ah, it's good to see you laugh instead of cry. I can't bear to see my girl unhappy. There are other men beside Lord Branford and we should try to find them."

"And on the invitation cards we could ask them for their measurements." If joking pleased him she could turn on the jokes.

Perhaps he guessed the effort she was making because he asked now, "Seriously, my Deb, did Lord Branford address you at all?"

"Yes, he addressed me as Deborah. We were Frederick and Deborah after the night of the fire."

"But that supposes a closeness, an intimacy –"

"But not love, Father. I think he *admired* me too much to love me."

That seemed to strike him forcibly. He pondered a little and

Height of Folly

nodded. "That may be very profound, my girl. I too was in awe of your mother for many years. I saw how strong she was and yet how dutifully she submitted to her father. Then she came through the plague, through loneliness and poverty, cruel servitude and then the fire. I almost dared not love her because how could I live up to her high standards?"

Deborah was thinking, is this the mother *I* know? And with that uncanny insight he sometimes showed he added as if he knew her thought, "It's much harder for your mother to show her true character in prosperity and comfort. If I were to lose everything tomorrow she would come into her own."

"I'm sure you are right, Father, but tell me how did you finally bring yourself to dare to love her? To believe you could be *married* to this *paragon*."

He was thinking, trying to remember. "I sensed she was *in love* with me, but for her that was not enough. I had to convince her I was a good man she could honour in the sight of God. She had promised that to her father who was always desperate to keep her from men. When I thought she had faith in me I dared to propose."

Deborah gave him an impulsive kiss on his cheek. "Dear Papa, that is very enlightening. But what I feel about Frederick is just the opposite way round. I didn't fall in love – not as I did with Ranald, God help me! But I already know he is a man I could honour in the sight of God. I believe I could have had a happy marriage with him – but for Ranald."

"Well, *he* is past history. You are older. That belief of yours in Frederick is a sound basis. If he knew you felt like that would not his admiration for you grow into the love you are seeking?" He straightened his long back and clapped his hands on his knees. "Surely our two families could arrange things between us. I am certain his grandfather had you in mind for him when he first wrote to your grandmother about him. It was the unlucky newspaper article that put a spoke in the wheel. Maybe your mother should not have urged you to leave him."

"His mother said the same thing – I suppose to protect my good name."

"But has he written to you since you parted?"

"Yes, to Rombeau to ask me to send Peter back to him."

"And did you reply?"

"Yes, I sent Peter."

"But a letter?"

"No, I felt it was all over."

"Well, why should I not write to his grandfather and say I understand you and his grandson reached a pleasant level of companionship on your travels and would he consider promoting a match between you. Words to that effect. These things are done mainly by approaches of this sort among great families."

"Oh no!" Deborah plunged her face into her hands.

"No?"

"I would feel so exposed. I was cold with him when we parted or I couldn't have gone through with it, especially when he said 'I can't bear this, Deborah.'"

"He said that!"

"Yes, he didn't want to be left with Will Smyth. He liked looking at things with me because I was enthusiastic. That's all he liked, my enthusiasm."

She was growing frantic now not to break down and upset her father again. Why had she not answered Frederick's letter? Peter could have delivered it. Now she didn't know their whereabouts or when they would be home. Maybe he would be caught up in the hostilities and arrested as a spy before he could escape from France. The word 'spy' jumped out of her thought and she saw how she could escape from this subject which was becoming too

Height of Folly

fraught with emotion.

Her father was looking tenderly into her eyes.

"Oh," she said, "I've just remembered something I wanted to say to you. Nothing to do with this silly matter. Much more serious."

His eyebrows shot up. "*More* serious?"

"Yes. You let John go off round the county and I didn't even know about it till he'd gone. What did you suppose he was doing?"

"John? How have we got back to John?"

"I'm worried about what he was up to."

"Up to? Why just an exploration of his own into the farming practices of Northumberland."

"And you believed him? When has he ever cared about such things?"

"Oh come now, Deb. I've been encouraging him to study agriculture for years. What did you imagine he was doing?"

"Stirring up a Jacobite rebellion."

"What! Now that *is* nonsense. The last time you raised such a preposterous notion was in this room on New Year's Day, seventeen hundred. Have you seen any signs since of such activities on John's part?"

Deborah hesitated. Anything she said about Monsieur le Vent or Vicomte Neury would sound improbable when John had stoutly rebutted her suspicions at the time. She countered rather weakly with a question, "Well, have you evidence that he learnt anything of husbandry?"

"Yes, indeed. He passed me his notes not ten minutes ago." He drew the scrawled entries from his pocket and looked at them. "Of course he was never much given to writing but he has set down here enough to expand into a scholarly paper if he chose. The notes would jog his memory."

Deborah was shaken. Was John really clever enough to disguise his activities and deceive father? And was there more to his sudden wish to depart to France than Jeanetta's pregnancy? They only had his word that she *was* with child. He could write a letter later that she had miscarried and they would all believe him. Perhaps he had met with le Vent by arrangement and was ordered to France with his information.

She got up, heaving a deep sigh. It was all too speculative and her father would grow angry. "Maybe I imagined it," she said.

He stood up too and patted her shoulder. "No, our talk of marriage was distressing you and you needed a change of subject. I understand. We will let John and the wee one get away home to France and return to your affairs later when we are all calm and rational."

She forced a smile and let him go. Her affairs, as he called them, were a tangle of fears and longings, regrets and might-have-beens. I will not question John, she decided. If he is innocent well and good. If he is not I will pray that his schemes end in failure. I do not want to make him lie to me. But how empty the Hall will feel when he has taken that precious child away − and Nurse and Matt have gone too!

CHAPTER SEVENTEEN

Horden Hall had its Harvest Ball on a cool September day when the rain just held off till evening. It was to celebrate not only the harvest but the birthday of the baronet's two daughters. News had also just come of the lifting of the siege of Turin which had been going on since May. Prince Eugene and the Duke of Savoy had inflicted a heavy defeat on the French army and there was talk that surely now France would sue for peace.

There was an air of light-heartedness. Many young men were looking for wives and a few had the boldness to ask the baronet's younger daughter to partner them in the country dances that were held on the lawns with the village pipe band playing. Ruth hardly sat down once on the benches that had been fetched from the schoolroom for the onlookers.

Deborah had been sitting with her mother and Grandmother Bel but they had been feeling chilly and had gone inside. Almost immediately she was approached by Bill Warner, the bearded mining engineer, but not to dance. He lowered his big bulk on the bench and stroked his beard.

"Look here, Mistress Horden," he began. "I know this is irregular but I'm a man of action. Too many words bother me. To speak plain why shouldn't you and I get together? You know I lost my good lady last year and have four children in need of a mother. Your father and I are in business together over the coal works which puts us on a sort of level. I've brought him a good deal of wealth so I don't feel it's impertinent to approach you. I thought I'd sound you out before I asked his leave, seeing we're both over the hill a bit."

Deborah was so astonished she didn't interrupt him till he paused for breath.

Prue Phillipson

"Am I to understand that this is a proposal of marriage, Mr Warner?"

"Well, ay. No offence meant. I have a good town house in Pilgrim Street in Newcastle. I keep a carriage and pair, a cook, two maids and a manservant. You wouldn't have to lift a finger. Mind, you could teach the children for you're famous for your learning and they're making little progress at school."

And you would want me in your bed, I suppose, Deborah was thinking. She tried to imagine him naked under those straining breeches and her gorge rose.

"Thank you." She stood up. "Thank you, Mr Warner, but the answer is no."

He rose too, his face red. "You've not had time to think about it. You're not like to get another offer at your age and I could make you very comfortable. I'm standing for the town council. Who knows? I might go for parliament yet."

"I'm sure I wish you every success but *I* have no wish to change my present status." She walked away. No one seemed to have noticed the little encounter and when she looked back she saw him hunch his shoulders and slouch off to the tent where jugs of ale were being handed out.

A cool breeze and a feeling of rain in the air dispersed the guests within the next hour and the family assembled in the parlour beside a good fire with a fresh brew of tea from the kitchen.

Deborah looked round at them all with a laugh. "Well, I had a proposal of marriage so the Harvest Ball bore fruit as you hoped it would, Father."

Ruth burst out. "I had *dozens!*" Then she sat up and stared at Deborah. "You're serious? You mean somebody really did propose to you? You!"

"You needn't be so astonished."

Height of Folly

"But who?" Grandmother Bel exclaimed.

"Mr Warner, the coal merchant."

Father leapt up. "Warner! He had the nerve – I'll turn him off my land."

"You'll do nothing of the sort, Father. You've always said he's a hard worker, he knows his business, he treats his men fairly and doesn't cheat his customers. What more can you want?"

"Dear God, you haven't accepted him, Deb?"

Their mother threw up her hands. "She wants a child. That's it."

Ruth exclaimed, "But what happened to that earl who helped you escape from the fire? Did nothing come of that?"

Deborah wished she had never mentioned Mr Warner's proposal. "Father, you may sit down again. Of course I haven't accepted him. And no, Ruth, nothing came of Lord Branford who is not an earl yet anyway. I shall continue as I am. But one thing I would really like to do, Father, is take John's place while he is away."

Daniel sat down, mopping his brow with relief. "What a fright you gave me there, Deb! As to John's place what had you in mind? Were you thinking of writing a memorandum from his little notes?"

"No, I told John in France that he should do more to help you. Last night I believe you sat up late working out the cost of the ball but that is only one small item in a year's expenses. I would like to take over the accounts if you'd let me."

"Let you! No one would be more pleased than I. I tried John with them when he left university but he wasn't even as good at the figures as myself. Well, we will go over them together. I'll show you the ledgers in the morning."

"Thank you, Father. And now Ruth can tell us of all *her* marriage proposals."

Ruth blushed and giggled. "They weren't exactly proposals but every man I danced with said I was the girl for him and I danced like an angel."

Their mother held up a warning finger. "Never, never let me hear you uttering a word in praise of yourself, even if you are quoting someone else."

I danced like an angel with Ranald Gordon, Deborah thought. He was so strong he made me feel as light as a feather. It would be impossible to dance with Frederick unless I took the man's part. "Who did you like best of your partners?" she asked Ruth, knowing who she would say.

Ruth's cheeks flamed up more than before. "That cousin of the Robsons from Upper Horden Manor, as you very well know, Deb. Simon Stephenson." She spluttered over the name. "But he's to go to Oxford soon and I won't see him for years and his home's in York. So what's the use of that?"

"I waited years for your father," Eunice said, "and Mother Bel here waited for Father Nat. If he's a worthy boy and a God-fearing and loves you as a man should love his wife he will be worth waiting for. We will not run before the Lord. You and he will still be young in three years' time. He must work hard and earn his living before we would even think of him for you."

Ruth looked up at Deborah. "But he's so handsome, isn't he, Deb? I saw *you* looking at him."

Grandmother Bel laughed. "The lad in the blue waistcoat! *I* was looking at him. He was beautiful! But, as your mother says you should go by the inside of a package not the wrapper."

"Enough," said Daniel. "We will not marry Ruth off on her seventeenth birthday. Let us have a bowl of punch and drink to the health of both our daughters."

"In moderation, of course," said Eunice.

Deborah retired that night excited about her new challenge. If John intended to spend half his time in France and Ruth would be

Height of Folly

married in a few years' time the running of Horden Hall would be in her hands as her father aged.

Before my travels, she recalled, I thought I was tiring of the place but if I am truly involved in the running of it I will have work with a purpose. The study of modern languages was useful but where was Hebrew leading? I can refresh my brain with figures. Dear Grandmother ran this place in days of poverty and helped to set it on its feet. Father has improved the farms and now has income from coal too. But our expenses have mightily increased in recent years. John has a much bigger allowance than we girls but Father found extra money for our late travels and must now pay for more journeys to and from France. John comes and goes without a thought for the cost. I want to know our total income and whether it can continue to meet so many outgoings. Can I help Father make savings? Can I increase our income in any way so he has a surplus for Ruth's dowry when the time comes? Mother is frugal since she has no ambitions towards grandeur but the administration of a large estate is not something her mind can compass. Father is beginning to find the work wearisome. I think I can forget love and babies and be very happy from now on.

Bel Wilson Horden, to her great annoyance, was becoming frail in body. She had been accustomed all her life to do things in a hurry but now it was only her mind that still rushed about. With no specific duties since her dear Nathaniel had died and she had had to move from the vicarage to the Hall it was her son's family who filled her heart and soul, but she knew she must give Daniel's and Eunice's marriage the space it needed. So she spent certain hours in her own room, looking out on the green sward, Sir Ralph's statue and the fields and woods beyond the gates. There she had too much time for thinking since her eyes soon tired of reading or sewing and the object of much of her thinking that winter was her granddaughter, Deborah.

Seventeen hundred and six turned into seventeen hundred and seven and she could no longer stop her scampering thoughts from demanding action. Suzette came early to her room as she did every day to see what help she needed.

"*Je veux écrire une lettre*, Suzette." To please the girl she liked to recall what little French she knew and Suzette had become totally devoted to her.

So Suzette made up a good fire and moved her chair so she could sit at her writing desk with her back warming. Then she fetched all the materials she needed, wrapped a shawl round her shoulders and tucked a rug over her knees.

"*Merci bien*, Suzette."

The girl had hardly closed the door before Bel's pen was writing the opening words.

'My dear old friend,

You know from my late beloved Nat and from my letters all these years since his death that I never stood on ceremony yet and am not like to start in my advanced years. Why have we heard nothing from Hertfordshire for a long time? I pray you are all in health and your grandson is safely returned from his travels. I looked to hear at Christmas but we are now into the New Year. I believe it was June when my last letter went off but then our Deborah and John were not returned so I had not seen my sweet great-grandchild blessedly named Nathaniel John but it is not about him that I am writing now.

' No one knows I am writing this and I am sure I would be mightily scolded if they knew but I have been observing Deborah since their return and she is not herself. Would you believe it she has from last September thrown herself into the management of this estate to help her father. My dear Daniel has a reasonably good head on him but she is phenomenal and has been through

Height of Folly

the accounts and sorted all the receipts and papers and everything so that nothing can be lost again which I fear was all in a muddle before. But you will ask why I am telling you all this and still say she is not herself though she has found a deal of pleasure in the work but it is all to hide and bury deep down that she is really fretting. The fact is she can manage everything but her heart.

'I know this is all wrong in the world's eyes what I am doing but Daniel told me that Deb said she had parted from your Frederick coldly and that he said to her, 'Deborah, I can't bear this' or some such words. Now it seems to me that the two of them reached a fondness in those days of travel and especially after the fright of that horrid fire and that fondness shouldn't be allowed to cool unless of course they lose their hearts elsewhere. If your Frederick is affianced to another since his return for God's sake burn this letter. Daniel did propose making an approach to you about arranging a match but Deborah wouldn't hear of such a formal thing though I believe her heart was weeping. I know there are troubles holding her back. One is what she calls her cursed inches. It's true she is a fine handsome figure six-feet tall and as strong as an ox. She is never ill and I'd wager she could still bear many fine children. But there is another trouble which she only could tell a prospective husband and I can't dwell upon it but if they could only meet up again I believe that would melt away like snow.

'Perhaps Frederick could not abide the difference in their height and if that's so there is nothing more to be said only I can't help saying that in a marriage made by God such a thing should be of no account.

'I know you will forgive this letter, Edward, my dear good friend, because you like me have passed our three score years and ten. I want to live to see my Deb truly happy and I know you wish an heir for your great estates but most of all to see the grandson you so miraculously discovered finding joy in life since the sad loss of

Prue Phillipson

his wife and child.

'I shall tell no one I have written this and I beg that if you or Frederick make any response to it you will not let it be known that it was prompted in any way by me. Let the response come from a heart of love or not at all. I value love more than wisdom as is plain from my writing all this.

'I thank you, dear friend, for the love you showed my Nathaniel at Cambridge when he was dispirited by worries. You were younger than he but he told me how he valued your generous open nature and could talk of things to you that he could share with no one else at that time. It was a great joy to him that our sons had a good friendship both at the university and in the navy and if it is God's will that our families should be united in the days to come there will be more rejoicing.

'I say again if circumstances are such that everything in this letter should never have been written pray destroy it at once.

Whatever you do I will remain your affectionate friend,
Bel Wilson Horden.'

By some strange instinct ten minutes after she had finished and laid her head back and closed her eyes Suzette came in with a dish of tea.

"My lady done writing?"

Bel couldn't make the effort to speak French. "I must look through it when my eyes are rested for I'm sure the writing is unreadable. But this letter is not to be put among any other letters going from the Hall. I want no one to see it till it is safely in the hands of the postboy. Can you make sure of that, Suzette? Have you understood?"

"Oh yes, yes. Letter very special, secret. I understand good."

"Understand *well*, my sweet girl. Now pour me the tea. My poor brain is desperate for it."

The letter was addressed to the Earl of Branford and safely

Height of Folly

committed to the post that very day without anyone else in Horden Hall knowing about it.

Bel came down to the family dinner in a very cheerful mood. She felt as if a huge weight had been lifted from her shoulders.

Frederick Branford carried the letter to his grandfather's bedside. He could see it came from Northumberland and was addressed in the wavering hand of an old person. He had heard his grandfather referring to the lady with whom he had been corresponding as Arabella Wilson Horden, the widow of his dear college friend, Nathaniel. "But I must always write to her as Bel," he would say with a throaty chuckle. "She told me she would not answer to anything else." This letter, Frederick felt sure, was from her, wondering why she had not heard from him for many months.

There may be news in it of her granddaughter, he told himself, but I dare not hope for a message in it from her to me.

Nevertheless his heart was thumping in his chest and his breath coming in short bursts as he entered his grandfather's bedchamber. The room was dim, unchanged for years, Will Smyth had told him. The velvet bed-curtains were drawn.

Frederick lifted a corner and peeped round.

The features were always like death, white and sharp, the eyes shut.

"Are you awake, Grandfather?" They opened at once and the slack mouth tightened and curved into a smile. "There is a letter for you from Northumberland."

"Ah my dear Bel! It is an age since she wrote. Did I answer her? I don't remember. You'll have to tell me again how long I have been ill."

"You were ill when I returned from Europe in September, sir. Mother's letters telling me of it had never reached me. We altered our route because of the fighting and then we were held back for many days while they investigated us. I was carrying your pistol and they were suspicious of us."

"Did they take it away? I was fond of that pistol."

"I'm afraid they did, sir. Do you want to read your letter? I can prop you up and bring more candles."

"No, no, no. You read it to me, boy. What day is it?"

"Wednesday."

"That means nothing to me. The date. I know not how long I've been ill."

"We are into seventeen hundred and seven. It's the beginning of February."

The old man tried to sit up. Frederick laid down the letter and helped him, pulling up his pillows. "How have I lived so long, dear boy? I held on to see you again, didn't I?"

"God be praised." He had taken up the letter again and it tantalised his fingers. "May I let in more light if I'm to read it? The sun is shining. It's a bright spring day."

"Yes, yes. I can shut my eyes if it hurts them."

Frederick went to the window and drew the heavy curtain. The blue sky, the swathes of snowdrops in the lawn and especially the small figure of his mother gathering some to bring into the sick room blessed his sight. He waved.

"Let's hear what dear old Bel has to say for herself then."

Frederick stepped back to the bed, breaking the seal. His eyes at once jumped to the capital D's on the page. He thought, it's about Deborah. Ought I to read it?

His grandfather made an impatient grunt and he plunged into the first lines, Bel's reproach for the long time without a word.

His grandfather broke in. "You must write at once and tell her how ill I was. Nay, if spring is here I must get well enough to write myself."

"Are you sure you couldn't read it, sir? I feel it's – the contents

Height of Folly

– may not be for my eyes." But his eyes were devouring it as he spoke. He was incapable of dragging them away. Deborah was not herself, she was fretting, she had thrown herself into work to still her heart. Could this be true?

"Why have you stopped reading?"

"Because it is private, for you alone." He was telling himself, have I not been fretting, have I not thrown myself into learning the running of our estates and find Grandfather's affairs are not well sorted? There are unpaid debts. There are uncollected rents.

His mother tapped on the door and entered the room just when he had seen his own name and the very words he had said to Deborah quoted back in the letter.

She was bearing a delicate Japanese vase full of snowdrops. "Look here, Papa Ted. From your lawns. Never fear, I have left thousands." His mother loved to have her own names for her intimates. Soon after she had acquired a new father-in-law and learnt that his name was Edward she asked him if she might call him Papa Ted and he found it charming.

"He won't read my letter from Bel. You take it. I've nothing private that my May can't see."

She looked laughing into Frederick's face. "Are you shy because it's a love letter between two old folks? Why not? Love doesn't suffer from illness you know."

He was blushing. "You'll see," was all he said and crept out of the room to go somewhere to think because his life might be on the verge of a great transformation.

His steps led him to the garden. Where better to think than in the clean swept winter light? What will she think of this place, he was asking himself. She has seen Versailles as well as the Chateau Rombeau's hopeful imitation. But here there is no pretence of a garden. Nothing has been disciplined. The lawn will be cut when the snowdrops and crocuses are over and there are some fine trees but they do not march in straight lines. There are hedgerows, not geometric hedges. Horses graze the paddock and there are hay meadows speckled all over with flowers in summertime. The gravel of the drive is raked at the front from time to time but there is no great vista from the gates. You wind your way among clumps of woodland and come upon the house by surprise. It's true there are a few evergreens in tubs by the steps and along the terrace but the stonework there is flaking and discoloured if you look closely. Inside, all along the gallery, there are portraits of ancient Branfords sadly in need of reframing. Some of the upper rooms are unusable from damp. Is this what a north-country girl would expect of an earl's mansion?

He came to the little summerhouse and yanked open the door. It scraped on the stone floor because the hinges were worn. The benches inside bore embroidered cushions, so faded that the scenes depicted were indecipherable. He sat down and it was there his mother found him, still thinking.

"Well," she said, "what are you going to do about Deborah Horden, Fred?"

She sat down by him, folded her arms and gave him her best slit-eyed, lips-compressed grin.

He shook his head. "I haven't got anywhere. All I've been trying to do is see her here, imagine her exploring and looking at everything."

"That's a good start anyway."

"Is it? You haven't seen *us together*, walking about arm in arm. People laugh."

"And isn't that a lovely thing? Don't we want more laughter in the world? *I* shall laugh and when I've done laughing I shall love her to bits."

"Oh, Mother. You make it sound so easy."

"Why make life difficult? You want a wife, she wants a husband.

Height of Folly

Your grandfather wants the Branford line to go on and on and I just want you to be happy."

"I was very happy with Mary."

"And will be again."

"But this one is not like Mary. She is strong, *formidable*, the French would say, quick-witted, a master of every task she undertakes and what a memory she has!"

"You are trying to frighten me. She is still a woman. How much of her grandmother's letter did you read?"

"I seemed to grasp it all in a moment before I knew I should not be reading it."

"I read it slowly aloud. Her grandmother has known her since birth and should have a fair understanding of her nature. She believes Deborah loves you. That girl may be all you say but if she loves you she has seen in you qualities she admires."

"Are they enough? Will she not come to despise me over the years when familiarity has overtaken us?"

"But you have left one thing out of the list of her qualities – her sense of humour. Have you not told me how much you laughed together over people and places and situations? It was that that warmed me to her. I thought if I have to yield you to another woman I could to her. I wouldn't intrude on your marriage. I might ask Papa Ted if there is a cottage empty that I could have."

"Oh Mother, I would never wish that. You have your own wing here."

"And I was hardly in it while you were away for he wanted me so much."

"That will always be the case. But Deborah lives with family members in a smaller place than this. How could she *not* love to have you here? But Mother, what did *Grandfather* say to the letter? Will Smyth warned me that Deborah was beneath me in rank and almost accused her of being a fortune hunter."

Prue Phillipson

"It was Papa Ted who planned it from the beginning when he first wrote to Bel about you meeting her abroad. He thinks you should take horse at once and ride to Northumberland to claim her."

Frederick sat up and clasped his hands to his face. "That was my very first thought as I saw the letter. A great urge gripped me to be with her, just to be in her presence again!"

His mother got up. "There you are then. It's getting chilly in here. A passing cloud. Shall I give orders to Peter to pack up and be ready to accompany you?" He saw she was laughing. "Two mounts and a pack animal should be sufficient or would you go by the stage?"

He pulled her down. "Don't tease. The sun is out again. Truly I don't know what Deborah feels. She parted from me so speedily."

"Tore herself away, against her will. It was that newspaper article and then my letter and her family's."

Frederick wanted to believe that. But now he saw his mother was looking suddenly thoughtful, staring ahead at a blackbird on the lawn.

She turned and faced him. "I've remembered what Bel said towards the end. Something holds Deborah back, something she would want to tell a prospective husband. Did you see that part of the letter?" Frederick shook his head. "Then you'd better go to Horden Hall and see her and hope she tells you and that it is no great matter after all. But mind, Bel says no one must tell about the letter. If you take any action at all it must be on your own initiative." She stood up again. "We won't give Peter orders just yet because the roads will still be bad, but Papa Ted says he is going to write to Bel to explain about his illness. So I say *you* should write for him – to Bel not Deborah – and apologise for the long absence of letters. Then add a note that you have business in Newcastle and would love to call at Horden Hall and make her

Height of Folly

acquaintance."

Frederick stood up too and squeezed her waist. "That I would gladly do, dear Mother, except that I have no business in Newcastle."

She gave her twinkling laugh again. "Of course you have, silly boy. You are going to find a bride."

"Oh! A six foot tall bride? Oh mother will I not be a laughing stock?"

"Well if that's of more significance to you than getting hold of a rare gem among women then, as Bel said in her letter, there is no more to be said and I am a little ashamed of my boy." She was still laughing but he knew she meant it.

CHAPTER EIGHTEEN

A packet of letters arrived at Horden Hall as the family was finishing breakfast on a snowy mid-February day. Bel was able to secrete hers into her lap while the others exclaimed over one from France.

"Can it be news of the baby?" Eunice asked Daniel. It was addressed to Sir Daniel and Lady Wilson Horden but Eunice always passed such letters to him first. Bel snorted a little at this but Eunice would quote the Bible. "'The husband is the head of the wife,' Mother Bel, and though I do not always agree with Daniel that precept keeps everything in order. Abandon it and families will be in chaos."

Daniel had the seal broken and unfolded the letter. John never wrote much but this time it was a eulogy on the new baby girl born that very day. "She is tiny," Daniel read out, "but perfectly formed with a fuzz of jet black hair. Netta was wonderful and the château is celebrating with freely-flowing wine. She is to be Diana Maria. I did press for Eunice or Deborah but they all feel those names are a little stiff and puritanical. I trust Mother and Deb will not be hurt."

Deborah shrugged her shoulders. "As both their children are to be French Catholics and we will scarcely ever see them it matters little what their names are."

Bel was impatient to read her own letter. She looked round the table and saw they were all finished. She got to her feet. "Let us give thanks anyway for a safe delivery."

They all rose and Daniel pronounced the thanksgiving they always spoke after meals at Eunice's insistence. He added their gratitude for the arrival of Diana Maria and a prayer for the health of mother and child.

Height of Folly

Bel always gave a secret grin at his efforts to be fluent extempore but now she was anxious to escape to her own room and without saying why she hurried out and began to mount the stairs before anyone could inquire if she wanted something and couldn't Suzette run and get it for her.

Safe at her desk under her window she cut open the seal. She feared the letter would say Edward Branford was dead because the writing was not his but she had no sooner glanced down it than she was laughing and clapping her hands.

After the preliminaries in which he had described his grandfather's long illness Frederick Branford had written, *'I am very happy that he now feels well enough to spare me for a short while and I wonder if I might presume on my acquaintance with your grandson and granddaughter to pay a call at Horden Hall in the spring when the weather is more clement. My grandfather says he wishes he could accompany me as he would be delighted to meet you after the long and pleasant correspondence you have had together and to share his memories of Cambridge days spent with your dear husband. He sends his greetings to you all and my mother asks me to add her good wishes too.*

I will await your reply before I make any arrangements to stay in Newcastle whence I might give myself the pleasure of visiting you, but pray tell me if it is not convenient or if there is any time when you may be from home.

I will be most honoured to make your acquaintance and that of Sir Daniel and Lady Wilson Horden and renew my friendship with your grandson and his wife and your granddaughter.

I am pleased to sign myself your humble servant,
Frederick Branford.

Bel hugged herself. What an intelligent boy! He has not mentioned my letter at all which means I can show *his* letter to Deborah and not be suspected of any underhand work. Stay in

Prue Phillipson

Newcastle indeed! With a little shuffling around we can make him and I presume his man very comfortable here. Well, if they have done rejoicing over another little Horden – more of a Rombeau Deb says quite bitterly – I will give them this news. Sweet girl, you may be on the way to having a babe of your own this year if things can be hurried along. I shall live to see it, God willing.

She trotted downstairs, her old knees suddenly frisky.

Deborah and her father had moved to the Estate Office while Eunice had taken Ruth to the kitchen for a cookery lesson.

"Never mind what servants you may have when you're married," Bel heard her saying, "you should be ashamed if you don't know what food goes into every dish and how to make them."

"Before you start," Bel said at the door, "I'd like you to come to the parlour for I have a piece of news in *my* letter."

"I didn't notice you had one, Mother Bel. Very well we will delay for five minutes, but, Ruth, *you* are making dinner today and a pudding too."

Bel collected Deborah and Daniel who were examining one of the rent books.

"I need you all," she said, "for I have to know what answer I am to make."

Curious, they sat down in the parlour and with no preliminaries she simply read out the letter. She couldn't help peeping over her spectacles to watch Deborah's face. From the moment she read, *Honoured Madam, My grandfather regrets his long silence* . . Deborah's flushed cheeks and brightened eye showed Bel that she knew who the writer was. When she reached the request to be allowed to come and pay his respects Deborah's hands were up over her face. They didn't hide her joy from Bel. It was everything she had longed to see.

Daniel was the first to speak, with his eyes too on Deborah's face.

Height of Folly

"Well, did I not tell you I would be happy to invite him here? I am glad he has invited himself. We can put him up, can't we Eunice? In fact he could have John and Jeanetta's room which is the biggest after ours. If they come back I am minded to make over Nether Horden Grange to them. Lord Branford will bring a man I suppose. There's Ursula's old attic but it's very small. Or he could sleep in his master's dressing-room or Matt's room over the carriage house.

"What interests me," Eunice said in her careful way, "is that he doesn't say he has *business* in Newcastle though he proposes to stay there. One doesn't *call on* people in Northumberland from Hertfordshire. The journey is quite an undertaking. But yes, I'm sure we can accommodate him for a few days."

Daniel laughed. "Some weeks, I hope, since he is coming so far."

Ruth said, "I think it's a cold letter. He speaks of his *friendship* for John and Deb." She peered at her sister's face. "Why didn't he write a love letter to you?"

Deborah had now put her hands in her lap and was trying to look unconcerned. She doesn't know whether to laugh or cry, Bel thought. I believe I was wrong not to show it to her alone first. Then she could have poured out her heart to me.

"I hope you will keep your tongue under control if he does come," Deborah snapped at Ruth. "If he asks me to marry him I haven't decided if I'll accept him." She rose, tall and straight, and stalked out of the room.

Ruth pouted. "Of course she'll accept him. She'll be a countess and never have to do any work. *I'll* have him if *she* won't."

Eunice began solemnly to upbraid her so Bel stood up. "I'll go to Deb. I shouldn't have done this so publicly. But Dan, I presume I may write and tell the man he has no need to reserve lodgings in Newcastle."

Prue Phillipson

He nodded. "God knows I don't want to lose her but it will be her decision."

Bel tapped at Deborah's door and went swiftly in. She was prone on her bed but not angry at the intrusion. She jumped up and flung her arms round Bel's neck.

"Oh Grandmother, I will have to tell him about Ranald."

"And he will say 'I too have loved and lost' and then you can marry him."

"*Will* he say that? The cases are very different. And if he does am I sure? Marriage is such a great thing. We are one under God for the rest of our lives. Have I been independent too long? I would be saying goodbye to Horden and all of you."

"Nonsense. The stage coaches are up and down the Great North Road all the time. Do you imagine your parents wouldn't come to see the grandchildren? And you would bring them up to see Northumberland. I wager the roads will be better cared for as soon as peace comes about."

"Darling Grandmother, you are always full of hope. I *do* want children and no one else wants to marry me. Indeed, as Ruth pointed out, *he* hasn't said so either. It is a courtesy visit which his grandfather has persuaded him to make on his behalf. He thinks John and Jeanetta are here and he would like to see their boy."

"He wants his *own* boy I wager. He wouldn't be going to this trouble to pay his respects to *me*! Look, let me just go and write a friendly reply. I shall start 'My dear Lord Branford, We will all be delighted to welcome you to Horden Hall and you must not think of staying anywhere but here when you visit Northumberland.' There it is half done already. Do you want to enclose a message yourself?"

"I had better not. Just my greetings of course."

Bel nodded and was trotting to the door when Deborah suddenly said, "I have to love his *body*, don't I? I loathed Bill

Height of Folly

Warner's. Did you love Grandfather's body?"

Bel stood still and tried to think. "*Before*, no, not in the way I think you mean. I just loved and wanted *him*. I didn't separate the man into soul and body. He was Nat and he had to be mine. That was all. I suppose he was not one you would turn to look at in the street. Fair like your father but not nearly so tall or handsome of feature, but pleasant-faced. I loved him but I didn't think about his body. *Afterwards*, yes I loved every bit of him."

Deborah looked down at her. Those sea-green eyes were full of gratitude.

"I knew I could speak plainly to you and you would be open with me. Do you see the difference between us? You were a virgin. I am not. There's no one else to whom I can say this. I think about the act. I think about it too much. Is that a sin?"

Bel was only a little disconcerted. This imposing woman could not shed the experience she had had as a young girl with a wild, towering hulk of young manhood. The girl was still inside remembering her brief and thrilling passion and wondering how it would be with a mature man, small and compact and of a quiet disposition, a man whose body she had thought about but without a feeling of arousal.

Bel beckoned her to the window seat and they sat down together. "Describe Frederick to me."

"Oh." She began hesitatingly. "Medium height for a man. Well, a little shorter than John. He's all of a piece, neat arms, legs, firm body, no sagging. His face? He shaves very smoothly, a neat round chin, upper lip a little long and nose straight but not quite long enough, which makes him stop short of handsome. Under his wig his hair is dark brown what there is of it and of course his ears stick out as Father always says Henry's did but his wig hides them."

"And the eyes?" Bel prompted and saw Deb's face light up.

"Ah, his eyes! I love his eyes. They are a clear light blue and so honest, so expressive of his simplicity, his sweetness. Oh!" Her tears welled up. "I do long to see him again! Why have I allowed all these months to pass? He thinks I don't care for him but something has moved him to want to come. Do you think it is only because his grandfather wishes it?"

Bel felt a stab of guilt at concealing the secret of her letter when Bel had so opened her inmost thoughts to her. I must admit it one day when their marriage is firm as a rock, she told herself. Now she just squeezed Deb's hand and got up. "I would say he has been longing to hear from you but his grandfather's illness has occupied him and he couldn't think of leaving him to come and find out your true feelings, but now he can. Be happy, my child. You did no wrong all those years ago and it is no sin to recall the act. If this comes to a marriage it will be different, more lovely because you will know all around you approve and rejoice with you. Now let me go and answer his letter and you can look forward to his coming without a qualm."

Deborah knelt on the window-seat when she had gone and watched the flurries of snow settling among the emerging crocuses below the window. The points of yellow and purple were still visible. The cold was not intense. Maybe the landscape would not be swathed in whiteness again. Frederick would be here in the spring. It was easy for dear Grandmother to say have no qualms. She still had to tell him about Ranald.

Work was the best distraction. She went downstairs to the Estate Office and sat down in her usual chair beside her father. He was surprised to see her but made no comment and they put their heads together over the rent book they had picked out.

"Quarter Day has passed," Deborah said, "and Charlton has been written to but has not paid yet. Looking back he was late with his rent twice last year."

Height of Folly

"And paid some in eggs which we didn't need for our own hens were laying well." Her father was smiling at her but she avoided his eyes. She had come to work.

He cleared his throat. "Did you know there is talk that we must keep the English Quarter Days when the Act of Union is passed? Up here we have followed Scotland but they will have to conform in that and many other ways I suppose. The Act will certainly be ratified by Parliament this year now both countries have signed and then we will all be British."

Deborah couldn't stop herself from showing off her knowledge. "The English first quarter day of the year is Lady Day, the twenty-fifth of March. Shall we give Jack Charlton till then to settle up?"

He chuckled. "Not this year. Next year he may have that grace. I suppose *you* know all the other dates."

She nodded. "Midsummer, Michaelmas and Christmas."

"What will I do without you?"

"Don't." Her voice shook. "I can't think of it. I can't imagine it."

"Will it not become clear to you when Lord Branford is here in person? It will be hard for you to resist passionate love."

She repeated the words with a burst of laughter. "Passionate love. I cannot picture Frederick expressing passion. Perhaps he'll come with a legally worded agreement from his grandfather for you to sign."

"Well, if there is not *some* passion I don't believe I shall sign my girl away."

She turned to him and hugged him. "You are only making it harder, Father. I have been truly happy working with you. Shall I write another letter to Jack Charlton or ride over to find out why he's in trouble?"

"Let us enjoy a ride round all our land when the snow stops. I pray that John will come soon and bring his family and settle here and then you can be free."

CHAPTER NINETEEN

John was strolling with Jeanetta in the château garden while Jean and baby Diana were in the care of the nurse. It was still only March but spring was stirring around them and John's thoughts were on stirrings of another kind.

"You know, Netta, Scotland is seething with discontent. We must not miss this chance. Le Vent has been there and I wager he'll bring news soon."

Jeanetta pursed her lips. "Scotland is always seething, is it not?"

"This is bigger. This is no less than the government trying to wipe Scotland from the map. The very name will go. No, I say Scotland is ripe for its own king again. If we can get him there with Louis's backing Scotland will rise."

"And my John will have helped put him there."

They were some distance from the door in the wall to the stables but they heard it clash and Matthew came running.

"Master John. It is he, just arrived, asking for you."

"What? Our windy friend already?"

Jeanetta gave a skip of delight. "Oh it is so exciting. You must let me come too."

"He is in the stables giving orders about his horse," Matt said. "He'll see you in the chapel."

"And you see," she said, "he comes to you first now, not Uncle Neury." John lapped up her admiration. She clung to him as they made their way to the chapel and stood in the cold stone dimness of the porch watching the door in the wall. In a few minutes the cloaked figure emerged. "Le Vent *looks* like a conspirator," Jeanetta whispered, "but see how he swaggers. He should creep, hunched up."

"That is his way of *not* rousing suspicion."

Height of Folly

"Even his moustaches march before him. He is splendid. You *must* let me stay to speak with him."

John resented her admiration though he was himself in awe of le Vent. The day was fresh but his armpits pricked with sweat. Had the moment of action finally come?

Le Vent swept off his hat on seeing Jeanetta. "*La belle* Jeanetta! I bid your ladyship good day."

"She wants to stay. She knows all about it." At that John saw a gleam of anger in those very black piercing eyes and his heart quailed.

Le Vent was immediately all smiles again, kissing Jeanetta's hand. "Ladies are to be beautiful. No more is asked of them. Your towering sister does not know all, I trust."

"Certainly not. She is at Horden well out of the way."

"Like all good ladies." There was something about his gaze that crushed Jeanetta though he was still smiling.

She cast John a pleading look, muttered, "You'll tell me," and turned and scuttled away along the broad walk.

I never have that effect on her, John thought. He saw le Vent's eyes turning on Matt with a questioning look.

"Matt will be at my side all the time," he said and Le Vent just nodded and sat down on the porch seat. Matt remained standing as a look-out by the door.

Le Vent motioned John to sit beside him. The stone was cold through his breeches but he was too keyed up to notice.

Le Vent's manner had an intensity John had never seen before. He placed one finger against the side of his nose. "Ah, *mon cher* Jean, you say Horden is well out of the way but that is where you will be going."

"But I went and recruited many. Only I could give them no clear word."

Le Vent moved his eyes back and forth like black beads. "But now they are to be ready for the king's landing. Louis has at last promised French infantry and ships to transport them."

"God! It is really happening." John trembled at the drama with which Le Vent hissed the words, barely moving his lips, but smiling at the same time. "When does it set sail, sir? I would like to be with this force."

"No no no, you will be with the Jacobites to meet it when it puts ashore. Your task is to get to England and gather the people you have already recruited with all the armed man they have promised and join up with the Scottish forces. Together you will meet the king to march with him to Edinburgh." He pointed his finger in a generally southerly direction. "Go and await my message at Horden. The king will put ashore in the Firth of Forth."

John thrilled to the tips of his toes but the words that came out shamed him.

"We have a very young babe. They are not expecting me at home yet."

Le Vent tut-tutted. "Women, babies. Thank God I was never cluttered with such things. But spare your blushes. It will be some time before the force is assembled. Give no such reason to your wife. Go when she expects you to go and tell her nothing more. If she is unwilling to go you must go alone."

John was thinking, Netta may not care for life at Horden Hall but she will want to be there when I lead an uprising. She may insist on riding with me and leaving the babes with Deb and Ruth and the two nurses of course. I understand Le Vent. Women and children are clutter, but Netta must see my triumph.

Le Vent stood up. "I have others to call upon."

"You will see de Neury?"

"Ah *le petit vicomte* who believes he is a vital cog in the wheel! That great desk he has with secret drawers! Is he safe to be trusted any more?"

Height of Folly

John was flattered that le Vent appeared to be asking his opinion but he answered himself. "I will have a word with the old man. If he thinks he is being left out he could be dangerous." He pulled his hat further down and clutched his cloak round him. "You need not come, John." He stopped at the doorway and demanded of Matt, "You can handle a weapon?"

Matt came to attention. "Yes sir." Le Vent treated him to one of his broad grins and a twirl of his moustaches and strode towards the house.

"I'll be glad to be back in England," Matt said. "I began courting Elsbeth the new chambermaid last time and I'm hoping she hasn't forgotten me."

John laughed. "You heard what Monsieur le Vent said about unnecessary baggage."

"Nay, sir, but I'll not board her till this excitement's over."

Horden Hall was certainly in a state of excitement. Sir Daniel was reviewing his household for the visit of an earl's son. He was aware that everyone believed the gentleman was coming to court Mistress Deborah. They had all heard of the San Remo fire and Suzette had found herself the centre of questions from the moment of her arrival. Her account had grown more graphic with every new telling. Daniel was happy that she had become close friends with Elspeth, the new chambermaid. They shared a room over the kitchen next to Jane's, the senior female servant who liked to call herself the housekeeper though not in Lady Horden's presence.

When he looked round at the number of his servants it came home forcibly to him that Eunice, far from being an aloof Lady Horden, was housekeeper, often cook, seamstress and even laundry-maid. Jane, who had long ago wanted to be lady's-maid to the young Deborah, had learnt to help her ladyship whatever she was doing. A cook-maid came in from the village daily who brought her twelve-year-old daughter with her as a kitchen-maid and general skivvy. Suzette was happy to do anything she was asked, particularly waiting upon his mother, Bel. But however he reckoned them Daniel was unable to make more than three living-in women servants and two dailies.

Outside in the stable block two grooms, Luke and Walter, shared a large room above the carriage house. Matt when he was at Horden had a separate room there to himself, but since his travels with John Daniel thought he might expect to be housed in the Hall as a personal servant, though the word 'valet' could no more be used in Eunice's presence than 'lady's-maid'. Daniel looked after the wine cellar himself so there was no butler. A man came from the village to look after the lawns, hedges and fishpond but Deborah worked in the flower garden and vegetable patch and frequently the woodland while his own mother, Bel, still looked upon the hen-run as her province. Ruth had been allowed to concentrate on lessons till Eunice had wakened to some of her deficiencies in household management and was now doing her best to put these right. Eunice made it very clear whenever they engaged a servant that they must expect to help in any task within their capabilities. "We do not stand on ceremony here. We help each other. Come to me if you have troubles but do not grumble at anything you may be asked to do."

Going about among other gentry Daniel saw this was not the way of things with most of them. In the 'best' houses footmen stood about idle and chambermaids would not touch a kitchen implement.

"What will Lord Branford think of us!" he exclaimed to Eunice a few days before they expected him.

"Are you forgetting he was brought up a farmer's boy? Has not Deb told us he *struggles* to be a nobleman?"

"Maybe so, but he has lived long enough now in a great house

Height of Folly

and our frugal, informal ways may surprise him."

She wagged her finger at him. "My Dan, what is troubling you is your own pride. You have had the painters and plasterers in touching up every place that is worn or marked. Now you think we have not servants enough. Do you suppose the man will be upset if it is Deborah who opens the door to him rather than a footman in livery?"

Daniel shook his head and drifted away from her but he was muttering to himself, "I'll wager the Branfords have a livery."

Deborah tried very hard to find her father's anxiety amusing. She kept telling herself, it is only comical little Frederick we are expecting and stammering young Peter who is an interesting blend of bluster and shyness. It was I who escorted him through France rather than the other way about. They will settle in quite happily for a while and we'll show them the local sights and then they'll go home again and life will go on as before. It is of much greater significance that the Act of Union has been passed and England and Scotland have become one nation. That *is* momentous.

On the morning of the day they were expected a letter came from John to say that he and Jeanetta and the babies would be coming in July.

"Where do we put Lord Branford if he is still here then?" Eunice exclaimed. "There are two other good rooms but they are barely furnished and Nether Horden Grange is not ready for them yet."

"Mother it is only early May," Deborah said. "You spoke of a week or two for our guests at first. I shall be delighted to see John's children and I hope he intends to be here for good."

Eunice stood back to look at the flowers she had arranged for the dining-table. "We will all rejoice at your brother's coming. As for the other business it is in your hands and I don't feel I have any say in the matter. You keep so close about it."

"Oh Mother, I'm sorry." Deborah was moved by a gleam of tears in her mother's eyes as she adjusted a trailing piece of fern. "I'm in such turmoil inside I scarce know how to contain myself."

"Ah well, that is all I need to know. I can pray now that the right thing will come to pass." Daniel came in to see how well the table looked with their only set of silver cutlery sparkling in the sunshine.

"I am sending the carriage to the Staging Inn in fifteen minutes. Do you want to go in it, Deb?"

"Oh, should I? Is it proper?" She knew she was as flushed and confused as a little girl.

He said, "You went round France and Italy with him."

Eunice looked at Deborah. "I think, Daniel, it should be only our coachman so there is plenty of room for their luggage."

Deborah nodded vigorously. "Yes, thank you, Mother. I think I'll just go upstairs and let Suzette brush out my hair. She's done it up tight." As she left the room she heard her mother say, "She wants to look younger."

Descending from the stage at the inn door in Newcastle Frederick wanted to go inside and find a mirror and see how travel-stained he looked but Peter had already spotted the carriage drawn up waiting and called out, "From H-Horden Hall?" The driver nodded and jumped down to help with the luggage and Frederick found himself seated in it in two minutes. He was too nervous to look about him. He kept his eyes straight ahead as they drove through streets which might be brick, stone or wattle and daub for all he noticed. They passed through the town gates and he became aware after a little while of trees and fields. The coachman addressed a few remarks such as, "I trust your lordship has had a pleasant journey" but it was Peter who had to answer. All he could see was

Height of Folly

the figure of Deborah towering above him.

They had turned off the main road onto a narrower one which soon branched and he read a sign saying Nether Horden to the left and another pointing down a lane saying Horden Hall. He swallowed. It was a real place and he was almost there. A small copse of trees and a farm cottage, a bend in the lane and there ahead were fine wrought iron gates, gleaming with a fresh coat of paint. There was no lodge but a man was there to swing them open with a flourish of his hat and a bow. A newly swept gravelled drive lay ahead and the house itself sat foursquare beyond neat lawns, a solid, stone-built mansion with twirling red brick Elizabethan chimneys.

His heart was pumping so much he couldn't think what he felt about it. He just saw it. And then as they drew near he saw something else. Seated on a bench to the right of the entrance was a figure in a green gown with fair hair charmingly arranged in green ribbons about her shoulders. He was above her looking down on her and she didn't rise until he stood up to descend as the step was unfolded for him.

She came forward, inclining herself towards him, not rearing up like the image in his mind. Her smile was gentle, hesitant as she held out her hand. He thought, she is neither cold nor aloof and he took both her hands in his. His eyes were brimming and he couldn't speak.

"I'm glad to see you, Frederick," she managed and then she couldn't speak either. Was it possible that she was thinking 'you have come for me at last'? So her grandmother had been right about her feelings and now he had revealed his just by being here. Out of the corner of his eye he sensed a family group on the steps: a tall fair man, too tall for him, a small plump woman, an old one as bright and scrawny as a little bird and a young girl trying to push between them.

Prue Phillipson

"Meet my family." Deborah must have realised his awareness of them and drew her hand from his grasp. They approached, the young girl leaping the steps and reaching them first.

"Welcome, Lord Branford. I'm Ruth, Deb's sister."

He bowed and kissed her hand. She giggled at that and blurted out, "You were gazing into each other's eyes. It was beautiful. Deb must be bending her knees."

Fortunately Sir Daniel and his lady were there then and the greetings became more formal. He couldn't see how Deborah took her sister's remark. The last to greet him was the old lady, obviously Bel, his grandfather's correspondent. There was a special squeeze of her hand from him and a meaningful look. 'We are in a conspiracy here but you will not betray me, will you?' He put all the reassurance he could into his smile.

All he wanted now was time to be alone with Deborah. Was she to be the wife of his bosom for ever more? It was very plain to him at the first meal that expectations buzzed in the air above him. Would he declare himself soon? Of course the subject was well buried beneath inquiries about his grandfather's health, the state of the roads and coaching inns and the reactions in southern England to the union with their northern neighbour. Ruth had obviously been rebuked and said not a word though she treated him to grins and winks when she thought no one was looking. If he could put Deborah into her sister's outward shape he would never have had a moment's hesitation. No doubt he would have fallen in love at the first meeting. But the character was not there. The character he loved was in the long being opposite him with the narrow nose, strong jaw, wide, generous mouth and those searching, liquid eyes with ocean colour and ocean depths that rested on his from time to time, saying what? That she was his for the asking? He couldn't be sure.

CHAPTER TWENTY

Deborah's first thought when he grasped her hand in his was 'He *has* come for me! What do I do?' Ruth she would have liked to slap hard but he seemed to take no notice. In fact he politely but firmly kept her at a distance after that for which she applauded him heartily. For the first two days of settling in he was the perfect guest, deferential to her father and mother, playfully at ease with Grandmother Bel and warm and gentle to herself. He admired everything, the house, his room, the cooking, the grounds, the kitchen garden, the stables, where Peter soon made himself at home with the two grooms, and even the hens, which were the finest birds he had ever seen.

I must break through this, she thought. I know they keep leaving us alone for a short while in the parlour but I am tongue-tied until I have time and space to tell him about Ranald and he is tongue-tied because he senses there is something holding me back.

The third morning dawned with a silken sky in which the sun floated like a golden flower on a lake. The light woke Deborah early and she looked out of the window to see Frederick Branford walking on the grass, his feet casting up tiny showers of dew. She dressed quickly, leaving off her corset, and ran downstairs. When he saw her coming to meet him he lifted his hat in delight.

"Ah the day has brought you out too. It is such a day as we have in Hertfordshire but I am ashamed to say I thought the north was cold, cloud and rain."

He was chuckling in just the way they had done on their travels. She must check this light-heartedness. The time had come. She said, "I will show you our woodland walk."

Without taking his arm she began to stride off towards the gate into the wood where Ranald had prepared a bed of leaves and would have had her if she had allowed him. This was the place to tell him. Ranald's presence was there whenever she passed that spot. She could see him beating his fists on the oak tree because she refused him.

Frederick kept pace with her, a little puzzled, she could tell, by her purposefulness.

They passed through the gate and walked into the cool fresh greenness of the new leaves. Sunbeams lit the floor of burgeoning woodland plants.

"Beautiful," he said.

"Frederick, the story I am going to tell you is not beautiful."

"Story? You are going to tell me a story?" He was looking up at her and his clear honest eyes were inquiring and a little anxious.

"You were so good as to tell me yours the very first time we walked in a garden together. I have held back but now we are together again after a long absence and this is my first chance to tell you mine. No one knows we are here and we cannot be interrupted." She stood still and faced him. "Ah that is what *he* said on this very spot."

"He?"

There was a fallen log in the sunshine. She walked over to it and sat down. He followed. Their eyes were more on a level. She sensed fear in his as to what was coming next.

"It begins with John as a boy of twelve, willingly kidnapped you might say by an older boy, Alexander Gordon, who loved him. John went with him into Scotland and was caught up in the rising led by the man who became known as Bonnie Dundee." Frederick nodded to show he had heard of this and she guessed he would connect it with le Vent's inquiries but she didn't want to pause. She pressed on.

"Alexander had an older brother, Ranald." She brought out the name with difficulty. "Between them they trained John to use a

Height of Folly

shield and weapons and he took part in the Battle of Killiecrankie. He was hurt and the wound festered. The brothers quarrelled over him because Ranald said he must be taken home but Alexander didn't want him to go. Ranald prevailed. Ranald brought John home to us at great peril of his own life." She paused. This was a hard thing to tell. "Frederick, he was a giant of a man, taller than my father and broad. I was seventeen but he had never seen a woman so tall. The first thing he said to me was 'Ye're a fine specimen of womanhood.' No man had ever been attracted to me before and I was certain no man ever would. No, let me speak. I loved him for that. I loved him because I was dressed up for a country ball which I missed because of John's homecoming and he made me dance with him on the grass. He could lift and twirl me and I felt as light as a feather. I was riding on air. I was intoxicated with his admiration. He stayed two days and I showed him this wood. On that piece of ground there he made a bed of leaves and wanted to lie with me. I told him no. He was angry and passionate but came away subdued. Then he had word that his brother had been killed in the battle for Dunkeld. He said he must go and find what they had done with his body. He loved his brother. I was desolate when he went. He told me I was the only woman for him. He said 'You're mine! You're mine!' and rode away."

Frederick murmured, "You were so young."

She held up her hand. She wanted no interruption or she would never be able to tell the rest. "Two weeks later he wrote a letter to my father that he was a prisoner in Edinburgh Castle and due to be hanged as a rebel. He had been betrayed by his brother before his death. That must have cut him sorely for he believed in loyalty above all things. My father wrote a letter to the keeper of the prisoners pleading that Ranald had fallen into their hands only because he had nobly brought John home to us. I saw the letter lying on the dish in the hall and I couldn't bear that it should wait

Prue Phillipson

till the morning to go by the carrier. I got Matt, then our new young groom, to saddle my mare, Bud, and I rode through the night, arriving at the gates of Edinburgh Castle late the next day." She heard a grunt of amazement from Frederick. "Oh, I had a change of mount, a few minutes' rest, and a drink and a little food or I would have fainted on the way. Inside the castle I was told the governor was out for the evening. I wouldn't give the letter to anyone but him. They said Ranald was to hang the next day. I begged to be allowed to see him. A group of drunken officers made a game of it. They would take Gordon his woman and watch him enjoy her."

"Dear God, you poor girl!" Frederick buried his face in his hands

"They took me down to the vaults where the prisoners were chained. Ranald was wild with joy at seeing me. He threw together some straw mattresses and blustered it out. Let them have their fun, he would give me a child to live after him. I refused. I told him I couldn't unless we were married in the sight of God. So he told their captain to fetch the prison chaplain. Oh you cannot begin to know what I felt like at the thought that I would become a wife, something I was so sure would never happen to me. And I loved him because he wanted me so much. They fetched a priest and there in the dungeon he married us. I was Ranald's wife. I loved him and he was to die tomorrow unless my father's letter and my own pleading could save him. Frederick, I spent the night with him."

She couldn't help glancing at his face. He had to meet her eyes. There was a listening intensity in his look. His lips were slightly parted. She hurried on.

"The drunken officers went away after a while. In the morning I was told the governor wanted to see me. I took him the letter but first he wanted to apologise for the behaviour of the officers. I

Height of Folly

pleaded for Ranald's life on the grounds of our recent union and I think he was minded to reprieve him. He read my father's letter but then Father arrived in person and of course he was appalled when I said I was married to Ranald. The governor gave him permission to see Ranald and said he would make his decision on his fate afterwards. We went down. I knew my father was already mad with anger against Ranald but then the corporal of the guard came in and told us that the priest wasn't a priest at all but a barber. He had been bribed of course but he had a Missal and cap and gown from when he had been an altar boy. He spoke it all beautifully in a soft Irish voice. So now I knew I was not a wife but I was sure Ranald was as much the victim of the drunken captain's trick as I." She took a deep breath. "He wasn't. He'd suggested they find anyone to impersonate a priest so he could enjoy me. That was when my father let rip his anger and Ranald, though chained up, managed to fall on top of him and nearly throttled him. The guards couldn't fire their muskets. The corporal drew his dagger. I told him to kill Ranald. My father would have died. He stabbed Ranald in the neck and there was blood everywhere. He died, looking at me with reproach in his eyes."

She stopped. Her breath was coming fast. She sucked in her lips with her teeth and stared unseeing at a primrose next to her foot. She couldn't look at Frederick. He had said nothing.

"That's the story I had to tell you." She heard a gulping sound and gave a quick glance at his face. Tears were streaming down his cheeks.

The sight of them released hers. The telling had been agony. Every picture had come back and with them all the hurt.

He found his handkerchief and wiped his eyes. His hand sought hers, pressed it and held onto it. He offered her the handkerchief. It was moist from his own tears and she suddenly thought, we can mingle ours, and she used it all over her face and managed to smile at him.

He found a husky voice. "Did you – was there – a child?"

She shook her head. "Thank God, no. I imagined a great rough boy and Ruth was a tiny baby at the time. I thought of them growing up together and mine a bastard like his father. But it didn't happen."

He had been sitting hunched on the log but now he straightened up and drew a long slow breath. When he had let it out again he said quickly, "Deborah, why did you have to tell me all this – to give yourself so much pain at the memories?"

She looked him very straight in the eye. "Oh Frederick, I think you know."

He got up and paced about a little. The sun had moved off them. He's cold, she thought. "Are you cold, Frederick?"

He came back and stood in front of her. "It makes no difference to me. Your story – except to fill me near to bursting with compassion and admiration – and love. But how can you – how can you – even think – after a man like that roused your love – how can you – *begin* to look –"

"I *am* looking. I'm looking up at you." She remained seated so that she could do so in truth. "I respect what I see. I am not a giddy girl any more and I thank God I was never married to Ranald and that he did not live to be a husband to me. God knows the good points he had and He will judge him but I believe I would have had no peace as his wife."

He held out his hands to her. She put hers in his but did not rise.

"Can *I* give you peace?" he said. "Will you trust yourself to *me?*"

Everything it meant rushed before her, leaving family, leaving Horden, especially leaving Father, a strange great house in Hertfordshire where she had never been, a mother-in-law she had never met, his aged grandfather, a whole household of servants, a

Height of Folly

society of snobbish southern grandees, presentation at court perhaps, keeping up being Countess of Branford, terrifying thought. Could it be done for this little man standing before her, his clear gaze pleading for her answer? He had spoken the word love. Yes it was truly happening, a man wanted her again, despite her long lanky body. It was possible for that word wife to apply again to her, even perhaps mother. It would be spoken over her and she would after all this time have the thing that she believed would never ever again happen, a man's love.

It was the height of folly but she had to do it. She stood up straight. Would he not change his mind? She looked down at him. "Are you still sure you want to ask me this question?"

He nodded. "I want you to be my wife. I will be most honoured if you will be my wife. I do not deserve you but I will go to your father and ask for your hand in the proper way. Only I would like to be assured that you will say yes."

"Then I will say yes." She drew an excited breath and gazed about in amazement. She was surrounded by the dazzle of green and gold in this spot which had only had autumn memories. She gave a skip of glee. The burden of the past had gone. She was a new young girl setting out on an adventure. She caught his arm in hers and walked him out of the wood.

They were late for breakfast.

Grandmother Bel took one look at their faces and exclaimed, "Daniel, Eunice, I believe they have something to tell us."

Frederick stepped forward. "Not tell. Ask for. Sir Daniel, I do apologise for not appearing at the correct hour but if I may have a private word with you afterwards I would be most grateful."

Deborah saw the smile on her father's face and the pain in his eyes as he looked up at her.

"Lord Branford" – he wasn't looking at him but still at her – "I have nothing more precious that I am free to give you than what I am looking at now. If she is willing then she is yours. We can speak privately about it afterwards but I think the family are too much on tenterhooks for us to keep them waiting."

She too looked at him with a loving smile and a spasm of sorrow. "I am willing, Father."

Ruth set up a cheer and clapped her hands. "I shall be a bridesmaid again!"

Her mother frowned her down. "Wait till you're invited." Then she looked up at Lord Branford. "There are many things I would like to ask you so I would wish to be present at this private meeting."

He bowed, a little nervously, Deborah thought. Then he held out his hand to her father who had risen to his feet. "Sir Daniel, I cannot begin to tell you how happy you have made me." They grasped hands and Deborah, looking from one to the other, thought, it is the men who are struggling with emotion. Mother is calm and I am just amazed that I have reached this point at thirty-five when I believed life held nothing more for me at all.

They sat down and the cook-maid and her girl were summoned to bring in fresh breakfasts.

Afterwards Deborah demanded to be present too in her father's study. "I am not a parcel to be bargained for but I must be there for our official betrothal."

Her mother looked doubtful but her father said, "Yes, you are entitled for no one knows our affairs better than you."

It was soon obvious why her mother didn't want her there. She put Frederick through what amounted to an examination of his spiritual life before she could feel happy to entrust her daughter to him. Deborah, watching his face and listening to his answers, given with complete openness and no resentment, was bursting with love and admiration. Did I take him just to get a man? Well, I have achieved a paragon among men. Her mother too was more than

Height of Folly

satisfied. She stood up so he immediately rose too.

"I welcome you as my future son." She took his hands and was then moved to embrace him. "Frederick." Deborah recalled she had not addressed him as 'My lord' since his arrival. "I have only one Lord," she would say.

He was moved too. "Lady Horden, I am honoured to have your favour."

"And if you can't bring yourself to call me Eunice," she laughed, "I will be happy with Mother-in-law when you two are married. Now I will leave you to do business for that is not the sphere in which I am greatly interested." She smiled round at them all and left the room.

As he sat down again Deborah took Frederick's hand and pressed it. "You have *flown* over the hardest hurdle there." She mouthed it and her father, gathering papers together, didn't hear.

"Lord Branford," he began, "our daughter is to be elevated to a life she is not accustomed to with the wealth and grandeur that accompanies it."

Frederick held up his hand. "Please pause there a moment, Sir Daniel. As you know I was in much humbler circumstances for most of my life, but since my 'elevation', if you like to call it that, I have realised that far from grandeur or wealth the house of Branford is teetering along. Now that I have seen the excellent state of Horden Hall I realise more strongly than ever how shabby and ill-cared for our place appears. My mother has done what she can with little touches to her rooms but my grandfather's age and recent illness have meant that she could not pester him for improvements and alterations that are necessary. Now I wish to go back and see what can be done to make the place fit for my bride. If Deborah were to come to me with nothing I would be rich indeed but any dowry however small would be used wisely for her comfort and happiness." They were still holding hands and he squeezed hers. "If it is necessary I would happily resume my profession as a lawyer but any advice she can give me about the management of an estate I will be most grateful for. I believe she has been helping you, sir, in the absence of your son."

Deborah saw her father nodding vigorously at that. "Indeed she has. Her abilities that way are extraordinary." He then named a sum which opened her eyes wide. "This is the dowry I intend to settle on her on her marriage." He smiled at her surprise. "Moneys for you and Ruth have been set aside from your births, very small at first but added to over the years and well invested. It did not appear in the estate books which you have so beautifully set in order and which I will hope to keep so and hand on to John in due course. As we've mentioned to you, Lord Branford, we are expecting him and his family in July and this time we trust his wife will agree to settle here with perhaps annual visits to her French family. I would want his boy brought up here to appreciate what he will one day inherit himself."

"Speaking of days," Deborah broke in before Frederick could reply, "when should we fix our wedding day?"

Frederick pressed her hand but he was looking at her father. "There will be more to settle, Sir Daniel, when I return to my grandfather with the news of our engagement." Then he met her eyes again. "As soon as possible, I hope."

CHAPTER TWENTY-ONE

Nathaniel Jean, always called Jean here in Rombeau, was toddling along the broad walk at the château having pulled away from Nurse Forêt's hands while John and Jeanetta followed, watching his independent steps with great pride. Nurse Capot, Diana's nurse was trailing behind them carrying the baby.

John had been handed a letter from England as they left the château but seeing only his mother's writing he was not in a great hurry to read it. His brain was full of a lightning visit he had had the day before from Edouard le Vent. He was recalling his excited whisper, "Colonel Nathaniel Hooke is this moment with King Louis at Versailles. He has brought a paper signed by many Scottish lords showing that the country will rise for James as soon as he lands with French support. The plan is to head south from Edinburgh and invade the north of England and occupy the coalfields which supply London. This will compel the government to capitulate. Did not the same thing happen in the time of Charles the First? Was not the port of Newcastle closed?"

"I don't know," John had said, "I wasn't born then but I think I heard of that from my grandmother."

"Well, it was so. It is a good plan. Military and economic pressure at one stroke."

John had not mentioned that his father was mining coal on his land. Le Vent would know that. He seemed to know everything. "Do you want me to go to England sooner," he asked him.

"July will be soon enough. Louis's force may not be ready before autumn. And if they miss that it will be the spring of next year. I will be in England ahead of the force but I will not come to you at Horden Hall lest your formidable sister sees me. I will get a message to you when I know the king is about to sail. To avoid detection the message will say nothing."

"Nothing?"

"The day you receive a blank sheet of paper with only my initials in the corner, that will be the day you are to set off from Horden Hall. Of course you will bring what force you can from your own tenants."

John's heart quailed at this. There were no Catholic families within their land. He knew no one but Matt who would attend him willingly.

Le Vent was still talking. "The task of shipping the French force may be given to Admiral Forbin. You have heard of his success at Beachy Head."

John nodded. The court at Versailles had been celebrating it with lavish parties. A naval defeat for England was a matter of great rejoicing, with two of Her Majesty's ships sunk and the Royal Oak only just escaping ashore at Dungeness with a hole in her side. Twenty-one sail of merchant ships had been carried into Dunkirk. John was a little guilty at his own delight but just now he felt more French and Scots than English. King James would have safer passage if the English navy was depleted.

Well, he would collect all the men he could as he rode north through Northumberland and le Vent would not know with how few he started out.

His thoughts now, roaming towards personal glory, were interrupted by a howl in front of them. Jean had fallen over and was being dusted down by Nurse Forêt. Jeanetta ran to him and called out to John, "There's blood on his brow. I can't bear to look."

John came up with her. "It's only a scratch. He must learn to be a brave boy."

Nurse Forêt took him in and Nurse Capot followed saying baby Diana had had enough of the sun.

Height of Folly

"Why don't we sit down and read your letter?" Jeanetta said. "Were they not having a visit from Lord Branford? Perhaps he has gone for Deb's hand after all?"

"Old Deb? I doubt it." But they found a seat and sat down.

"Well, it is so," he exclaimed after opening it up. "I never thought that little fellow would stand being overtopped by so much. They are talking of a wedding in the autumn so that Deb can be shown first to his mother and the old earl for their approval I presume. They may find we have a change of monarch by then."

"But that means she will leave Horden Hall. Will you be glad of that? Will you expect us to go and live there all the time?"

"Father has promised us Nether Horden Grange so we will be on our own as a family. You'll be happier there."

"It's only an ordinary house. Where will the servants sleep?"

"Nay, it's much bigger than you think. You have only passed it at a distance."

"We must have our own carriage. When Deb is married why shouldn't the old people go and live in the Grange and we in the Hall. There must be room for Ruth there too and I'm sure she won't be as much trouble for a husband as Deb has been."

"Netta, my father is the baronet. He's in charge till his death or till he's too old to carry on."

"But we have everything *here*."

"And I am nobody but your husband. Your brothers are growing up. Pierre is your father's heir and already giving himself airs. I'll answer Mother's letter and tell her we expect to have Nether Horden Grange when we come. That should give Father time to see it's fit for us. When we are there I can come and go on the true king's business without any interference."

Jeanetta went into a long sulk. "I will have Maria and you will have Matt and there will be the two nursemaids. What other servants will we have? I hope you're not expecting me to cook and clean."

John got up. "Oh Netta, there are much more important things to plan for. You were as excited as I about le Vent's news."

"I was but I can see it now. I will not be allowed to ride with you. LeVent does not trust women around and it is he and this Colonel Hooke who will lead the expedition, not you. I think they distrust you because your family is not Catholic."

John stamped his foot. "I will not have you say that. I shall go in and write home now."

She shouted after him, "You see you call *that* place *home. This* is home to *me*."

He didn't look back. He marched into the château, hot and angry. It was true that Le Vent had not addressed him as if he were the leader. Colonel Hooke had the nobility organised and Le Vent like the wind moved everywhere. The lowlier gentry that he had stirred up himself would mingle with their superiors when the great march began and it would be the standards and banners of the great ones that would be carried in front. "I *will* make my mark," he told himself as he went from the heat of the garden to the cool of the library to write his letter.

Deborah walked over with Frederick and her father and mother to look at Nether Horden Grange when they received John's letter. "It is just such a place as you and I could be happy in," she said to Frederick.

"And much bigger and grander than where *I* was brought up," he said.

If only we *could* live here, she thought fleetingly, only a mile from home and my beloved father! But my new life is to be Countess of Branford. I mustn't be afraid.

Eunice was running her finger along the window ledges. "There are cobwebs and damp everywhere. I think, Daniel, if you really

Height of Folly

promised it to John we should have concentrated our improvements here these last months. At least the Hall was clean if not shining."

They explored every room and descended to the big kitchen which had a heavy trapdoor in one corner.

"A cellar as well!" Frederick said.

Her father laughed. "Nay, it is more than that if I remember rightly. I'll show you." With the help of Frederick he lifted and dragged the trapdoor along by its iron ring, revealing stone steps down into the depths. "Wine has been kept here but these were actually dungeons. There was a medieval castle here once but it fell into ruin and much of the stone was taken by villagers. The site was cleared long before Sir Ralph's time and the Grange built for a yeoman farmer. The dungeons were all that remained and were kept for storage."

The heavy door was dragged back and let fall into place with a hollow sinister clang that reverberated beneath their feet.

Eunice shivered. "How could anyone be so cruel as to shut someone up in there? Let us get out into the sunshine again."

They walked round the outside in the overgrown garden. Daniel looked up at the wing that had been added by Sir Ralph's grandfather whose mistress occupied the Grange and produced a large illegitimate family.

"It occurs to me, Lord Branford, that if we have the place done up for John and his family he wouldn't need that wing at first. You and your man could occupy it in the days leading up to the wedding so that you and Deborah were not under the same roof beforehand. I believe some people think that unlucky."

"I would say, *unseemly*," Eunice said. "Luck is not an idea I approve of. Everything is overruled by our Father in heaven."

"Whatever arrangements you make will be acceptable to me, sir, but I would be most grateful if you would address me as

Prue Phillipson

Frederick."

Deborah saw her father smile. "I will come to it in time."

"I would like to start work on this garden," Deborah said. "I wonder if there are tools in that shed." She went to look.

"And there's nothing I would like more than to help you," Frederick said, following her.

A few minutes later as Daniel and Eunice were walking back to the Hall, they glanced over their shoulders at the two figures attacking the overgrown shrubs, Lord Branford with his coat hanging on the gate post and his shirt sleeves rolled up and Deborah in an apron she had found in the kitchen.

"An answer to prayer," Eunice said.

"Indeed." He heaved a great sigh. "I still can't conceive how I am to part with her."

Letters had been written to the old earl and Lady Branford, his daughter-in-law, and they were to expect to meet Frederick's betrothed at the beginning of June. Deborah would make the return journey to Northumberland after a month's stay and prepare for the wedding in September. Setting off for the journey south took Deborah back to the excitement of the start of her travels. She had never seriously imagined she would end up as an affianced bride. Such a hope she had told herself was the height of folly. She was only seeking new scenes and adventure and after meeting Edouard le Vent on the packet boat she had vowed to have nothing to do with men. Yet here she was now with Lord Frederick Branford sitting beside her in the stage coach and Suzette and Peter up top, three characters who had come into her life in these last two years. She was heading for a first look at the place which was to be her home for the rest of her life. The two years were an age and yet the time had brought so much change so quickly that she felt out of breath just thinking about it.

Height of Folly

"Frederick," she said suddenly, "I want to ask you two questions." No one else could hear for two men passengers, a Scot and an Englishman were engaged in a lively discussion about the Act of Union. Frederick had evidently been listening to them but he immediately inclined his head to her. There was an anxious crease to his brow and an unusual wariness in his eyes.

She said, "Did my tale of Ranald Gordon truly make no difference to you?"

His face cleared at once. "I told you. I was only filled with greater love."

"Even though I had loved another man and he had me."

He shook his head. "We are both shaped by what has happened to us but our future together is a new thing for us both."

She nodded. That chimed perfectly with her own sentiments. "The other question is, what made you come to me when you did?"

The anxiety returned. He hesitated. "My grandfather had been ill."

"You could have written to me."

"I did – from Rome – and you sent Peter but no letter. I felt – when we parted in Florence – that our friendship was becoming too close for you."

"I know. I was unkind to you. I was fearful of meeting your grandfather's titled friends. Who would they think I was? And then Will Smyth –"

He managed a rueful smile. "I fell out with Will Smyth. We were never close before but after that the rest of the tour was more of an endurance than a pleasure. Before I left home this time to visit you he thought he would be coming too but I told him his duty was to stay with my grandfather."

"But I still wonder what inspired you to write to my grandmother and suggest the visit after so long a silence."

He was definitely uncomfortable now. "Your silence held me back."

"But something stirred you into action."

"My grandfather improved. I could leave him. The silence had become a pain to me. I needed to know if there could still be hope for us and the moment I saw you I felt sure there could be, despite everything."

"Despite my ridiculous height."

"Ah, no." His eyes were bright and clear again. "Despite the months of doubt."

She ought to be satisfied but she was not. She had felt he was a man who would never have anything to hide from her. It had been his chief attraction, utter honesty and simplicity. Well, she had a month to get to know him in his home surroundings. "Tell me about your mother," she said.

The Branford carriage had been sent to the staging inn and she renewed her acquaintance with Joseph who was driving it. It was very newly painted and polished and Frederick laughed when he saw it. She joined in. "Your family has behaved just like mine. I hope you didn't imagine dear old Horden Hall was usually so smart." It was lovely to feel that bond of amusement with him at the ways of the world.

He said to Joseph, "Castle Branford couldn't possibly be like this all over?"

"Why no, my lord, but there's been a deal o' effort made."

The first thing Deborah saw was that there was a solid lodge house at the gates and a stout lodge keeper, in a livery far too small for him, bowed his way out and flung back the gates.

She chuckled to Frederick. "We had to send one of our two grooms to open ours for you and then he had to run back to help with the carriage horses. As you saw later our gates are usually left

Height of Folly

open." She looked about. There was a fine park with many trees but no sign of the house. "Yours is a long drive. And you call home a castle. I ought to be very nervous but somehow I'm not."

"That's one of the things I love about you. Your serenity, your humour. You do not know fear."

"Oh come, I told you on the way that I was frightened to meet your society friends."

"And I didn't believe you. If you had met them you would have done it with charm and dignity."

They were holding hands and she laughed and pressed his. They rounded a bend, passed through a great avenue of oaks and beeches, and rounded another bend.

"Oh!" Her hand flew to her mouth. "Oh!" She swallowed and turned her gaze on him. "Now I *am* frightened. It really *is* a castle. It's – it's huge!"

"That's just what I said when *I* first saw it. I'm still a little frightened but it's truly just a rambling old place and most of it is hardly used."

"Well, that's a shame. It's a waste of a fine building."

The central castellated pile had spawned long wings in both directions. Could not one wing be a school? It began to dawn on her that the day would come when she would have a say in the management of this place. Frederick had never disagreed with her about anything yet. Was that how it would always be? For the present she kept silence though she could feel many plans stirring in her brain. But first she had to meet his grandfather, the earl.

It was his mother who came to the great pillared entrance to greet her. Oh, she could see her as a farmer's daughter, rosy-cheeked, with Frederick's light blue eyes, her grey hair unpowdered and neatly pinned behind. She was short but sturdy and looking younger than her age which must be late fifties. Deborah at once saw her as easier to deal with than her own mother, Eunice.

Prue Phillipson

From the step she was standing on she could look straight into Deborah's eyes and her first words were spoken with laughter.

"Fred did warn me. I think we'll always have to hold our conversations out here." But she came down and took Deborah's hands. "You don't look tired but come in and have a dish of tea in my little parlour." She waved her hand towards the vast building behind them. "Don't take any notice of all this. We can be quite cosy." She gave her son a swift, passionate hug and then turned to Suzette, hanging back several paces behind her mistress as usual.

"You must be Suzette. Welcome, my child. There is a snug little bed in your mistress's dressing-room for you. Follow us and I'll show you where it is."

Then she led the way up a wide staircase talking all the time. "You know, Deborah, I'm supposed to hate you for taking Fred from me but I won't be that sort of mother-in-law. I wasn't with Mary but she was a mere twig to your tree. She *asked* to be bullied so I made sure I didn't." She turned her bright face up to Deborah and laughed freely again. "I wouldn't even try with you."

They had been settled in the small parlour for five minutes and Lady Branford had poured tea with her own hand when a knock came on the door and a grey ancient face peeped round.

"Oh come in, Papa Ted," cried Lady Branford. "Meet our Deborah."

He had been quite a tall man but was very bowed now and leaning on two sticks. Frederick jumped to his feet and helped him to a seat. Deborah rose too but seeing how hard it was for him to turn his head to peer up at her she crouched before him and took his hand.

"How are you, my lord? I trust you have not risen from your bed because of my coming?"

"No no no." His voice was faint and husky. "I am trying to get out and about now. How is Bel? She writes me such letters and I

Height of Folly

am not to call her anything but Bel though we have never met." He managed a laugh which ended in a cough.

"She sends you her loving greetings, sir."

"Ay, she would, she would. Full of love she is. My dear friend Nat was fortunate to get her and to have her all his life. I lost mine not so long after this one's father was killed." He looked at Frederick. "And we never knew he'd had this boy till so lately." He shook one of his sticks towards Frederick's mother. "Her fault you know. All her fault and she's the light of my life now." There was more laughter.

Now he studied Deborah closely. "You look well, bright eyes, clear skin and lovely flaxen hair. She thought you were fretting but I don't see that."

Deborah stood up and looked at Frederick who had gone bright red. "Who thought?" she asked.

The old man answered, "Why Bel of course. Isn't she your grandmother?"

Deborah understood it all in an instant. Lady Branford was laughing and shaking her head at Frederick. "We might have known it would come out. He's forgotten it was to be a secret. But there's no harm done, is there? Everyone's happy."

Frederick had risen, still hot and flushed. "Deborah, she made me promise to say nothing. She didn't know how much it would hurt me not to be open and honest with you. But I told you no lies in the coach coming here. I *was* longing for you. Her letter gave me enough hope to write and beg to be allowed to come."

Deborah felt a spurt of anger at Grandmother Bel for daring to guess her feelings and at Frederick for not having written till he was prodded, but how could she keep that up in this company and in the face of his obvious shame and sorrow. Now, she resolved, they would never again keep anything from each other.

The old earl was looking about in bewilderment. "What did I

say?"

She bent down to him again. "Nothing sir. Yes, Bel is my grandmother and very dear indeed to me. And your friend, my Grandfather Nat, was very special all my life. He taught me Latin and Greek and always had time for my questions."

He nodded, happy again. "Yes, he was cleverer than I. Many a Greek exercise he helped me through at Cambridge." He waved a hand at the wall. "I have his papers there that he wrote on Job and other texts. Nay, we're not in my library are we? Her parlour. Poky little room but she likes it."

"It's the size of our parlour at the farmhouse," Lady Branford said, "biggest room in the place it was and only ever used for best."

Deborah resumed her seat and muttered to Frederick, "I suppose you think I've forgiven you?" He looked alarmed till she gave him a merry smile. Laughter seemed to be the order of the day at Castle Branford. The only stiffness was the meeting with Will Smyth. "Mistress Horden." A deep bow and that was it.

In the next weeks she was shown at her own insistence every part of the building and supplied with a handsome mount to explore the grounds.

I can grow into this great responsibility, she kept telling herself, but there is so much I need to know. I gather there are properties in neighbouring counties too and Frederick is only beginning to work with the earl's lawyers to find the whole truth of the Branfords' position. I can see he wants to take over from them and save the fees they charge. I'm sure he has the ability and I will enjoy helping if I can. They are arranging a marriage settlement now with Father's lawyers. Letters are going back and forth and I believe I am to take the final document when I go home. It makes me feel like a piece of property but I have to accept this is what happens. A good laugh with Frederick disperses such thoughts. I have to remember too that the earl, fragile as he looks, still has his faculties and understands what he is signing. Frederick defers to him very properly in all decisions.

Each night she went to bed and lay awake marvelling at the new room she was becoming accustomed to, the new people with whom she already felt intimate and the uncanny distance that now seemed to lie between her and Horden Hall. She would go back for a few weeks before her marriage but nothing now, it seemed, could come between her and her new life.

CHAPTER TWENTY-TWO

Deborah was home at Horden Hall a few days before the arrival of John and Jeanetta with the children. She threw herself at once into helping her mother with the last minute preparations at Nether Horden Grange and was only a little hurt that this was in the forefront of everyone's minds.

She had one intimate moment with Grandmother Bel who was eager for her to describe Frederick's mother and the old earl.

"Frederick's mother talks much and laughs even more," Deborah told her. "She was prepared to love me before we even met. The old earl is a poor bent stick but quite alive to what is going on. Only his memory lapses occasionally. He forgot that a certain letter was supposed to be a secret."

Grandmother Bel hid her face in her hands, then peeped out between them. "Oh sweet Deb, you are not going to be angry with me I hope?"

There were hugs and tears and Deborah took her chance to share some of the myriad new impressions that had crowded upon her over the past month.

"They were so good in *not* inviting their neighbours, but that is to come after our wedding when I must be shown to Hertfordshire society. It took me all the time just to find my way around and learn the names of their household. Oh, Grandmother Bel, it *is* daunting but I believe I *can* live this new life and find it most exciting."

"And, my Deb, you look ten years younger, your eyes are brighter, your skin glows and you carry yourself joyfully. I thank God I've lived to see this. Now I only want to welcome those sweet babes and see John and Jeanetta as wise, loving parents and I will go to my Maker any time with great contentment."

Height of Folly

Contentment was not what John's family brought with them. Jeanetta was cross. The journey with the children had been most trying and both were fretful. John seemed very much on edge.

Deborah was disappointed but her mother surprised her by her tolerance.

"They will take time to settle in. Having two babies close together is exhausting. Nathaniel is a vigorous little boy. He wants to be exploring everywhere and Nurse Forêt is too old and fat to be running after him. When little Diana is weaned Nurse Capot should have Nathaniel."

"And why is Jeanetta not caring for them herself?" Deborah demanded. "I suppose we have to accept it is the way of French grandes dames."

She was not very pleased with John either. He had not greeted her with the brotherly congratulations she had expected.

"Well, so you caught your earl, eh Deb? That'll set you even further above your humble family. Taller, cleverer and now grander."

"Oh John-Jo, how can you say such a thing?"

"Don't John-Jo me. You made me feel a baby all my childhood. At least I'm a father before you're a mother and when I'm master of Horden Hall I may not stay a mere baronet. You'll see."

Deborah was shocked at this display of envy but his outburst made her look back at their youth and realise she had resented her mother's tenderness for John from the moment he was born. That's why I made him feel stupid, she reproached herself, and teased him into thinking he was a Catholic when he was only three. 'Caflick' he used to say and I must have driven the word into his little soul. If the Lord does give me any children I must strive to keep them free of jealousy. Jealousy corrodes.

Ruth, she was pleased to find, was genuinely happy for her. Perhaps that was because she was in love herself and all the world was sunny for her. The handsome Simon Stephenson had come to Upper Horden Manor to stay with his cousins for the summer vacation and was very attentive to Ruth.

"I wager we'll have another wedding in a year or so," their father predicted. "He's to go into his father's business in York and Ruth is likely to turn out richer than all of us."

Jeanetta was fretting, it was obvious, because Nether Horden Grange was so small after Château Rombeau. She wanted more servants to live in the wing Daniel had allocated for Frederick to occupy before the wedding.

"When you can afford more you can have more," he told John. "At present you have what I can allow you and it is plenty for your needs. I expect you to manage with one nursery maid when the babes are a little older, and I hope an English one."

John said in a portentous tone, "Well sir, whether we stay here or go back to France may depend on what happens in the next sixth months."

Deborah who was present saw her father flush with anger at what sounded like a threat. She herself had an uneasy feeling that it might relate rather to the political situation than the amount of John's allowance. Everyone in the north of England was aware of the Scottish discontent with the Union. Was it possible that a rising was imminent and John was involved? She had tried to forget her suspicions when he had appeared to have dealings with the Vicomte de Neury. Playing chess? Was that credible? Nothing, she prayed fervently, must upset her joy in her coming wedding.

But an upset of a different kind appeared in a letter from Frederick just eight weeks before the wedding date.

'My dearest One,

I send sad news. Last week Grandfather would go out himself to inspect the stables. He was determined to approve the mount you rode when you were here, intending to send for a better if he

Height of Folly

thought Snowdrop not tall enough for you. I assured him you had been very happy with her but he went out on his own and not surprisingly had a fall before he even reached the stables. The concussion he suffered rendered him insensible for two days before he quietly passed away from the shock, the doctor said, to his heart. For him it is a joyful release from a body that had become a painful burden, but to us all a great sorrow which I know you will share.

There are some, Will Smyth is one, who think anything less than a year's mourning would be disrespectful. Mother and I do not agree but feel that under the circumstances we should postpone our wedding till the spring. It gives me great heartache to say so but there is much to attend to consequent on his death which will keep me busy over the winter.

It is impossible for you to be at the funeral, the distance being so great but you will never be out of my thoughts. You were so loving to him while you were here that he said my choice of bride gave him the utmost joy.

I would wish the funeral to be a quiet affair but Will Smyth believes all should be done with great and solemn pomp and in this I will not oppose him.'

He finished with his loving greetings to all the family and his longing for her which he would bear with what patience he could.

"It is my fault then," Deborah exclaimed when she had read it to the family. "If he had not been worrying about my horse he would not have gone out."

"Nonsense," said Grandmother Bel. "It would have been something else. No one's fault. Not his either. We old folk are blamed for our obstinacy but the truth is we forget that we are old and our still young minds urge us to do what our bodies are not capable of. He thought he could stride out to his stables as he used to do and his poor legs let him down. God rest his soul."

Prue Phillipson

Deborah was sad because she had taken a genuine liking to the earl but she was uneasy too. Marriage had leapt before her eyes in so short a time but was now receding. Would it truly happen? There was a long winter to get through and she missed Frederick's reassuring presence.

John's temper was soured by frustration. There had been no word from le Vent. The weather which had been hot in the earlier summer was cold and wet in August and though Jeanetta heard from her family that it was even worse in France and was impeding Marlborough's movements there was no sign of an end to the war. He balked at his father's efforts to interest him in Deborah's work on the estate books.

"You see how it is," he said to Jeanetta one evening when the babies were in bed and the nurses dozing by them, "Deb's wedding will fall just when Louis's forces are ready to move. I will not shirk my duty if I am called to march to meet the king but it will be deuced awkward if it happens at the same time. And it won't do me any good to be brother-in-law to an English earl who supports the Protestant succession."

She crept onto his knee and twined herself round him. "Could we not go back to France before then and pretend one of the children is ill so we don't have to come to the wedding?"

He gave her a perfunctory kiss. "Silly goose. My duty is *here*. James will be king *here* and it is here that he will raise me to Baron Horden or even higher for my service to him." She pouted. "But Netta," he urged, "you like being here better than with the family in the Hall?"

"I suppose so but it's so dull. There are no parties and festivities. The English court is so far away and no one cares about fashions here."

"There'll be a Harvest Ball as soon as the weather clears."

Height of Folly

"A lot of peasants prancing about on the lawns."

"Well, come to bed. You enjoy that anywhere and any time of the year."

"I'm not in the mood," she said.

Of the family only Ruth enjoyed the Harvest Ball although the day was one of sudden crisp autumn sunshine after grey clouds. It was done for the sake of the village though the family were not in a festive frame of mind. Deborah was not pleased to be accosted by Bill Warner, stouter than ever and with streaks of grey in his beard.

"Well, Mistress Horden, I know now why you wouldn't look kindly on my proposal last Harvest Ball. You had an earl up your sleeve. Ay, when I heard about that I says to myself, no wonder she looked down on me. But I reckon with the way coals are in demand that I'll have more to my name and more in my coffers than many an earl has before I'm much older."

"I congratulate you, Mr Warner." She turned on her heel and left him standing.

Ruth came afterwards to Deborah's bedroom, a thing she rarely did. She curled on the bed and pulled Deborah down beside her.

"I'll only tell *you* because I trust you to keep a secret. Simon declared himself in the middle of a dance. He said, 'I'm going to make you mine, Ruth Horden. No one can stop me.' Wasn't that masterful!"

Deborah hugged her. To her Simon and Ruth seemed absurdly, delightfully young. All the same she had never felt so close to her sister in her whole life.

"Of course we can't be betrothed properly," Ruth babbled on, still in her arms, "till he's graduated and asked Father properly and all that but everybody likes him and it's wonderful that I won't have to wait for a husband all the years you've had to wait and then have it put off just 'cos an old man dies who was hardly alive at all."

Prue Phillipson

Deborah had to laugh or she would have wept. Life had not begun to buffet Ruth in any way and now she was looking to be a wife. I think I am glad to be older, she told herself. Imagine if I were facing being Countess of Branford at Ruth's age!

The new closeness to Ruth helped her to endure the long winter without Frederick. In these extra months she had been given she also set herself the task of rousing John to his responsibilities at Horden. She positively *ordered* him to sit in on business talks with their father and despite Jeanetta grumbling at being left alone he complied. She guessed he had realised it was politic to please their father. He even alluded to his efforts the previous summer to find out more about husbandry.

"You know I did try, sir, and I've come to the conclusion that we should have more milking cows on our flat meadows. Sheep are fine on the moors but we are so near Newcastle and the population is growing so fast with the coal mines bringing people in, that I reckon we should increase our milk production."

"Have you really thought that out for yourself, son?"

Deborah loved to see her father innocently delighted. She had noticed one of the tenant farmers talking to John at the Harvest Ball. John had looked bored but had luckily remembered something of the conversation.

Her father went on, "It is what Deborah and I have in mind for this summer – an enlargement of the herd on Turner's farm and an extension of his dairy."

"There you are then," John said. "We are all agreed." And he grinned hopefully at their father for the first time since he and Jeanetta had come home.

At last the winter snows melted into the grass and a wedding date was fixed for Deborah and Frederick towards the end of March. Frederick would come north and bring his mother to meet the family two weeks before. They would travel in the Branford

Height of Folly

carriage with Will Smyth, who refused to be left behind, and Peter and Joseph to share driving and guard duties.

"So May Branford is not bringing a lady's maid," Eunice exclaimed. "I applaud her heartily. She can share Suzette and Jane with us."

Deborah found her mother's refusal to say 'the countess' delightfully consistent. She was confident that the farmer's daughter and the street preacher's daughter would get on well. May was light-hearted and Eunice puritanical but neither had any pride to disrupt harmony.

"They can all be accommodated in the wing of Nether Horden Manor," Eunice told Daniel, "but apart from breakfast they could take their meals in the Hall with us. Do you agree?"

"I think the countess should have our best guest bedroom – John and Jeanetta's old room. If she's at the Manor she would have to share Jeanetta's maid, Maria, and that would please no one."

"Very well, though why we so called ladies can't manage ourselves, as maids have to, I can't imagine."

Deborah and Ruth giggled at each other. "Because we have to wear the most impossible clothes, Mother dear," Deborah said.

"And where does it say *that* in the scriptures?" Eunice said and joined in the general laughter.

CHAPTER TWENTY-THREE

Frederick was happy to point out the sights of Newcastle to his mother. Before her new life as daughter-in-law to the earl the only urban scene she had ever known was that of Cambridge. To see a northern town vibrant with industry on a river alive with sea-going vessels as well as coal barges was a new and exciting experience. Her head turned this way and that as the carriage horses struggled up the steep bank from the bridge and headed for the Pilgrim Gate into the Liberties.

Frederick was alert too to the people in the streets and as they rattled past the staging inn he sat up suddenly, making his mother look up and exclaim, "What is it?"

"I saw a man I know. I'm pretty certain it was he. A man I am wary of whom I last saw at Château Rombeau." The carriage had slowed as a carrier's cart turned in the street and, without letting himself be seen, he pointed out to his mother the tall figure of Edouard le Vent in conversation with a carrot-haired youth.

She chuckled, "He has very fine moustaches. Why do you not like him?"

"Deborah and I think he is a government agent on the look out for Jacobites."

"Well, you are none so you don't need to mind him."

They were passed and on their way out into the country. He put the encounter behind him, overwhelmed now with the thought of seeing Deborah again. Not even Will Smyth's comment as they turned into the gates of Horden Hall, "No lodge house, but a pleasant modest little mansion I see," could diminish his joy.

"Oh and look at the stone statue of some ancestor," his mother cried. "The flamboyant way he brandishes his sword! I like that."

The whole family including John and Jeanetta and the babies

Height of Folly

greeted them. As he had expected his mother was instantly at ease with them all. Over the babies she cooed with delight. That is how she will be with ours, he thought. Pray God we can be soon blest with a child.

While his mother was being conducted to the best guest bedroom Deborah took him out to see the Branford carriage inserted into the carriage house and the extra stable that had been added for guests' horses since his last visit.

"We won't need it again I expect," she said, "until the new earl and countess pay their next visit. I wonder when that will be."

"You won't have too much heartache at leaving here?" he pleaded.

"Some, but it will be overlaid by the thrill of my new position, not the finery but the duties."

He pressed her arm tucked in with his. In the next breath he was exclaiming, "That's odd. I saw that lad with Edouard le Vent in Newcastle as we came through."

A carrot-haired youth was hesitating at the open back door.

He felt Deborah stiffen in alarm. "Le Vent! In Newcastle!" She drew away and marched up to the lad. "What do you want?"

He looked up at her startled by her height and tone of voice. "Please, my lady, I'm to hand this to Master John Wilson Horden and no one else." He was holding up a paper and looking at Frederick, evidently wondering if he was the man.

"That's all right. I'll give it to him." She took it from his grasp and stepped back to hand it to Frederick. "Do you expect payment?" she said as the boy paused open-mouthed.

"Nay, I'm paid already." And he ran off round the house.

"John was to return to the Grange before dinner," Frederick said, "but we might catch him before he goes. Shall I take it?" He looked up and saw her shaking her head. Her face was suddenly quite grey with anxiety.

"No, indeed. This worries me sorely. Let us see what it says."

"You'll open it up?" He was quite horrified at the idea of intercepting someone else's letter.

"There's no seal. It's just a paper folded together. Why should John receive a message from le Vent? This confirms all the fears that have haunted me since we were in France. Maybe this is a warning to John that le Vent knows he has had dealings with Jacobites."

"But why would he warn him? Why would he not arrest him straight away if he thought that?" Frederick was watching her fingers itching to open up the paper.

"That is what I would like to find out." And then she did unfold it, turning it inside out and upside down. "There is nothing on it at all!" She handed it to him and he examined it carefully, holding it so that the sunlight shone on it.

"There is a tiny monogram in one corner – ELV."

They stared at each other. "What can it mean?" she said. "Is it a magician's ink that will shine in the dark?"

The grooms had dispersed from their duties so they took the paper into the dimmest recesses of the carriage house but still nothing appeared on the paper.

"You'll have to give it to John I suppose," he said. "Maybe he will understand that a blank sheet means no news of any sort."

She stood still and looked solemnly down at him. "Do you realise what you are implying by that remark?"

"That John and le Vent are hand in glove. John is also secretly working for the government?"

"Or that le Vent is secretly working for the Jacobites? Oh Frederick, I fear that more. John would never work to catch or entrap the rebels. He has always professed his loyalty to the Stuarts."

"To pull the wool over your eyes perhaps?"

Height of Folly

"No, never, never. He could not dissemble all his childhood and right up to the present. You remember his visit to Saint Germain? But le Vent! He is capable of anything. He could have infiltrated the Jacobites only to betray them at the last minute."

"Will you confront John then when you take him the paper?"

"I am not thinking of taking it to him. Le Vent doesn't know that John is now living at Nether Horden Grange. We have an advantage in that the messenger almost certainly believes that *you* are John Horden. If le Vent sends again we have a chance to intercept it and find out what is going on. I will not have John's folly upsetting our wedding plans. If we can save him from some mad enterprise it will be all the better for him too. I have such a sickening feeling that something could still prevent our marriage."

"We will not let that happen. We are both here and in health and the church and the parson are ready. All the same" – Frederick stroked his chin – "perhaps it is my lawyer's training that makes me mighty uneasy at the idea of interfering with another's correspondence."

She shook her head. "No, it is your utter integrity. I admire it, I applaud it and would always share it – except this once. I will be watching John and will keep an eye out for any further messages."

"That will be hard amidst our wedding preparations and with John not living in the Hall."

"I'll try. If John was expecting a message he may come inquiring for one. Then I may have to force a confession from him. Last summer he rode round the county. I wondered at the time what he was up to. I even voiced my suspicions to Father but he pooh-poohed the idea. Oh Frederick! If this is all true that he is part of a rebel plot I feel ashamed of him, not so much for his passion but for the lies he has had to tell. And you! You will not want to ally yourself with one who might be arrested as a traitor any time. I *am* afraid that all our joy is to be undermined. It was too good to be true. I never did deserve such happiness. I was not a loving, understanding sister to John and now he will not care if he destroys my life."

She clung to Frederick and he found her weakness filling him with strength and love. "You are mine whatever happens. Nothing can take that away."

Peter came out of the house. "There you are, my lord. Sir D-Daniel wants to walk over with you to the G-Grange where we are to stay. Jo has taken our luggage there by c-c-cart. It's a m-mile by the road but they've lately had a p-path c-cut through the w-wood which is not above six m-minutes."

"Very well. I'll come. You did well to get all that out, Peter." He pressed Deborah's hands. "I will be close to John. I understand your concerns. I'll keep alert."

As he walked through the sultry woodland with Sir Daniel Frederick was uncomfortable. He had wanted nothing to disturb a pleasant relationship with his new family. The knowledge he now had of a mysterious liaison between his future brother-in-law and the sinister le Vent troubled his innate openness and honesty. What could a blank missive really mean? If it meant no news, why send at all?

He found the wing of the Grange spacious enough for his needs and for Will, Peter and Joseph, with horses in the stables for them if they wanted to ride out. Will met him in the dressing-room to the largest bedroom, looking into the wood.

"Not what you are used to, my lord, but it's only for two weeks."

"On the contrary, Will, I shared a bedroom smaller than this all my childhood with my mother's two brothers." He couldn't resist teasing Will with such memories. Now that he had succeeded to the title Will wanted to treat him with even more deference. Mischievously Frederick, and his mother too, enjoyed frustrating him.

Height of Folly

"I have set out clean linen for you to change after the journey, my lord," was all Will said by way of answer.

Through the walls they could hear both young Nathaniel and baby Diana howling.

"I trust that will not occur too often, my lord."

John was increasingly desperate for news from le Vent as the wedding day drew near. The news sheets reported nothing of French troops gathering at a channel port but surely the expedition must be setting sail soon. Lord Branford was very affable with him whenever they met in the Grange or the Hall but his anxiety cast a wedge between himself and the wedding preparations which made him stiff and nervous in his presence.

The wedding was only three days off and he was to see the tailor from Newcastle who was to supervise the final fitting of his wedding suit. Lord Branford had purchased his in London but two of the gold knots at the hem of the coat had suffered in the packing and unpacking.

"If you are seeing him, John, he might as well put these right for me."

Everywhere I go, John thought, Branford seems to be there. He's always so deuced friendly too. My hope is that the wedding will be over and he and Deb will be gone before the summons from le Vent comes. I won't see her this morning. She's having the last fitting of her wedding gown. We are to see the tailor in the library. I must try and find out if any message has come for me to the Hall and not been sent round. This is what I feared when Louis' plan was put off till spring and Deb's wedding too.

He walked in silence beside Frederick as they set off on the path through the woods. They had not gone far before he glimpsed a gleam of coppery red hair through the trees.

"Hello. Is there a stranger coming? We have no red-heads at

Prue Phillipson

Horden."

"Red!" Lord Branford exclaimed. "Ah I see him. I'll chase him away. Must be an intruder."

John was astonished at Frederick's agitation and the sudden bound with which he ran towards the figure that now appeared on the path, a carrot-haired youth.

"What's up? He looks harmless enough," John called out, following him.

Frederick had taken from the boy what looked like a letter and the boy, seeming frightened, had run away not by the path but through the wood.

John stood still, struck by a terrible thought. *He* was the one expecting a message and it would come by a stranger. Why had Frederick grabbed it? He leapt forward.

"Is that not for me? Give it to me."

He was astonished to see that Frederick had opened it up and was rapidly scanning it. He put it behind his back as John confronted him.

"Surely that is mine."

"There was no name. The messenger handed it to me."

"You snatched it."

"John, I beg you." Lord Branford's agitation was intense. "Do not ask to see this. It is best you know nothing of it. Let us proceed quietly to the Hall to see the tailor. The wedding is in three days' time."

John was now absolutely certain it was the long awaited call. Nothing was going to rob him of this. He had waited all his life for this moment.

"Damn your wedding! That letter is mine." He tried to reach round the little earl for it but he turned, dodging him.

John drew back his fist and clouted him on the jaw. It was a wild movement but so sudden that it knocked Frederick clean off

Height of Folly

his feet. John was onto him at once and wrenched his arm behind his back. His hand was gripping the letter so tightly that it tore as John snatched it away. But the moment he had most of it he turned to run, just glancing back to see Frederick staggering to his feet.

I'll hit him again if he tries to stop me, he told himself as he reached the stables behind the Grange and saw Matt emerging in surprise at the noise of the commotion. "Saddle both our mounts. The call has come," he yelled at him.

"Right, yes sir. Oh, but what about the wedding?"

"We'll miss it. This is the king's work."

"Sir!"

As he said it John bethought him to look at what there was of the paper in his hand. There might be a mistake and he would look an unutterable fool. Frederick was approaching with wavering steps. John cast his eye over what lines he could see.

'Where have you been? I sent you the blank.' Then there was a tear and the end of the line below said 'delayed by measles' – that was what it looked like. But the tear had ripped the first part of the next line which ended 'can still come.'

His thoughts galloped. I can still go then. Le Vent must be desperate to have written this not in code. But why did I not get the blank message? Ah, it came, but Branford stopped it! He recognised that boy. Or Deborah has suspected me all along and put him up to it. Curse them both.

He had reached the Grange back door which led straight into the kitchen. He could see Will Smyth there and crates of wine in the centre of the floor. While Matt was saddling the horses he must get to Jeanetta and grab some clothes and weapons – his sword and a pistol. He dodged round the wine crates. There came a squawk from Will Smyth and the floor opened beneath his feet. He had fallen through the open trap door into the dungeon.

Prue Phillipson

Frederick, panting in, met a horrified Will Smyth. "My lord, Master Horden came rushing in and before I could warn him he fell down the hole. We had just brought up the wedding wine." Frederick saw Peter and Joseph, their faces aghast, peering over the piled up crates.

Frederick looked into the vault. There was a lit lantern still down there and he saw John spread-eagled on the last three stone steps opposite him. He had fallen forward onto them, hands outstretched. But now he was scrambling to his feet at the bottom, gasping for breath. He was winded, that was all. He turned right round and saw Frederick looking down.

"You did this," he breathed. "But you'll not stop me." Now the steps were behind him and he flapped his hands about, looking for them.

Frederick saw the trap door lying on the far side of the hole. "Joseph, Peter, Will, push it over. Be sharp." And to John he called down. "Cool yourself there awhile."

The men were staring at him. He stepped round the hole. "I order you. Close it." He bent down to it himself.

Then Will said, "Your chin? You've been fighting, my lord."

"He attacked me. He's to have a short punishment."

They all pushed then with a will and the heavy door ground its way over the stone floor and banged into place, but not before they heard John's furious yell.

"What are doing? Let me out!"

Frederick straightened up. He was shaking. Will Smyth led him to a kitchen chair. He sat down. They heard a hammering on the trap door.

"I don't think he can move it but put two crates over it. And give me a glass of brandy if you please. He is not to be released without my say-so. Do you all hear?"

They nodded solemnly. Their faces showed that they were

Height of Folly

flabbergasted at their master's behaviour, so out of character.

At that moment Matt appeared at the back door. "The horses are ready." He looked about and saw only alien faces. "Where's Master John?"

"The horses will not be needed today." Lord Branford took a sip of the brandy and spoke in a commanding voice. "You may unsaddle them and return them to the stables."

"I only take orders from Master John."

"You will not be receiving any today."

"You'll not stop him from serving his king."

He had become aware of the banging from below. "God in heaven! You've not thrown him into the dungeon?"

"He fell in, but he is staying there and there will be a guard on him."

Nurse Capot, the young and almost pretty nurse, came in the other door from the hallway. She was cradling baby Diana who was wailing.

"What all the noise? Baby waken." She at least had learnt some English. "Who make banging?"

Lord Branford turned to her. "Take the baby back to bed. There will be no more noise. Is your mistress up there?"

"She trying on dress."

"I will not trouble her now but I will wish to speak with her later." She hesitated a moment but the habit of obedience was strong. She slipped away.

He looked back at Matt standing pugnaciously at the door.

"I told you to unsaddle the horses."

"Master John will kill you for this. He'll never ever forgive you, that's certain. And neither will I, my lord."

Will Smyth drew himself up to his full height and breadth and confronted him at the door. "How dare you speak to his lordship like that? If I report you to Sir Daniel he will dismiss you on the spot."

"I will tell him you have all conspired to imprison his son and he will send *you* all packing. There will be no wedding."

Matt turned and strode away down the path.

Frederick took another sip of brandy to control the shaking. He had never been involved in such a scene in his life. He had never taken such a sudden rash decision. His jaw ached and now he realised that his three men were staring at him inquiringly.

Will Smyth, with the utmost respect in his voice, asked, "There is more in this than Master John attacking you, my lord. What did that ruffian Matthew mean by 'his king'?"

"He meant King James or rather the aspiring King James. You three must not mention this outside the family. I fear John Horden was caught up in some Jacobite plot which must even now be afoot somewhere. For his own sake I had to stop him." He realised he had put in his pocket the scrap of paper he had been clutching. He took it out and uncreased it and studied it. The tear had left him the bottom end of the message but included the beginnings of two lines above. These read 'KJ was' and 'so you'. Then there was the whole of the last line: 'Meet by the F of F.' and the letters ELV. There was vital information here which government forces should know but just for the moment he felt too sick with apprehension about what Matt was saying in the Hall at this moment to bring his mind to bear on that question. Nothing must stop his wedding to Deborah.

There was quiet below. The trap door with two crates upon it would not let shouts through but hammering had been plain enough before. John might be prowling about to see if there was any other way out. He had a lantern there. That was something, and not all the liquor had been brought up. He could knock the head off a bottle and drink himself into insensibility.

Will Smyth was speaking and he hadn't been listening.

Height of Folly

"My lord," he repeated urgently, "can we do anything to foil the plot? What information have you there?"

"Not much, but I will do nothing to incriminate John Horden. That is why I have kept him out of this. If rebels are taken they are like to hang."

Will Smyth shook his head. "It was a bad day when you ever got involved with this family, my lord."

"You will not say that, Will, or you'll no longer be in my service."

"My lord, I beg your pardon."

Frederick could say nothing more. He was overcome with horror at what he had done and fear of the consequences. Sir Daniel, Lady Eunice, the old Grandmother Bel, what would they say? Would anyone be in a fit state to hold a wedding in three days' time? Would they banish him from Deborah for ever? He sipped the brandy as if it could stifle his dread. At the same time the thought drummed in his head: it would be a poor introduction to society if my brother-in-law was hanged as a rebel.

Will tapped his shoulder. "I see Mistress Deborah and her father approaching by the path."

Frederick swung round and there they were almost at the door which had stood open all this while.

He got to his feet and clutched at the back of the chair as a wave of dizziness struck him. She was into the room and threading her way between the crates.

"Frederick! Are you hurt? What did John do to you?"

"It's nothing," he gulped out. "I am devastated. That is all."

She looked at the crates over the trap door. "He is in there? What is he doing? Oh poor wretched boy!"

Sir Daniel was looking round at the three idle men. "These crates are to go to the Hall. The cart is being brought round by the road. Get them outside ready to load."

Peter and Joseph leapt to the task.

Will Smyth, evidently feeling the work was beneath him, addressed Sir Daniel warily. "Sir, my lord has some information which might help to foil a rebellion against our lawful Queen. Can I be of service in communicating it to the authorities?"

Frederick snapped at him before Sir Daniel could reply, "That is a matter for Sir Daniel to consider when I have had a chance to speak of it with him. Pray find some other work."

Deborah said, "The tailor is waiting in our library. Perhaps you, Mr Smyth, could inform him that there will be a delay and if he wishes for some refreshment you could give orders for it from our kitchen."

The sound of 'giving orders' seemed to please Will and Frederick saw him bow and take his departure, if a little unwillingly.

There came some banging again from below. John must have found something heavy with which to strike the trap door.

Frederick bit at his lower lip. "You cannot tell how bad I feel about this, Sir Daniel. I acted without time to think. I am truly sorry. Shall I let him out?"

"Certainly not. Where can we go to speak of all this?"

Frederick drew a long breath of relief. He was not in total disgrace. "There is my room in the wing, sir, but might not Matt return and release his master?"

"Matt is in disgrace and locked in his room above the stables."

Joseph and Peter were in and out carrying the crates. "Leave those two there," Sir Daniel said, pointing to the two on the trap door. "They can go later. Make sure they are not moved." He led the way from the kitchen and Frederick still not quite sure of Deborah's view of his action ushered her ahead of him.

As they all three turned aside to the door that led from the hallway into the wing, Jeanetta came tripping down the main staircase in the gown she was to wear for the wedding.

Height of Folly

"Has John not come back yet from the tailor? I wanted to show him how I will look."

Frederick was struck with her beauty. Her colour was high and her black hair charmingly coiled up with golden ribbons. The low-cut dress was a pale gold over a white petticoat spangled with embroidered roses in gold thread. She carried her fan in her white-gloved hands. Diamonds glinted on her white bosom.

What a horrible shame to have to upset so lovely a picture, he thought.

He looked at Deborah, his eyes asking, will you break it to her?

She obviously wanted to go with him and her father but she nodded and took Jeanetta's arm. "I'll come back up with you, Netta. John will be a little longer."

Frederick watched them go. His bride was still in her working dress, her fair hair tumbled about. She must have been about to try her wedding gown when her father called her to come. Beside Jeanetta's immaculate figure she looked a sad sight.

He followed Sir Daniel and waved him to the comfortable chair by the window in his room. The sunlight had set the tiny leaf buds sparkling in the wood. He sat on the stool by his bed and looked at them and wished time could go back to the early morning so the day could start afresh.

"I need to know exactly how this thing began," Sir Daniel said. "All I got from Matt was that you had shut up his master in the dungeon to prevent him serving his true king. I had no idea that John was mixed up in this cause nor that he had infected Matt who was always easily led. I should have listened to Deborah who has had her suspicions for a long time."

Frederick with great thankfulness uncovered everything from the encounters with Edouard le Vent to the carrot-haired boy he had sent with two messages.

"And John knocked you down to get at his letter. I am ashamed of my son."

"Nay, he was desperate, sir. The letter was rightly his though it bore no name. I knew it was his and opened it without his permission." He showed Sir Daniel the scrap he had retained. "I had only the quickest glance at the whole thing but the word 'measles' caught my eye. I wondered if a delay had occurred in France because young James Stuart caught measles. Some French ships must be at sea now. Le Vent seemed to be telling John there was still time for him to take part. The meeting place is to be at the F of F, whatever that means."

"The Firth of Forth I'll wager. French ships would not venture to put in at an English port. John and Matt could have ridden there in less than three days if they changed mounts often enough. But it would take us as long to send a warning message and doubtless the force will have landed by then. I warrant our navy will have been shadowing them too. It will all be general knowledge now."

"In all honesty sir, do you think they will have any success?"

Sir Daniel shook his head. "I know not what government forces are in the area but I think James' main support is in the Highlands. Deborah was telling me coming along that she is sure John was trying to raise our county last summer. It's true there are Catholics a-plenty in *north* Northumberland but who wants more turmoil after the wars we've seen?"

"Excuse me, sir, but the young men do. They have grown up in comparative peace and want action."

Sir Daniel arose and ran his hand through his cropped flaxen hair. Frederick realised he had not put on his wig. He too must have left in a mighty hurry.

"I'm afraid you are right, Frederick." He had risen too and to his delight Sir Daniel from his great height grasped him by the shoulders and exclaimed, "Thank God you did what you did. John would have been twenty miles up the Great North Road by now. I

Height of Folly

believe you have saved our house from terrible danger." He dropped his hands and exclaimed, "I forget, those poor horses are waiting saddled still. May I use one of your men to stable them again? There are only women servants here and they must be with poor Jeanetta."

"Indeed, sir. I will tell Joseph. He is not so strong for humping crates about but he can manage horses."

"And now, somehow I must talk to my wayward boy without letting him give me the slip." Sir Daniel shook his head sadly and hurried ahead of him downstairs.

CHAPTER TWENTY-FOUR

Deborah had not fared so smoothly with Jeanetta.

"John has not seen the tailor yet," she told her, "and he can't come and look at your dress. At this moment he is being prevented from ruining himself and his family."

"Ruining? What are you talking about, Deb?"

"Did you know he was mixed up with the Jacobite movement?"

Jeanetta's head jerked up. "What! Well yes, of course I did."

"You supported him in it?"

"Why not? It was to make his fortune. When James is king he could be made an earl like your funny little Frederick. He's taller and handsomer and will deserve it for his work for the king." She flapped her fan vigorously and sat down abruptly on her bed. "What do you mean 'he's being prevented'? How did you find out about the plot? What's *happened*? Has his call come and he didn't tell me? I know he wanted me to ride with him at first but that horrid le Vent wouldn't have it."

"Oh Netta, you met le Vent too! You – a mother of two lovely children – yet you wouldn't dissuade him from so mad an enterprise?"

"What have the children to do with it? And who says it's mad? Le Vent thinks it has every chance of success. The Scots will rise and an army will take the English coalfields and that will make London give way."

She flung down her fan and sprang at Deborah ignoring her beautiful dress.

"Tell me what you have done to him. Prevented him? How?"

"He's in the dungeon below this house." Deborah had to put up her hands to stop Jeanetta tearing her face with her nails. She gripped her wrists and held her firmly. Jeanetta glared up at her,

Height of Folly

her eyes like black daggers.

"You mean they are all riding to the muster and he will be left behind. It will kill him. He will die of fury and frustration. How dare you? Who put him there? He would fight them to the death, my John."

"He fell in himself so my Frederick closed the trapdoor."

"Hateful Frederick! My poor darling! He will go mad in there."

"And he will thank us all for saving him from disaster." Still gripping her wrists she forced Jeanetta's compact little form back onto the bed. "Horden is John's inheritance and you speak lightly of the Scots overrunning it and seizing the coal workings. Last time the Scots took Horden Hall Grandmother Bel was cast out into the snow with nothing. For the love of God, have you and John gone mad? England is at peace again and can prosper now. No, England and Scotland together, one nation, Britain. Together we can prosper in friendship as Christian peoples should. Do we want the clash of arms again and blood spilt in our fields? Do we, Jeanetta? Is that what you want for John, wounds or death and your children left fatherless?"

Jeanetta was whimpering now. "I only know he wanted so much to ride into battle again and do great deeds and win honour and glory. He wanted to show you all what he can do."

"Was that it? Well, we will revere him much more if he cares for his land and his tenants and brings up his children in the fear of God."

"But he will be so ashamed if he has missed it all, if someone else gets all the glory. He will be wretched. He'll be quite impossible to live with and he's so much more fun when he's happy."

"He would be more wretched dangling on the end of a rope. Don't you know that's what happens to traitors and rebels?"

"Deborah, you'll eat your words if James is made king. And if

John has no part in it he'll kill himself for shame."

In her heart Deborah was weeping for them both. Jeanetta was a poor thing and selfish but she loved John and only dimly understood the world. But John's ambition was so sad. He had tasted battle when he was thirteen and remembered the excitement more than the suffering. Was she herself to blame because he still hankered after glory? Oh she must tell him what she had just been telling Jeanetta. Surely he would see sense.

She released Jeanetta's hands and stood to her full height. "If *you* support him – whatever the outcome – he will come through this without shame. It is *your* love and admiration that will help him over his disappointment. But disappointed he will be because Father will not let him go and join the rebels even if he has to keep him locked in there during our wedding."

"Oh Deb, he wouldn't do that! John has a fine new suit and I must wear my dress. Do you think I could go to the festivities if he was locked away?"

"We'll go downstairs and see what father has decided? Where are the babies? They are very quiet."

"Oh the two nurses have them. That big attic room is the nursery. Jean makes noise enough when he toddles about up there. He usually has an afternoon sleep. Is it afternoon?"

"No, it is not yet dinner time. Should you not change out of that dress? It is too fine for the kitchen."

Jeanetta shouted for Maria who appeared from the adjoining dressing-room where she and the Grange cook-maid and scullery-maid must be hiding, Deborah realised. She supposed they had been invited to see Jeanetta dressed. No doubt they had heard every word.

"Come down when you're ready, Jeanetta. I'll see what's happening." She added to herself, God knows I would hate to be shut up in that place.

Height of Folly

She ran downstairs and found her father sitting on a chair by the trap door which was open a crack. Frederick was outside. She could hear his voice as he gave Joseph orders about the horses.

She heard John's voice. "Father, you have to let me out. I can't bear this. The oil lamp has failed and it's pitch dark."

"I am giving you a taste of what you would have suffered if you had been taken prisoner in this mad escapade. It would have been the Tower till they decided whether you deserved to hang. A night or two in the cellar of your own house is nothing compared with that."

"A night or two! You would not do that to me."

"I can't trust you not to break out and ride to join the rebels. If you could punch your brother-in-law for trying to stop you how do I know what you will do next? The longer I can keep you under restraint the safer we will all feel. If you know you will come too late there will be no point in your going."

"You cannot keep me here for ever. When they march south I will join them. Do you want me shamed before all those who made their pledges at my request?"

"That was what you were doing last summer then? And in France? Does it never occur to you that you have lost my trust for ever? That my own son could tell so many lies – do you not think how that has wounded me?"

Deborah sat down on another of the kitchen chairs. She wanted to join in, but her father was speaking her own thoughts. She could hear the crack in his voice which showed how cruelly he was tormented by what had been revealed.

John had heard it too. He shouted up, "*You* wounded? And what is my own father doing to *me*? Keeping me from my sworn duty, making me betray my comrades! And what about my sister and her man, seizing my letters so that I cannot reply, cannot fulfil my pledges, making me out a coward to all the world. I can never trust *her* again"

He seized some implement he had found and crashed it against the walls and ceiling of his prison. Then he burst out in a passion of tears, "Mother of God, I can never live this down. I will be branded as a traitor to my king and my faith for ever."

Deborah's heart was wrenched. "John," she cried out. "I hear what you are saying and I feel for you deeply. I am sorry I had to do what I've done but it was to save you from a terrible mistake. And don't blame Frederick. He was uneasy about intercepting your messages but I told him we must. You would have gone away on a wild goose chase and I wanted you so much to be at our wedding. To think you didn't care – my own brother –"

"No, Deb," her father broke in, "that is not the point. He believed in a cause that was bigger than a mere ceremony."

"I did, I do," John cried. "James Stuart is our true king under God. How can it be denied by anyone? He is the direct line, the divinely appointed. When Anne dies they are going to bring in a German prince. How can that ever be right?"

Deborah was compelled to respond. "John, you are living in the past. The law is above kings now and the law says we cannot have a Catholic monarch. If the second James had been wise and practised his faith quietly this would never have happened. Father is only trying to stop you from breaking the law. Would you not do the same if young Nat put himself in danger of arrest?"

Her father shook his head at her. "I fear he is too angry for a history lesson, Deb. John, I will give you time to cool down and reflect." He stood up stiffly.

"No, don't shut it. Don't go away. Talk to me. Tell me why you think the rising will fail. Scotland will flock to their true king when they see his standard raised on their shores. I *must* be there. And don't you see, when the king comes into his own *I* will be able to save all of you from retribution for opposing him. If I ride now I

Height of Folly

can be there to greet him. Don't you recall that day when I was three? You told me I would one day kiss his father's hand and I was to remember how he waved to me. *He* is dead but I can kiss his *son's* hand, my lawful monarch. How dare you deny me that? Did you not boast that you kissed *Charles'* hand? It impressed me so much. You spoke with your true king, face to face. Oh let me go, Father! For pity's sake, open that trap and let me out."

Jeanetta appeared at the kitchen door. She had heard the last words. Deborah saw that she had taken care with a pretty coral pink dress and matching ribbons and touched up her face again.

"John!" she screamed, running to the slit where she could just make him out and turning furious eyes on Daniel. "You brute, how dare you keep him down there. John, are you starving?"

"Why should he be starving?" her father said with astonishing coolness after the passion that had been poured out. "He has had the same meal as all of us and it is still not quite the hour for dinner. What I have done, Jeanetta, has been for you and the children as well as for John himself."

Deborah could see how her beauty moved her father. He had always loved to look on her, whatever her mood.

John shouted up, "You've not done it for our children. Do you think she wants them to be ashamed of his father?"

"That's it," Jeanetta said. "We want to be proud of him and you're stopping him and we'll all be disgraced with him. How can I go back to France and tell my family he wasn't there when the king came?"

"Did they know he was a Jacobite?"

"Well no, only my Uncle Neury."

"And would they have approved?"

"My father and mother are not much bothered about politics. King Louis would because he's sent troops to put James back on the throne. And King Louis would have made John a Chevalier of

France or something."

John yelled to her, "Don't talk to them of France, Netta. They don't care about France or the true faith or anything. Just get me out of here or I'll go mad."

Deborah could see that Frederick was hesitating outside. The March day was bright but cold. She got up and went out and brought him in. He looked down at the tiny gap by the trap door and spoke softly to her father.

"Sir, Lady Horden has sent from the Hall to know when dinner is wanted. We were all to go over there for it. And the tailor is still waiting."

"Tell her half an hour," her father said. "And, Frederick, you go and have the tailor do your repairs. The wedding preparations are to go ahead as planned."

John must have guessed who was there. "Branford, you villain, I'll never forgive you for this."

Deborah murmured, "Don't answer him. The day will come when he'll thank you." She took his arm and walked outside with him. "I can't imagine how much everyone at the Hall understands of what has happened. Will Smyth is still there. Will he have told all he knows?"

"No, he'll press his lips together and look sly."

"But talk must be buzzing among the servants if Matt is locked up. Mother and Grandmother and Ruth will be completely bemused. And oh Frederick, what about your mother? Will she still want you to marry into this madhouse when she knows all?"

He pressed her hand on his arm. "I'll warrant she'll enjoy the excitement. But I will paint John in the best light I can, a man who believed whole-heartedly in a cause and was ready to die for it."

She nodded. "Good. I love you. Go now." He went.

In the kitchen she saw that Peter and Joseph had eased the trap door open a little more, enough to pass in a fresh lantern and

Height of Folly

a hunk of bread and cheese and a flask of ale.

John's upstretched arms could just reach them when he stood on the bottom step. The stone steps came up to the side that was still covered. Deborah was amazed to see him accept the gifts in silence.

"How have you quieted him?" she whispered to her father.

"I told him that if his friends knew he was imprisoned they would not look on him as a traitor. He knows I will not let him out unless he swears a solemn oath that he will never again join them and that he will not do."

He ordered the trap to be closed.

"Oh Father it seems so cruel."

"I never thought I would do such a thing to my worst enemy, let alone my own son. You two," he said to the men, "are to take turns on guard. Cook should be about somewhere and will see you are fed, but take no strong drink."

"Yes sir."

"Where has Jeanetta gone?" Deborah asked.

"I suggested that to save John's blushes when this is all over she should go and dine at the Hall and behave as naturally as possible. She has gone to get ready."

"Ready! She preened herself just to come down to the kitchen. What more does she need but to put a cloak on against the chill."

"Then that is what she has gone to get and to bring Maria who trails everywhere with her. She says she will say John is unwell. I cannot condone lies but I'm sure she will find the truth is already known. You go ahead, Deb. I will bring her myself to see she is not intending to try her charms on these men to let John out."

When she had gone Daniel felt uneasy at John's sudden submissiveness. What if the shame was too great to bear? What if he had the means there to take his own life? He heard the mincing step of Jeanetta on the stair and went out into the passage. Maria was carrying her shawl but he could see no other change in her appearance.

Cook and the scullery maid crept behind, looking guilty at deserting their kitchen. He told them to go in and give the men something to eat. They slipped past Jeanetta who had stopped on the stair when she saw him.

"Oh!" She ground her teeth at him. "So, you're still here."

She *was* planning to bribe Peter and Joseph to release John.

"I wish to escort you to dinner at the Hall."

"And leave John to starve."

"He has been given better rations that he would get in a real prison. Come. This is a sad business but you are going to be calm and brave for John's sake before servants and our guests." He took her arm firmly and walked her through the kitchen. She was dragging her feet and looking back. Peter and Joseph sat on the wine crates munching on bread and cheese and regarding her with stolid faces. Cook and the scullery maid busied themselves cutting more bread and trying to look as if everything was normal.

When they were outside Jeanetta looked up at him, her eyes huge and pleading. "I would never have believed you of all people, always so kind and generous, could have tortured your own son like this." He set his face and kept walking her along the woodland path. She persisted, "Do you think I can sit in company and eat a dinner with my beloved shut up in a hole?"

She continued like this all the way and he patted her hand from time to time but could think of nothing to say. His thoughts were now on what Eunice would say to him. Deborah would have told her everything. John was her precious baby. He was surprised she had not already come running to demand his release.

They emerged from the path onto the lawn before the Hall and Eunice was there on the doorstep watching for him. She would see

Height of Folly

how he was almost dragging Jeanetta along, ignoring her upturned face and her frantic pleas and she would know he was hating it all. But what she would say herself was, despite their years of marriage, a mystery to him.

She took Jeanetta's other arm. "Come, you must put a good face on it, my dear, for all our sakes." It was what he had said himself.

"But do you know what he has done? Put my John in that horrid dungeon."

"I know." Eunice was looking up at him with a very steady gaze. "I didn't know you had so much strength of will, Daniel. You have surprised me."

"You are not angry?"

"Angry! That you have almost certainly saved his life? No, I admire your courage because I know how much your soft heart must have loathed to do it."

"Soft heart!" cried Jeanetta.

"Hush. They are all ready for us in the dining-room. Now for John's sake behave with dignity, my dear. When he comes back into the fold he will be glad to know you bore yourself well."

Daniel, blessing Eunice in his heart for her words of praise, saw that his mother, Deborah, Frederick, Ruth and Lady Branford were already seated. There was no place laid for John. They had obviously fallen silent as soon as the front door opened and they must have heard what had passed in the hallway. So there were five faces turned to them as they came in. Each seemed to be waiting for someone else to speak first in this extraordinary situation.

Eunice broke the silence. "Daniel, will you say grace?"

He stumbled through his customary words without adding anything special and they sat down. Jeanetta was quivering with suppressed sobs beside his mother. She put an arm round her shoulders and gave her a squeeze. Deborah and Ruth who always served the dishes from the side table rose to do it.

It was Lady Branford who broke the awkwardness of the occasion. "You mustn't mind me being here you know. Deborah has made it all clear to me. As long as we can still see these two safely married I can only say I will grieve with those who are grieving and laugh when it is all resolved and we can rejoice together. At least I can say of the dear boy who is missing that I admire his clinging to his principles but admire even more the steadfastness of all of you that want to save him from them. There now, have I spouted a paradox, Fred. Is that what you call a contradictory sort of saying?"

Daniel had to admire her. She was actually smiling round at them all and trying to raise a laugh under the most inauspicious of circumstances. Frederick he could see looked a little embarrassed, but Mother Bel was happy to put in her word.

"Thank you, May, you've put that beautifully." Gracious heavens, they are May and Bel already, he thought. "But I would like to visit the dear boy who is missing," she added.

Then Eunice had her say. "Mother Bel, I claim the right of first visit. Our Lord told us to visit prisoners but I never thought my son would be in such a predicament. I can barely eat for thinking of him cold and alone and suffering in his mind and if you will excuse me in five minutes I will go to him. He needs to hear that his mother endorses heartily the action taken – as I understand it – first by you, Frederick, in response to Deborah's anxiety and wisely continued by you, Daniel. Jeanetta, I know you will not agree with that –"

She squeaked, "I didn't want him to go unless it was a great success."

"No, well that we won't know for some days, but I beg you to believe that what has been done has been done out of love, for him and for you and the children."

Height of Folly

She took two more mouthfuls of the beef stew that Cook-maid had had gently cooking on the trivet over the kitchen fire for two hours. "Tell cook it was very good but I will miss her pudding today. Will you let me leave you?"

It crossed Daniel's mind that if Peter and Joseph moved the trap door a crack her anguish at seeing her boy in such a strait might overcome her and she would have to let him out. It was a risk but he must trust her after what she had said to him.

"Yes, go Eunice. The men there will give you a slit to speak through. It takes two to move the door."

Eunice rose. As she went out she said, "I can pray with him through a slit."

Deborah waited till they heard the front door shut, then she said, "It's all right, Father. Don't worry about Mother. She's not going to let him out."

Jane tapped and looked round the door.

"If you please, Sir Daniel, Cook says has she to send a bowl of stew to Matt in the stable block? Elspeth's crying that he'll be hungry."

"Tell Elspeth she may take him some but Luke and Walter must go with her to see he can't break out. I will come and speak with him later."

Jane bobbed and went out.

"Matt became very close to John when we were in France," Deborah said. "You won't let him go yet, will you, Father? If he was free he might ride off to join the rebels and report how we prevented John from going. And if he was arrested Horden Hall would be tainted with the name of treason."

Ruth sat up, open-mouthed. "Oh Deb, that mustn't happen or Simon won't marry me. His father is on the council in York and supports the Whigs in Parliament."

Daniel looked at his younger daughter in surprise. "That's the first time I've ever heard you mention politics."

"They've never been exciting till now."

Daniel looked at his mother. "Are *you* finding this disaster exciting, Mother Bel?"

"The only excitement *I* want is my Deb's wedding. I shall tell John that he has no right to spoil the occasion for her."

Jeanetta spoke up. "It won't be John who spoils it. A great Jacobite army may come marching by and take prisoner all who don't support them. Then *I'll* tell them how you stopped John from joining them and you'll all be sorry. They'll probably fire the Hall."

Daniel frowned her down. "Jeanetta, when Eunice comes back don't you dare say such a thing in front of her. You know Deborah was born when the Hall was on fire. I will not have fire mentioned at her wedding. We have talked enough of this wretched business. If there *is* a rebel army it will only fight if opposed by government troops. It would be madness for them to alienate the civilian population." He stood up. "I think we have all finished. Let us disperse."

CHAPTER TWENTY-FIVE

When John heard the trap door being scraped back he was ready for it. He had eaten every scrap of food and drunk the ale. If I am to ride I must be fortified, he told himself. And I will ride. If I have to knock Father to the ground I will do it. He has no right on earth to stop me.

The iron bar he had found in a corner of the dungeon and which he had used so far in wild hammerings, he would wedge in the gap when it was next opened. He had upturned an empty crate on the bottom step and climbed onto it. He planned to manoeuvre the bar so far into the gap that he would be able to lever the trap door along. Of course they would try to stop him. They would grab at the bar and he would strike their fingers with it. It was a wild hope but they would see how desperate he was. If he could get his hands over the lip they would not dare to crush them. There must be limits to how far they would go.

The scraping sound was accompanied by a voice as soon as there was the tiniest of openings. His mother! That was a blow. He couldn't risk hurting his mother but surely he could move her by persuasion not force. Standing on the crate he lowered the bar and laid it by his feet.

"Mother! You've come to let me out of here?"

"No John. Unless you will give me your word not to run away."

"I can't do that. I am pledged to the cause."

"A Bible oath?" She sounded horrified.

"No, but some chose to swear to me on their Bibles that they would come when called. What will they think of me if it is I who fail?"

"It is pride that feels shame at failure. If you had been humble you would never have found yourself in this predicament. I come only for your physical comfort while we restrain you from this desperate enterprise. I will insert this thick woollen rug through the hole. Wrap yourself in it and I will find another for you to lie on at night."

"Night! You will not leave me here all night."

"If we must to save your life, we will."

"Why do you all speak of this thing as if it would end in bloodshed? You will look fools if Deb is wed in Nether Horden church while a great army of Scots, French and English are marching by on the road from Edinburgh to London. More will join at Newcastle and from all the towns on the route. And of this family I only will be on the side of right and truth."

"But it is not right to take up arms against your lawful government."

"Father thought it right that Cromwell's government was overthrown. The true king came back then and was welcomed by the whole nation. The same will happen this time and you are stopping me from being there by this cruel restraint."

He was proud of this argument. She must be wavering.

"John, you have judged history wrongly. Cromwell was corrupted by power and had become a cruel tyrant. Our present queen is ruling with parliament and the consent of the nation."

"And when she dies without issue the crown should go to James where it should have gone when his father tamely abandoned his duty as king. The nation will not accept the rule of a German prince."

"The nation will not accept a Catholic who will put it in thrall to the Pope in Rome. John, it has grieved me to the core that you have deceitfully gone over to the faith of your wife without a word to us. I was always fearful when you married her but I believed you would still attend the church of your family. I cannot speak of these things to you now. What has grieved me even more are the

Height of Folly

lies you have told. Surely you see that a thing that has caused you to lie so often must be of the devil who is the father of lies."

"I only lied because you would have stopped me doing what I knew was right. Those are not bad lies then. How can they be?"

"Oh John, all lies are evil. Nothing can justify them. You could have spoken honestly of your opinions and we could have shown you the folly of them. Here take this rug and the Book of Psalms. You have light. Read and pray. Think about others and the distress you have brought on us all on the eve of your sister's wedding."

"Ah that's it, isn't it? Deb's wedding to her precious earl. That must not be upset. If you let me go I would be safely out of your way. Would that not be happier for you all?"

She was easing the book through. He took it and let it fall to the ground. Then came the rug, unfolded. It landed on his shoulders. Instinctively he drew its warmth round him. Now he could hear her giving unseen men orders to close the trap. No, he couldn't bear that. He bent down and snatched up the iron bar and pushed it into the gap. He heard a little shriek from his mother.

"Oh you have cut my chin. You might have put out my eye."

He dropped the bar. "Mother, I'm sorry, but you mustn't let them close it. Don't!"

All he heard then was the grating of the wood on the stone floor and the slit of light vanished. Had he scarred his mother for life? His wretchedness increased a hundredfold. He took his supporting hand from the stone wall to hold the sides of the rug together but only succeeded in drawing it round his legs in a tangle. He shifted one foot. The crate overbalanced and tipped him sideways so that he landed not on the steps behind him but directly onto the floor of the dungeon. The Book of Psalms was crushed under him but he knew nothing of it. He had knocked himself insensible.

Prue Phillipson

Daniel came over to the Grange when the meal was over and found Eunice dripping blood into a basin while Nurse Capot tried to staunch the flow with rags from a torn up sheet. Eunice half turned her head to him.

"It seems worse than it is."

Nurse Capot looked up at him. "My lady has so great courage!"

Peter and Joseph were standing about looking helpless.

Joseph said, "I'm afraid Master John thrust up an iron bar he had found down there."

"An accident," Eunice said. "Of course I was bending down to speak with him. I am afraid he is not reconciled to missing this uprising."

"Well, *he* will not be uprising in a hurry, after this. Can you put a pad underneath her chin, Nurse, and bind it on? If you lie down, my darling, it might stop bleeding."

A wad of cloth soaked in vinegar which Joseph said was used on wounds in battle was pressed on the place and strips of cloth round her head held it in position. Daniel fastened these round with his own hands and told Nurse Capot she could return to baby Diana.

"I can't talk," Eunice mumbled through closed teeth. He led her through to the Grange's downstairs sitting-room where there was an old couch brought from the Hall. The drawing-room on the first floor he had had elegantly papered and newly furnished for John and Jeanetta.

"I wish to God they had stayed in France," he said, settling her to lie flat on the couch. She made negative grunts. "I know, he is my heir and we are to lose our precious Deborah. Let us pray he has learnt a lesson from this and will devote himself to Horden. Or should I buy him an army commission so he can work this longing for glory out of his system? Let him serve his country on the right side." Eunice tried to shake her head and growl her disapproval again. "The navy cured me of *my* restlessness but he is older than I was and a married man with children. Do you feel, my darling, that he never really grew up?"

She turned pleading eyes on him. "I'm sorry, you can't answer." She looked a pathetic sight. He tucked a blanket round her and kissed her on the forehead. Some blood had stained through the wad but no more was dripping out. Perhaps she would not be too marked for the wedding.

Voices came from the kitchen and his mother and Jeanetta appeared in the doorway and looked down at Eunice.

"Joseph told us what happened," Mother Bel said. "There's Frederick with a bruise on his chin and now poor Eunice. Jeanetta, your sweet John has turned into a wild beast. I had thought to talk some comfort to him if he's to stay where he is but I shan't have my ancient looks spoilt for the wedding and Deb had better not go near him."

Jeanetta broke into sobs. "He didn't mean – he's not a wild beast. You've all driven him to this."

"Nay, I am trying to make light of what is a bad business. What can we do, Dan? When will there be some news do you think, if French troops have landed?"

Jeanetta brushed aside her tears with a wild gesture. "They will come here and take over the coal works, so John told me."

"I see," said Daniel, "and that is what our son would like to happen to his inheritance, is it? So if they land on the south bank of the Firth of Forth and march at once I would say three days from disembarking perhaps."

"They will arrive on the wedding day," his mother said.

"I will send into Newcastle tomorrow and see if any news has come. Eunice I will have the carriage brought round to take you back to the Hall."

Her eyes said no. His mother laid a hand on his arm. "Let her lie a while here and then you can walk her gently along the path." Her eyes said yes to that.

"Very well. I will sit by her." And he drew up the worn basket chair. The room had only a window seat and some bookcases that had been considered too shabby for the Hall library.

"It's cold here," his mother said, "those men of Frederick's in the kitchen are doing nothing. I'll tell one of them to get a fire lit in this hearth." And she bustled out, glad to have something to do.

Daniel looked up at Jeanetta. "Why do you not go and play with your babies? They never see you."

"Nurse Capot has gone back to Diana and Nurse Forêt may be settling Jean for his afternoon sleep."

"*Nathaniel*," he said pointedly, "needs his mother especially when his father is not about. I have seen John throw a ball to him and Nat loves to run and fetch it just like a little dog. Nurse Forêt is too slow and heavy to play with him properly. You could have fun with him."

"How can I play when John is shut up in there? He will die of cold."

"No, his mother lowered a rug to him. If I release him he will take horse and join the rebel army. He has told me he will. Would you have me tie him up and set guard over him? No, I will go and speak with him again when he has had more time to consider and realise that his whole plan was the height of folly."

Peter came in bearing a bucket of kindling and one of coals.

Jeanetta glared at him. "You and Joseph will be gone soon but if you ever tell anyone in Hertfordshire of this day's work I will bring a curse on you."

She flung up her head and stalked out of the room and up the stairs calling for Maria.

Daniel got up and pushed Eunice's couch, which was on little wheels, towards the blaze Peter was creating in the hearth. She

Height of Folly

waved her hand from side to side and he remembered her terror of fire and stopped it at a safer distance.

"How are you, my love?" he asked her and she managed a crooked smile.

It was not till late afternoon when he had escorted Eunice home that Daniel came back and ordered the trap door to be opened enough for him to look in. At first he could see nothing. The lantern must have burnt itself out.

He called, "John, have you had time to reflect? I would wish to release you if you are prepared solemnly to swear not to ride away to join the rebels. John?"

There was no answer. Was it a trick? He could be hiding behind the stone stair and come rushing up if the trap was completely opened. Will Smyth was now in the kitchen, Joseph and Peter having been given the task of cleaning and polishing the Branford carriage ready for the wedding. Will Smyth's bulk was reassuring.

Daniel, crouched by the hole, looked up at him and spoke low. "Will, I'm minded to open the trap fully. If Master John tries to make a run for it will you help me restrain him?"

"Better than that, Sir Daniel. I am armed with the old earl's trusty pistol."

"Heaven forbid! It has not come to shooting."

"Nay, sir, I wouldn't fire it but there's nothing like the sight of one to check a runaway."

"Well, lay it on the corner of the table and help me move these crates."

In a moment the opening was clear and the afternoon sunlight streaming through the kitchen window was enough to lighten the dim depths.

"What! He is there. Is he sleeping?" Then Daniel noticed the tipped up crate. "Dear God, he has fallen." Icy fear gripped him.

Prue Phillipson

Was he dead? Had this horrible series of events ended with the very thing they had tried to prevent?

Sick at heart he began to descend the steps.

"Beware sir," Will Smyth called down. "It may be a trick."

"It's not." Daniel was turning his son's body over to see his face. It was white and cold to the touch. "Oh God, John!" He took him up in his arms.

Will Smyth was cautiously descending. He pushed aside the crate and lifted John's limp hand.

"There is a pulse, Sir Daniel. See he has a bruise on the side of his head. He is concussed, but very cold, lying on this stone floor."

Daniel felt the blood in his own face beginning to flow back. "We must take him up quick." He put his hands under John's shoulders.

"If you'll allow me, sir," Will Smyth said, "I will carry him up on my back. That will be easier than two of us together." He crouched down and Daniel helped him to get hold of the flopping arms and heave the body into position. He followed with his hand on John's back as Will mounted into the kitchen. They took him to the couch where Eunice had lain earlier and pushed it close to the fire. Will went back for the rug that had fallen off him and found the Book of Psalms. He brought up the two empty lanterns as well and closed the trap.

"No one will ever go in there again," Daniel said as he reappeared. "Someone must go to the Hall and tell his mother. No, she is resting. Tell Deborah. I will fetch Nurse Capot from upstairs. Jeanetta will come down too but the nurse and Deborah will be more useful."

"I'll send Peter to the Hall, sir, but meanwhile we must get Master John heated up. Brandy and warming pans I suggest."

The nurse came, Jeanetta came, screaming that now they had killed John between them. But it was Will Smyth's ministrations

Height of Folly

that were the most helpful. By the time Peter had come back bringing both Eunice and Deborah John had opened his eyes and was drinking the brandy Will held to his lips. Eunice had discarded her bandages.

She said, "The bleeding stopped. See it is but a small cut. How is my poor boy?"

John was staring about him over the glass at all the faces looking down at him.

"What's up, what's wrong? How did I come to fall asleep in here?" His voice sounded thick and slurred. Daniel wondered if Will was being too generous with the brandy.

"I thought to send for the physician," Daniel murmured to Eunice, "but we don't want any of this known outside."

"No no," she said, "all he can ever think of is to open a vein. The boy needs all the blood he's got. He's not in a fever. We can nurse him as well as anyone."

Deborah whispered, "He knows us but he has forgotten he was ever in the dungeon."

Jeanetta moaned, "What else has he forgotten?" and she ran upstairs and brought little Nathaniel down – the only time Daniel had ever seen her carrying one of her children. "Jean," she said, "va au Papa."

"Eh bien, Jean." He took the boy up who began pummelling his face happily. "Non, papa mal au tête."

He set him down again and put his hand to the side of his head. "I've a big bump here. When did I fall over? Where? I don't remember."

Nurse Capot came in from the kitchen with a pack of something to lay on the bruise.

"Let us leave him in peace," Eunice said but Daniel feared Jeanetta would try to awaken his memory of what had passed.

"You stay, my dear." He drew her aside. "I am going to speak to

Matt and tell him there is no question of his master riding anywhere for several days after a blow like that. His duty is to stay and minister to him when I think I can safely release him. I am minded to ride into Newcastle myself and see if there is news of a French landing. Luke can accompany me."

Eunice begged him to leave it till the morning. "For it may be dark," she said, "before you could be home and I would be fearful. The good Lord has saved our boy till now and we must be thankful for that."

John was very giddy when they got him upstairs to bed but that, Daniel thought, was the effect of the brandy. He seemed only to want to go to sleep. He asked once for Matt but seemed satisfied when Jeanetta said, "I want to take care of you myself."

Downstairs Daniel had a word with both Will Smyth and Frederick. "I cannot see that he will stir all night but as a precaution will you not only bolt the doors but take the keys out and look after them in your own room. I feel I cannot trust him not to ride away if he recalls what has happened."

Will Smyth nodded. "He will not get past me and his lordship, Sir Daniel."

CHAPTER TWENTY-SIX

At first light next day the fields and woods lay at peace under a pearly sky. Wars and rumours of wars could not have seemed further away when Daniel accompanied by Luke, the groom, rode into Newcastle.

There were government troops in the town and a general air of relief and excitement. Shopkeepers stood at their doors and cheered as a body of soldiers marched past heading north.

Daniel dismounted at the staging inn and asked a gentleman who had alighted from the coach from Edinburgh what the news was of a French landing.

"Nay," he laughed, "they never landed. They've scuttled back to France."

"Never landed? Where heard you this?"

"In Edinburgh. They were sighted off the coast and there were Jacobite forces drawn up to meet the so-called King James. But boats that put out to meet him were turned back. Royal navy ships had shadowed the French from Dunkirk where unlucky young James caught measles I understand, so their ships were held up with our navy just waiting to follow 'em when they came out. They say the French Admiral took fright that he would lose half his fleet and has turned about. They were pretty battered by a storm coming here but I reckon it was Her Majesty's ships scared them off."

Daniel heaved a huge sigh of relief. "So our troops have no need to march to control a rebellion." He was watching another well armed band marching past with colours flying and drums beating.

"Ay, but they're going to round up the rebels. I wager they'll hang most of 'em to stop it happening again. But I doubt old

Louis will want to send again. His military have no stomach for a fight here the way our great Duke is knocking 'em about over there."

"Well, I thank you, sir."

They touched their hats to each other and Daniel remounted eager to head home with the news. Then he remembered a list of errands Eunice had asked him to do for things for the wedding. He turned to Luke and gave him the orders and rode back alone.

When he reached the Hall he could see through the library windows many animated figures, hands waving about, heads moving. Everyone seemed to be there. Deborah's flaxen head appeared above everyone else. She too seemed to be talking with great vigour. In fact judging by the sounds he could hear even before he dismounted and Walter came to take his horse, they seemed all to be talking at once. The news he brought would surely silence them all. He strode up the steps, flung down his hat on the hall table and passed under the right hand archway to the library door which stood open so the whole household could listen in. He stepped inside and shut it firmly behind him and now it was he who dominated the room as all eyes turned to him. The only words he had distinguished as he came in were John's in a furious tirade against Lord Branford.

"Even when you are married to Deb I never want to see you again."

Eunice looked up at Daniel with a face of woe. "It has come back to him, all of it. He still thinks Frederick arranged the dungeon to be open so he would fall into it. He won't listen to any of us."

Deborah said, "Frederick and I were sitting quietly in here looking over the list of expected guests when he came in with a face of thunder. Poor Netta was running behind him worrying he would do himself an injury. And of course the noise brought

Height of Folly

everyone else from the parlour."

John glared defiantly round on them all and then poked Frederick in the chest.

"I can still ride. Somewhere I will meet them. I've told Matt to saddle up again. If you try to stop me this time I will draw my sword on you." He swung round to Daniel. "And I will find it hard to forgive *you*, Father, for keeping me here under duress."

Mother Bel, from the corner chair where she had seated herself said, "John, say no more words you will regret bitterly very soon. Your father's face is full of news. Dan, you have been to the town. Have you heard anything of this rebellion?"

"Well John, there *is* no rebellion for you to join. There has been no landing. The French ships have been chased away by the Royal Navy and the rebels are being rounded up by government soldiers at this moment."

Everyone in the room uttered exclamations of delight, even Jeanetta, Daniel noticed.

John's mouth hung open for a second. Then he straightened his back and glared at his father. "You are lying to me. That cannot be. They would not come so far with their precious cargo and not set him ashore."

"But they have. For all we know he may have been pleading with them to land but the fact is they have not. So you can get down on your knees and thank God for your family that has saved you from a certain and ignominious death. I am told the rebels they catch are likely to be hanged as traitors."

John did not sink to his knees but he did sink to the nearest chair and bowed his head on his hands. "I cannot believe it has all come to this. The months, nay years of preparation!" He looked up. "No, Father, they will be landing elsewhere. They will put ashore on the highland coast. Loch Tay perhaps. They could not abandon it. I was told twenty-three ships and thousands of troops.

Prue Phillipson

Who has told you they have returned to France? It cannot be."

"A gentleman just arrived from Edinburgh. Newcastle is in happy mood. Did you ever think the population here wanted their lives disrupted by war again?"

Eunice went over to John and put an arm round his shoulders. He shrugged it off. "You too connived at my imprisonment. Was that done like a mother?"

Daniel, still standing opposite the window, saw Matt approaching warily from the path to the Grange. "I am sorry you involved Matthew in this, John. He must be coming to tell you the horses are saddled again." John looked round as Matthew passed the window, his mobile face showing alarm at the gathering of people in the library.

"Stay there, John. *I* will speak to him."

Daniel went out and called to him. "I let you out in good faith. You can get back and stable those horses again. Master John has accepted that there is nowhere for you to ride today."

Matt looked suspicious. "I'd like to hear that from his own lips, begging your pardon, Sir Daniel."

"Now Matthew, just you understand this. You were allocated to accompany Master John on his travels because you are our most experienced and longest-serving manservant. But it is I who still pay your wages. You answer to *me*. You have your quarters at the Grange and look after the stables there but it is I who will discipline you if you step out of line again. Just tell me, were you yourself convinced of the rightness of the pretender's cause?"

Matt hung his head. "It seemed like a bit of adventure, sir. Life's mighty quiet here."

"You've said enough. The rebellion has failed. Be thankful you were not there and if Master John ventures on any more wild escapades come and tell me."

Matt touched his hat but couldn't bear not to put in a word

Height of Folly

more. "That could sound a bit like spying on him, sir."

Daniel lost patience. "Then spy on him for God's sake, rather than you and he should dangle together on a gibbet."

At that Matt fled back to the Grange.

Back in the library Daniel found his mother hard at work on the task of reconciliation, aided – or possibly impeded – by the efforts of Lady Branford who seemed to be trying to persuade John to laugh at the whole thing. That he could not do. His mind was full of fears for the families he had visited the previous summer and what they would think of his non-appearance. Had the men ridden off themselves without a word from him and were they now being hounded down and taken prisoner?

"I wonder about le Vent. Did he rouse them in my place or will he still come seeking me and upbraid me for my disloyalty?"

He looked up at Deborah. "You are going to say this is not the atmosphere for a happy family wedding."

"I am and I do say it. We are rejoicing because the nation is at peace again and because of that and the happiness Frederick and I are looking forward to we are ready to forgive and forget the lies you told us in France and the trouble you have caused here."

"Well said," cried Lady Branford. "Fred, come forward and shake John's hand."

"Nay," Daniel said, "if you'll pardon me, madam. John must be in a better frame of mind first. He might shake hands now but does it come from his heart? I heard him say he never wanted to see Lord Branford again. There are things you must take back, John, and there is a thing you must do to satisfy me. But first stand up when I'm speaking to you."

John looked at Jeanetta. "You see they treat me like a little boy here."

"Yes." She twined her arms round his waist as he grudgingly rose to his feet. "We had better go back to France at once."

Prue Phillipson

"I'll treat you like a man when you act like one," Daniel said. "This place is your inheritance and if I am to feel comfortable leaving it in your hands I would want you to swear a solemn oath you would never again think of taking up arms against your lawful monarch. I fear these fanatical people will not accept this setback quietly but may again be plotting and scheming to put James on the British throne."

John stared at him. "Are you saying, Father, that you will disinherit me if I can't take such an oath?"

Eunice looked up nervously. "I like not taking oaths. John's word should be enough."

"It would be if he had not told us so many lies. No, John, believe me, if I doubt your commitment to this place and observe you hankering after rebellion and sedition and your strong connections with France I would do what I said. I will not leave what I have built up here to one who cares nothing for it and who would gladly remove his family abroad."

"Who could you leave Horden to if not to me?" John shouted at him.

"Ruth may have a family. Deborah and Frederick may produce sons and daughters. If they have an heir to the Branford estates they may be able to spare one for Horden. At least I am surer my Deb will never lose her interest in the place."

Deborah stepped to his side with tears in her eyes. "That I won't, Father, but I fear my presence has always overshadowed John as I have always overtopped him. When I am in Hertfordshire he'll come more into his own. Is that not possible, John?"

John looked up at her with a mixture of longing and desperation. It was the same look she had seen so often in her childhood when she set him goals he knew he could never attain to. He didn't speak.

Jeanetta sobbed, "I want to go home. I want to take my babies

Height of Folly

back to Rombeau. Oh," she put her hand to her mouth, "I've just had a fearful thought. We must tell Uncle Neury to destroy all his papers. Someone might find them and know what you were up to."

"Indeed, I might have to go," he said then. "At least till all this has blown over. But will they ever forget I let them down when the call came? And if some are imprisoned and some hung the families will never forgive me for being still alive. They will come for me."

Jeanetta jumped up and down like a child. "We must go at once. You won't mind if we miss your wedding, Deb, will you?"

"I will, very much."

"And the ports will be watched for fugitives," Daniel said. "That is what you must *not* do. Your safety is in having been here all the time and life being as normal as possible. It would be very odd to our friends and neighbours, who are *not* among your so-called comrades, if the bride's brother and family were not at her wedding."

"Then I must *write* to Uncle Neury," Jeanetta said.

"That is also what you should *not* do. Letters to France are likely to be opened here and read. Your uncle will have heard of the failure of the plot and will have the sense to destroy anything that might incriminate John. The French government will not punish their *own* people for being involved since the expedition had King Louis' backing. He may punish the admiral who turned tail, that's all."

"So what *should* we do *now?*" Jeanetta turned her big black eyes, filmed with tears, up to Daniel as she still clung with her arms round John's waist. He felt her power and her helplessness both at once. She had not been the wife John needed but that could not be undone now.

He softened his voice. "Why don't you go and dress up again?" and to John he said, "I sent the tailor away yesterday but when I heard the news I told Luke to call on him in the town and ask him to come today for your fitting. I assumed you would be in a proper state to see him and I will expect you to behave – as I have already said – quite as normal. This is for your own sakes."

Jeanetta was excited again. "Oh yes, John you must see my dress and I need you to choose between two hats."

She pulled him towards the door. As he went, Daniel heard him mutter, "Dress, hats. Today should have been my day of glory."

Daniel addressed the remaining company. "Our servants have seen and heard too much. Except for Maria and the two nurses I need to summon them all together, including your men, Lord Branford, if that is agreeable to you, and explain as best I can what some of these unusual goings-on have signified. I trust they will never be questioned by the authorities, but at least they can say with truth that John has never left these premises. I will do that now and then I trust we can proceed to dinner at peace as one family."

"Amen to that," said Eunice.

Before he left the room Daniel felt he must say something to Lady Branford. She had bobbed up from the stool she had found to sit on and was approaching him with her cheerful smile.

"I do beg your pardon, Lady Branford, that you have had to witness something that I assure has been a rarity in this house – a family dispute."

"Bless your heart, Sir Daniel, you have handled it beautifully. As for me, well, it was better than many a play I've had to witness on the London stage."

It was not quite what he wanted to hear but the compliment to himself was very comfortable. He bowed and left them all to make his way through to the kitchen where cook was beginning to prepare dinner. He gave orders for all the servants to be fetched, from the stables, the Grange, the gardens and to assemble in the

Height of Folly

Hall kitchen.

As he feared Eunice came through after him. In her presence he could in no way smother the truth. As they were assembling, all agog and whispering, she said softly to him, "Daniel, as your housekeeper may *I* be the one who speaks to them?"

He was startled, but as he didn't know what he was going to say he thought he might risk it. "If I can add anything that I see fit afterwards."

She nodded. Her small size meant there were several who couldn't see her so she got up on the sturdy steps used to reach the vessels stored on the top cupboards.

They were all assembled now and gazing up at her in silent surprise.

"Friends, I speak to you as Eunice, mother of John."

Daniel cringed. This was her leveller background speaking.

"Those of you who are parents know that children can be troublesome." She glanced at cook whose son had been caught by a gamekeeper stealing pheasants. "My John was led astray in France by those who want James as our king. When we found this out we stopped him from going to meet with others over here who support James Stuart's claim. We have heard today that James has *not* been set ashore in Scotland and the French ships have taken him back again. We hope to learn more later but that appears to be the end of the matter. All you need to know is that no one from Horden Hall has been involved or will be involved in this. As it is all over we trust you not to speak of it outside our little family gathered here today. We are all sinners in one way or another and will be judged by God at the last day. Let us be glad if anyone holds us back from committing a wrong. Now we are looking forward to the wedding of Deborah and Frederick the day after tomorrow and you all know what duties we expect from you to make it a happy day. Daniel is in charge and has promised you an extra day's pay as part of the celebrations. Marriage is a holy ceremony so I trust you not to spend it in strong drink. May God bless you all."

She held out a hand to Daniel and stepped down. There was silence as she did so, the silence of astonishment at the bare Christian names and the simplicity of the statement. As she had announced the little bonus Daniel had nothing more to say.

"Thank you all, you may return to your duties."

To his surprise it was Matt who set up a cheer and then they were all joining in, except he noticed Will Smyth whose face was stony. The sooner he is back in Castle Branford, Daniel thought, the happier he will be, though whether Frederick and Deborah can ever meet his idea of an earl and a countess I cannot imagine. Perhaps he should retire to a cottage and live on memories.

"Was that to your liking?" Eunice peered up at him.

"It was to *their* liking certainly. But will they follow *John* as devotedly when *his* day comes? I shall certainly require a solemn promise from him that he will live here and serve his Queen and country faithfully if he is to inherit Horden."

"This place means much to you, I know, but you will enjoy it for many more years. You are in good health. John will be a different man when he takes over."

"I believe he will. I had to grow up before Horden mattered so much to me."

They returned to the library where Mother Bel, Deborah and Frederick were showing Lady Branford the guest list. She looked up as Daniel and Eunice came in.

"They are mostly farmers I hear. I shall get on with them splendidly."

CHAPTER TWENTY-SEVEN

Deborah stood at her narrow arched window on the morning of her wedding day and remembered the first day of the century when she had wondered if life would ever change for her. She went to her cheval mirror as she had done that day.

"Today it will happen, Scarecrow," she said aloud. "Today you will be a wife of the sweetest-tempered man in the world. Two days from now he and I will go a long way south and inhabit a room four times the size of this in a castle five times the size of Horden Hall. I will look out on a vast, lush parkland with great oaks and beeches as far as the eye can see and I will be called the Countess of Branford. But all I can think of is our bodies, his and mine. We have never seen each other naked. What will he think of mine, long, small-breasted, strong-limbed? And his? Neat, firm, athletic. We have ridden together and he sits a horse well, brought up on a farm. I have never known him ail anything and nor have I. Surely we can produce a child."

There was a tap on her door as there had been eight years before but this was her mother's knock not her father's. She took one stride and opened the door.

"I thought you were talking to someone." Her mother was not yet dressed for the wedding but some ointment obscured the mark on her chin. A grey wool bed-gown was wrapped round her. She reminded Deborah of a dumpy little pawn in a chess set.

"Just myself. Come and sit on the window seat."

Eunice sat, becoming smaller than ever. "I should have so much to say to my daughter on her wedding morning but I find myself only thinking of my wedding to your father, the same church, the same villagers, a generation on. And you could say too we were a mismatched couple, he six-foot-three, me five-foot-one."

Prue Phillipson

"Did you wonder how it would be in bed with him?"

Her mother's eyes opened wide. "Not for a minute. I thought of my tiny hovel with my father compared to this great mansion and prayed not to become proud. And now you are to go from this to something so much grander. People will say our family is going up in the world. In the *world*, yes."

Ah now, Deborah thought, she is on safe ground. But she and father did the other thing or John and Ruth and I would not be here.

"Yes," her mother went on, "that is what I should be saying to you, never let the world swamp the things of the spirit. Yet I don't fear you with that, Deborah. You don't speak much of your faith but I feel it is strong and I believe Frederick's is a solid rock. I don't show my feelings very much as you know but I love Frederick. I love his mother too although she is so different from me, so light-hearted, so care-free, but that too rests on a sound base. She seems without pride, except in Frederick himself. She wouldn't let him go to his true family when he was a baby. She feared he would be taken from her and brought up in the world's ways. Like me she made nothing of the grandeur of his title. When he was grown she knew she had to give him to Mary – she has talked with me of Mary, a quiet, meek little thing. And she remained at hand herself though she made them have their own home. Now she has accepted you, so different from Mary and says she may choose a cottage on the estate to give you your own life together."

"She has no need. She has her own separate suite of rooms. The place is vast. You and father must come and see it soon."

"We will." She stood up and took Deborah's hands. "I can let you go to your new life with an easy mind. It was so hard when John married Jeanetta. I was unhappy at Castle Rombeau on their wedding day. I felt it was all wrong and would come to no good.

Height of Folly

And it hasn't." Her chin quivered.

"It may not be so bad, Mother. They love each other in a wild passionate way and I trust they will both grow up as they watch their babies grow up. They will be so proud of them for they will be handsome children, that's certain."

"But John will not give your father the solemn promise he requires for him to have Horden and that will drive them back to France where John seems to live a life of idle pleasures. John needs to have demands made upon him or he will be lazy and that makes him unhappy and restless."

Their hands were still clasped. Deborah pressed her mother's and withdrew her own. Was John still to be uppermost in everyone's minds even on this day?

"Shall we go to breakfast? Suzette has been to me twice already to know at what hour she can begin dressing me."

Eunice pulled herself together. "Yes, yes of course. The Grange party will not appear till we all go to church. I trust all is well over there. That Will Smyth likes everything to be done properly and will keep them all in order."

She hurried out and Deborah followed slowly. She knew her father would not come. He would be busying himself over arrangements. What she dreaded was the morning of the day of their departure. He would struggle and fail to contain his tears and that would trigger hers when she wanted to show Frederick unalloyed happiness.

Suzette took half an hour to dress her and another half hour to do her hair. All the time Ruth kept looking in to have this or that adjusted in her own dress and to assess Deborah critically.

"Bride's headdresses are often tall but I suppose you didn't want that. You need more flowers in your hair, then. I worry that in some lights the dress looks more green than blue. And you know green is unlucky. It will bring rain on the wedding if nothing worse."

"Well, my eyes are neither green nor blue but in between."

"I suppose you'll do. I shall wear pink when I'm married to Stephen, perhaps a deeper pink than this. This is too pale to set off my golden hair."

Deborah smiled. Ruth had begun lately to refer to her hair as golden when it was no more than a browner shade of fair. Stephen had written a sonnet to her golden hair and blue eyes. Frederick, she reflected, has written nothing to my flaxen locks but then we are middle-aged. She regarded herself in the cheval mirror. I am no longer a scarecrow. I look stately, a floral goddess.

"Is it time we went downstairs?"

At the foot of the stairs she found Lady Branford holding a jewel-encrusted box.

"You look splendid, Deb. Wear this for the dear old earl's sake. His wife wore it on their wedding and it matches the ring Fred has given you."

Deborah looked into the box. It was a diamond necklace. When it was fastened round her she thought, I have at least a thousand pounds dangling round my neck. How does that make me feel?

The Italian mirror that adorned the central archway showed her the effect.

Oh dear, its beauty shows off my plainness, she thought. Diamonds should set off a face of perfection. She sighed. Of course I must wear it. She embraced her mother-in-law to be and her father walking in the door that moment from inspecting the carriage arrangements exclaimed, "My Deb, you are a queen!"

His eyes were immediately brimming with tears.

At the church Frederick, with John at his side – had they shaken hands yet she wondered – were just as resplendent. Frederick's

Height of Folly

coat was royal blue, embossed with the repaired gold knots around the hem. His waistcoat was ivory worked with a pattern of gold threads. His shirt cuffs turned back over the jacket sleeves bulged with lace. How will he eat his dinner without soiling them, she wondered.

John was in purple and silver. He looked pale and tense. His hair was brushed over the bruise but Frederick's chin showed a slight discoloration from John's blow. Can we put on a show of a happy united family, she asked herself as her father handed her from the carriage.

The crowds round the church cheered her appearance. I never supposed I was much loved in Nether Horden, she thought. It just shows what dressing-up and a bit of ceremony can do. All this was pleasant and reassuring but it was when her father took her arm and led her into the church and symbolically handed her over to Lord Branford that it came upon her that she had been at this very point all those years ago. Then it was a place of horror but she had believed she was about to be made a wife. The words were spoken and she had thrilled at the thought that the huge man at her side was her husband.

Now it was a bright March day in the church of her childhood with her family and friends surrounding her and it was really going to happen. There was no trickery, the words were being spoken again but this time from the English prayer book. All was open, honest and transparent. Frederick was agreeing to worship her with his body and she was agreeing to love, honour and obey him. They would hold together till death parted them.

They were pronounced man and wife. It had happened, nothing could undo it, nothing could mar it in any way. The surge of happiness that went through her nearly unbalanced her.

And then from outside came the sound of marching feet and the clang of weapons and shouts and squeals from the crowds who had not been able to squeeze into the church. She and Frederick exchanged a look of shock and bewilderment.

A red-coated officer appeared at the church door. Everyone turned and stared in alarm. John's face was ashen. The parson went forward to meet the officer.

"What is the meaning of this? You are interrupting a wedding service."

"Captain Lawrence at your service, Reverend. We want to see Sir Daniel Horden to find out if he knows the whereabouts of his son John who was involved in the late rebellion. We believe he has escaped to France. He has a French wife. The ports are being watched."

The officer's voice rang clear through the church. Deborah tried not to look at John's face. She held tight to Frederick's hand and could sense his body quivering like hers.

"Whereabouts!" repeated the parson. "John Horden is where you would expect him to be, here at his sister's wedding. The gentleman in the purple coat."

Jeanetta came rushing forward, hiding John from view. "And I am his French wife and there with their nurses are our two babies. John is heir to Horden and why would we be running away to France? We live here at Nether Horden Grange. Take your silly soldiers away from my sister-in-law's wedding."

Deborah, her heart lifting at Jeanetta's words, saw that her father had stepped forward and now approached the Captain.

"You asked for me. I am Sir Daniel Wilson Horden. May I ask what reason you can have for saying my son was involved in the late rebellion?"

Oh father, let it alone, Deborah was praying. The captain looks dashed by Jeanetta's outburst and might have gone quietly away.

"Why, sir, forgive me but we were given a list of names by a prisoner who hoped to gain his freedom by betraying others. It is

Height of Folly

true we have found most of them quietly at home and begin to suspect the man of lying to save his own skin."

"And who is this traitor?"

"He calls himself Edouard le Vent."

Now Deborah did send a stabbing look at John to make no sign. His lips were parted but he snapped them shut. Jeanetta poised herself to block the officer's view of him. Deborah was impressed with her.

But le Vent, she thought, must have been a Jacobite himself. John let us think he was a *government* man. He said he had heard his name bandied about. Yes, among *Jacobites*. He has been in league with him from Rombeau days. Oh the lies he has told us! And that villain with his flamboyant moustache and exaggerated gestures, his teasing grins, he was playing with us all. And John knew it!

The captain went on, "We believe his real name is plain Edward Brown – an Englishman masquerading as French. He was a nobody who wanted to be somebody in a romantic cause, deceiving the gullible. He liked play-acting but we have blown his cover. He thinks turning informer will save him but I wager he'll hang anyway. Well, Sir Daniel, I will just apologise to your son." He stepped nimbly round Daniel and Jeanetta and confronted John. "Master John Horden!"

Sweat glistened on John's forehead. The captain looked suddenly round at the local gentry in the pews and the villagers standing round the walls. "You all know this is John Horden?" There was a general sound of affirmation. Isolated voices called out "Known him from a baby!" and "Get your men out of the church" and "The service ain't over yet."

Deborah had a sickening dread that he was about to ask John how well he knew Edouard le Vent but he seemed to make up his mind to leave the matter. Perhaps the fierce looks of the gentlemen farmers and the splendid plumes in their ladies' hats intimidated him as well as the sheer numbers of people inside and outside the church.

"I beg your pardon, Master Horden, and you two," he bowed to the bridal couple, "for disturbing your wedding."

The parson had followed him back up the aisle and addressed him severely.

"Let me tell you, Captain, that far from harbouring villains here in Nether Horden *I* have just had the great honour of marrying the Earl of Branford to our own Mistress Deborah Horden, now the Countess of Branford. It is *their* wedding that you have so rudely interrupted."

The captain bowed low. "My lord, my lady, forgive me. I was obliged to carry out orders to investigate the prisoner's information. Sir Parson, we will withdraw at once."

One of the soldiers lined up behind him was grinning and pointing at the bride and groom. Lady Branford stepped out of her pew and, singling him out, said, "Enjoy your laugh, my man, and I will enjoy a laugh at your big red nose which tells me you drink a deal more than you should."

The men turned on their comrade with grins at his expense, the captain glared round at them and called them to attention and marched them out of the church. The congregation could hear the crowd outside jeering them on their way and chatter broke out within the ranks inside. The parson begged for order and quiet for the conclusion of the service. The wedded couple were prayed for and blessed and at the end everyone inside and outside clapped and cheered.

When would Nether Horden see such another wedding, Deborah asked herself.

They came out into the sharp spring air and she turned to Frederick. "Are we fast married do you think?"

Height of Folly

"We are fast married."

John was the first to come up to them, his face crumpled. He kissed his sister and shook Frederick's hand. "You heard that? Le Vent turned informer. If that is the character of Jacobites I will swear Father's oath today to have nothing more to do with them ever again. Was not Jeanetta wonderful?"

Deborah hugged him, her sweet, silly, persuadable little brother. "She was – if she will now live out all she said."

"And did not the officer say he found most of le Vent's list quietly in their homes? They didn't march. Were they waiting for me? Will they now be grateful that I never called upon them?"

"Their wives will I am sure. And are you grateful? To me? To Frederick? And you'll stay and learn to run Horden?"

"Yes." She could see it tore him to say it. He lowered his voice. "Deb, I have to admit it. To bring in King James was the height of my ambition but the mountain of a rising has turned into a mouse. I will never trust the French again but believe me, there never was any play-acting with me."

"Was there not? Well, if you can admit that all the deception you were driven to was the height of *folly* rather than *ambition* I shall have great hopes of you in the future, John."

Frederick took her hand. "Come to the carriage, wife. It waits to take us back to the Hall."

CHAPTER TWENTY-EIGHT

November 1715
Horden Hall

Frederick, Earl of Branford, Deborah, his Countess and their three children, Edward, Daniel and Bella, along with May, the Dowager Countess, are at Horden Hall for the funeral of Lady Arabella Wilson Horden. They came at her request so she could see them before she died and now they have the sad duty of following her coffin to the grave of her beloved Nat in Nether Horden churchyard. It is a bitter November day. The Branford children have stayed at the Hall with their tireless nurse, Suzette.

Lady Eunice Horden uncharacteristically is weeping. "I felt the warmth of her nature the first moment we met. I knew if I married her son she would love me truly."

It seems strange to Deborah that her father, Sir Daniel Wilson Horden, is dry-eyed. He has an arm round her shoulders and is murmuring, "She wanted to go once she had seen your latest child. The trial of living in a frail body was too much for her busy soul and I am thankful she is joining my father. They never wanted to be apart."

They are looking across the grave as the coffin is lowered. At the other side stands John Wilson Horden, the heir to the Horden estate with his wife Jeanetta and two children Nathaniel Jean, a leggy boy of nine, looking thinner than usual in his black suit and clutching the hand of his little sister, Diana Maria. She is a perfect replica of her mother and grandmother Diana, now dowager Comtesse of Rombeau since the death of Comte Rombeau five years before and the marriage of her eldest son Pierre. Jeanetta and the children do not look sad, only cold.

Height of Folly

Deborah cannot help but see the torment in the face of her brother. It is not for the death of his grandmother though he loved her well but for the solemn promise he made to his father seven years before on the day of her wedding to Frederick. At this moment she knows his heart is with the band of Northumbrian Jacobites under the leadership of the Earl of Derwentwater who raised the standard of James Stuart at Warkworth Castle on October the ninth. He has followed all he could learn of their progress and setbacks day by day. They headed for Newcastle but found it well-prepared. The known Catholics in the town had already been arrested and the militia and train-bands were mustered on Killingworth Moor, a formidable force. The little Jacobite band retreated and linked up with another group on the Scottish border. Together they were now known to be marching into England by the west coast route via Carlisle and hoping to gain more recruits in Lancashire.

"They have done this without French help," John had told Deborah before the funeral. "I have lain low all these years as most of my former comrades have but now they have risen and I am held back by my cursed promise. I have had messages calling upon me to come and I was near breaking my word to Father but Netta begged me not to go. She is more timid than she used to be and fears failure. But I believe there is a real chance of success this time. The Earl of Mar has raised a great army in the Highlands. You Branfords who support the House of Hanover may find George the First toppled before you can get home to Hertfordshire."

"I applaud Jeanetta for saving you from the height of folly once again," was all Deborah answered.

Now she can see in his face that her poor brother is torn apart.

She knows how much has changed for him and Jeanetta in the past seven years. He has 'lain low' as he put it in France as well as in England but the delights of the Château Rombeau have faded. Pierre is master now and their mother Diana is subdued. Pierre barely tolerates his sister's English husband about the place and his new wife cannot stand the noise of children. The Vicomte de Neury has burnt all the papers from his desk and is now a little mad because he has no exciting games to play. Madeline has succeeded in marrying Sophia's two daughters to French noblemen of higher rank than John Horden and her triumph and the comte's death have crushed Diana's spirit. Sophia is melancholy since her daughters left. The air of bustle and gaiety is lost and its loss has communicated itself to the whole household. Jeanetta cannot feel light-hearted there any more and prefers her own place at Horden.

She is pale, today, Deborah thinks. She is having a hard time with John. She once told me he was only fun when he was happy and now he is not. She is also shivering as we all are. Do funerals always have to happen in winter? There is no place colder than a graveside.

The service over they are all thankful to return to the warmth of Horden Hall and a hot dinner.

Deborah, who knows her father so well, is aware that he is on edge. Something momentous is gripping him and she wonders a little anxiously what it is.

When they have well fed, and the children have been sent to the library to play games with Suzette he clears his throat and Lady Branford's chatter dies away.

"May and Frederick," he begins, "I wish to make a proposal which I am happy for you to hear although it does not directly concern you."

Lady Branford breaks in happily, "Daniel, I *love* other people's business."

It is not quite the note of solemnity he is seeking but he presses

Height of Folly

on. "I look on you both as family and it is a family matter."

They compose themselves to listen. Deborah sees from her mother's face that she knows what is coming.

"The fact is," he says "that I am minded to make changes at Horden if John and Jeanetta agree. I would not disturb Mother while she was ill but Eunice and I would like to end our days in the peace and quiet of Nether Horden Grange, further from the coal workings, and because we need less space and attendance than your family, John. We have both passed our three score years and ten and though I will be ready with advise at any time, I believe I should now give the reins into your hands and you should live here as Master."

He looks at Deborah who has stirred in surprise and some concern. "Why do I propose this, you may wonder. It is entirely because John has kept his word to me, at great cost and heart-searching over the present and still ongoing rebellion. We do not know how it will turn out and people are needlessly dying as we speak for the sake of James Stuart who as far as we are aware has not yet set sail to take his part in it. But even before we know the outcome I wish to show my son that I believe he can and will take charge and fulfil his duty to all for whom Horden is their livelihood. I will not see it but I have faith that he will pass on the baronetcy to young Nathaniel in good standing with the community at large. What do you say, John?"

Deborah has already seen that Jeanetta is all smiles and is prodding John to make a grateful and gracious reply. He is flushed and tongue-tied for a moment. His mother is nodding at him. He looks up at his father.

"But I don't know that I will have any standing at all if King James wins the throne. I will be ostracised in Northumbrian society. I will receive none of the rewards I hoped for as his loyal servant. I alone will be left out."

"Nonsense!" Deborah intervenes. "If it ever happens that we exchange George of Hanover for James Stuart, you will be among the vast majority of the population who have *not* helped him to the throne and don't particularly want to see him there. Should you not be happy that you were not hanged in seventeen hundred and eight like that wretched Edward Brown? You would not be here today if Frederick had not dropped the trapdoor on you."

"Come, we won't bring that up," says her mother. "All our lives have moved on since then. I believe in living in the present moment while making wise plans for the future when necessary. So answer your father, John. I can see Jeanetta's answer in her face."

John draws a deep breath. "Well, Father, I am grateful for one thing. I think it is the first time in my life I have felt that any of the family believed I could do anything at all."

"Oh John, is that my fault?" Deborah cries.

"It's the way things happened. More my own fault I suppose. But I will accept everything you suggest, Father, and I will work hard and try to leave Horden more prosperous even than you have made it."

As the words are spoken there comes a knock on the door. Matt's face appears. His expression mirrors the conflict in John's.

"Sir Daniel, I thought you'd want to know. Luke has been to the town and there's word going around that the Jacobite force that reached Preston has surrendered and the Earl of Derwentwater is taken prisoner."

John buries his head in his hands.

"O'course there's still the Earl of Mar's force in Scotland," Matt says by way of comfort.

"But the other is where you would have been, John," Deborah points out. "Thank God for Father's wisdom in extracting a promise from you."

"Thank you, Matt." Sir Daniel dismisses Matt with a wave of his

Height of Folly

hand.

Lady Branford looks round the table with her bright smile. "Does anyone else have a sense of *déjà vu?* Have I used the right expression, Fred?"

"Quite correct, dear mother." It is the first word he has spoken since the subject came up. He has been thinking though, thinking that Sir Daniel would have liked to keep Deborah to manage Horden Hall if he himself had not whisked her away to Hertfordshire where she has spent seven years bearing him two sons and a daughter and helping him to put the affairs of Castle Branford in fine order.

He looks at her, sitting tall, her flaxen hair still untinged by grey, her blue-green eyes alert. As a mother she is passionate for her children but now, past forty, has accepted she will have no more. At the least naughtiness she can be very firm. Edward and Daniel, close together in age, are highly competitive and Frederick often wonders how to keep the peace between them. He can usually succeed by warning them that he will tell their mother they have been quarrelling again. Then he makes them, at six and five, shake hands and vow friendship. Three-year-old Bella is beginning to assert herself too. She is clever and eager to do all that the boys are doing but she is not, Deborah assures him, unusually tall.

Her own height has been the talk of the court.

"Have you seen the Countess of Branford?" "She makes the poor little earl into a dwarf." "But what a presence she has, how she carries herself!" "And they say there isn't a university man who can surpass her in learning."

"Ay," says one wag, "If Branford had passed her over it would have been the height of folly."

She is rising now the speech-making is over. "If you'll excuse me, Father, I'll see that the children are not being too much for Suzette." They have brought with them the one maid to help with the children and act as lady's maid and two men, Peter and Joseph to man the carriage. Frederick knows that his mother-in-law heartily approves the small retinue.

Now his sister-in-law, Ruth, round with her own first child, rises too. "Let me come, Deb. Simon told me to learn everything I could from you about children since his business keeps him in York today."

The sisters leave the room together.

John and Jeanetta excuse themselves too, John pausing at the door to address his father. "What will you say if the Earl of Mar wins a great victory in Scotland?"

Sir Daniel just shakes his head. He can't believe it will happen.

Next day they hear that the Duke of Argyll, heading the government forces has defeated Mar at Sherrifmuir. Although James is still to land in Scotland and be proclaimed at Scone, it is in fact the death-knell of the uprising. Lacking support he escapes back to France and the cold bleak winter that follows sees him banished from St Germain to Avignon.

The same cruel weather at Horden Hall keeps the Branford family from returning to Hertfordshire. They celebrate Christmas quietly, conscious of Bel's empty place.

Frederick has left the faithful Will Smyth in charge at the castle. He stubbornly refuses to retire and has reluctantly become reconciled to a new style of master and mistress. He finds the place very empty without them and when the snowdrops are all over the lawn and he hears the rattle of the carriage wheels on the drive he is a happy man again.

"My lord, my lady," he exclaims, "it is good to see you safe home. We have had a narrow escape from a civil war. Was Master John Horden persuaded not to join the uprising, my lord?"

"Indeed. That is all past history, Will."

"I am glad to hear it, my lord. Hordens and Branfords in

Height of Folly

harmony. How that would have rejoiced the old earl's heart!"

He pays less attention to the dowager countess who is always laughing at him but to Edward, who bears the old earl's name and who is to be brought up aware of his inheritance, he is deferential to a fault.

"And how has my young lord enjoyed his journey?"

The boy, brown-haired with the round Branford face and slightly protruding ears, grins at him. "Mamma tried to teach me a game called chess but I didn't understand it so I threw up the board and the bits all fell about."

"I will retrieve them for you, my lord."

"No, Will. Edward will find every piece himself *now* before the carriage is put away."

Deborah looms over the small figure and he knows he will have no supper until he does.

As they walk inside, Frederick says, "I think, Deb, he is a little young for chess."

Deborah smiles ruefully. She is not going to find a prodigy among her children or one of exceptional height. Perhaps, she thinks, it will be just as well. If they turn out like their father I will be very satisfied.

She looks about at the gardens she has created and sees the winter has been kinder here than at Horden. Good, she thinks, I am home.

ABOUT THE AUTHOR

PRUE PHILLIPSON was born and reared in Newcastle upon Tyne in northern England. Prue enjoyed writing historical novels from an early age. She trained as a teacher, taught full time for four years and was a freelance writer during this time. She took a correspondence course in creative writing and honed her craft.

She is married and has reared five children. Her current occupation is writing articles, short stories and novels.